LETTERS TO CUPID

ALSO BY MIRANDA MACLEOD

Stand Alone Novels:

Telling Lies Online

Holly & Ivy (cowritten with T.B. Markinson)

Love's Encore Trilogy:

A Road Through Mountains

Your Name in Lights

Fifty Percent Illusion

Love's Encore Omnibus Collection

Americans Abroad Series (stand alone romances set across the globe):

Waltzing on the Danube

Holme for the Holidays

Stockholm Syndrome

Letters to Cupid

London Holiday

Check mirandamacleod.com for more about these titles, and for other books coming soon!

LETTERS TO CUPID

MIRANDA MACLEOD

Apple Blossom Press
Boston, MA

Letters to Cupid

Copyright © 2018 Miranda MacLeod

All rights reserved. No part of this publication may be reproduced, distributed, or transmitted in any form or by any means, including photocopying, recording, or other electronic or mechanical methods, without the prior written permission of the publisher or author, except in the case of brief quotations embodied in critical reviews and certain other noncommercial uses permitted by copyright law.

Find out more: www.mirandamacleod.com
Contact the author: miranda@mirandamacleod.com

ISBN-13: 978-1721576548

ISBN-10: 1721576541

This is a work of fiction. Any resemblance of characters to actual persons, living or dead, is purely coincidental.

Apple Blossom Press
PO Box 547
Bolton MA 01740

ABOUT THE AUTHOR

Originally from southern California, Miranda now lives in New England and writes heartfelt romances and romantic comedies featuring witty and charmingly flawed women that you'll want to marry. Or just grab a coffee with, if that's more your thing. She spent way too many years in graduate school, worked in professional theater and film, and held temp jobs in just about every office building in downtown Boston.

To find out about her upcoming releases and take advantage of exclusive sales, be sure to sign up for her newsletter at her website: mirandamacleod.com.

LETTERS TO CUPID

ONE

VALENTINE'S DAY, twenty years ago.

Valentina held her breath as Francesca teetered along the outer rim of the fountain that dominated the cobblestone piazza at the heart of their Tuscan village. Her best friend balanced on the tips of her leather loafers, toes pointed for maximum extension as she paused to plot her next move. In the middle of the swirling waters, the famous Cupid of Montamore looked down on them from his perch, high above the water's spray. His expression was as inscrutable as ever. Was his laughter-filled smile meant to encourage them in their efforts, Valentina wondered, or to mock their inevitable defeat?

Because despite Francesca's boundless optimism for this afternoon's task, defeat *was* inevitable. At least, that's how it appeared from where Valentina stood with the other girls, all craning their necks to watch while remaining huddled together for protection from the raw winter day. No matter how much their friend wanted to believe otherwise, Cupid's crumbling stone pedestal, Francesca's ultimate goal, seemed destined to remain impossibly out of reach.

La Fontana di Cupido was the star attraction in Montamore, the single thing that enticed tourists to visit the otherwise sleepy hilltop town. Legend had it that the life-size carving of Cupid had once resided in an ancient Roman temple that had stood on this spot. The temple had long since vanished, along with the gods it had served, so that now only the statue remained.

Eventually, the carved Cupid had become the centerpiece of a marvelous fountain which had been constructed in Montamore at the height of the Renaissance, making it practically new by Italian standards. A bowl-shaped pool formed the fountain's base, its outer lip standing knee-height with a width about the same as a person's foot. The distance from the lip to the center, where the statue resided, was maybe a bit more than both of Valentina's arms stretched out wide, but it was hard to know for certain. This was because of the steady flow of water that rushed out from beneath the statue's pedestal, well above head height for even the tallest adult. But whatever the exact measurements, the chances of a fourteen-year-old spanning the distance successfully were slim.

Foolish Francie! The tang of blood registered on Valentina's tongue as it slid across the rough spot where she'd worried her lip with enough force to break the skin. *She's going to get herself killed!* Not that anyone had ever died before, at least not that she knew of. On the other hand, there was a first time for everything. But regardless of the evident dangers, she knew there was no way to talk her friend out of what was a time-honored local tradition.

Francie and the other girls possessed more guts than good sense, leaving Valentina alone in her concern.

Without warning, Francesca gave a final lunge. For a moment Valentina's heart stood still, only resuming its rapid staccato rhythm when her best friend's hand came safely to rest against the cold stone pedestal, as strands of dark hair whipped wildly around her face in the punishing wind. Valentina let out a puff of steamy breath as she blotted her hands along the stiff corduroy of her trousers. Her palms had grown sweat-dampened despite the considerable cold. The fountain was hard enough to climb in the summer. No one in their right mind should be trying it on a day like this.

But rain or shine, stopping at the fountain on the way home from school had become a ritual for Valentina's circle of friends, ever since the subject of boys had become their main topic of conversation. As she looked at them now, Valentina felt nothing but confusion over the sudden transformation that the others had undergone. They were completely boy-crazy now, to the point that any one of them would gladly risk an accidental dunking or worse, on one of the coldest days of winter. But the boy-crazy phase had either passed Valentina by or was greatly delayed in its arrival, and at times this worried her.

"I made it!" Francesca cried, flashing a triumphant grin as she turned to look at her friends.

All four of them, Valentina included, continued to observe her actions with keen interest, as Francesca took the scrap of paper she'd kept grasped in one hand and poked it into a crack in the weathered pedestal, before giving her handiwork a satisfied nod. It was just one of many such scraps, in varying states of disintegration. During the height of the tourist season, a special crew had to be dispatched nightly to scoop paper pulp from the edges of the basin before it turned to glue. The reason for this was a simple one. It was common knowledge in Montamore that when it came to matters of the heart, if you left a letter for Cupid at the base of this sacred statue, he was obligated to help. The quest for true love made Cupid's fountain one happening spot.

"Let's see Paolo try to escape *that!*" said Mia with a cackling laugh. "Or was it Lorenzo's name you wrote instead?" she teased. That *someone's* name had been scrawled across the slip was a given. Francesca wouldn't tell them whose, of course. They all knew the rules. Whatever was written was for Cupid's eyes alone. That wouldn't stop them from teasing.

"It was probably Marco," Sofia suggested. It was devilish of her, since they all knew Mia had a huge crush on Marco. Bianca, who had watched the spectacle with rapt attention, giggled, and Mia's cheeks turned scarlet. The gentle ribbing did little to hide the envy on all of their faces. It was obvious that they'd each secretly hoped Francesca would fail and give them the opportunity to be the first among their group to harness Cupid's power. Only Valentina looked neither impressed by nor jealous over her friend's accomplishment. Instead, she was studying the girl's precarious foot placement on the slick stones with a frown.

"Careful, Francesca!" Valentina warned.

"Quit being such a worrywart." Francesca wobbled as she tried to shift her weight away from the statue, and Valentina's arm flew out to steady her.

"It's the middle of February," Valentina scolded. "I don't

care *whose* name you wrote on that scrap of paper. No boy is worth tumbling into freezing water in the middle of winter."

As she helped her friend down, Valentina's gaze was drawn to the spot where Francie's thick wool skirt had ridden up several inches and now clung to her tights in a way that showed off the better part of one thigh. *Goodness!* Her eyes lingered. *Francie's thighs aren't at all chunky like mine, but shapely and beautiful, like a girl in a magazine.* She dug her front tooth into the sore spot on her lip and winced. What a shame that Francie didn't wear her skirts short like that all the time.

"If he's your true love, *of course* he'd be worth it," Bianca said, continuing the argument that had been raging while Valentina was preoccupied with Francie's thighs. Mia and Sofia nodded solemnly in agreement. "And it's not just the middle of winter. It's *Valentine's Day*. Everyone knows that's the best day to do it."

"Bianca's right." Mia pointed accusingly at Valentina. "*You're* just too chicken to try. We come here every day and you won't so much as throw a few lire into the water to make a wish, let alone try to leave a letter! Why are you so scared?"

"I'm not scared," Valentina muttered. In truth, just being in such close proximity to the mystical fountain filled her with unease. That smiling Cupid, with all his secret knowledge about the desires of their hearts, gave her the creeps. But she wasn't about to let on. Girls at fourteen—even friends—could be merciless when they smelled fear. "I just think it's stupid."

"Do you think *I'm* stupid, then?" Francesca demanded. She'd realized her skirt was askew and set about the task of repositioning it, once more hiding her thighs from public view.

"No, of course not." Valentina reluctantly refocused her attention, giving her chin a defiant lift and looking directly into Francesca's eyes. They were the deep, rich hue of chocolate ganache, her favorite. Valentina was an expert on chocolate, as her family owned the local confectionary shop where she worked every day after school. Valentina loved chocolate ganache, but she didn't care one bit for the hurt look in her best friend's eyes.

Valentina's tummy tightened and her palms grew sweaty again. Whether displeased or approving, it seemed that everything Francesca said or did these days prompted this type of physical response in her. *It's normal for a best friend to have that effect on you, though, right?* Yet the other girls never mentioned it, and recently she'd begun to suspect that it was not normal. Not normal at all.

Francesca continued to sulk. "Well, that's how it sounded."

"It's just, I don't see how it's supposed to work, is all." Valentina's teeth sank mercilessly into her lip once more as she struggled to strike the right tone to smooth things over. "We're fourteen. The only boys we know are the ones from school, and to be honest, I'm not sure I fancy any of them enough to risk slipping, hitting my head, and drowning in the middle of the town square."

"Oh, be serious, you drama queen. It's not *that* dangerous." But Francesca's pout had begun to fade at the wild exaggeration, just as Valentina thought it might.

"I *am* being serious," Valentina insisted, encouraged by the twinkle of amusement in Francesca's eyes. "Okay, not about drowning. But we're all headed off to different schools next year, and what if the right boy for me is someone I'll meet there, or maybe not until college?" *That has to be it, right? I'm not so different from them, after all. I just haven't met the right boy yet.* Because the last thing Valentina wanted was to be different. In a town as small as Montamore, being different was a curse. "If I don't have a name to write down, I don't see the point of any of this."

"You don't have to write down a name." All eyes turned to stare at Mia, who had just dropped this news like a bombshell in their midst.

Valentina frowned. "What do you mean? Of course, you have to."

"Yeah," Sofia added. "I mean, that's how it's done."

But Mia shook her head vigorously. "No, there's another way. You can just tell Cupid you want to fall in love and ask for his help."

"That doesn't sound right," Bianca said, voicing the skepticism that was clear on all the other girls' faces. "If that were true, one of my older sisters would've told me by now."

"It *is* true," Mia reiterated. "My grandmother said so, and she should know because she did it herself. You leave a letter asking for help, and after that, you drop a coin in the fountain and look down right away into the ripples. If you do, you'll see the face of the boy you're going to marry."

The frown lines in Valentina's forehead deepened. "Why haven't we heard this before?"

Mia shrugged. "I don't know, but I guess that's what everyone used to do back in her day. Don't any of you ever listen to your grandparents when they tell stories? My grandmother went to work in a café in Rome after the war, and as soon as my grandfather walked in, she recognized his face from the fountain and knew it was him, even though they'd never met. They were married three months later, so there's your proof."

"I guess…" Valentina swallowed roughly as she considered this troubling new evidence. "I guess, in that case, it might be true."

Privately, Valentina had always thought the presence in their village of Mia's somewhat brash though friendly American grandfather, threw a long shadow of doubt over the whole magical fountain nonsense. After all, it's not like Mia's grandmother could have known to ask for him by name when she was a girl, and yet they'd been happy together for fifty years. But to her annoyance, Mia's revelation had just made the whole thing much more plausible and blew a supersized hole in her argument against participating.

Francesca must have realized the same thing, because seconds later, she nudged Valentina toward the fountain. "Now you don't have any reason not to try."

Valentina shook her head. "It's not a good day for it."

"Of course, it is. It's your birthday! That has to make it extra lucky."

This stopped her short. Francesca had remembered it was her birthday. With a name like Valentina, it seemed that more people would remember that her birthday landed on Valentine's Day, but so far, Francesca was the only one who cared enough to mention it. That's why they were best friends. Of course, now that they'd been reminded, the rest of the girls backed Francesca up with great enthusiasm, and Valentina eyed the fountain with growing dread. *Drat! How do I get out of it now?* She let out a breath as an idea came to her. It wasn't perfect, but it would hold them off for a while.

"I mean, I would, but I don't have a letter or anything. I might not need a name to write down, but I still need some kind of letter."

Her excuse was instantly countered by Francesca, who held out a blank piece of notepaper that she'd seemingly conjured from thin air. "I brought an extra."

"And I have a pen," Bianca added helpfully, pulling the item from her pocket.

"Well. Great." Valentina's hand shook as she took hold of her friends' unwelcome gifts. "But are you sure one of you doesn't want to try? We only have one spare note." She swept an imploring look across the group. "Mia? It was your idea, after all."

"It's no use. I've tried and tried," Mia said, "but I'm way too short to reach."

As Valentina gave her friend's stature a critical appraisal, she was forced to admit that Mia would be lucky if she could reach Cupid's pedestal by the time she was eighteen. Even then, she might need to bring a ladder. "What about you, Bianca, or Sofia?" But each girl made an excuse, and it was soon clear that they were all determined for her to be the one to go, as a special treat for her birthday. *Some treat.*

"Fine." Out of options, Valentina sighed dramatically. "But what do I even write in this letter?"

"Just say that you want to see your true love's face," Mia suggested.

Wrinkling her nose, Valentina scribbled down the words, then folded the paper quickly so she wouldn't have to look at it any longer than necessary. She took a single, resigned step toward the fountain, as if approaching an enemy for battle. Every nerve ending fired on high alert as she propped one foot onto the stone rim. She shivered as she looked into the water, yet it wasn't the icy blast of a dunking she feared most, but something else. Something Cupid might know, that she'd only just begun to realize.

"Don't forget this!" Francesca pressed a coin into her palm. Valentina gave her friend's fingers a light squeeze under the guise of grasping the cold circle of metal, and warmth radiated from fingertips to shoulder at the touch. Holding her breath, Valentina hoisted herself onto the fountain's ledge, swaying gently as she sought her balance. Once steadied, she looked upward, narrowing her eyes into a stern stare as she sought the statue's face.

"Look, Cupid," she muttered under her breath, "let's just get this over with. I don't want any funny business, okay?" It must have been a trick of the light, yet she could've sworn he winked.

With the coin in one hand and the note in the other, Valentina sized up the distance between herself and the pedestal's base. Though it had appeared impossibly far from ground level, it turned out to be more illusion than reality. From her current vantage point, she could see that it would only take one good stretch of an arm and a little luck to reach her mark.

Though still wary, the thrill of succeeding at a challenge that had long stymied her friends, urged her on. *If I do manage it, won't Francesca be so proud?* Focusing all of her attention on the goal, she leaned her weight forward, more and more, until she was past the point of no return. Her heart clenched at the dizzying sensation of her body in free fall, but it only lasted a moment before her hand made contact with reassuringly solid stone. She scrambled to find a crack and shoved the corner of the note in as far as it would go.

"Got it!" she called to her friends. "Now what?"

"Drop the coin," Sofia reminded her.

"And don't forget to look into the water," Mia added.

Right. Look into the water and see my true love's face. She peeked at the swirling water below, her breath a series of shallow bursts as she anticipated what might happen next, if anything at all.

Steeling her nerves, Valentina pushed back from the statue with one arm while holding the hand that clutched the coin out over the water, but despite her best efforts, her fist remained tightly clenched. She knew that her palms had become damp again, as they always did under pressure, and for a moment she feared the sweat had caused her hand to freeze shut, though of course that was impossible. *Oh, come on,* she chided herself silently. *Get it over with.* Her muscles relaxed just enough that the coin slipped out and landed with a *plunk* on the water's surface. It shimmered for a moment in the weak afternoon sunlight before slowly sinking to the bottom. Valentina watched its descent, mesmerized, as a shape began to form in the gray pool.

What she saw was not a face, but as the ripples spread in concentric circles from the point where the coin had entered, it was clear that *something* was there that had not been before. The sound of her own blood pounded in her ears, blocking out all other noise. Squinting, Valentina thought she could just make out the outline of a wooden door, heavily carved and rustic in style, like something belonging to an old Tuscan farmhouse. The fact that she saw anything at all was startling. Truly, she'd been counting on the whole thing being nothing more than an old wives' tale. But as she continued to stare, the door appeared to move on its hinges, the gap widening in excruciatingly slow motion as it prepared to reveal the face that waited on the other side: the face of her true love.

It won't be Francesca! In a flash, something elemental became clear. That was the name Valentina would have written if she'd dared. Hers was the face she wanted to see. *But that's ridiculous! What's wrong with me?* She shouldn't so much as be *thinking* something like that. None of her friends ever would, not even for a second. It wasn't normal at all, just like her sweating palms around Francie weren't normal, or her fluttering tummy, or how she'd been mesmerized by those shapely thighs…

Oh God. I think I'm in love with a girl. The revelation tolled with the force of church bells at noon, echoing inside Valentina's skull in an endless carillon. Though deep down she may have guessed already that there was nothing she could do about it, in the panic that overtook her, her only thought was to make it stop. If only she could reach that blasted note and steal it back before Cupid finished his mischief, she could make like the whole incident had never happened. She could go right back to being just like everyone else, like all those other girls who would never even consider falling in love with their best friends. She'd learn to be boy-crazy, if she had to. How hard could it be? Everyone else managed it.

Blind to the precariousness of her position, Valentina swung both hands at once, wildly aiming for the scrap of paper that dangled so tantalizingly close. She missed. Though her palms landed with a thwack against the pedestal, their sweat-drenched state, along with the layer of ice that had formed on the stone from the fountain's constant mist, was a treacherous combination. For a brief second, time stood still, and then she hit the water and could feel nothing but the stabbing pain of thousands of frozen needles jabbing at her skin as the water saturated her clothing.

What happened next went by in a blur as a flurry of hands and arms pulled her from the water and attempted to shield her from the biting wind. Her friends whisked Valentina across the piazza and into the welcoming warmth of her family's shop. She was vaguely aware of her mother's voice calling her name, and then of being bundled and carried up the stairs and into the safety of the spacious apartment on the second floor that she and her mother and father called home. She shut her eyes against the roughness of the towels that her mother and grandmother used to dry her soaking wet body, but all she could see behind her lids was that carved door, and Cupid's mirthful face, and the corner of the note that she had failed to retrieve. *What will happen now?*

Alone, she stared out the window in her bedroom that afforded a view of the piazza. In the center of the fountain, Cupid rose above the spray and laughed. He always laughed, but this time she knew it was at her expense. Teeth chattering, she pulled on a dry turtleneck and jeans, all the while keeping her adversary in her sight. "Listen here, stupid Cupid. You're going to forget this ever happened," she muttered to the statue, expecting no response and not getting one. "You got that? As for me, I'll never tell a soul."

"WHAT WERE YOU THINKING, VALENTINA?" her mother asked when Valentina, dried and dressed, ventured sheepishly back down the stairs and into the store. She poked at a strand of her daughter's still-damp hair and clucked her tongue in that disapproving way she always had. "You caused quite a commotion coming in here half-frozen, and on the busiest day of the year!"

Valentina's cheeks burned as she looked around the crowded chocolate shop and registered the fact that at least half the village was there. Valentine's Day was always a busy day for them, but she'd never seen it like this. A few of her neighbors had the courtesy to browse the merchandise, or pretend to be engrossed in their coffees and baked goods while seated at one of the shop's half-dozen café tables, but from the way the majority of them stared so openly at her, she knew that shopping for last-minute gifts or grabbing an afternoon snack was not what had brought them in. Word of her exploits had traveled fast in their quiet town. "I'm sorry, Mama," she mumbled, hanging her head.

"Well," her mother replied, "we'll sell a lot more chocolate today because of it, anyway." Her usually dour expression was softer, so perhaps the prospect of an overflowing till had mellowed her response. "Why don't you go join your friends? I'm sure they're dying to know who you saw."

"Who I saw?"

"They're not the only ones," her grandmother, interjected. She regarded Valentina with what could only be described as a knowing smirk.

A furnace of embarrassment engulfed her. Of course, her mother and grandmother knew exactly what she'd been up to out there. All of Montamore knew. She shot her grandmother a dirty look. There was little doubt in her mind that the tiny woman who stood so innocently behind the truffle display was single-handedly responsible for the current crowd size. *Nosy old gossip. She probably phoned every house in the village before I was dry.* Sometimes the old woman carried her self-appointed position as town crier a bit too far.

From the looks on their faces, it was clear that every single occupant of the store was about to expire from the strain of waiting to hear the details. But what could she say? *I've fallen in love with a girl?* That would be a conversation stopper, all right. No, that would never do. Dragging her feet, Valentina joined her friends where they waited at a white-painted wrought iron table by the window, too busy watching her approach to even pretend to sip the mugs of hot cocoa they clutched.

Francesca looked up, her chocolate-ganache eyes wide with worry, and perhaps a little bit of guilt over pressuring her the way she'd done. "What happened? What did you see?"

"I…"

Valentina swallowed hard. In the pause that followed, one thing became clear. There was no way she could explain the revelation she'd been given, or even hint at it. Never. There'd been no fooling Cupid, but she'd die if anyone else so much as suspected the truth about what her heart desired most. There was nothing to do but lie.

"I saw a boy, but no one I knew. He had, uh, dark hair," she added lamely, knowing she was a terrible liar and hoping the random detail added some measure of legitimacy to her story.

But Francesca cocked her head to one side and made a face. "Dark hair? Just about every boy in Italy has dark hair."

"And his eyes were brown." *Also, just like every boy in Italy. Dang it.* She'd need to make up a more remarkable detail or she'd be found out for sure. "Brown like…" *Don't say chocolate ganache.* Only one person had eyes like that, and she was currently using them to squint at Valentina as if seconds away from calling her out. "Like hazelnut cream. And he had a little mole, right here." For good measure, Valentina pointed to a spot just to the side of her right eye.

"He sounds handsome." Francesca gave a dreamy sigh that was echoed by the other three girls, along with about half the adult population of the shop, poor saps.

"Oh, yes. Very handsome," Valentina agreed quickly, her pulse racing. *They're buying it!* "A real Prince Charming." And why not? If she was going to make up a story, she might as well make it a fairy tale while she was at it. Looking around the shop, it was plain on their faces that it's what they all wanted to hear.

Nonna was positively beaming, which wasn't surprising. The old woman loved that Cupid statue more than anything. But the rare glow of approval on her mother's face was something else. Was a made-up story about a dark-haired boy really all it took to win her favor? She looked ready to hand Valentina the moon. The revelation sparked an ingenious, if devious, idea.

"I think he may have been wearing a white coat, like the type students wear at the *istituto professionale*. Mama!" Valentina forced her eyes wide in feigned surprise. This was it. This was her one shot. "Do you think that means I'll meet him there?" She held her breath as she waited for her mother's response. She'd been begging to enroll in the school's special culinary training program in the fall, but so far, her mother had dashed her hopes at every turn.

"I don't know, Valentina. It's so far. Your *babbo* is already on the road so much getting new contracts and meeting with suppliers for the shop. He shouldn't have to drive you there every day, too."

"But, Mama..." Though Valentina knew it was true how hard her father worked, she refused to allow her mother to pile on the guilt. She cared as much about the shop as he did. "The culinary training offered at the istituto professionale would help all of us. I'd learn everything I need to know about making chocolate and running the shop."

"I can teach you what you need to know about that. Your grandmother, too!" Her mother dismissed the thought with a laugh. "Who needs a fancy school?"

"I do, damn it!" Valentina froze. She hadn't meant to curse. *Oh, I'm in for it now.*

"Valentina!" The expression on her mother's face was somewhere between shock and rage. "Language!"

"Sorry, Mama." Valentina took a breath and tried again. "I'd learn new ways of doing things, and how to make my own recipes. I could help *babbo* expand distribution, the way he's always dreamed. Someday, *Cioccolatini di Venere* could be famous all over the world!"

Her mother, whether skeptical of her daughter's grand plans, or just lacking faith in her ability to pull it off, rolled her eyes and remained silent. Oh, how Valentina wished her father were home. They were two peas in a pod when it came to the family business, but then again, he had a hard time standing up to her mother. He'd be on Valentina's side in this matter, but he might not have her back. With heart-thumping agony, Valentina was on the brink of admitting defeat, when her grandmother spoke.

"Show me the application tonight, *piccolina*, and then, we'll see." It wasn't quite a yes, but it wasn't a no, either. Valentina's mother opened her mouth as if to object but the older woman gave a thoughtful glance out the window to where the fountain stood and shook her head. "If *La Fontana di Cupido* says it, then maybe it's meant to be, *cara mia*."

She waited for her mother to strike a final blow to her plot, but instead the woman nodded solemnly. "Maybe."

Valentina's fingers were still stiff with cold as she poured herself a steaming hot chocolate and sat to join her friends, but inside she glowed. Her mother's tepid 'maybe' had as good as sealed the deal. *I'm going to culinary school!*

And what of her discovery that she was in love with her best friend, *a girl,* and if not for that reason alone, then she was probably going to hell for all the lies she'd just told? In the excitement of youth, it was already nearly forgotten. It didn't matter anyway. With culinary school on the horizon, her immediate future was safe once more. Safe, and above all, normal. Attending the istituto professionale would make her the envy of all her friends. Maybe there'd even be a boy with hazelnut cream eyes to meet when she was there. Who knew? Frankly, she didn't care. Let the other girls have their letters to Cupid. Whatever it was the ancient god had been trying to tell her, Valentina was no longer willing to listen.

TWO

VALENTINE'S DAY, present day.

Andie's back pressed against the unobtrusive gate that punctuated a long, plain wall which stretched the length of a city block on either side of her. Behind it was one of the most luxurious hotels in Florence, a converted palazzo and convent whose grounds were a series of world-renowned formal gardens shaded by centuries-old trees. But from this side of the wall, you'd never know it was there. The building in front of her was as unassuming as the wall behind her. Both were coated with flaking paint in at least three different shades of beige that made only a passing attempt at matching one another. Despite the exclusive neighborhood, the wall and buildings had been tagged here and there with scrawls of black graffiti. She understood almost no Italian, but it was still enough to know the sentiments being expressed were crude in nature. It did little to improve the opinion of Italy that she'd formed during her visit to this city that many considered to be its jewel.

It was a rare chef who didn't elevate this country and its

cuisine to near-divine status, but Andie was hardly a typical member of the profession. She'd never had formal training, and the only chef she'd heard of growing up was named Boyardee. His spaghetti and meatballs in a can had been a menu staple in their tiny Brooklyn apartment on the all too frequent nights when her single mother lacked the energy to fix anything else. Ever since Andie started picking up shifts at a local restaurant as a teenager and learned to cook for herself, tomato sauce was the one thing she still took pains to avoid.

She'd come a long way from those days, and in just the past twelve months, her career had skyrocketed. It had been a long shot for a self-taught rookie to take first place on the Sizzle Network's most popular cooking contest, but she surprised them all. Hell, she'd even surprised herself. Her life had changed in an instant. Gone were the days of sweating in other people's kitchens. Thanks to that win, she was the host of her own cooking show, *The Quick and Easy Queen*, and had the publication of her first cookbook on the horizon.

No one could deny that Andie was a bona fide chef at last. But even now, Italian cuisine was one of the few things she took great pains to avoid. Too many tomatoes. Too many memories of dinners from a can. Too many foreign terms and techniques waiting to expose the gaps in her knowledge. Her visit to Italy had been a minefield of potentially awkward situations, and after two weeks in Florence on a contractually mandated PR blitz for her network, she was counting the seconds until she'd be on a plane back to the States.

Andie checked her watch, noting the time with an exaggerated sigh, though it was only two minutes later than the last time she'd looked. Her driver had yet to arrive. She stared one way and then the other down the impossibly narrow street—because, though it would have been little more than an alleyway back home, there was a fair chance in Italy that a road like this would be expected to handle two directions of traffic, with a line of cars parked along both curbs. She was hardly a fan of driving in the best of circumstances, but in this environment, it was near impossible. No wonder the limousine was late. It was probably trapped down some even narrower street, wedged in so tightly that it would need a shoehorn and a tub of grease to get it unstuck. Chalk up one more reason she was glad to be leaving.

Of course, her destination didn't hurt, either. In less than a day, she'd be in Los Angeles, eating sushi and soaking up the sun at the start of her three-month, all-expenses-paid sabbatical. It was by far the biggest and best of the prizes she'd won. The network had arranged a stunning rental, just steps away from the beach, with a professional kitchen that would make developing and testing the recipes for her cookbook a breeze. Assuming, that is, that she ever made it to the airport.

Reaching a hand into her coat pocket, Andie rooted around for her phone, then dialed a number from memory. "Tracy? It's Andie," she said when the call went straight to voicemail, though leaving her name wasn't really necessary. After a year of working together, the woman assigned to be her network liaison and all-around personal assistant should know who she was. "I've been waiting by the gate on Borgo Pinti for almost ten minutes and there's no sign of the car. Call me, okay? Better yet, could you call the driver and tell him to hurry? It's freezing out!"

She stuffed the phone back into her pocket but left her fingers buried deep inside the fleece lining, as she debated whether to shove her other frozen hand in alongside it or try to thaw them both with the warmth of her breath. Neither alternative seemed likely to do much against the biting wind. On top of the tomato-slathered food and the insane traffic, the unexpectedly cold winter weather had earned the entire region of Tuscany its third strike. Wasn't Italy supposed to be warm?

Based on the photos she'd seen in tour books, Andie had been prepared for rolling vineyards lined with towering cypress and dazzling sunflowers. Despite any other misgivings, she'd been looking forward to sitting on a sun-drenched patio and sipping wine in the afternoons. She had *not* expected snow. If she'd wanted her cheeks chapped so badly that the air hurt her face, she could've stayed in New York, where at least most of the graffiti was in English.

Her phone buzzed with an incoming call, and relief filled her at the sight of the network's number. *Keep it together, now. Just twenty-four hours and you'll be in the land of golden sunshine.* Tracy was a wonder. She could be trusted to get to the bottom of this missing ride situation, and Andie would be settling herself into an oversized leather seat in the Masaccio VIP lounge before she knew it, downing a well-earned cocktail or two while she waited for her flight to board.

"Tracy, what's the deal with the car? You know how I feel about this place. If I have to hear from one more Italian grandmother what a bad influence I am on the younger generation, I may lose it completely."

Of all her experiences in Italy, being told off by a bunch of old grannies had been the worst. Andie swore she could still hear them. Had it been her spiky hair with the flame-orange tips that they objected to, or her reputation as a famously out and proud lesbian that was too much for their Old-World sensibilities to handle? Oh, no. It had been her endorsement of the microwave oven. The microwave! One of the most important inventions of the twentieth century, and one would think she'd suggested killing someone.

Sure, it wasn't as traditional as a regular oven, but sometimes that's just how she rolled. They called her the *Quick and Easy Queen* for a reason. Practicality, baby. But apparently, any cooking method or recipe that hadn't been in use for as long as the Pope had been Catholic was a capital offense in these parts. Andie was just trying to offer reasonable alternatives so that people like her mother didn't have to turn to cans of spaghetti and frozen dinners to feed their kids. The way those old ladies carried on, she was single-handedly destroying a generation of young Italian cooks by teaching them how to make a healthy dinner in under three hours. The horror.

It's not like I don't know other methods, Andie fumed. Despite being self-taught, hadn't her win proven that she could cook with the best of them? But being the *Quick and Easy Queen* was all part of the image the network had cultivated for her. Viewers loved someone a little rough around the edges, someone who'd pulled herself up by her own bootstraps. She would've been happy to change it up a little, show a bit more of the wide range of skills she'd mastered over the years, but the executives had been adamant. They'd called it her *brand*. If she wanted to enjoy the perks of being a winner, she'd have to play by their rules.

"Miss Bartlett?"

Her spinning brain had momentarily forgotten about the

phone in her hand, but now an unfamiliar male voice cut through her mental rant. Andie frowned. "You're not Tracy."

"No, ma'am. This is Todd from the network legal department."

"Why am I talking to the legal department?" While the lateness of her ride was an inconvenience, she had no intention of suing, if that's what the network was worried about. They were always worried about something, but she was certain she'd done nothing to give the legal department a reason to notice her.

"It's about the story in the *Star Post*, Miss Bartlett."

Andie's frown deepened to a scowl. She'd heard nothing about any story, but if it involved that trashy tabloid, experience told her it wouldn't be good. "What is it this time? Was I dancing topless on a bar? No, let me guess. I'm going on psychotic rampages backstage on my show? Poisoned a guest star? Duncan King's behind this. His father's money is the only thing keeping that pathetic rag afloat."

Duncan had been one of the other contestants on the show. Entitled trust fund baby that he was, he'd expected to win. Too bad for him, that had been Andie's plan, too, and ever since, he rarely passed up an opportunity to make himself a nuisance in any way possible. But this was the first time the legal department had become involved. "It's not a big deal, Todd," she added, guessing at the reason for the call. "I'd rather not pursue any legal action against Duncan or the *Star Post* at this time."

"You misunderstand, Miss Bartlett. Duncan King is involved, but he's the one trying to sue you. I'm calling to advise you of your options."

A lawsuit? Christ. Andie leaned against the wall to support her wobbling knees. "Duncan's suing me? What the hell for?"

"Like I said, it's to do with the story in the *Star*."

"You'll have to fill me in, Todd," Andie snapped. She regretted it immediately. Legal was *not* the department to piss off. Not at Sizzle Network. "Sorry about that. It's just, I have no idea what that story's about. They don't exactly have the *Star Post* on every street corner in Florence."

"Do you know Jessica Balderelli?"

"Of course. She was one of the judges on the show." Not just any judge. Jessica was the reason she was here. After voting against Andie on every challenge, by some miracle she'd had a change of heart at the end.

"That's right. Specifically, she was the deciding vote on the final round of the competition, is that correct?"

Andie straightened up from the wall, adrenaline providing renewed strength. The way he conveyed that fact was very different from how she'd heard it in her own head. Somehow Todd made it sound dirty. "I suppose that's true."

"And did you know she was gay?"

"Jessica Balderelli?" Andie snorted despite herself as she recalled the prim and proper judge and her Suzy Homemaker image. "Well, I certainly don't recall seeing her at any of the annual lesbian membership picnics."

"It's a serious question, Miss Bartlett. Were you aware of Miss Balderelli's sexual orientation while you were a contestant on the show?"

His tone was deadly serious, and Andie's gut clenched like a child on the receiving end of a lecture from her teacher. "No. I had no idea. Why?"

"Miss Balderelli was giving an interview on a national morning show earlier in the week when one of the hosts inadvertently outed her by asking about her girlfriend, who'd been visiting her backstage. Rather than deny it and give the papers a field day, Miss Balderelli thought it best to issue a statement confirming that she was, in fact, a lesbian."

"Oh, that poor woman." Though she'd never felt compelled to hide such a basic fact about herself, Andie's heart went out to the unfortunate judge. It wasn't fair for anyone to be forced into revealing more about their personal lives than they were ready for, especially in such a public way. "Look, she never said a word about it during our time on the show, okay?"

"So just to be sure I understand your position, at no time while you were a contestant on the show did Jessica Balderelli proposition you or in any way suggest that she would vote for you in the final round in exchange for sexual favors?"

"In...in exchange for..." Andie spluttered as the rest of the picture came into sharp focus. "Jesus, is *that* what Duncan's saying happened?"

"In part," Todd confirmed.

Her anger burned so hot that Andie forgot she'd ever felt cold. "That son of a bitch! I knew he hated me for winning, but I didn't think he'd stoop so low as to suggest the only way I could do so was to sleep with one of the judges."

"And blackmail her," Todd added matter-of-factly.

"What?" Andie cringed as she heard her own shriek echo back across the line.

"Miss Balderelli had gone to some lengths to hide her sexual orientation publicly. And up until the last episode, she'd shown her support for every contestant except you. Duncan King alleges that you slept with her and then threatened to go public if she didn't vote for you in the final round."

"That goddamned—" Andie choked, at a loss for words. She'd been about to call him a weasel, but she stopped herself as she realized the comparison wasn't fair. She had no desire to insult the weasel community. "I would never do something like that."

"I will say, it's unfortunate that you're not in a serious relationship."

"I beg your pardon?" Okay, sure, she hadn't been on a date in over a year, but that didn't make her the charity case his condescending tone implied. Since her win, she'd been on the go constantly on behalf of the network. It left her with precious little energy to spend worrying about her love life. "Duncan's running a tabloid smear campaign that's threatening my standing with the network, and you think it's my love life that's unfortunate?"

"It's just, it would make the story less credible—"

"You know what else makes this story less credible, Todd? Reality." Andie squeezed her words through a jaw that was tightly clenched. "Please understand me when I say that I've never even spoken with Jessica Balderelli except for on camera during the show."

"I understand, Miss Bartlett. And you'd be willing to file a formal statement to that effect with the network legal department?"

"Yes, of course." Andie pinched the bridge of her nose with her free hand. *Legal departments and formal statements?* Duncan was a real piece of work, but she'd never dreamed he'd take it this far.

"Great!" Andie could almost hear Todd's grin through

the phone. "Then I'll just pass you back over to Tracy and she can help sort things out with your car."

The car. Andie blinked as she realized that she'd been on the phone with Todd for at least ten minutes and, in all that time, her ride to the airport had yet to materialize. Her pulse began to race as she reviewed her options. She was running beyond late, and there were no cabs in sight. Though she was a born-and-bred city girl, catching a bus with no knowledge of the schedule or how to ask for help in Italian was beyond the scope of her abilities. She needed help.

"Tracy," she said as soon as the line was picked up, "where's the car?"

"Hi, Andie! Hell of a thing, all this, isn't it? I'm so sorry."

"Thanks." Andie's anxiousness abated at the genuine sympathy in Tracy's tone, and the clicking of a keyboard in the background reassured her that the network's resident miracle worker already had the situation well in hand. "Look, if it's too late for the flight to LAX, why don't you book me on one to New York. I wouldn't mind a night in my own bed. Or maybe Miami, instead?"

That last one was a flash of inspiration. It was just as warm in Miami as LA, with the added bonus of dropping in on her mom. Andie had been promising for months to visit her mom in the Florida retirement community Andie's winnings had helped her move into. It was way overdue. Miami was perfect.

"Miami?" Tracy's tinkling laugh rang out at the other end of the line. "I'm afraid that's out of the question."

Of course. The spring break crowds. Andie had forgotten how popular the sunshine state could be this time of year. "Fine, fine. LaGuardia, then. Or JFK. I'm not picky."

"Didn't Todd explain?" This time there was no laughter.

"Explain what?"

"He was supposed to tell you that, for legal reasons, the network would prefer for you to stay out of the spotlight for a little while, until all this blows over. New York's out of the question, and Los Angeles is crawling with paparazzi."

"Okay…so where?"

"I've found you a really nice apartment about an hour away, and I'm setting up the transportation now."

"You're telling me I'm stuck in Italy. For how long? A couple days? A week?" she cringed as she said it. She'd never survive a week.

"Three months."

"What?" Andie yanked the phone from her ear and gave it a shake to make sure it was functioning properly. Perhaps she'd misheard.

"I could kill Todd for leaving it to me to tell you. That goddamned weasel!" Tracy let out a frustrated cry, though it was nothing compared to how Andie felt inside.

Yeah. Todd and Duncan, both! After the blow of this terrible news, Andie no longer had the energy to defend the reputation of some pesky little rodents. The weasel community was on its own. She had bigger issues to deal with. "But Tracy, three months is the entire length of my sabbatical."

"I'm afraid so. Under the circumstances, the powers that be all felt it would be better for you to spend it in a more out-of-the-way place. It gives legal enough time to sink Duncan's lawsuit, and keeps fresh photos of your face out of the tabloids while they do, which is the real key. It's a win-win, really."

"Twenty-four hours from now, I was supposed to be on the beach. I haven't had a single carb in months, just getting ready for bikini season, so forgive me if I fail to see how I'm winning in any part of this."

"Let's try to stay positive, Andie. I found a great little place for you to stay in a village so small that no one will ever think to look for you there."

"Fantastic." From the complete lack of enthusiasm in her voice, Andie was fairly certain Tracy knew how she really felt. "What am I supposed to do to stay busy in the godforsaken place you're sending me?"

"Work on your cookbook, obviously. It's Italy! It's a paradise for cooks. I'm having all the boxes that were being sent to Los Angeles rerouted to your new location. You'll have them in a week or two."

"A week or two. And what do I do until they arrive?"

"Whatever you'd like. It's called vacation, Andie. Rest and relax. You should try it."

"Rest and relax isn't really my style. Is there at least some entertainment in this place?"

After a pause, during which Andie could hear more keyboard tapping, Tracy exhaled a pained sigh. "I'm afraid there's not much. The town website is crap, but it looks like there's a farmers market in the central piazza a few times a week, and hey, some sort of old Roman fountain. That sounds kind of interesting, don't you think?"

"Thrilling." Andie swallowed the rest of her opinions on the location of her exile, knowing it wasn't Tracy's fault, even though doing so left her with a bitter taste in her mouth.

"There's a pizza place that gets some good reviews. And a chocolate shop. Andie, you love chocolate!"

Tracy said it as though it was a marvelous coincidence, one that redeemed the entire fiasco, but Andie wanted no part of her delusion. "Everyone loves chocolate. But chocolate is loaded with carbs, so I'm afraid that's right out."

"But you're not going to the beach, remember? You don't have to worry about that bikini now."

"Oh, no. No way. I didn't suffer through the entire holiday season without bread or sweets to give up now." Andie patted her hip with her free hand. She wouldn't describe it as skinny by any means, but there was definitely less jiggle, which was a real accomplishment. "That means no pizza, and no chocolate."

"But you're in Italy!"

"The camera adds ten pounds, Tracy, no matter where I happen to be. Did you watch last season? I looked like a whale."

"Man, Andie, you chose the wrong place to be on a low-carb diet."

"I didn't *choose* to be here at all! And I'll be avoiding the chocolate shop like the plague if I want to fit into my wardrobe on the show next season."

"Well, you can't avoid the shop completely, because that's where you'll pick up the apartment key. It may also be the only place in Montamore that sells coffee."

Andie groaned. "Beaches and sushi, Tracy, that's what I signed up for. And gyms filled with sexy women in skimpy sports bras so that I'm motivated to actually work out before we start filming. And a Starbucks on every corner. Instead, you've banished me to a land of bread and chocolate."

"And wine. There's a vineyard. I was saving that part as a surprise. But, wait. Isn't wine a carb?"

"Wine is an exception to the carb rule, that's what wine is. And for that one reason, I will go. That, and because I literally have no choice since my contract says that the network has final say over everything I do for the next three years. So, when should I expect to see the limo?"

After another long pause came a strangled groan. "That's the other thing Todd was supposed to mention. It's a hilltop village and the roads are far too narrow for such a big car. We've found you something a little smaller."

Andie gaped at the thin ribbon of pavement in front of her that was already insufficient for travel. Then she shut her eyes tight to block out the view. Just what she needed, a town with even smaller roads than Florence. "And when should I expect this smaller car to arrive?"

As if on cue, a high-pitched beeping sound caught her attention, and when she opened her eyes, she was amazed to see something that looked like an old VW bug, but one that had accidentally been put in a hot dryer until it was one-third its original size. As she stared unblinking, it zipped up to the curb just a few feet away from where she stood. She watched in growing horror as, instead of a side door, the entire front end of the car swung open to reveal a smiling man with a mustache and a red-and-white-striped shirt. He looked like a misplaced gondolier, seated on a tiny bench with a steering wheel and pedals mounted to the floor on one side. "You've got to be kidding me. What the hell is this, Tracy?"

"A micro-car!" Tracy responded, with much more enthusiasm than the toy vehicle merited. "I was assured by the agency that it's the perfect size for navigating even the smallest streets."

Andie looked from her suitcase to the minuscule car and

its average-sized driver, who took up more than half the seat all by himself. "How am I supposed to fit in this thing?"

"You just have the one bag, right?"

"Yes, but between it, and me, and the driver—"

"Oh, dear. I hadn't gotten to that part yet. You *are* the driver. He's just dropping it off for you. You're going to need something to get around in while you're there. You've got your license, right? All the rest of the paperwork is set."

Andie's heart rate ticked up as the driver unfolded his legs from the front of the car like an origami frog and hoisted himself to his feet. She knew how to drive, fortunately, but living in Manhattan, she tried to use public transportation when she could. And, not that she was a diva or anything, but since her win, she'd grown rather fond of the limousines the network shuttled her from place to place in. Now she was supposed to drive *this*? In disbelief, she scribbled her signature on half a dozen documents she didn't bother to read, then took the keys he offered and nodded dumbly as he said something in Italian before heading off down the street on foot. When he'd disappeared from view, she turned her attention back to her phone call with a growing appreciation for the seriousness of her situation. "I'm screwed, aren't I."

"Don't think like that!" Tracy had no doubt meant her words to be reassuring, but Andie couldn't help but notice that it wasn't exactly a "no."

"What am I supposed to think? One baseless accusation of cheating, and suddenly the limo's gone and the network's sending me into exile on a riding lawnmower."

"Look, we all know there's nothing to this. It's just, after the fallout from that whole sexual harassment mess last year, if the network so much as hears the word sex, they freak out. And given the influence Duncan's dad has at the *Star Post*, they're not taking any chances of the story getting out of hand. That's all this is."

Andie hoisted her suitcase into the passenger side of the car, letting out a puff of breath that froze in the air. "You're sure?"

"Positive. Everyone who knows you, or Duncan, knows that what he claims couldn't have happened. They're taking this seriously, but they'll get to the truth eventually. In the meantime, make the best of it. Do you have any idea what I wouldn't do for three months in Italy on the company's dime?"

Settling herself into the driver's seat, Andie hoped she could get the door closed without having to press her knees up against her ears. "Wanna trade?"

Tracy laughed, but the sound was more like a warning bell, one that signaled that the network was taking Duncan much more seriously than his accusations should have merited. Was there something that Tracy wasn't sharing? But instead of offering any more details or reassurances, Tracy simply sent her the directions to the chocolate shop and then ended the call.

Slamming the front of the car back into the closed position, Andie wasn't certain whether she felt more like she was encased in a coffin or a cocoon. This could be the end of her dreams, and she knew it. Fame was fickle, and if the network cut her loose, there'd be a thousand fresh faces lined up to replace her. She'd done nothing wrong, but it didn't always matter. That meteoric career she'd been granted could flame out in a heartbeat.

She frowned at her destination on the map. Montamore. It was barely a dot, hardly a place that would hold any promise. And yet, as she pulled gingerly away from the curb to begin her journey, she found herself praying to be wrong. This couldn't be the end. Whatever it took, she needed to emerge from this exile as the biggest, most beautiful damn butterfly the world had ever seen.

THREE

PARTICLES OF DUST lingered in the air as Valentina rested the broom against the old peach-tinted plaster wall inside her shop. The checkered floor tiles shone brightly, and she gave a satisfied nod as she surveyed her little kingdom. If her father was looking down from heaven, he, too, would be proud. Valentine's Day was the biggest day in a chocolate maker's year, and Cioccolatini di Venere was up to the challenge.

The copper and brass espresso maker shone brightly in its corner. A petite hot chocolate kettle sat ready for use beside the behemoth machine, glittering from a fresh polish. They were both vintage models with an appearance like something straight out of a Jules Verne novel, but surprisingly simple to use. A teenager could be trained to do it, that is if the shop ever had enough customers to require another hand besides those of the four generations of women who kept it running now.

Beside the coffee station, a glass case filled with her mother's delectable pastries awaited the influx of customers who would arrive in the afternoon, to indulge in a quick pick-me-up and a few minutes of gossip. Valentina could just about match each baked good to the local patron who would buy it. Despite her mother's constant insistence that they'd be swarmed on any given day by some new tour bus that was bound to happen through, Valentina had convinced her over time to make exactly enough of each kind to satisfy their regulars, with just a few extras of the most popular ones in case of surprise guests. No one ever went without, and there was rarely any waste. Despite this, her mother still resented her for it, as if Valentina's frugality was what kept the tourists at bay.

The shop's specialty chocolates, the ones their reputation was built on and which Valentina now mostly made herself, in the very early mornings when the temperatures were just right, were piled high on silver trays in a different case. This one was an art nouveau masterpiece made of solid carved oak and curved glass that her great-great grandfather had purchased when he opened the shop at the turn of the last century. There were always more chocolates on display inside it than they would sell in a day, or even a week, but chocolate lasted longer than most people realized, and Valentina knew as well as her mother did that abundance created an atmosphere of decadence that encouraged sales. She just favored a more sensible and measured approach.

Across the back wall, rows of glass apothecary jars lined the shelves of a heavy and equally ancient wooden cabinet that stood nearly as tall as the ceiling. It was stocked with more brightly colored candies than they were likely to sell in a year, but it gave the otherwise dark interior of the shop a festive pop of color, and Valentina enjoyed handing out the occasional free treat to the local children as a way to keep the contents of the jars refreshed. It was a tradition her father had started, and every time she gave away a brightly swirled lollipop or speckled jawbreaker, she thought of him. Just because she'd grown into a shrewd businesswoman didn't mean she lacked a heart.

Reaching into the window display at the front of the shop, Valentina adjusted the single gold-wrapped box that formed the apex of a perfect pyramid. All around its base she'd arranged delectable chocolates shaped like hearts and birds, and—after her objections had once again this year gone unheeded by both her mother and grandmother alike—dozens upon dozens of smiling Cupids. How she hated their smug little faces, nearly as much as she hated the view of their oversized counterpart in the piazza. He was still frolicking out there in his stupid fountain, twenty years to the day since what she'd come to think of as *The Incident*.

It had been her first and only encounter with the impish god. She'd learned over the years to look past him when she gazed out the shop window, avoiding eye contact. It worked for the most part, but every February, these edible versions invaded her space with their bows and arrows. They were like a miniature chocolate love army ready for battle, and she their foe. It was all Valentina could do to keep from going insane just from looking at them.

She stepped back from the window and glanced at the clock behind the register. It was nearly noon. After the typical morning rush of people in need of coffee and breakfast, plus maybe a last-minute gift for a lover or friend, she'd been alone for several hours. She expected another crowd in the late afternoon, perhaps a bit bigger than usual because of the holiday, but like any other day of the year, the shop stood much emptier than she would've liked. The whole town was like that these days. There just weren't enough people to keep things bustling as they once had. She and her family managed to stay afloat, but only barely, as the number of tourists and residents alike decreased each year. Theirs was far from the only business struggling.

Surrounding the central piazza were dozens of buildings, painted in shades of golden yellow and arranged at the edge of the cobblestones in a gentle curve. It was as charming a spot as any Tuscan village could hope to offer, with potted plants and café umbrellas aplenty, and yet it seemed each year, another landmark of her youth went out of business, and nothing new ever came along to fill the space. There were so many darkened windows in their once vibrant main street that when the lights came on in the evening, it resembled a gap-toothed grin. But there was nothing funny about the steady stream of families packing up and leaving for better opportunities. A few managed to sell their homes, but many others were stuck trying to rent them out to vacationers when they could. Valentina had recently started making a little money on the side by managing those properties for neighbors who'd gone elsewhere. Perhaps she should've considered going elsewhere, too, but she had the shop to think about. And Chiara.

The front door jingled and Valentina's head snapped up. Having just said her daughter's name in her mind, she almost expected to see the little girl running through the door in her bright blue school smock. But this was one of the nights she spent with her father, and so she wouldn't be home until after dinner. Instead, it was Valentina's mother who entered the shop with a bundle of blood-red roses nestled in her arms. The cloying stench of romance made Valentina's nose itch.

"These will make it more festive in here, don't you think?" her mother asked as she sat the paper-wrapped bouquets on the counter and began hunting for a vase. Why was it that the woman, who'd made being in a bad mood an art form, was always so chipper on *this* day? *Does she do it just to piss me off?* "Maybe add a few to the new window? Anything to encourage those last-minute sales!"

Valentina raised an eyebrow at the abundance of flowers but held her tongue. She knew her disdain for the traditional trappings of romance was irrational. She made her living off chocolate, for heaven's sake. What could be more symbolic of romance than that? But she couldn't help how she felt. Ever since she'd become the only divorced woman in Montamore, everything about this holiday—from the flowers, to the heart-shaped boxes, to those horrible little Cupids—made her skin crawl.

Romance. What's the big deal, anyway? Valentina was certain she didn't know. Even when she'd donned a white dress and veil on the day she'd married Luca, she'd suspected there was something missing from inside her that other brides felt. Was it any surprise, then, that her marriage had ended? She simply wasn't cut out for it. Being alone again wasn't so bad. She had her daughter and her shop. She didn't need anything else.

I'm fine, really. Happy even, Valentina assured herself. *Of course, I am.* She simply preferred when the whole romance thing wasn't shoved in her face. Truth be told, she was counting the hours before she could rip down every scrap of pink and red crepe paper and replace it all with the cotton-tailed bunnies and fluffy yellow chicks that would herald spring. As for the roses? Oh, how she wished she could tell her mother to throw them all in the trash.

"I need to go out for a minute," she told her mother instead, knowing from experience that saying anything else would be pointless.

"Out? It's the busiest day of the year, Valentina!" A crease formed in her mother's brow, so deep it looked like her head was about to fold itself in half. It was exactly the same response she would have received if she'd told her mother to shove the roses up her ass, and oh how she wished now that she had. Her mother hated foul language with a passion. How satisfying that would've been.

"Yes, I can see how busy it is." Valentina made a point of visually examining every corner of the empty shop. "But I need to go check on the Rossini place across the square. I got a notice a few hours ago that someone's rented it. I'll be back in plenty of time for the afternoon rush."

"Oh, I hadn't seen that." The deep forehead lines receded and her mother's expression brightened with a smile. "Someone new is moving to Montamore? Things are finally turning around!"

But Valentina shook her head. "Just a short-term rental. Three months. It's been empty a while, so I need to make sure it's presentable before I hand over the key."

"Well, at least so many empty places means it will be easier for you and Luca to find something nice when you're ready."

Valentina gritted her teeth. "We're divorced, Mama. We won't be looking for a place together. You know that."

"You never know. People reconcile all the time, and think how happy Chiara would be not to go back and forth between you."

"It's been a year, Mama. Is this about you wanting to move back to the second floor?" When she and Luca had married, her mother had moved in with her grandmother to the smaller apartment on the first floor. Valentina suspected she'd been rethinking the deal ever since the divorce.

"No, of course not. I can barely make it up and down the stairs." This was a lie. The stairs had never stopped either of the old ladies from barging in, day or night, like they still owned the place. "I just know you'd be happier together. It was meant to be."

"And I know we wouldn't be. When are you going to accept that for what it is?" But of course, Valentina knew the answer. Her mother would accept it when hell—or that damned fountain—froze over. Both scenarios were equally unlikely. Even in the dead of winter, the water never stopped flowing. Proof of Cupid's power, the neighbors claimed. More like proof that the source was a hot spring and their ancestors had been clever with plumbing, but Valentina's way of looking at it was definitely in the minority.

"Valentina, can you check to see if we have enough Cupids in the basket by the register?" her mother asked, ignoring her protestations about Luca completely.

Valentina glared at the basket, which was overflowing with dozens of factory-produced copies of her shiny, foil-wrapped nemesis. Swiping one from the basket, she ripped the foil from the top and bit off his head while her mother watched in horror. "There were too many. Now it looks better." She grabbed up the keys to the Rossini place and shoved them in her pocket. "I'll be back in a bit."

VALENTINA'S EYES swept across the apartment, which belonged to her old friend Sofia. Sofia and her family had left for Rome the year before. She inspected it from top to bottom, taking in the traditional terra cotta ceiling tiles, the compact but efficient kitchen with its hooded stove, and the sliding glass door that led to a balcony overlooking a communal herb garden. It was a charming little place, and yet most of the year it sat empty, like so many others in town. Valentina guessed that about half the people she'd gone to school with had left since the start of the last economic downturn, which in truth had never really come to an end in small villages such as hers.

Their best hope for a revival was a resurgence in tourism, but without a decent website and a smart marketing strategy, that was unlikely to occur. Valentina had looked into such services for her shop, but both cost a whole lot more cash than she, or virtually anyone in town, had to spend. There was little hope left for Montamore. Losing the shop her father had spent his life building up, the one she had promised him on his deathbed to take care of, was more than she could bear. The question of how to turn it around was one that kept her tossing and turning through far too many nights, and as much as she sometimes complained about the place, the prospect of leaving Montamore broke her heart.

Valentina sighed as she finished her once-over and shut the front door. The intoxicating scent of freshly cooked pizza tickled her nose as soon as she hit the stairwell. The town's lone pizzeria occupied the ground floor of the building, and she knew that Francesca would be hard at work inside preparing tables for the lunchtime crowd. Her husband, Paolo, worked the ovens. Theirs was one of the few places where business was reliably brisk year-round. After all, everyone had to eat, and pizza was a favorite no matter who you were, maybe even more popular than her own offerings of coffee and chocolate.

Valentina hesitated in the building's small entryway, her rumbling stomach at odds with her heart. Though Francesca had remained her best friend all these years, lately their relationship had been strained. It wasn't Francesca's fault. While Valentina had been married, she and Luca and Francie and Paolo had been thick as thieves. But now, certain feelings for her best friend that she thought she'd gotten rid of for good had bobbed back to the surface like the bloated carcass of a fish. In her heart, Valentina knew the only way to deal with it was to keep her distance for a while, and yet it made her lonelier by far than her divorce had done. Francesca wasn't just her best friend, she was just about her only friend, or at least the only one who hadn't moved away. Smart or not, she couldn't continue to stay away.

Entering the pizzeria, Valentina nodded at the man behind the counter. "Hey, Paolo! Any chance you have one of my favorite calzones ready, or will I have to wait?"

"Valentina! If I'd known you were coming by today, I would have popped one in already. But go sit down. I'll have one out as soon as I can." Paolo grinned broadly as he spoke, erasing all traces of age to reveal the boy her best friend had fallen in love with, and risked her safety to beg Cupid for, twenty years before. *Lucky bastard.* Though she loved him like a brother, there was a heaviness in her chest sometimes when she saw them together. But Valentina had to admit that he'd made Francesca happier than anyone she'd ever seen. They had a home, and a business, and three adorable children with another on the way. What more could she want for her friend?

She pulled out a chair and had just lowered herself into it when Francesca emerged from the kitchen, heading toward her with the distinctive pregnancy waddle. It had been ten years since she'd experienced it herself, but Valentina remembered the sensation well. She shook her head in wonder at the swelling bump that was baby number four. "Look at you! You're showing already?"

"I should hope so." Francesca eased herself into the chair on the other side of Valentina's table. If it weren't for the way her friend avoided direct eye contact, it would have seemed that nothing was amiss. "I'm nearly in the third trimester."

"Already?"

"I guess you lost track. It must be really busy in the shop. I haven't seen you in a while."

"Well, it's the high season, you know. Christmas through Easter, it's chocolate, chocolate, chocolate. We've been crazy for weeks." Valentina squirmed. It was a stretch of the truth to say the least, but if her friend was willing to toss her a life preserver, Valentina was going to grab hold. "You know as soon as the little one gets here, you won't be able to shoo me away. I love babies."

Francesca perked up at this. "Enough to have another?"

The very thought made her blanch. Valentina loved her daughter dearly, but unlike her best friend, she had no desire to go through the whole pregnancy experience more than once. It had been just one of the hundreds of ways in which she'd discovered that she and her ex-husband were completely incompatible. He would've been happy trying for half a dozen. She would've been happier sleeping in separate bedrooms. Needless to say, it had eventually become an issue.

"Definitely not!" Valentina shuddered in the overly dramatic way that always made her friend laugh. Soon they were both smiling and the tension between them, at least for now, was water under the bridge.

"Just stopping in for lunch?"

"No, I was making sure Sofia's apartment was ready. You're going to have a new neighbor upstairs for a few months."

"Really?" Francesca's dark eyes blazed with curiosity. A newcomer, even a temporary one, was a major source of interest in a town where very little happened. "Who?"

Valentina frowned, trying to recall the details. "Honestly, I'm not sure. It was booked by an American company, something called Sizzle Network. But in the notes, it mentioned an *A. Bartlett*. That's all I know."

"Wait, Sizzle Network? Are you serious?" Francesca's eyes were wide.

Valentina translated the English words into Italian and a horrible possibility crossed her mind. "That's not an adult entertainment channel, is it?"

Francesca laughed. "That would be a clever name, wouldn't it? But no. They do cooking shows. We've just started getting them here. You don't think your A. Bartlett could be *Andie* Bartlett, do you? I love Andie Bartlett!"

"Andy Bartlett…" Valentina squinted as she tried to place the name, but nothing came to her. "Who's he?"

"The American celebrity chef! And *he* is a *she*. She's fantastic. How do you not know who Andie Bartlett is?"

"Maybe because I'm a single mother who works twelve hours a day."

"But that's why you should watch her! She makes cooking a healthy dinner feel easy. You'd like her. She's funny and entertaining—and a lesbian, if I recall correctly..." The pensive expression that passed over her best friend's face made Valentina's pulse quicken. *Why would she mention* that, *of all things, and what does she mean to imply by that look she's giving me?*

"Well, I already know how to cook just fine, thanks," Valentina hurriedly assured her, wresting control of the conversation before either of them had time to see where Francesca's thoughts might lead. "I have about as much use for cooking shows as I do for an adult entertainment network."

"Sounds to me like a little adult entertainment is *exactly* what you could use," Francesca said with a suggestive raise of the eyebrows.

"Francesca!" Heat flushed her cheeks in the way it always did when anything to do with sex was brought up. *And a lesbian, if I recall correctly...* Why did those particular words have to choose this exact moment to echo through her mind?

"I'm serious!" Francesca laughed impishly. "I know you don't like talking about it, but everyone needs sex."

"Yeah, well, just look where it keeps getting you," Valentina grumbled, still squirming in her seat.

Francesca patted her round belly without a hint of regret. "Clearly, I know what I'm talking about. I mean, it's not like you're a nun. Unless..." She clapped her hands together, eyes wide. "You and Luca aren't back together, are you?"

"I swear, between you and my mother!" Valentina pretended outrage, though what she felt was relief that they'd moved safely away from anything to do with the

American chef and her sexual preferences. "Why is everyone so hell-bent on me getting back with my ex? It's not normal."

"Because splitting up isn't normal," Francesca said softly, and in a way that made it clear she said it without judgment. "Not around here. You and Luca are meant to be together."

"Trust me, we're not."

"But the fountain—"

"The fountain?" Valentina sighed. "I know everyone here believes in that thing but look at this place. It's empty. If we really had the secret to everlasting love flowing through the middle of our town square, don't you think word would've gotten out? We should have tourists lined up all the way to the main highway, waiting for their chance to give Cupid their letters."

"You're right, we should." Francesca's reply was more pensive than combative. "I don't know why we don't, but I do know this: the fact that people outside of Montamore don't know about it doesn't prove anything. Just look around you at all the happy couples. Cupid's never been wrong."

"Present company excluded." Valentina stood abruptly and pushed in her chair. She didn't want to talk about this anymore. "I need to head back."

"Without your food?" Francesca stood as well and studied Valentina with troubled eyes. "I'm sorry. I didn't mean to make you upset."

"It's okay, you didn't," Valentina assured her, forcing a smile. She couldn't bear to see Francesca look sad. "It's Valentine's Day. I really do need to get back to the shop."

"But you haven't eaten!"

"I had a chocolate Cupid on my way over." *Bit that sucker's head clean off, and it served him right.*

Francesca laughed, and for a second, Valentina worried that she'd said the last part aloud. But then her friend reached out and touched a fingertip to a spot just beside Valentina's lip. "I see that. You still have a little bit, right there."

Francesca gave the spot a gentle dab, and when she'd removed her finger, Valentina touched her tongue to the spot self-consciously, alarmed not so much by the fact that she'd been walking around with chocolate on her face, which was a common occupational hazard, but by how aware she remained of the tingling sensation where Francesca's finger had been. *This is why it's better to keep my distance,* she reminded herself. *It's safer that way.*

After she'd married Luca, she'd convinced herself that those feelings she had for Francesca—and not *just* Francesca, if Valentina were brutally honest, but sometimes other women, too—simply didn't happen anymore. She'd trained herself not to feel that way about her best friend, or any female. Mind over matter. It's what everyone wanted for her, and it made life in Montamore so much easier. But every so often, she slipped. The inability to control her desires troubled her as much now as it had when she was young.

"Right. I'd better go." Valentina took a nervous breath as the significance of the day's date struck her. Now that she was grown, she tended to forget that the fourteenth of February was not just a busy day at work, but her birthday, too. "Uh, I know I haven't been around much lately to mention it, but, tomorrow night—"

"Your annual birthday dinner?" Francesca's expression

reflected Valentina's own uncertainty. "I was wondering if you were still...that is, if we were still—"

"Invited? Of course!" Some of the tension flowed out of Valentina's muscles as Francesca flashed a smile in response. "Same time, same place. After all these years, I figured you'd just know, but I should've mentioned it earlier. And I should've been around more, no matter how busy things have been. I'm really sorry."

"Well, you know we wouldn't miss your dinner for anything." Francesca's assurance filled her with relief, along with a host of other emotions that were harder for Valentina to put a name to.

Back outside again, instead of racing across the square to her shop as she normally would, Valentina's steps slowed as she neared the fountain. When she was just a few feet away, she stopped, and for the first time in twenty years, she looked directly into Cupid's face, staring him down. "You've caused a lot of trouble for me," she informed him, not breaking eye contact.

It was clear from Cupid's expression that he disagreed with her assessment.

"Don't tell me you've forgotten *The Incident*."

He remained stony-faced and unrepentant.

"And how about Luca, the dark-haired boy with hazelnut cream eyes? What do you have to say for yourself about that?"

I had nothing to do with that, Cupid silently chided. *You're the one who made up that story, all by yourself.*

"Well, I wouldn't have had to," she pointed out, muttering under her breath, "if you hadn't started showing me things I didn't want to see. And if you hadn't done that, I wouldn't have fallen in, and if I hadn't fallen in, then half the population of Montamore wouldn't have ended up in our shop, and I never would've made up that story in the first place."

The statue was speechless, which left Valentina feeling vindicated.

"Besides," she continued, "are you telling me you had nothing to do with bringing Luca here? Not even the slightest bit?"

Again, Cupid said nothing, but his cherubic face was guilty as sin, and Valentina gave him a satisfied nod. "That's what I thought. Never in my life had I met anyone with hazelnut cream eyes. I didn't even know they really existed! And yet, out of all the villages in Italy, a boy with hazelnut cream eyes just *happened* to move to Montamore, exactly when he did?"

The year leading up to Luca's arrival had been a particularly rough one for Valentina. She'd been in her last year at the istituto professionale and had just been accepted for an internship with a master chocolate maker in Belgium, but then her father had had a heart attack. Her mother blamed it on all the extra driving back and forth to Valentina's school, and by extension, on Valentina herself. Deep down, Valentina did, too.

Her father had survived for a time, but never quite recovered. Guilt had overwhelmed Valentina, and with only her mother and grandmother left to run the shop, there was no way she could go to Belgium. After graduation, she'd stayed in Montamore. And one by one, she'd watched her friends get engaged. First it had been Mia, then Sofia and Bianca. Finally, it had been Francesca's turn. That had been the last straw, the one that plunged her into a major panic, as she truly realized that everyone she loved was leaving her behind. Then a new young man moved to town, and it escaped exactly no one's attention that he matched Valentina's description of the boy from the fountain, down to nearly every detail.

She could have argued that Luca's hair wasn't dark enough or pointed out that he lacked the tiny mole beside one eye. She could have come clean and admitted she'd made up the whole vision in the first place, that she'd never seen a boy at all. In retrospect, that would've been the smartest move, even if she had lacked the courage to confess the deeper truth about herself that she'd been trying to hide. But she hadn't. To this day, she wasn't sure why.

Maybe some small part of her wished her made-up story had been real. How simple that would've made things. Instead, she'd done the next easiest thing and just kept pretending. She'd let her mother and grandmother, along with all the old ladies in the village, push her and Luca together until finally she'd agreed to a date, and then another. Were there sparks? No. But he was nice. They got along. As her father's health declined, he started helping out in the shop. By the time Luca proposed, she'd nearly forgotten that her vision wasn't true.

On her wedding day, she'd felt relief. She didn't have to worry anymore. Her choice was made, her future secure. It was good enough. She had no need for whatever hid behind the mysterious door that Cupid had once tried to show her, if indeed the whole thing hadn't been a figment of her own youthful imagination. Any lingering concerns about her sexuality had remained unexamined, buried deep. Until now.

Inexplicably, as she stood face-to-face with the fountain she'd refused so much as to look at for twenty years, curiosity burned her from the inside. Maybe it was all that talk of sex, or the forbidden flush she still felt from when Francesca's fingers had brushed her skin. Perhaps it was the auspiciousness of the anniversary—twenty years, nearly to the hour. It was a long time to go without facing the truth, and the longer she stood there, the more the questions weighed on her. Was there really someone out there for her? If she hadn't panicked and fallen in, whose face would have greeted her in the ripples? Valentina looked from Cupid's face and down to the water, which gurgled and bubbled as it always did. *Probably no one's,* she reminded herself harshly. *What makes you think there's anyone special out there for you?*

Even so, Valentina drew a breath and squared her shoulders, giving Cupid her best no-nonsense stare. "I told you back then, and I'll say it now. I don't want any funny business. I don't want you doing anything, or heaven forbid to go summoning anyone like you did with Luca, got that? No interfering. I'm just fine with the way things are. I like being alone. I just...want to know." She inhaled again in an effort to ward off the shakiness she felt. "If the door had opened all the way, what would I have seen?" Despite her erstwhile conviction that it was nothing but hogwash and old wives' tales, her stomach churned alarmingly as she reached into her coat pocket and pulled out a shiny euro coin.

Clenching it in her fist, she took a step closer to stand over the basin of swirling water, but her knees trembled to such an extent that she quickly sat, perching on the fountain's damp stone rim, for fear that she wouldn't be able to support her weight. She hadn't brought a letter. It's not like she'd planned this out, and she didn't exactly walk around town with letters to Cupid in her pockets. Maybe it wouldn't work without the letter. But even that happy prospect didn't do much to stop her from shaking.

It was foolish to be scared. She wasn't a schoolgirl anymore. At thirty-four years old, with both a marriage and a divorce under her belt, it wasn't like she didn't already know, deep down, the nature of the attractions she felt. She wasn't that unaware. The only thing that had changed is that finally, she was willing to face the facts head-on. Sort of, anyway. She'd face them, as long as she wasn't required to do anything about them.

Swallowing hard, eyes shut, she tossed the coin into the pool and then forced herself to pry her eyelids open and look into the water. Her breath froze in her lungs as, clear as day, she saw the image of a woman with brilliant orange hair, cropped short and spiky, almost as if her head was on fire. *A woman, for sure. Well, you already knew that, didn't you?* The image was not precisely what Valentina might have pictured as being her type had she ever given any thought to such a question, but the woman was stunning in her own way.

Valentina stared at the vision, unable to turn away. *She looks so real, like she could be standing right behind me.* As she stared, her heart seemed to cease its beating in her chest, and the world around her slowed to a crawl. There was no denying it. Cupid's magic was real, after all.

The sound of a clearing throat prompted Valentina's heart to move from still to racing. Someone *was* right behind her. She spun around and found herself facing a very real woman with flame-orange hair.

"Valentina?"

The shock of hearing her name on the woman's lips threw Valentina off to such a degree that she jumped up, and before she could put her arms out to regain her balance, she felt her body falling backward, well beyond the point of no return. For the second time in her life she experienced the weightless sensation of being suspended in air. She tensed, waiting for the stab of a thousand icy needles that she knew would come next as her body hit the water. But it never came.

FOUR

WITHOUT PAUSING A SECOND TO THINK, Andie's arms shot out, her fingers digging deep into the wool sleeves of the woman's coat as she grasped her upper arms and wrenched her away from the frigid, swirling water. "Are you okay? You nearly fell in!"

The woman didn't reply. Instead, she drew several ragged breaths as she sank low, her whole body shaking badly as her bottom came to rest at the edge of the fountain. As Andie took in the sight of her, her own breathing grew shallow and her pulse quickened. Seated as she was, and so bundled beneath her heavy black coat and fur-trimmed hood, it was all but impossible to make out any details of the woman's height or figure. It didn't matter. That wasn't what captured Andie's interest. It was her eyes.

Even if the stranger had been standing there naked, Andie was sure her gaze never would've traveled any further than those midnight eyes. The woman's pupils were especially wide from fright, with the deepest shades of brown surrounding them so that they appeared nearly black, like a perfect dark-roast espresso—about the only thing in Andie's opinion that Italy consistently got right. The woman stared up at Andie without blinking, and Andie found herself incapable of looking away. The moment stretched out for so long, charged with such intensity, that it became thoroughly unnerving.

Andie cleared her throat and tried addressing her again, if only to break the spell. "I'm sorry, do you understand me?"

"How..." The woman broke eye-contact long enough to shoot a suspicious glance over her shoulder in the direction of a stone Cupid that smiled down on them from some distance above. Ordinarily, this wouldn't have struck her as odd, only Andie could've sworn the woman had been talking to that very same statue as she'd approached. "How do you know my name?"

"Oh, good. I was afraid you might not speak English, although the woman back in the shop seemed to speak it surprisingly well."

"My family has owned Cioccolatini di Venere for generations. It's popular with tourists, and most of them speak English, so of course I do, too. But you still haven't explained how you know who I am."

"It was on the rental agreement for the apartment. I asked at the chocolate shop and they told me I could find you out here."

"Ah." The wariness slowly subsided from Valentina's face, replaced by a cautiously polite smile and an outstretched hand. "Yes, I'm the property manager. Valentina Moretti."

"Andie Bartlett. Nice to meet you."

It was only when she went to extend her own hand for a

shake that Andie realized she was still holding both of Valentina's shoulders in an iron grip. Her fingers sprang open at once and Valentina wobbled at the suddenness of the release, but managed, much to Andie's relief, not to topple into the fountain. Overcome with awkwardness, Andie stuffed her hands into her coat pockets and took a step backward to create some distance between them.

"Andie Bartlett?" Valentina lowered the hand that had been left hanging and tucked it behind her knee. "The American from TV?"

Andie smiled broadly. "Yes, that's me. Are you a fan of the show?"

"Never seen it," Valentina mumbled with another look back at the fountain, "but my friend Francesca watches it. She, uh, told me about you."

"Good things, I hope?" Andie's too-loud laugh echoed in her ears as the woman fidgeted but didn't answer. Andie pinched the lining of her pockets, twisting the fabric anxiously while she waited for Valentina to say something else. *Could I have sounded any dorkier?* Andie was adept at keeping her cool in many circumstances, but two seconds in Valentina's presence, and she found herself demonstrating all the smooth moves of a high school freshman. All the while, the woman watched her, unblinking, her wide, dark eyes leaving Andie with the heady sensation of gazing into a distant galaxy. She forced herself to look away. "The key?"

"What? Oh, of course." Bright pink circles colored Valentina's cheeks as she rose to her feet. "Why don't I show you the apartment, just in case you have any questions. I apologize that the kitchen isn't stocked very well. I'm afraid I only received the booking a few hours ago and there's no grocery store in town. I can bring over some essentials if you need anything."

"No grocery store?" Thinking of the dozens of recipes she had to test over the coming months, Andie stifled a groan. She was already looking at a delay of a few weeks while she waited for her boxes to arrive. Now there was no place to get supplies? What was the network thinking, sending her here? She'd be lucky to get any work done at all. "But where do you shop?"

"There's a farmers market tomorrow in the piazza. Your apartment is just over there, above the pizzeria, so you can make do with that for tonight, and get whatever you else you need in the morning."

"Oh, I don't eat pizza. Too many carbs." Valentina said nothing in response, but her raised eyebrow left Andie with little doubt that the woman thought she was nuts. They'd probably never heard of a low-carb diet here.

Valentina led the way across the square and Andie followed. As she caught a whiff of baking dough outside, her stomach let out a sound like a truck going over gravel. She'd driven all the way to Montamore without stopping. In truth, she'd been afraid to stop, as she hadn't been convinced she'd get the toy car started again. That she'd made it all the way to her destination in one piece, and without snapping the steering wheel in two from how tightly she'd been clutching it, was a miracle. But now, the sharp pang in her gut was a reminder that she had yet to spare a thought for lunch. She took a deep sniff. "That smells divine."

"Best place in town," Valentina replied as she opened the door to the building. "Also, pretty much the only place in town, if I'm honest," she added with an apologetic shrug, "but even if it wasn't, it would be the best. I may be a little biased, though, as I'm very good friends with the owner."

Andie breathed in again and tried not to swoon. *Pizza. The forbidden food.* At least in LA, she could have ordered it with a cauliflower crust. But as they made their way to the second floor, even the stairwell held the heavenly, yeast-filled smell of baking bread. The intense gnawing in her belly, coupled with the emptiness of her new pantry, told her that resistance would be futile. After the stress of her morning, the prospect of indulging in a slice of crispy carbs topped with gooey cheese was more temptation than she could withstand. *Okay, maybe just one slice.* "I wonder if they could make one without tomatoes?"

She'd muttered the question to herself, but Valentina looked back with a curious tilt of her head. "Why, are you allergic?"

"No, I just don't like tomatoes," Andie replied, joining Valentina in front of the door to the flat.

"You don't like tomatoes? And you don't eat carbs, either." Valentina blinked in surprise, then gave a hearty laugh. As she did so, one hand came to rest on Andie's shoulder, setting alight a string of desire that burned from her skin to her innermost depths. Unable to form a coherent response, Andie just shook her head, the movement nudging her shoulder deeper into Valentina's palm. The woman's dark eyes widened, as if only just becoming aware of where she'd placed her hand. She pulled it quickly to her side, leaving Andie's shoulder bereft of warmth. "What on earth are you doing in Italy?"

"I've been asking myself that since I arrived." Andie swiveled her head so as not to stare at the spot on her shoulder where she could still feel the ghost of Valentina's touch. Though her skin cooled rapidly, a fire continued to burn inside. She glanced surreptitiously toward Valentina's fingers, which were fumbling with the key in a clumsy way that was oddly endearing. Clumsy or not, she wouldn't mind feeling them against her bare skin, should the opportunity arise.

The door swung open and Andie followed Valentina inside, though not before attempting to catch a glimpse of Valentina's bottom. Sadly, the bulky black coat obstructed her view, and so she turned her full attention to scoping out her new abode. Despite her reservations about the country as a whole, she was forced to admit that the apartment was much nicer than she'd expected.

It was tastefully furnished with an overstuffed sofa and matching chair, covered in a floral upholstery in shades of red and yellow that conjured up thoughts of the type of warm weather that was sorely lacking on that particular mid-February day. There was a sturdy table of weathered boards that stood in the dining area, flanked by two equally sturdy chairs. With a table like that, the possibilities were endless. An intimate dinner for two with her lovely landlady was just one idea Andie's imagination presented for her consideration. As for the rest of the images that quickly flooded her brain- of her, the landlady, and that particular table- they were shockingly explicit, and Andie shooed them right back out before they could make her blush. *If this is where my brain goes the minute I'm forced to take a vacation, I'd better get back to work soon!*

Fortunately, it turned out that the kitchen was the best and most unexpected feature of her temporary home. Though smaller than the kitchen she would have enjoyed in Los Angeles, it was still more spacious and well-appointed than anything she'd ever had in New York. She just might get some work done here, after all.

"Is that a six-burner gas stove?" Andie asked, looking from the gleaming steel appliance to the tile backsplash and rustic Italian-style hood. "Impressive. The owner must like to cook."

"Everyone likes to cook," Valentina replied, as if it were an established fact of the universe.

"Yes, I've noticed that around here," Andie said flatly. "So traditional. All that Italian food." She caught her nose starting to wrinkle and hoped that the pretty Italian lady hadn't noticed.

"Well, this *is* Italy." Valentina chuckled, her dark eyes even more captivating with the spark of amusement in them. "Maybe you could give it a chance. You know, there are dozens of Italian dishes that don't have tomatoes in them."

There was that amusement again, and this time Andie couldn't shake the feeling that maybe she'd sensed something more intimate, besides. Something that wasn't just a product of an idle imagination. Combined with the memory of Valentina's hand on her shoulder, it was enough to make her insides buzz and hum.

"I don't believe you," Andie teased with what she hoped was an irresistible grin. The practical part of her brain told her that the chances were remote that Valentina had any interest in her, regardless of what she'd thought she'd sensed. *It was probably nothing,* she reminded herself. *After all, if you never had an inkling about Jessica Balderelli in all the months on the show, it's safe to assume your gaydar's busted.* And yet, her grin grew wider until it teetered on the edge of goofiness. It couldn't hurt to be charming, just in case. "I thought tomatoes were the only crop you grew here."

"Hardly." Valentina laughed, a bit more boisterously than the observation called for, and Andie couldn't help but wonder if perhaps she too were trying to appear at her most charming. If so, it was working.

The woman grew quiet for a moment, her gaze becoming distant and clouded, though Andie had the distinct impression that it had come to rest, intentional or not, upon her chest. Valentina had been leaning against the sofa, and now she reached down idly to fluff and stroke the corners of the pillows, as if tidying them up. Still pensive, she cradled one of the little cushions to her own chest, a particularly plump and rounded one, pressing it just to the spot where the swell of her breasts must be. *Ah, if only such a wonder were visible*, Andie thought, *through the bulk of her winter clothing*.

The fingers that had appeared clumsy when holding the apartment keys were long and graceful now as they the cheerful fabric in slow, firm circles that immediately brought to Andie's mind images of their doing the same on her. How she longed to use her own hands in exactly that way, right upon the part of Valentina's anatomy for which the pillow had become a tantalizing proxy. "I could show you half a dozen things to make with fresh, local ingredients and not a tomato in sight," Valentina said, her voice low and dreamy, with a lustful quality that tomatoes, or the lack thereof, rarely inspired.

Andie swallowed roughly, barely registering the words as her eyes remained glued to the pillow, which she would never be able to look at in the same way again. She'd be seeing that pillow in her dreams that night, among other things, that was for certain. Her libido was desperate to interpret Valentina's actions as flirtatious, to tease out the coyness hidden in her words. Was it something about Valentina that was doing this to her, or had it just been that frickin' long since she'd been on a date?

"Is that an invitation to dinner, or were you offering me private cooking lessons?"

Andie had meant to keep the comment just to the right side of innocent, but her less than pure thoughts had introduced to her voice an unusually husky quality. No sooner was the question out than Valentina stiffened, a deep crease marring her brow. She seemed to become aware just then of the pillow clasped against her chest. Perhaps she'd also grasped how suggestive her interaction with it might have appeared to an onlooker, because she instantly let it drop to the floor. "Oh!" Her eyes darted from left to right and her cheeks flushed alarmingly. "That is…I'm sorry. How stupid of me. You're a professional chef. You don't need me to tell you how to cook."

Andie's pulse raced at the unexpected reaction, and she scrambled to smooth things over. "It's okay, Valentina. In fact, I think it would be—" But the woman's agitation only increased until she cut Andie off mid-sentence.

"I should go. Here's the key." She fumbled with the key ring and it slipped from her fingers, falling to the floor. Her hands flew to her cheeks as if uncertain what to do next.

Andie swooped down to retrieve the keys. When she straightened up, Valentina was already gone. "Valentina, wait!" she called out, but the only response was the sound of footsteps scurrying down the stairs.

Sensing that racing after her would only spook her more, Andie crossed the living room and peered out the window onto the piazza below. She heard a door slam shut on the first floor, then saw Valentina emerge into the outdoors, clutching her arms close to her chest and looking shaken. The weight of regret settled into Andie's chest.

The attraction she'd felt had been plain in her voice, and no doubt was all over her face, as well. She could be an open book like that, much to her chagrin. She'd obviously scared the woman by revealing more than was wise, though she would've tried harder to control it if she hadn't been increasingly convinced that Valentina returned her interest.

Below, Valentina had taken several steps in the direction of the fountain when a man came out of the pizzeria. He appeared to call to her, because she stopped and turned in his direction. Moments later, Valentina was caught up in his embrace and a chill swept over Andie. Whatever she'd thought was happening between them moments before, she'd been sorely mistaken. The closeness of the couple's embrace was irrefutable evidence that there was no reason to indulge her fantasies any longer.

A husband? No. Valentina had worn no ring. And yes, Andie had checked, first thing, just to know where the situation stood. She raked her fingers through her short crop of orange-tipped hair as she watched Valentina clasp the man tightly, her laughter audible through the closed window as the man lifted her so high that her feet dangled above the ground. *A boyfriend, then?* That was the most likely explanation.

With palpable disappointment, Andie turned away from the window and went back to shut the apartment door. No wonder Valentina had become so ill-at-ease. Coming from such a small and traditional town, it must have been a shock to her sensibilities to realize a woman was interested in her, even if Andie's behavior had been mostly innocent.

*Still, it really did seem...*Andie rolled her eyes at her overeager imagination. It may have seemed for a moment like Valentina returned her interest, but that clearly was not the case. More likely, she'd just been lying about not being familiar with Andie's show. She'd seen that type of thing before, a star-struck fan trying to play it cool could sometimes come across as flirtatious instead. It was probably nothing more than that.

Andie slid the deadbolt into place with a loud click. Turning away from the door, she spied the brightly colored pillow on the floor. She could hardly leave it there, and yet the idea of picking it up somehow seemed wrong, considering the lascivious thoughts it had so recently inspired. Instead, she prodded it with her foot, pushing at it until the last of it disappeared beneath the sofa's ruffled bottom. Then she set off to explore the remainder of the apartment, determined to put the Italian chocolate maker with the amazing eyes out of her mind for good.

FIVE

STUPID! Stupid, Valentina! What had she been thinking, allowing herself to behave that way, both horrifyingly awkward and brazenly forward at the same time? *I nearly asked a stranger out to dinner. And a woman!* She'd taken leave of her senses in the American's apartment—never mind whatever it was that she'd been up to with that pillow, which even now sent a wave of embarrassment through her strong enough to make her toes curl inside her shoes. It was all Cupid's fault.

Though it had never completely gone away, that magnetic pull she felt toward women had mostly faded over the years to little more than a dull and manageable hum. It helped, perhaps, that she rarely met anyone new. A new woman in Montamore was like the introduction of a virus to which she'd yet to build up an immunity. She'd been infected the moment Andie's reflection had appeared in the fountain, instantly developing a fever that had clearly fried her brain circuits and left her incapable of rational thought or dignified behavior. *Why, oh why, did Francie have to tell me about Andie Bartlett being a lesbian?* It had to have been that little bit of knowledge that had done her in.

The chilly air as she stepped out into the piazza dealt an unexpected blow to her lungs, forcing Valentina to pause, massaging her side as she struggled for breath. High on his perch, Cupid laughed his usual stony laugh, directed squarely at her. She fixed him with a look of indignation.

Is this your doing, you troublemaker? Did you bring her here?

When that woman's face had appeared in the water, the pale skin and the shock of insanely orange hair, she'd truly believed for a moment that she was having another vision. When she realized it was the reflection of a real, live person, she hadn't been certain whether to be relieved or terrified. Was it just lucky timing, this woman showing up like that? Or was it something else? The possibility that it was not a coincidence at all, but part of some plot that wretched statue had set in motion, was what had kept Valentina tripping over herself throughout their entire interaction, riling her up and stirring her most hidden desires until the only safe choice had been to flee.

A voice called her name and a shot of adrenaline sent her heart rate, which was only now returning to the non-life-threatening range, soaring skyward once more, but it wasn't the clipped American accent she'd expected to hear. Instead, it was the deep and reassuringly familiar voice of Paolo, who had just emerged from the pizzeria with a bag in hand.

"Valentina, wait up a minute! I have your lunch."

She plastered a smile on her face and turned to face him full-on with one arm outstretched to grab the bag. Instead she was immediately caught up in a massive hug that lifted her feet straight off the ground.

"Paolo!" she screeched through laughter, clutching wildly at his broad shoulders as she dangled in the air. "What have I told you about those bear hugs of yours?"

"That they're your favorite things ever?" He grinned impishly and Valentina rolled her eyes as he set her back down on the ground.

"It was your calzones that I said were my favorite things ever."

"Oh, that was it!" He smacked his forehead playfully and Valentina couldn't help but laugh some more. Valentina was generally fond of the big goofball, and even more so now that his antics had returned a small sense of normalcy to her. She was back to a version of herself that she recognized and knew what to do with.

Paolo pressed the paper sack into her hand. "For you."

"Thank you. You and Francie take such good care of me."

"You may need to eat fast. Looks like business is starting to pick up over at the shop."

Valentina glanced across the piazza in time to see a customer disappearing through the front door. She groaned. "It'll be a late night."

"Got a hot date?" he asked, as incapable as ever of resisting an opportunity to tease.

"Who would I...I..." Valentina's usual denial turned to a stutter as an image of the American chef with the hair that looked like a lit candle came, unbidden, into her brain. "No. I just meant we'll be open late. It's our busiest day of the year."

Paolo nodded. "Us, too. Ever since the last of the nice restaurants in town closed, we get lots of husbands picking up dinner to take home to their wives. No plans with Luca? I didn't see his name on the order list."

"And if you had, it wouldn't be me he was bringing dinner to, remember?" *Honestly, can no one in this village wrap their heads around the concept of a breakup? Surely, they've seen one on TV.* "I'd like nothing more than to see him move on, find someone to be happy with. And if you see him, tell him that for me, will you?" With that, she said goodbye and sped the rest of the distance across the square.

Half a dozen customers were milling around the shop when she entered, but her mother had things under control, and waved her on toward the large commercial kitchen where they prepared their homemade chocolates and baked goods each week. Valentina had been hoping for a few moments of quiet to eat, and maybe to check her phone. *For messages,* she hastily reminded herself, *and definitely not to look up information about a certain American celebrity chef.*

But it wasn't meant to be. She stifled a groan as she caught sight of her grandmother, a bird-like woman with thinning silver hair pulled back in a bun, who was seated at a folding card table that they used for breaks. Disappointed, Valentina sat and unwrapped the calzone while her grandmother silently sipped her coffee. As soon as the food reached her lips, the old woman set down the cup and fixed her with the look that signaled she was in the mood for some serious gossip.

"So, did you get a look at her?"

"At whom, Nonna?" Valentina asked, knowing full well to whom she referred.

"The American! And I already know you did. I saw you talking to her myself."

Which of course meant that her grandmother had been spying on the piazza from the upstairs apartment again. Her grandmother had been spying out that window forever and wasn't about to let a little detail like the fact that it hadn't been her apartment since the 1980s keep her from her routine.

"She's renting Sofia's place."

"Well, I know that, child. She came in here first, asking for the key. I'm the one who sent her out to find you."

And then ran up to the second floor lickety-split for a better view. Jesus, Mary, and Joseph! One of these days, the woman's going to break a hip!

"What was she like?" her grandmother prodded.

"Nonna, you just said you met her yourself. Why are you asking me?"

Her grandmother pressed on without bothering to answer. "She's famous. Did you know that? Has a cooking show for people who don't like to cook?"

"I've heard."

"Can't imagine what that's all about," her grandmother groused, though it was hard to tell if it was the subject matter of Andie's show, or the fact that her granddaughter had already heard the news about their famous neighbor elsewhere that had put her nose out of joint. "Why would you need a cooking show for people who don't cook?"

As her grandmother chattered on, Valentina only half listened as she chewed her calzone and gave the occasional obligatory nod. Her thoughts were on her near-miss in the piazza, her emotions awash in gratitude toward their new arrival. Andie had charged in out of nowhere, saving her from a most embarrassing plunge into the fountain. If she'd fallen into the water for a second time—and both times on Valentine's Day—Valentina could never have lived it down, not to her dying day. Her own grandmother would've been just one of the many gossips who made sure of it.

Valentina's heart fluttered as she remembered the strength of Andie's hands pulling her up, conveniently forgetting that it was her unexpected appearance behind her that had caused her to lose her balance in the first place. Valentina smiled wistfully. *Andie Bartlett is definitely—*

"...a lesbian," her grandmother said with a nod, finally completing her monologue.

Valentina choked as a piece of calzone lodged itself momentarily in her throat. "A what?"

"A lesbian, dear," she said, taking great care to enunciate each syllable. "You know, that's when two women—"

"Yes, Nonna," Valentina rushed to cut her off, the thought of her grandmother going into greater detail on the topic being too awful to contemplate. "I'm well aware of what it means. But, how would *you,* of all people, know something like that about our new visitor?" *Does everyone know? Are they all talking about it? Is this just going to come up in conversation all willy-nilly from now on?*

Her grandmother shrugged. "I heard it somewhere." Valentina held her breath, awaiting the details, but her grandmother pushed her chair from the table and hoisted herself to her feet. "Well, back to work."

Valentina stood as well, following in stunned silence back to the shop. *I heard it somewhere?* Was that seriously all she planned to say? In all her thirty-four years, this had to be the very first time the Nosey Parker of Montamore had failed to dish the dirt. Was she seriously not going to say another word?

Halting beside the still-overflowing basket of chocolate

Cupids beside the register, Valentina's eyes narrowed. *What are you up to, you devil?* The Cupids in the basket all stared back as wide-eyed and innocent as their counterpart in the piazza, clearly denying her accusations, but Valentina knew in her heart that they were all a bunch of liars.

SIX

ANDIE OPENED ONE EYE, uncertain whether the clattering outside her bedroom window had been real or only a dream. The first rays of morning sun streamed through a crack in the curtains. She squinted at the bedding that was tangled around her limbs as her brain struggled to make some sense of the unfamiliar surroundings in its woefully un-caffeinated state. Another loud sound, longer this time and like metal wheels bumping across an uneven road, drifted in from the window, along with a man's booming voice. Though the meaning of his words was unclear, Andie was able to make out that they'd been shouted in Italian, and all at once her foggy head cleared.

Montamore.

It all came flooding back, the call from the network lawyer alerting her to the ridiculous story in the *Star Post*, her harrowing journey by clown car to a hilltop village that was too small to find on a map, and her encounter upon arrival with a particularly sexy local chocolate maker. Most *especially* that. Those dark-roast espresso eyes had been the last thing she'd thought of as she'd drifted off to sleep, and if the total chaos of her bedsheets was any indication, they'd made their way into her dreams and kept her tossing and turning all night. But the last thing she needed to do was dream the day away too. It wouldn't lead anywhere, not with the existence of that boyfriend of hers putting a damper on things, and besides, Andie's stomach felt hollow with hunger.

Swinging her bare legs out from their nest of sheets, Andie lunged toward the suitcase she'd left open at the foot of the bed in hopes of retrieving a robe. As she tossed items of clothing onto the floor, the relative warmth of the air on her skin informed her that the previous day's chill had disappeared. With that happy discovery, Andie left the room in her nightshirt and bare feet to search out something that could pass for breakfast in the foreign kitchen.

Valentina had been telling the truth about the state of the pantry. The pickings were slim. After devouring an entire small pizza in the middle of the afternoon—because it turned out that eating a single slice was much harder than she had remembered—Andie had settled into a comfortable, carb-induced coma and hadn't bothered to give groceries another thought. She regretted it now, both her inability to limit herself to a sensible portion where certain junk food was concerned, and her lack of planning for a healthy morning meal.

Though there was little in the way of nutrition, a search of the cupboards turned up an unopened bag of finely ground coffee. Andie quickly added several scoops to the moka pot, an old-fashioned aluminum device she hadn't seen in years but knew to be standard equipment in every Italian kitchen, and placed it over a burner to heat. The only other item to be found was a partially eaten box of cereal left behind by some previous tenant. The brand was unfamiliar and the fuzzy photo on the box left more questions than it answered. Andie opened the flap and gave the contents an appraising sniff.

She wasn't a fussy eater. People often expected her to be because she was a chef, but aside from tomatoes, there was little she wouldn't eat, her current anti-carb phase aside. Perhaps it was the years she'd spent as a latchkey kid, or the fact that any of her cooking skills that weren't self-taught had been learned on the job, slaving away for minimum wage during long hours in a hot kitchen. Andie wasn't snooty. Sure, she loved a spinach and goat cheese frittata as much as the next chef, but celebrity or not, she could still appreciate the value of a box of foil-wrapped toaster pastries. Preferably the strawberry ones with that hard coating of icing and the rainbow sprinkles. *Damn my carb addiction!* A protein bar was what she should be eating, but cereal would do in a pinch.

Andie fished out a handful of nondescript flakes, popping them into her mouth. The regret was instantaneous, the taste that enveloped her tongue being as stale as it was bland, and she realized right away that even with her iron stomach, there was no way she could choke down more than a single bite. Her belly rumbled in protest. Thankfully, a cheery gurgling from the stove announced that the coffee was done, and the strength of the brew would almost certainly chase away the last of the unpleasant cereal aftertaste. She eyed the miniature stack of espresso cups on the shelf before opting for a generously proportioned mug instead. She filled it to the top with the entire contents of the pot. Was there such a thing as too much caffeine? She thought not.

All the while, as she'd been puttering around the kitchen, the racket in the piazza had continued unabated. A quick check outside the living room window revealed a steady stream of tiny trucks piled high with boxes. They were filing into Montamore's center like brightly colored ants heading to a picnic, along with pushcarts and wagons pulled by hand. Andie rubbed her eyes, still a little blurry from sleepiness, but the vehicles did not increase the slightest bit in size even as her vision cleared. She checked her watch and found that it was only just past seven. *What are they all doing out there so early?*

Her question was answered moments later when the first few tents popped up and crates of produce began to appear on the tables underneath. Andie recalled that Valentina had mentioned a farmers market. Given the sad state of her food options, it had arrived just in time and would save her the trouble of hunting down a store in a larger town.

After a quick shower, Andie dressed in her favorite jeans and a loose-fitting chartreuse tunic before heading out the door. Her taste in clothing was like her taste in food. The jeans had come from a Manhattan boutique, the tunic from a discount store. She loved them both equally, though this morning she was particularly grateful for the way the tunic hid her bloated pizza belly. Her head was still damp, with her hair turning a particularly jarring shade of tangerine as it reflected the bright sunlight, but it was a mild morning so she had no worries about getting cold.

Pausing to survey the piazza, Andie caught her breath, barely able to believe the rapid transformation that had taken place. All around the fountain stood stalls overflowing with produce, baked goods, and even freshly cut flowers. The market was ready to open, and a crowd of shoppers had begun to make their way into the rows of stalls. A snort of laughter escaped her as a minuscule truck rolled along the perimeter of the square. It had only three wheels, and Andie was fairly certain the average six-year-old would tower over it. The vehicle was painted a garish shade of pink, and a pair of equally bright fuzzy dice dangled from the rearview mirror. *These toys make my rental look like an SUV!*

Andie sucked in her breath at the sudden memory of parking that very rental car on a side street several blocks away the previous afternoon. The street had boasted at least half a dozen signs with an impressive list of parking restrictions—all in Italian, naturally. As best as she'd been able to translate, the car was safe from towing for the time being, but she'd meant to ask Valentina about a more permanent parking arrangement before the abruptness of the woman's departure had swept the issue from her memory.

The thought of how quickly Valentina had fled the day before made Andie frown. Once again, she wondered how much her own actions had been to blame. There was no question she found the woman attractive. But between the temporary nature of her stay, not to mention the insurmountable hurdle of Valentina having a boyfriend, it's not like she planned to act on those feelings. It didn't mean she hadn't shown her cards, and in fact she almost certainly had. Her larger than life personality may have helped her win fans to her show, but it had caused its share of troubles, too. Without meaning to, she'd come on too strong and frightened Valentina away.

She sighed, the car no longer her biggest concern. If she

hoped to have a peaceful stay for the next three months, she'd need to patch things up right away. It didn't pay to be on the outs with the landlady. She didn't know if the chocolate shop would be open so early, though she did recall Tracy saying something about coffee, too. More coffee was the last thing she needed. After consuming a pot of espresso, she could feel her pulse in her teeth. She wouldn't need sleep for a week. *Perhaps Valentina will be at the market?*

She'd no sooner thought it than she caught sight of a figure exiting the shop's front door. She recognized the black wool coat with its fur-trimmed hood from their encounter the day before. Once outside the shop, Valentina paused and then removed the hood from her head, as if deciding that the weather was pleasant enough to go without. With her chestnut ponytail set free, she headed in the direction of the market.

Andie set off as well, determined to meet up with her in the middle, but when she reached the first row of stalls, she found that Valentina had disappeared into the crowd. She peered down one row and then another, and finally saw a familiar-looking black hood bobbing along a few stalls ahead. Had she put it back on? Andie followed with renewed determination, but by the time she reached the spot where Valentina had been, she'd once again disappeared.

Disheartened, Andie was about to give up when she turned and spotted the peak of a fur-trimmed hood sticking up from behind a stall on the opposite side of the aisle, and the tip of a shoe poking out to the side. Andie approached cautiously, uncertain what to expect, until she was close enough to the table to see over the top, to where Valentina sat crouched on the other side, her face pulled deep inside the hood like a turtle in its shell.

Andie cleared her throat, then addressed the lump of hooded black wool with a puzzled frown. "Are you hiding from me?"

THERE WAS A BRIEF MOMENT, between the clearing of a throat and the unmistakable sound of Andie Bartlett's voice speaking to her from several feet above her head, where time slowed to a crawl. It gave Valentina just enough time to suffer serious misgivings over her choice of hiding place, but not enough time either to escape or come up with a clever explanation as to why she was crouched on the ground with her head inside her coat on such a mild day. All she could do was stare dumbly up at Andie from beneath her hood, sweltering under the head covering and yet frozen in place by a blinding panic unlike anything she'd experienced since that time in her youth, when she'd been caught by Father Francisco with a Playboy magazine in the back pew of the church after mass.

Somehow, I got out of it that time, but I doubt I'll be so lucky now. As she recalled, she'd sworn the magazine wasn't hers, and it had never occurred to the flustered priest to press the matter, nor to her to question her own motivations for wanting to see all those pictures of naked women. She'd forgotten about the incident until now, like so many others that had led her, inevitably, to this moment—praying to be made invisible as she crouched behind a table to hide from the new lesbian in town.

"Are you okay?" Andie cleared her throat once more, her

puzzled expression deepening to concern. "You're sweating like you have a fever. What are you doing down on the ground?"

"Just looking for a contact lens," Valentina replied hastily, grasping at the first thought that entered her head.

"You wear contacts?"

"No." *Merda!* The truth had just slipped out before she could stop it. She was awful at lying. The story about seeing Luca in the fountain had been the only falsehood she'd ever really gotten away with, and that had been told in a moment of supreme self-preservation. If Father Francisco had thought to ask whether she'd in fact stolen that Playboy magazine from the back pocket of one of the boys on the way into church, she'd have cracked like an egg, just as she was doing now. In fact, she was fairly certain the only reason the whole world didn't already know about her attraction to women was that no one had bothered to ask.

"I'm sorry. I'm not sure what I'm doing down here." As she looked up into Andie's eyes, Valentina knew how pathetic her cowering form must appear in them, and yet she had just enough presence of mind also to note how unusually brilliant a shade of blue they were, and to be oddly relieved that they didn't resemble a single variety of chocolate in any way. Chocolate eyes in their many shades had given her enough trouble for one lifetime.

"No, no. I'm the one who needs to apologize." Andie held out her hands as if to stop her before she could speak again. "You see, I'm American. I've been told my personality can be overwhelming, and I think it's probably true. If I did anything to make you uncomfortable yesterday, I really didn't mean to."

Is that all it was, her strong American personality, that's thrown me off so completely? Valentina knew it wasn't, but she nodded anyway as she rose to her feet. "Maybe we could just forget any of this silliness ever happened?" Forgetting was something Valentina felt confident she could do, and relief flooded her when Andie responded with a smile and a nod. When the woman failed to turn and leave, however, some of Valentina's worry returned. "Was there something else?"

"As a matter of fact, yes. I need to know where I can park my car."

"Is it very large?" Valentina knew enough about American tourists to know they loved their massive cars, which could be a real problem on narrow old streets.

"No," Andie said with an unaccountable snicker, "it's not large at all."

"Well, where is it now?"

"I folded it up and put it in the living room last night for safe keeping."

Folded? Valentina frowned, wondering if she'd gotten her translation right. "You're on the second floor. How could you get it up the stairs?"

"That was a joke."

"Oh." Valentina suspected her cheeks were glowing as brightly as Andie's hair.

"Sorry. I'm doing that overwhelming thing again, aren't I? I promise I'm not usually this bad. I'm a little hyped up on caffeine."

As if to demonstrate, Andie's fingers drummed against the dark blue denim of her jeans. They were the skinny kind, the type that left little to the imagination, even when topped as they were now with a shockingly bright tunic. Predictably, Valentina's eyes became glued to Andie's thighs, which were thick and meaty, though firm. Valentina had always thought she favored thin thighs, like Francesca's, but she was rapidly changing her mind. Andie had a pleasing figure overall, Valentina couldn't help but notice. She wasn't skinny, but who could trust a skinny chef? The fact that she wasn't too large, either, was probably a testament to the effectiveness of that war on carbs she'd been waging. Which was a pity, because Valentina loved carbs, and knew she could never make avoiding them work for her.

"So, the car?" Andie's fingers had stopped drumming.

Valentina's eyes, which had not stopped staring, grew wide as she realized she'd spent an unknown quantity of time scoping out her new tenant's legs. "You can park it in the alley behind your apartment building. I'll get you a resident permit," she added, doing her best to sound like the professional property manager she was supposed to be. "I'll bring it by when I've finished my shopping."

"What are you shopping for?"

"Tomatoes." Despite her lingering embarrassment, she couldn't resist some teasing of her own. Andie grimaced, and Valentina giggled. "That was also a joke."

"Very funny."

"I thought so. Actually, I'm looking for *cinghiale*. The hunting season's over in a few weeks, so it won't be around again until the fall. It's—what would you call it in English—wild boar?"

"Boar?" Andie asked with evident interest, and just a hint of suspicion. "What do you do with it?"

Valentina's stomach fluttered, suddenly self-conscious about discussing cooking with a professional chef. "Just about anything, I guess. I'm sure you'd have plenty of ideas."

"Maybe, but I still want to know what *you* plan to do

with it." The way she said *you* sent a tingle along Valentina's spine.

"Well, Nonna loves *pappardelle al ragù di cinghiale*, served with a local wine. Maybe a nice *Brunello di Montalcino*? So, anyway, that's what I was going to make."

"I haven't a clue what any of that is, but it sounds really nice when you say it. I had no idea how absolutely delicious Italian could sound."

"Ah, but you'd hate it." Valentina laughed at Andie's confused expression. "It's basically a tomato sauce over pasta."

"Again, with the tomatoes. I swear. So, what should I buy that isn't tomatoes? Because to be honest, I'm more of an Asian market girl. Love my fresh veggies. I was all set to shop in several of the larger ones in Los Angeles this week, but instead I'm here. Now I'm looking around at everything and I'm a little embarrassed to confess, I have no idea what half this stuff is. Like, what is this?" Andie gestured toward a bin on the table that was filled with small white beans.

Valentina studied Andie's face for a moment, wondering if this was another joke, but the woman seemed sincere. "Those are beans."

"I know that. But what type? I was thinking cannelloni, but they don't look quite right."

"No, they're a local variety called zolfini. They're similar to cannelloni, but smaller and more tender. You might put them in soup, or you can boil them with some sage and peppercorns." Valentina pointed to another bin, warming to her lecture as it dawned on her that Andie might actually appreciate the fascinating details about local foods that usually bored everyone but her to tears. "And these are special chickpeas that grow in Chianti. They have a strong flavor and are wonderful if you cook them with rosemary."

"I think I'll try these for now," Andie said, grabbing a bag of zolfini. "Any suggestions for what to make to go with it?"

Valentina thought earnestly for a moment before answering. "There's a stall down the next row that sells Valdarno chickens. If you stew them, they're delicious."

"And that chin-gay-lee you mentioned—"

"The wild boar? You really want to try it?"

"Well, is it good?"

"It's excellent, and a real Tuscan tradition. It's just…" Valentina pressed her lips together, uncertain how to express the sense of sadness she was experiencing at the thought of Andie cooking alone in her kitchen, just for herself.

"Afraid I'll screw it up?"

"No!"

"Are you sure? Your face got all funny there for a second. I know you've never seen my show and have no reason to believe me since I can't even pick out my own groceries today, but I really do know my way around the kitchen." She punctuated her assertion with a wink.

Valentina's cheeks grew hot and flushed. "I swear that wasn't what I was thinking. It's just that the beans will have to soak overnight, and the way my family likes to eat, we're already making enough cianghiale to feed a small army. If you really want to try it, why not just join us for dinner tonight?" It was, in fact, her birthday dinner, belated as usual because of the busyness of the holiday the day before. But Andie didn't need to know that part.

"It's a very kind offer, except for the part where you told me I'd hate the food."

"I'll grill it instead, no tomatoes. I like it that way better, anyway. Nonna will just have to make do."

"You're sure you really want to invite me to have dinner with your family?"

Valentina hesitated. The prospect of spending an evening with Andie made her heart race, but that was just the problem. Racing hearts were to be avoided at all cost. Besides, what would everyone else think? *It shouldn't matter what they think,* a long-silent voice opined from deep within Valentina's head, croaking like a frog from years of disuse. *It's your birthday party, so technically, you can do what you want.* Valentina blinked, uncertain where the thought had come from, but unable to argue with the logic.

"Yes," she said, before any other voices could pop in with a counter-argument. "Yes, please join us. It will be good for you to meet some neighbors, and besides, Nonna will love it. She's a fan of your show." Okay, maybe not a *fan,* but she'd certainly heard of it, and the excuse gave cover for any of the more personal motivations for the invitation that Valentina harbored.

"Well, in that case, what time should I come over?"

Valentina swallowed hard, fighting to maintain her nerve. "How about seven?"

"Great! It's a date."

"A—" Date? *Wasn't that the English word for—*

"It's just an expression," Andie hastened to add, with such speed that Valentina guessed at least some of the terror she felt must have shown on her face. "It means yes, seven will work just fine for me. Thank you." She smiled broadly, and there was a twinkle in her eyes that caught Valentina by surprise and made her whole body feel wiggly.

"Okay." Valentina's throat was tight, and it was a struggle to squeeze out the word. She was about to put her hand out to shake Andie's when she realized her palms were drenched with sweat, so she stuffed them into the pockets of her coat instead and gave a nod. "I'll see you then."

And though they'd just established that it absolutely wasn't, even so it felt for all the world like they'd just set up a date.

SEVEN

LATER THAT SAME EVENING, the church bell had just tolled seven times as Andie stood before the intricately curved frame of deep cherry wood set with gleaming glass that formed the chocolate shop's front door. Ornate lettering on a sign above announced the place as Cioccolatini di Venere. The design hearkened back to an earlier era, and Andie reckoned the shop had been there at least a hundred years. Beside the door was a bowed window that formed a display case, one that overflowed with delectable chocolates of every possible variety. Though it was only the fifteenth of February, the window had already been switched over to an Easter display. Andie marveled at the shop's efficiency, being fairly certain there was still a plastic pumpkin left out from Halloween in her apartment back in Manhattan. Long days at work left her little time to worry about things like that.

There was a small sign on the window that read *chiuso*. It was one of maybe three words in Italian that Andie could recognize on sight, (*gelato* and *vino* being the other two, as a girl must always have her priorities). It meant "closed," which gave her a moment of doubt, but when she tried the shining brass door knob, it turned easily in her hand. Stepping inside, she was struck at once by the heavenly scent of chocolate that perfumed the air.

It was like stepping into heaven. She'd been inside the shop briefly the previous day while in search of her key, but perhaps the crowd had lessened the impact of the aroma. Alone now, it felt as though she were discovering its magic for the very first time. In the quiet semidarkness, the sweetness was so intoxicating that it was all she could do to stop herself from letting out a moan. Her senses were overwhelmed.

And here I thought the smell of fresh pizza dough would be the biggest challenge to my willpower, she thought, conveniently forgetting that since her arrival in Montamore, she'd had no willpower. With the calzone she'd consumed for lunch, that brought her tally to two forbidden foods in thirty-six hours. It was less than an ideal start to her stay. But if she woke up to this smell every morning, she'd easily weigh a thousand pounds. *Like it or not,* she informed herself as she purposefully walked past a display table without a second glance, *these sweet treats are strictly off limits.*

The lights were off in the main part of the shop, but a glow came from a partially open door in the back, through which was a staircase. Andie could hear voices coming from upstairs. As she placed her foot on the first step there was a loud creak, and a man's voice responded in English, inviting her up. The scent of chocolate gave way to that of garlic and grilling meat as she climbed. When she reached the top, all sense of joy evaporated as she recognized the man from the piazza who had given Valentina the embrace. *Oh, right. The boyfriend.* She'd conveniently put him out of her mind, but here he was, a reminder that, like her chocolates, their maker too was off limits.

He smiled warmly and held out his hand. "Paolo. Nice to meet you!"

"Hi. I'm Andie Bartlett. It's a pleasure." She returned his smile, but it was hardly with pleasure. She'd known already, of course, having seen them together the day before. But based on the sudden crush of disappointment, the moments she'd shared with Valentina in the farmers market must have rekindled a flicker of hope.

"Of course, Andie Bartlett! My wife is such a huge fan of your show."

Andie swallowed down a bitter tang that coated the back of her throat. *Not just a boyfriend, but a husband? Man, it's more than my gaydar that's broken.* "Valentina's your wife?"

"No, no- Francesca! That's my wife, over there, with the big belly. She's Valentina's best friend."

"Oh!"

Andie glanced at the rosy-cheeked mother-to-be, currently conversing with a little old bird of a woman while doing her best to ignore the three children pulling on her legs. Andie's spirits soared. *No husband, after all!* She *knew* there'd been something there between them yesterday at the fountain, and again this morning in the market. *There's nothing broken after all!* Straight women simply didn't blush the way Valentina blushed each time they made eye contact, not to mention the way she'd hidden behind that table. And the pillow. *Dear God, the pillow!* If copping a feel from a throw pillow didn't signal unbridled attraction, she hardly knew what did.

Paolo motioned to his wife to join them. "*Cara mia*, come meet Andie Bartlett!"

"Isn't it funny," she remarked to keep the conversation moving, "I happened to see you with Valentina yesterday, and I just assumed you were a couple."

"Me, Valentina's husband! Ha, ha, I'll have to tell Luca that one."

"Who's Luca?"

"Valentina's husband."

Paolo's news instantly delivered a boulder to Andie's stomach, dragging her spirits right back down to the ground. "Oh."

She managed a stiff smile as Francesca approached, while reminding herself that a three-month sabbatical was hardly the time or place to look for love. She ought to be grateful to Valentina for turning out to be a straight married lady. This trip was about producing a best-selling cookbook. It was about planning the next season of her show. This was make-or-break career stuff, and here she was letting herself get distracted at such a crucial moment just because a dark-eyed Italian woman with lovely fingers knew how to do provocative things to a piece of stuffed upholstery. What had she been thinking?

"My goodness, you really are Andie Bartlett!" Francesca used one hand to hold back the most exuberant of the three children who still clung to her legs, while extending the other in greeting. "I absolutely love your show. It's so wonderful to have you here in Montamore. If you have a moment later, I'd love to talk to you about the town's spring festival."

"Now, Francesca, I thought we agreed you weren't going to pester her with that right out of the gate." Though his words were scolding, the affection shone through in his eyes. "Have you seen Luca? I have a funny story to tell him."

"He's in the back, I think .Why don't you take the kids and go see?" With a practiced maneuver, she transferred the two older children from her own legs to their father's, leaving her with only the smallest, whom she scooped up into her arms. Andie watched, impressed. "They can keep busy watching Chiara in the kitchen."

"Wow, you've got your hands full," Andie commented to Francesca with heartfelt sympathy as Paolo and the older children wandered off. She knew very little about children, having never given much thought to becoming a mother herself, but just observing Francesca's brood prompted the need for an exhausted yawn that she barely managed to stifle.

"Oh, I'm used to it. And those two will disappear for the rest of the evening watching Chiara."

"Chiara?" Andie wondered what sort of magical television show this Chiara might be. A singing cartoon dinosaur?

"Yes, that's Luca and Valentina's daughter. Have you met her yet?"

Andie stared at the floor as she mumbled some sort of nonsense in reply. With a sizzle and a pop, any last romantic daydreams she'd harbored about Valentina went up in smoke. A husband was bad enough, but a daughter, too? Before she'd fully processed this disappointing turn of events, a woman's voice announced the start of dinner, her lightly accented English familiar and sweet.

Andie's downcast eyes shifted to the doorway where her interest was immediately captured by a pair of strong and well-formed legs. The Mediterranean skin, left bare despite it being a wintery evening, still retained a faint bronze glow that must have been stunning at the height of summer. The voice sounded again, this time calling Andie's name, so familiar and sweet.

Valentina.

Her eyes continuing in an upward sweep, Andie took in the way the hem of Valentina's simple black dress floated just above the knees, skimming the graceful curve of generous thighs and hips before nipping in to accent a surprisingly narrow waist. It then swelled again around breasts that a v-shaped neckline fought valiantly, but not altogether successfully, to contain. Andie swallowed hard. That sofa pillow back in her apartment had nothing on the real deal. It was the first time she'd seen Valentina without the shapeless padding of a bulky winter coat, and what was now revealed to have been hidden beneath, set her pulse racing.

Of all the variety of female shapes and sizes in the world, Valentina's was precisely the type that Andie appreciated the most—amply voluptuous, with just enough firmness of tone to look vibrant and healthy. Andie's fingers twitched at the imagined softness of those pleasantly plump curves, and as she dug her nails into her palms, she cursed the cruelty of the moment. It struck her as especially unfair that she'd just been made aware of all this loveliness at exactly the same moment she'd learned it was hopelessly out of her reach.

She forced herself to drag her eyes to safety, zeroing in on Valentina's face and hoping she hadn't lingered too awkwardly on any bits and pieces along the way. But the view here proved to be just as tortuous, as she discovered that the once unremarkable mass of hair that had been stuffed in a hood or bundled into a ponytail against the wind had now been smoothed into long, spiral curls, shining like silken skeins that all but screamed to be caressed. Andie clenched her fists more tightly at her sides, ordering her hands to behave.

"Andie, have you had a chance to meet everyone?" Valentina asked. As her head shifted slightly, the light from the chandelier sparkled in her eyes like stars at midnight. Andie's breath caught, a dull pain squeezing her chest, and all she could manage was a mute shake of her head as she struggled to keep her mouth from falling open.

If Valentina had noticed that Andie was scoping her out or was aware of her marked shortness of breath, she didn't let on. Every bit the gracious hostess, she simply motioned Andie into the dining room, ushering her toward a chair at one end. "There's Paolo and Francesca and their children." She gestured around the table where the rest of the guests were already taking their seats. "This is my mother, Celeste. That's my grandmother, whose name is Regina but mostly everyone in town just calls her Nonna, and then my daughter Chiara, and her father Luca."

Pulling herself together, Andie acknowledged each one in turn, taking especially close notice of the final introduction: Luca. He seemed pleasant enough as husbands went, if you were into that sort of thing, and yet something about his curly dark hair and soft brown eyes gave Andie the impression that he'd arrived as a result of an order placed from a catalog. She'd never seen a more stereotypically handsome Italian, though it wasn't his blandly generic good looks that most caught her focus at that moment, it was how he'd been introduced. Had she heard incorrectly, or had Valentina called this man Chiara's father, as opposed to her husband, *caro mio*, the love of her life? It seemed...odd. Her thoughts on the subject yo-yoed once again. Could it be that the interest she'd sensed from Valentina hadn't been completely imagined after all?

You're grasping at straws, she scolded herself as she took her seat. It was only semantics, and though the woman spoke it well, English was Valentina's second language. In all likelihood, how he'd been introduced made no difference to the loving reality of their marriage. *But then again*, that drama-loving voice inside her head niggled, *what if it did?* If nothing else, it was a distinction that Andie found worthy of a closer look, and she grew determined to get to the bottom of it during the course of the evening.

Her attention, however, was soon diverted by a flurry of platters and bowls being passed around family style. Grilled wild boar, fresh vegetables, pastas, and sauces all made their way around the table and onto Andie's plate, with not a single tomato anywhere in sight, just as Valentina had promised.

"Valentina," Andie said as she took in the massive feast in front of her, "you outdid yourself! You didn't need to go to so much trouble."

Valentina laughed. "It's just a simple dinner. We do it all the time, and tonight I had plenty of help. I barely lifted a finger."

"You mean you eat like this every night?" She was about to wonder aloud how any of them managed not to weigh as much as a horse, but as she looked around the table, she realized that her plate had twice as much food on it as anyone else's. "If that's the case, I guess I should learn to pace myself. Not to imply that I'll be eating with you all the time, or anything," she added hastily when she realized how her words may have come across. Valentina lowered her gaze in apparent shyness as bright pink spots bloomed on her cheeks. It was a response which Andie would normally have interpreted as a sign of her attraction, if it hadn't been for the confounding presence of Luca, her other half.

"Nonsense, Valentina," Francesca chided. "You know very well that tonight's special. Your birthday only comes once a year!"

Andie's head swiveled from Francesca back to Valentina, her mouth falling open. "It's your birthday? Why didn't you say? I shouldn't be intruding on you and your family like this."

"No, it's okay. It was yesterday." Valentina's cheeks had grown even rosier, if such a thing were possible, and her eyes were glued to her plate. "Besides, I wanted you to come."

For a moment, no one said a word, until Valentina's mother addressed her granddaughter, breaking what had become a charged silence. "Chiara, tell Miss Bartlett how you helped chop the vegetables for your mama's special dinner."

The girl, whom Andie had up until this point not given much attention to, gave a grumpy reply in Italian even though her grandmother had spoken in English. Studying her now, Andie saw that she appeared to be about nine or ten, and had the same shining hair as her mother, though her light brown eyes seemed to have come from her father's side. The child stared daggers at her from across the table.

It should have added just one more reason to be grateful that the ill-tempered child's mother was off limits to her, and yet somehow it had the opposite effect. Andie was gripped with the determination to endear herself to Valentina's child. As if reading her mind, Chiara's eyes narrowed in an unspoken challenge. *Before I go back home, I'll win her over,*

Andie promised herself, though she wasn't certain why it felt so important to do so. It's not like she was a natural with kids, or even liked them much. The girl's eyes became little more than slits, and Andie swallowed. *Or maybe I'll just die trying.* Based on the present moment, death was the more likely option.

The old woman, who until now had appeared to be dozing in front of her plate between bites, snapped to attention and put an end to the adolescent's attitude with one withering look. "Yes, Chiara. You have to answer, and in English, too."

"But she talks funny," Chiara countered with a noticeably British accent.

"It's not funny. It's just American," Valentina explained, shooting an apologetic look across the table to Andie.

"Well, I don't like speaking in American or English," her daughter replied, defiantly crossing her arms.

"It doesn't matter if you like it, Chiara," Celeste scolded in a harsh tone that made the hairs on Andie's neck stand up. "You still have to practice, because of the tourists. If you're going to run the shop someday with your mama, you have to be able to talk to the tourists, no matter how funny you think they sound."

"I don't want to run the shop," the girl huffed. "I hate Montamore." Silence returned to the table, more charged than before. Andie couldn't help but admire the girl's courage. Her grandmother was a little scary.

"Does Montamore get a lot of tourists?" Andie inquired, in part to move past the sudden awkwardness, but also because she was genuinely curious. What she'd seen so far of the little village was charming, but if there had been tourists prowling around, she'd missed them.

"No," Luca said, speaking for the first time. "It doesn't."

The bitterness was unmistakable, and Valentina shot him a scorching look over Chiara's head that gave Andie the impression this was a fight that had played out between them many times before. But with guests at the table and their daughter between them as a sullen but effective buffer, nothing more was said. Was she the only one who found it strange that the couple didn't sit together? Despite having three children to manage, Paolo sat beside Francesca and had his arm draped around her shoulder. Valentina and Luca had barely interacted with one another, and unless there was something Andie had missed, she was increasingly convinced that their marriage was less than happy.

"Andie," Francesca asked, "what is it like to cook for television?"

"Well," Andie answered, grateful to the woman for breaking what had threatened to become an even more uncomfortable silence after Luca's outburst, "it's very different from cooking at home. For one thing, I have assistants who prepare everything ahead of time. All the chopping and the measuring, and—"

"Yes, we have that, too," the old woman cut in, and Andie realized that despite her diminutive size, she was quite formidable. "We call them children. On your show, you always tell people how to do less and save time. Why not tell them to use their children?"

"Well, uh..." No answer sprung to mind, so Andie changed course. "So, you're familiar with the show?" Valentina had said her grandmother was a fan, hadn't she? Listening to her now, Andie had her doubts.

"Oh, I've heard of it." Her tone left little to the imagination as to what she'd thought, confirming Andie's fears. "All the talk about people not liking cooking. Here, people like to cook and eat with their families. Maybe you should make more Italian food. Then you'd see."

Andie shifted a little in her seat but kept her composure. She'd heard it all before. The criticism was almost word for word what every other old woman on her visit had said. People like to cook, they'd tell her, not zap things in microwaves. Meanwhile, Andie's life experience told her otherwise. In fact, she'd built a successful career on it.

But as she looked around this typical Italian table, for the first time she began to wonder if the Nonnas might have some small point. Maybe here, some people did still enjoy the simple pleasures of preparing meals and eating them with family. She watched the children, especially, in amazement. Chiara's moodiness aside, they all had good table manners, and all four of them were eating everything on their plates, despite not a single item being shaped like a cartoon animal or swimming in ketchup. And they helped to cook, too? It was a much different childhood than what she'd experienced, that was for sure. Maybe it led to a different outlook as adults.

When the meal came to an end, Francesca and her family left for home. Valentina's mother and grandmother, plus Chiara and Luca, all made their way into the living room, inviting her to join them, while Valentina headed toward the kitchen to clean up. Andie hesitated a moment, then followed Valentina. After the evening's conversation, her mind was buzzing with questions about Montamore, tourists, and cooking, along with curiosity of a more personal nature where Valentina's family life was concerned. After the swirl of dinnertime conversation, she'd welcome a few moments of quiet to chat with her new friend. Though they may never be anything more to one another than friends, Andie did hope they could be that.

"You're a guest," Valentina argued as Andie came to stand beside her at the sink. "You don't need to help."

"It's the least I can do," Andie told her, and instead of protesting, Valentina handed her the scrub brush. Her fingers brushed across the top of Andie's hand in the process, and Andie virtuously ignored the all-too-pleasant tingling even that little bit of contact produced. *Friends, just friends.* "It's your birthday dinner, and though you've denied it, I know it was a lot of work. You shouldn't do dishes, too."

"I appreciate it, though it's just that one pot. My family barely let me lift a finger tonight, I swear. And Chiara will load the rest in the dishwasher, after Luca goes."

Andie's interest was piqued. "Goes…where?"

"Home." Valentina turned to get a towel as she answered, and so Andie knew she couldn't see the look of shock that must be evident on her face at the news. "We're divorced."

As quickly as that, Andie's heart soared like a kite in a strong breeze. *Divorced! Of course!* That explained everything, the tension at dinner, the coldness between Valentina and Luca, even Chiara's sour mood. More importantly, it meant that everything was back to square one. This attraction she'd sworn was building between them might not be just a figment of her imagination after all. She couldn't know for certain how it would turn out, but ever the optimist, Andie rejoiced in the fact that at the very least, all her previous assumptions were null and void. All options suddenly and delightfully were back on the table.

"Oh, I'm so sorry to hear it." Andie hoped she'd filtered

all traces of glee from the response, as she knew her elation was highly inappropriate. "I guess that sort of thing happens, but—"

"Not around here, it doesn't." Valentina's tone was flat, a thin veneer that failed to fully cover the hurt beneath. Andie regretted her earlier joy. A child of divorced parents herself, she knew how hard it was. "No one gets a divorce in Montamore."

"Traditional values?" Andie ventured, knowing how small towns could be.

"It's a little difficult to explain," Valentina sighed. "What bothers me is nobody gets how it doesn't work between us."

"I'll be honest, I did wonder about that. It seemed a little tense at dinner."

"Every week, it's the same."

Andie's heart broke at the sadness evident behind the simple statement. What torture it would be to have to spend time with an ex, week after week. She didn't have a lot of exes, but the ones she had, she was just as happy to have left in the past. What could keep Valentina on such close terms with Luca? But of course, Andie was fairly certain she knew. "I think it's great that you invite him over, for Chiara's sake."

"Yes, well I'm not sure how well it's working, but that's why I let him come. Only I don't invite him." Valentina sighed again as she handed Andie the final dish to dry. "It's my mother and grandmother. They're convinced we'll get back together. They refuse to listen when I say a husband is not for me."

"Is that just Luca, or any husband?" Andie held her breath. She shouldn't have said anything at all, but Valentina's phrasing had been so convenient that she hadn't been able to resist. Would Valentina answer the question she was really trying to ask?

Valentina's face was scarlet, her eyes fixed on the empty sink. The silence was thick, and the electricity that always seemed to hum between them kicked up several notches in intensity. Andie's insides grew so jittery that she reached for the bottle of wine that was mostly empty from dinner and drained it directly into her mouth, just for the distraction. Valentina laughed.

Andie laughed, too, as she set the bottle down on the counter and wiped the dribbles from her lip. "Hey, this is really good! You know where I can get some more?" She picked the bottle back up, squinting to make sense of the foreign label. "Does this say it's made in Montamore?"

"As a matter of fact, it does." Valentina bit her lower lip, as if weighing her next words carefully before speaking. "The vineyard's not too far, and they do a nice wine tasting."

After pausing a beat in the hope that an invitation would be forthcoming, but determining with no small amount of disappointment that one would not, Andie nodded thoughtfully. "I'll have to add it to my list of things to do while I'm here. Well, thank you for dinner. I should probably head home." Andie took a step toward the door.

"Sunday."

Andie's heart beat a little faster as she turned back around and saw the look of surprise on Valentina's face, as if she wasn't certain how that word had slipped out of her mouth. "Pardon?"

"Sunday is when they do the tasting, starting at noon." Valentina's hands were clasped together, her fingers fidgeting. "It's also the day the shop is closed, so we could go sometime on a Sunday. That is, if you wanted…"

Andie's heart thudded like a kettle drum. "I'd love to. How about this Sunday? We could meet by the fountain in the piazza?"

"No!"

The forcefulness of Valentina's refusal chilled Andie's blood. "Oh, uh, right. That's just a few days away. You're probably busy."

But Valentina's mouth was open wide, her expression apologetic. "No, no, I didn't mean it like that! I just meant not the fountain. This Sunday is fine. Come by the shop at eleven."

As Andie made her goodbyes, Celeste urged her to take some chocolate with her on the way out. Heading back through the shop to the front door, she paused by a basket of foil-wrapped Cupids, deliberating. She'd sworn the chocolate would be off limits during her stay. Then again, she'd said that about Valentina, too. But, the truth? If given the opportunity, she had little intention of keeping her word on *that*. The Cupids shone and sparkled in the dim light from the stairwell. *Who am I kidding?* she thought as she plunged her hand into the basket of chocolates, grabbing up two. *Since when can I resist something shiny?*

Nibbling a piece of chocolate, it was all Andie could do to keep her feet from skipping across the cobblestones as she crossed the piazza toward home. It wasn't what had been said, but what she'd sensed beneath the surface that sent her hopes so high. *I could be wrong, of course, but I think I was just asked out on a date!*

Andie paused to grin at the statue of Cupid, which upon her arrival had initially struck her as an odd choice for such a prominent location in the center of the town square. Why him, and not a town founder or, given the proximity of the church on one end of the square, a saint? But now she saw the wisdom of the choice. Love was in the air in Montamore, romance embedded in its stones. Though her time there would be brief, she saw no reason not to enjoy a little bit of that uniquely heady sensation that came with falling for a pretty girl. It could be fun while it lasted.

She was struck by the desire to jump onto the fountain's stone ledge and give the ancient deity a high five. In her elated state she just might've done it, too, except she thought she'd caught a glimpse of Valentina's grandmother hiding behind the curtain in the second-floor window as she left, and she didn't want to look completely insane. She settled for snapping her hand to her forehead in a mock salute. Sunday was just three days away, and it couldn't come soon enough.

EIGHT

SHE'D ONLY MEANT to watch one episode. Valentina rubbed her bleary eyes and lifted her head from the back of the couch just enough to see the clock. It was a little before five in the morning, and she hadn't slept a wink. Thankfully Chiara was with her father, so Valentina could still go to bed for an hour or two. But she'd have to draw the curtains tight, as the sun would be up soon.

She knew the exact timing of the sunrise for a fact, because it was the third night in a row that she'd done this. It had started as a mild curiosity about Andie's show. She'd felt her grandmother's tirade at dinner had been unfair, but without ever having watched the show herself, she could hardly take sides. She'd found the reality show contest on a streaming site later that night and decided to watch the first episode, just to see for sure. Then she'd kept going. And going. She'd gone right through until she'd watched every episode of the contest, and of Andie's cooking show, too. Visions of Andie's signature "quick and easy one-pot dinners" would've invaded her dreams, if only she'd managed to get enough sleep to have any dreams. But she hadn't. Seven hours after pressing the play button, she had faced the work day with bags under her eyes, still wearing the same dress from the night before.

It wasn't that the shows themselves were so engrossing. They were professionally done, with easy-to-make recipes that had Valentina wishing their local market carried more of the ingredients so she could try them at home. But with her own education in the culinary arts, it wasn't like she was seeing recipes she'd never heard of before.

No, what kept her watching hour after hour was Andie herself—her bubbly laugh and overall vibrancy, the larger-than-life personality that even through the television screen could dominate the room—that's what she found addictive. Andie fascinated her. In person, Valentina was too self-conscious to do more than sneak a glance or two when Andie wasn't looking. But on TV? She could watch the woman as much as she liked. And so, she'd just kept watching, and sleep be damned.

Valentina yawned and groaned. This hadn't been a well-thought-out plan, to say the least. Three nights of no sleep was bound to take a toll. *This is why you should never have watched the first one,* she scolded herself. *Once you give into temptation, you're powerless to stop.*

She would pay for her indulgence today, for sure. She'd sneaked upstairs to doze through her lunch break on workdays, and occasionally caught a little sleep behind the counter, too, since business was back to its usual post-Valentine trickle. But today was Sunday, and in six hours, Andie would be there, in the flesh. The realization, along with the tantalizingly suggestive word, *flesh,* sent a shiver through her core. Her droopy eyes shot open as if from a jolt of caffeine. *She'll be here in six hours!* Joyful anticipation filled her heart, as if she were about to be reunited with a long-lost friend. It was a dangerous feeling.

What Valentina had not realized until that moment is that there is a dark downside to binge-watching someone on television for eighteen hours. Especially if you know them in real life. Just from the simple act of watching, Andie had transformed from a relative stranger to someone who felt like the closest of friends. Over the course of three days, Valentina had experienced a year of Andie's life.

She'd heard hundreds of her jokes and had learned to recognize at least three distinct laughs. She'd watched her hair color change and had caught on to how her sense of style fluctuated depending on whether or not she was trying to hide a few extra pounds. Not that she needed to worry on that front. Valentina firmly believed one should never trust a skinny cook, and if Andie was carrying any extra weight, the way she did it was sexy as hell. But Valentina found her attempts to hide it adorable.

Merda. Did I just use the phrases 'adorable' and 'sexy as hell' to describe Andie Bartlett? And *that* was the other reason giving into this particular temptation had been such a dangerous move. Had Valentina ever looked at a woman on television and thought something like that about her? Of course, she had. Had any of those women ever stood inches away from her at the Montamore farmers market and winked at her? And called her invitation to dinner a "date," and then claimed that it wasn't a date in a way that made Valentina certain that a date was exactly what she wanted it to be?

And now she'd just spent three nights in a row watching that woman's face on her television, like a junkie. That's exactly what it felt like, that desperate scrabbling inside as she sought out more, and just a little bit more, of Andie Bartlett. Even worse, her most recent binge had left her fresh out of episodes, and there was only one way to get her next Andie Bartlett fix. In the flesh. *Damn it, there's that word again. Now I'm picturing her thighs.* The whole thing left her with an anticipation for their trip to the vineyard that was well out of proportion to what was appropriate for a casual outing with a person she'd only just met.

I should cancel our plans. I should go back to bed and sleep. It's the only smart thing to do.

There was a slight chill in the apartment, and Valentina nudged the thermostat until she heard the heat click on, then wrapped a blanket around her shoulders and stared out the window into the piazza. Dawn had not yet arrived, and no lights shone from the windows that faced the square on the opposite side. The spotlights that surrounded the fountain provided the only illumination, and from her vantage point, Valentina could see Cupid's face clearly. Smiling. Taunting.

You know you want to ask me something. From high on his pedestal, Cupid seemed to wink.

"No, I don't," Valentina informed him.

You do, Cupid countered. *You're dying to write me a letter. It's all you've been thinking about while watching that show.*

Valentina stiffened. "How do you know that?"

I'm a god, remember?

"Yeah, well, you had no right to eavesdrop on my thoughts. If I want you, I'll ask."

So, just ask already! Come out here and ask me if she was the one behind the door.

"That wasn't what I was going to ask. I guess that's why you were only a minor deity at best."

Hey!

Valentina rolled her eyes, refusing to apologize to a chunk of stone. "I already know she wasn't the one behind the door. She's an American tourist who's going home in a matter of weeks. Not a lot of long-term potential there. If I were looking for that kind of thing. Which I'm not."

But there's still something you want to know. What is it? Are you wondering for certain if your true love is a woman? Come and ask.

Valentina clenched her hands, twisting them until the skin was red and raw. She had a question, all right. It was one she'd been asking herself since she was fourteen, or perhaps even younger than that. But it wasn't whether or not she had the capacity to fall in love with a woman. Cupid had been wrong again, because the answer to that, she already knew, was a resounding yes. No, the question that had plagued her thoughts into the early hours of morning was something else, something that the god of erotic love just might have an answer to, in fact. But did she have the guts to face him and ask?

Down in the piazza, not a soul was in sight. Since it was Sunday, Valentina knew it would remain that way for some time. The earliest risers wouldn't be at the church until seven o'clock mass, and most of Montamore's less faithful would have the good sense to sleep in. If she acted fast, she could slip out and back without anyone being the wiser.

Valentina went to her desk and pulled open a drawer filled with odds and ends. Near the bottom was a tiny pink card and matching envelope. It had originally been meant as a gift tag but never used, and she wasn't certain what had possessed her to keep it all these years, except that deep down she'd always known it would be perfect for a moment such as this. She'd just never been ready to use it before.

She pulled out her nicest pen and scribbled her query, just a few words that she didn't bother to sign. Why should she? If he was really all knowing, he'd know who'd sent it. She placed the card inside the envelope and licked the seal, but the glue was brittle with age and wouldn't stick. Another search of the drawer turned up a sheet of stickers that Chiara had brought home from a Valentine's party at school. She placed one—heart-shaped, no less—on the flap to hold it closed, then stuffed it into her pocket, slipped on her shoes, and was out the door.

She scurried across the piazza with her arms clasped tightly across her chest, as in her impulsivity she'd forgotten to grab a coat. Though the afternoon was forecast to be pleasant, the predawn air remained too cold for bare arms. When she reached the fountain, she stopped and stared up into Cupid's face. He was no longer taunting and teasing her as he'd done upstairs. He was just a statue now, a silent and unresponsive piece of art, poised in the center of a fountain that was no less forbidding than when she'd been young.

There was no ice this morning, but the ledge around the basin was as slick as ever from the water's constant spray, and though she knew from experience it was mostly an illusion, the pedestal above her head appeared just as impossibly out of reach as it always had been. Valentina slid her foot along the pavers, testing her grip and discovering that the soles of her shoes were smooth and completely wrong for the task. She'd end up in the water for sure, and this time there'd be no one to save her.

Valentina looked across the piazza to the darkened windows of the pizzeria and then upward to the apartment where she knew that Andie slept. She closed her eyes and tried to picture her lying in the bed. What would she wear to sleep in?

A T-shirt.

It was her brain's first, purely practical response, but as her eyes popped open, Valentina batted the image away. If that was the best she could do, she might as well have stayed inside where it was warm.

A bra and underwear, then? The corners of Valentina's mouth twitched, her lips spreading into a slow, sly smile. Now she was getting somewhere, but could she do better? *How about nothing at all?* She sucked in her breath, the air whistling against her teeth. Could she picture that, what Andie would look like in bed wearing nothing at all? Allowing her lids to shut once more, Valentina quickly discovered that she could.

In the picture in her head, Andie's skin was pale, with swathes of freckles that crossed her collarbone and shoulders. She pictured herself running a finger along the surface of Andie's skin as she slept, tracing a line across the smoothness as she followed the path of tiny dots along a bicep that was firm and well-defined from mixing batter and lifting heavy pots. That detail caught her by surprise. She'd obviously put way more thought into this fantasy than she'd realized. *And now to move onto her breasts, which are...*

Here Valentina frowned, finding herself at a loss as the image in her mind grew fuzzy. Andie's breasts were of a moderate size from what she'd been able to gather. Not so large as grapefruits, but perhaps like a pair of navel oranges? Only, how would they look? Round and hard? Plump and soft like dough? Try as she might, the only image she could conjure was the aforementioned oranges, stuck comically on

Andie's chest like a game of pin the tail on the donkey gone terribly, tragically wrong.

Valentina let out a frustrated growl. A woman's breast would neither look nor feel like a navel orange, that much she knew, nor would it have the citrusy scent that she swore was teasing her nostrils at that very moment. She owned a pair of breasts herself and saw them in the mirror every day. They were nothing like citrus. It shouldn't feel so mysterious, and yet she remained baffled.

And there was the problem that lay at the heart of the matter, the root of the burning question that had brought her to stand at Cupid's feet. For years, she'd tried to imagine what it would be like to be with a woman in the most intimate of ways. She'd seen pictures of naked women, and could conjure up a reasonable facsimile, current navel orange fiasco aside. She knew that Andie's calves would be strong, her naked thighs delightfully thick and fleshy. She even understood the mechanics of what might happen if they found themselves alone, naked in that bed she'd just been picturing. But without experiencing it firsthand, there was something that remained forever just outside her reach.

You want to know what it's like to make love to a woman?

Valentina's eyes flew open, her head snapping up to stare at the impudent statue. "Excuse me?"

Well, that's a new one, I'll admit. Let me see, how to answer...

"No, that's not what I was going to ask!" Her hands nearly flew to her ears to block out his words, just in case he insisted on giving her an answer to the question she hadn't asked, but then she remembered that he was just a hunk of marble and the voice she'd heard was all in her own head. Which meant, of course, that what it was like to make love to a woman was at least *one* of the questions that plagued her, though it was not the one she'd written down.

Reaching into her pocket, Valentina drew out the pink notecard and turned it around in her fingers, contemplating the seal. There was no need to open it. She knew what it said. In the end, she'd boiled all the uncertainty of thirty-four years, and all the inner turmoil of the past four days, down to six simple words. *Would Andie be worth the risk?*

Valentina knew that Andie couldn't be the one behind that door, the one who was meant for her, if such a person existed at all. She lived thousands of miles away and was only passing through. Valentina's home was in Montamore, and nothing would change that. There was no future for them, no happily ever after in the cards. And yet she liked her. More than that, she desired her.

Since the moment the American with the crazy orange hair had arrived in town, her body burned just to be near her, and trembled at the thought of her touch. Valentina didn't know a lot about these things, but she knew enough to understand the attraction she felt, and to sense that Andie felt it, too. And so maybe for the first time in her life, with just a little luck, the answers to some of her questions —questions like what would it feel like to caress a woman's breast or bury her hand deep between the cleft of her thighs —were right there at her fingertips, so to speak. But a bigger question remained. If it was destined to end, was it worth it at all?

Her life in Montamore was quiet and uncomplicated, and she liked it that way. The divorce had been bad enough, but as the memory of it faded, she and Chiara mostly fit in and got by just fine. Why risk all that by opening herself and her daughter up to scandal and gossip, for nothing more than a whim? And yet how could she bear it if she didn't take the risk?

"Well?" Valentina demanded of the statue, but though she waited for what seemed an eternity, Cupid's lips remained sealed.

"This is stupid. You're not even real." She made sure to say that part extra loud, just in case Cupid was listening, though she no longer believed there was even the slightest chance that he was. He didn't exist. It was only her. "There's nothing you can say to help me with this. It's something I have to figure out on my own."

Thrusting her hands back into her pockets, Valentina turned her back on the fountain and headed home.

NINE

SUNDAY MORNING HAD ARRIVED, but only just. For the third night in a row, Andie had barely slept. Nursing a steaming mug filled to the brim with espresso, she stared out the window into the shadow-filled piazza and waited for the first rays of sunlight to announce the morning properly. She'd left the lights off, trying to ease her body gently into the day. Her plan to go to bed extra early the night before, in anticipation of her trip to the vineyard with Valentina, had been useless. Her excitement had kept her staring at the ceiling most of the night.

She hadn't seen Valentina since the dinner they'd shared in that cozy apartment above the chocolate shop. At least, she hadn't seen her while awake. At some point each night, and often more than once, she'd seen Valentina in a dream. Inevitably each time, Andie had tried to kiss her. Half the time she'd been met with willing lips, the other times rebuffed. Both outcomes were torture. Either she'd awoken filled with the sting of rejection, or immediately been swamped with the disappointment that their steamy encounter had been nothing but a product of her own imagination. The fact that she couldn't predict what the outcome would be if she dared attempt a similar action in real life plagued her with doubt and kept her tossing and turning well into the night.

Needing a distraction, Andie picked up her phone. The brightly lit screen informed her that it was a little past five o'clock, and that the forecast for later in the day was sunny and mild with a high of fifty degrees. With a tap of the screen, she opened her email and frowned as she saw one that had come from Tracy a few hours before. It would've been past eight in the evening New York time when it was sent, and her stomach knotted at the possible calamities that might've kept her assistant in the office so late. As she read the email, the knot grew.

Andie—

This whole Jessica Balderelli situation has become a real mess. It's moved way beyond Duncan's initial story. Accusations are flying all over the network, and some of them might stick. There are rumors of a big shake-up in management from the top down, and even talk of shows getting the ax. Don't worry, your name's been kept out of it for now, and your boxes will arrive soon. My advice is to keep your head down, focus on your work, and wait for me to be in contact when I know more.

—Tracy

Andie drew in a deep breath and let it out slowly, focusing all her energy on remaining calm. *Don't worry? Keep my head down?* She breathed in again. How could she be expected to remain calm when Tracy had so much as said outright that shows were on the chopping block? Her show, her career, was her life!

Andie hadn't gotten as far as she had by sitting still, or

by keeping her head down. Playing it safe was the exact opposite of her natural instinct. Andie was a fighter. Duncan's story had been in print for less than a week. If she went back to the States now, she could confront his baseless accusations, tell her own side of the story, and expose him for the rat he was. If she followed Tracy's advice, wouldn't it look like she had something to hide? *I should fly back to New York today.*

Legs twitching from a combination of distressing news and way too much espresso, Andie stood and paced the length of the living room and back several times before pausing to lean against the window. It was still dark in the piazza, and the spotlights that were trained on the fountain cast inky black shadows across the stones. There were no lights on in the windows on the opposite side of the square, but as she looked on, a figure emerged from the chocolate shop. Though she couldn't see her face, Andie knew in an instant who it was.

Valentina. They were meant to meet up for their trip in just a few hours' time. That couldn't happen if Andie followed through on her plan to return home. Should she run right out and tell her? The thought left Andie feeling far emptier inside than it should have. She'd only been in Montamore for four days, and she didn't even know if the pretty chocolate maker was interested in her. Whatever crush she'd developed on the local woman was a one-sided affair and couldn't be allowed to influence her decision. *I should go tell her I'm leaving,* Andie determined, but her feet remained firmly in place.

Then again, Tracy says to stay. Her assistant was a network insider. In the past year of working together, she had saved Andie from her own reckless impulses more than once and had yet to steer her wrong. If her job was in danger, Andie would do whatever was necessary to save it. Even if, counterintuitively, that meant taking no action. If hiding out in Tuscany, testing her recipes, and carrying on as if nothing was wrong was the best way to save her career, that's what she would do. Her body relaxed against the curtain, and she smiled with a much more intense feeling of happiness than could rightfully be attributed to a decision that amounted to doing nothing at all.

Valentina was still outside, and by now she'd made her way to the center of the piazza and had stopped, looking up at the fountain. Andie watched with interest as she stood and once again seemed to speak to the statue, though her voice was lost across the distance. Maybe she was talking to herself. Whichever it was, the conversation came to an abrupt end as Valentina turned and marched back in the direction from which she'd come. She shoved her hands into her pockets, and as she did, Andie saw something drop to the ground, but Valentina neither appeared to notice nor alter her pace.

As Valentina disappeared into the dark interior of her shop, Andie's attention remained on the object that had been left behind. It was small and square, and appeared to be some sort of note. She watched it for a solid minute. It didn't move, and no one came by to notice or retrieve it. Finally, her curiosity got the better of her and she padded down the stairs to get a closer look.

Thankfully she'd thought to put on pajama bottoms, as she discovered upon opening the door that it was nowhere near the promised high of fifty degrees outside. Still, now that she was so close, the mystery object called to her and she couldn't go back without retrieving it. Ignoring her lack of shoes, she dashed across the uneven cobblestones and grabbed up the little square card, racing back so quickly that the soles of her feet barely registered their discomfort.

Retreating to the warmth of her apartment, Andie stared at her prize. It was a pink envelope, a few inches square, with a heart-shaped sticker sealing the flap. Could it be a miniature love letter? Andie felt a stab of jealousy at the possibility that Valentina had left it there for a lover, and a bristle of apprehension over the fact that she'd just stolen it. Should she put it back, or take a peek inside? The answer was obvious.

Bracing herself against whatever she might find, Andie peeled the flap open with a fingernail and pulled out the card. As she scanned the note, her laughter echoed through the empty apartment. The joke was on her, because it was written in Italian, and so scribbled and smudged that when she tried to type it into a translation app, the best she got was something to do with roller skates.

Andie returned to the window and looked out, but the piazza was empty and still. For a moment she was consumed with the urge to wait, watching for the lover who would come to retrieve the missing note. *Get a grip on yourself! Do you know how crazy you sound?* Even in her sleep-deprived state, she knew that spying would be taking her interest in Valentina a step too far. She had no idea why the woman affected her this way. It had to be because, for the first time in a year, she had nothing else to do. Until her boxes arrived and she could begin testing her recipes, Andie's work was on an involuntary hiatus, and Valentina was by far the most interesting thing in town.

She stepped away from the window, determined not to let a week of vacation turn her into a stalker. If Valentina was leaving notes for a lover, it was none of her concern. Pity, though. At least seeing if it was a man or a woman who retrieved the note would answer one burning question—whether she had a snowball's chance in hell with this woman. Maybe then her brain would finally let her get a good night's sleep.

Still chilled from her trip outside, Andie cranked the thermostat, then made her way to the bedroom. She slid the note back into the envelope and tucked it into her wallet, placing it on the nightstand. She'd return the note to the fountain as soon as the sun was up, and no one would ever know.

Weary from her early morning exertions, Andie stretched out across the bed and closed her eyes. For the first time in several nights, she felt her muscles relax, and as the heat hummed in the radiator, warmth spread through her tired limbs and she soon drifted into a deep sleep. It was so unexpected that she didn't have a chance to set an alarm.

FOR A MOMENT ANDIE was certain she was in Miami. A gentle warmth surrounded her like hot sand beneath a beach blanket, and even through her closed lids, she could sense the brilliant sunshine of midday. There were voices in the distance, the sound of children at play, counting along to some sort of game. *Uno, due, tre...*

This was definitely *not* Miami.

Andie's eyes shot open, remembering. She was still in Italy, in an apartment where some dummy had turned the heat to eighty degrees before taking a nap. Despite the turmoil at her network, she'd opted to remain in the sweet

Tuscan village that was home to an even sweeter chocolatier, the very same woman who was expecting her to be at her doorstep at eleven o'clock sharp. Andie gasped as she realized she had no concept of the time. Rolling over, she patted her hands frantically across the mattress to retrieve her phone, but before she could turn it on and check the time, the church bells began to toll. *One, two, three...*

By the time the eleventh chime rang out, Andie was racing around the room in a mad dash to locate a pair of pants. She paused, pajama bottoms dangling off one leg, cringing in anticipation of a twelfth chime. Her breath escaped in a rush when it didn't ring. She'd be late, but not *that* late. She wriggled into a pair of jeans and a bright blue knit shirt simultaneously—not so much a fashion statement as simply being the first two pieces of clean clothing that made it into her grasp—and ran toward the bathroom. There was no time for a shower, so she simply doused her head with water from the sink and gave it a vigorous shake, letting the short locks fall where they may and hoping she didn't look like a complete lunatic. With a windbreaker in one hand and her purse in the other, she was down the stairs and halfway across the piazza by eleven seventeen.

"I'm so, so sorry," she announced as she burst, breathless, into the shop, which once again had been left unlocked despite the notice of *chiuso* being posted on the door. Valentina, who'd been perched against the edge of the display table that was loaded with the last of the discounted chocolate Cupids, sprang to her feet. The look on her face let Andie know just how worried she'd been. "We're not going to be late, are we? I can drive extra fast!"

"No, we'll be fine." Valentina's beaming smile was unexpectedly bright, and Andie wondered if it was relief over not having been stood up for their not-quite-a-date. "But if you don't mind, I thought we'd go by bike instead. It's not that far, and Signora Zitelli is known for her generous hand with the wine. We'd be safer getting back without a car."

"Really?" Andie thought back to the snooty wine tasting tour she'd taken through Napa Valley as a contestant on the show. "The only vineyards I've been to give you a couple of drops and expect you to spit it back into a cup."

"Spit out the wine?" Valentina looked horrified. "Don't even think of doing that today. Signora Zitelli might slap you on the head! Don't worry, though. She always serves a little snack so it won't make you *too* tipsy. And if it does, I'm sure she won't mind if you nap by the fireplace for a little while."

Andie shook her head. "I think I've had enough napping for one day. I'm sorry again about being late."

"I'm just glad you made it." Valentina lowered her eyes quickly to the floor, but not before Andie saw a flash of something in their depths, something that gave her hope that if she played her cards right, there might be an actual date in their future. "That is, I wouldn't want you to miss out on the local wine."

"No, I wouldn't have wanted to miss this," Andie replied, not really referring to the wine.

In the back alley behind the shop, two bicycles waited against a stucco-covered wall. They were old but not so old as to be vintage, just two well-used cycles in shades of teal and canary yellow, with dark leather seats. Valentina swung her leg over the yellow one, hopping onto the seat like a pro, as Andie held back, sparing a brief moment to enjoy the view of Valentina's bottom as it settled onto the seat, then surveying the teal bike gingerly as she contemplated her own far-too-tender derriere.

"You do know how to ride, don't you?" Valentina asked, her concern colored by a hint of teasing.

"Of course, I do, but it's been a while. I'm afraid I may be a little out of shape." Andie eased herself onto the bike, for the first time sincerely regretting all those spin classes she'd never managed to attend at her gym back home. "Do you ride a lot?"

"All the time. It's the easiest way to get around. You may have noticed that some of Montamore's streets are a little narrow."

"Oh, are they?" Andie asked in mock-innocence.

"Yes," Valentina continued, not picking up on Andie's sarcasm. "Sometimes tourists complain that they can't get their car doors open without scraping the wall on the other side. Americans especially. So many big cars."

"I guess it's a good thing mine opens from the front."

"*That* tiny thing is your car?" Valentina laughed. "I saw it the other day but hadn't realized it was yours."

"Don't tell me that even Italians think my car is small," Andie said with a groan. "How embarrassing!"

"No, it's just a little unexpected for an American," Valentina assured her. "But then again, I'd hardly say you were typical in many ways."

Andie wasn't certain, but she hoped it was meant as a compliment. Pushing off with one foot, Valentina began to pedal. Andie followed, uncertain whether her breathlessness came more from exertion, or anticipation of the day ahead.

TEN

AS THEY RODE ALONG, the pedaling became easier and Andie's breathing returned to normal as she adjusted to the exercise. Soon the streets of Montamore, which were every bit as narrow as Valentina had promised, gave way to a single road. It was deserted except for them, winding on a gentle downward slope into the valley. Though clearly a country road, Andie was surprised to find the pavement smooth and fresh.

The fields they passed were bare and yellow, but all around the hills were shockingly green, a brilliant emerald unlike anything Andie had ever seen. "Are they always so lush?" Andie asked, riding up along Valentina's left side, taking the position closer to the non-existent traffic as a show of gallantry. "I can't imagine what it looks like in the summer!"

"Actually, not nearly so pretty," Valentina said. "They're brightest in the winter, when it's wet and rainy. Everything else comes alive in the summer, but this is the season to enjoy the hills."

Andie lagged back, allowing Valentina to lead the way once more as she took her time and soaked in the countryside. As they rounded a bend, the whole valley was visible, and Andie noted how puffs of fog had settled into the low points like a blanket. All around them it was silent, with no sound except for the occasional squeak of their bicycle chains as the pedals spun.

After a ride that was nearly as short as Valentina had promised, though long enough to make Andie's thighs begin to ache, they came to the edge of the vineyard. Row upon row of grape vines, dormant now and bare of leaves, covered arbors that were laid out in neat rows. Along the hills, there were olive trees in abundance. Several yards ahead, towering cypress lined both sides of a long driveway where Valentina stopped her bike and dismounted.

"It's beautiful here," Andie said. She slid off the bike and winced, her bottom smarting from the hard leather seat. "But so quiet."

"It's my favorite time of year. I like the quiet of winter, but I guess it's very different where you live?"

"New York's anything but quiet," Andie agreed, and though she loved the hustle and bustle of the city, she had to admit that the silence had a certain charm that she never would have expected.

"We'll need to walk from here," Valentina said, pointing down the cypress-lined path. "It'll be too muddy to ride."

They pushed their bikes slowly along the gravel path, deftly sidestepping sloppy puddles along the way. The walkway sloped toward a large stone farm house, where white smoke curled from the chimney and perfumed the air with the spicy scent of burning wood. Andie took a deep breath, savoring the heavenly smell that was a rarity in New

York. Though she'd never imagined herself as anything but a city girl, she was beginning to understand the appeal of country life.

They reached the end of the drive and were just leaning their bikes against a stone wall when a woman emerged from the house to wave hello. She was short and plump, with curly hair that billowed out from her head like a halo. She greeted Valentina with a warm embrace and a kiss on each cheek, then turned to inspect Andie with open curiosity.

"This is the American I told you about," Valentina explained, "Andie Bartlett. Andie, this is Signora Zitelli, the owner of the vineyard."

"Welcome, welcome!" Signora Zitelli smiled warmly as she ushered them inside.

What had appeared to be the entrance to a rambling farmhouse was actually a working winery, and on the other side of the door, they found themselves in a cavernous room filled with giant oak casks. Signora Zitelli led them through at a brisk clip, their footsteps echoing off the vaulted stone ceiling. They exited a door at the far end and emerged into an open courtyard, across from which was another door that took them into the great room of the farmhouse proper.

The walls inside were a combination of plaster and stone, the plaster painted a cheery shade of apricot. The fire that had been hinted at outside, roared in a fireplace with an opening as tall as Andie herself, with a large sun made of terra-cotta hanging above the mantel. The hearth was surrounded by several tables and chairs. Despite the rustic surroundings, a white cloth had been draped over one of the tables, and it was set with plates and silverware as if for a meal, with four wine glasses per setting. A narrow sideboard along one wall nearly groaned from the weight of platters of meat and cheese, baskets of bread, and trays of olives.

"I thought you said this was a tasting. It looks like a full dinner!" Andie looked around with some confusion, noting that only one out of half a dozen or more tables had been set. "Where's everyone else?"

"No. No more today," Signora Zitelli answered as best she could in English. "Tourists? No."

"It's the off-season," Valentina explained. "In the summer there will be more of a crowd."

"Not so many," the signora added with a sad shake of her head.

"No," agreed Valentina. "There aren't nearly as many as there used to be."

"Sit, sit," Signora Zitelli instructed them, and immediately began piling their table with food.

Andie's stomach growled as she loaded her plate with an assortment of delicacies, noting with great appreciation that there were no tomatoes in sight. "Was that your doing?" she asked, mentioning the lack of the food she abhorred.

"I may have told Signora Zitelli about your tomato allergy when I called ahead for a table."

Signora Zitelli made a *tsk*-ing sound and patted Andie on the shoulder as she walked by. "So sad."

With a pang of guilt, Andie leaned closer to Valentina, so close she detected a whiff of vanilla perfume behind her ear. "You know it's not an allergy. I just think they're gross."

Valentina stifled a laugh. "I know that, but Signora Zitelli doesn't need to. You want her to like you, don't you?"

Andie glanced behind her to see the signora coming toward them with a bottle of wine in each hand. "If it means she'll fill my glass up to the top with that, then yes. Also, has anyone ever told you that you smell like a sugar cookie?"

"Excuse me, what?" Valentina spluttered, though judging by her expression, she was far from offended.

"Your perfume. It smells like vanilla."

Valentina nibbled her bottom lip with her front teeth. "I'm not wearing perfume."

"Really? Then I guess you must just be naturally sweet. Sweet enough to eat."

From the sudden flush of her cheeks, there was little doubt Valentina had understood the double meaning of her words, and yet her reaction was inscrutable. How could she remain so measured and controlled? Andie had always believed the stereotype of the fiery, passionate Italian woman existed for good reason, and yet here was Valentina, the very opposite of that.

In response, Valentina pinched a piece of bread off her plate and held it out across the table. "If what you have on your plate isn't enough, maybe this will do?"

The corners of her mouth twitched, and reassured that Valentina found humor in the situation, Andie felt emboldened to treat the offering as a challenge. Instead of plucking the bread from her fingers, Andie closed her hand around Valentina's wrist and held her steady as she leaned in to retrieve the morsel with her mouth. She wasn't lewd about it. She didn't wrap her lips around Valentina's fingers or run her tongue along the tip in search of crumbs. In fact, her mouth didn't touch her at all, save for a soft exhale of breath, but when that warm air hit Valentina's skin, Andie was almost certain she felt her tremble in the fraction of a second before she pulled her hand away.

"Signora Zitelli? More wine, please?" Valentina avoided eye contact, but her cheeks had deepened to a brilliant scarlet as she waited for their hostess to bring another bottle.

Andie laughed heartily. "Giving me *more* wine? An interesting choice."

Having regained a measure of composure, Valentina looked Andie in the eyes and arched one eyebrow. "Yes, you hardly seem to be in need of liquid courage, but you did say you wanted to keep your glass filled to the top, so I felt the need to oblige."

Andie had been joking about keeping her glass filled to the top, but seconds later as their hostess poured, the wine in her glass floated dangerously close to the brim. Andie's jaw slackened. "I didn't mean it literally."

"I told you," Valentina said with a shrug, clearly finding nothing out of the ordinary, "she's generous." Valentina lifted her glass and took several large gulps, leaving Andie to wonder if her companion was experiencing the need for a little liquid courage of her own. It didn't hurt to hope.

Andie lifted her own glass, making a pretense at sniffing it in the way one is supposed to at wine tastings, then took a sip, much smaller than Valentina's had been. "How is it possible that this place isn't packed every day?"

A somber expression settled over Valentina's face. "It started with the recession. Even when the economy improved, the tourists never came back. For businesses like this, it's not so bad. They can send their wine to restaurants and stores all over Italy. But for businesses like mine that rely on tourists, times have been rough."

Andie nodded. "I got that impression from your ex at dinner the other night."

"I'm sorry about that." Valentina bit her lower lip. "It's an old argument. Before we split up, Luca thought we should move to a bigger city and open a factory so we could make enough chocolate to widen our distribution."

"You disagreed, I take it?"

"He never understood. Cioccolatini di Venere has been a Montamore business for over a hundred years." The pride of ownership was infused in her words "A factory? That's just not how *my* chocolates are made. When I make chocolates, they're small batches from a kitchen, as my family has done for generations. You can't mass-produce that tradition in a factory." Valentina frowned, looking unsure of herself. "That probably sounds foolish to you."

"No," Andie assured her, "I know exactly what you mean. I was approached by a major food company a few months ago that wanted to produce a line of Andie Bartlett frozen dinners. I mean, it made sense. I'm the *Quick and Easy Queen*, after all. Wait." Andie's nose wrinkled, her lips puckering. "I never realized before how bad that sounds, taken out of context."

Valentina choked back a laugh. "That does kind of sound bad."

"Just so you know, that's in reference to my cooking show. Nothing else."

"Of course."

"I don't deprive myself, but I'm not easy. And I can guarantee that none of the women I've been with would accuse me of being too quick. Not a chance."

"Erm…" Valentina's words jumbled on her tongue. "So, those frozen dinners. Did you end up doing them?"

Andie chuckled. *Frozen dinners, my ass.* Andie had given her plenty to think about other than frozen dinners, and the fact that she looked like she was about to swallow her own tongue was a pretty good indication she was doing just that right now. "No, I passed. It would've made a lot of money, probably. But I have high standards and take pride in what I do. This company just wanted to put my name on any old product, and that wasn't for me."

"Exactly!" Valentina's face was returning to its normal color as the conversation shifted back to business. "It's not that I'm against expansion. I've dreamed of it! I even told Luca once, maybe with a bigger commercial kitchen and some modern equipment, I could hire people and train them, and we could increase production that way, but..." Her voice trailed off. "So, you do like to cook, don't you? Nonna swears you don't."

"Of course, I do!" Andie paused, her brow furrowing as she thought back over the months of meals eaten on the road. "Only the funny thing is, I can't remember the last time I *cooked* something. You know, from start to finish, just for my own satisfaction."

"You like cook?" Signora Zitelli asked haltingly, obviously overhearing her last few words as she leaned over the table to fill Andie's remaining two wine glasses well beyond a reasonable limit. "You want take lesson?"

"No, no, Signora Zitelli!" Valentina looked horrified. "Andie's a—"

"What kind of lesson?" Andie asked, interrupting before Valentina could reveal that she was a professional chef. Perhaps it was because she was enjoying the rare chance to be incognito, or it could've been the fear that if this nice old lady actually had heard of her show, she'd be as uncomplimentary as all of her contemporaries had been. Whatever the reason, she didn't want Signora Zitelli to know who she was. "Is there a cooking school nearby? I don't know a lot about Italian food." That part, anyway, was very true.

Signora Zitelli's lined face lit up. "Yes! My cousin has best one."

"Her cousin, Simonetta, has the *only* one," Valentina corrected. "It's just down the valley, still in the countryside, but a bit closer to the main highway, so they get more tourists stopping in, I think. There used to be another one, pretty out of the way, at an old farmhouse near here, but it closed. With a beautiful kitchen, too. I never saw it in person, but the photos they posted when it went on the market were amazing. You should've seen it." The wistfulness and longing in Valentina's deep brown eyes made Andie wish she'd had the power to give her that kitchen, all wrapped up in a bow.

"Here," Signora Zitelli urged. "You sign up?"

Andie looked down as the signora pushed a trifold brochure into her hand. "When is it?"

"Couple weeks." Signora Zitelli handed her a pen. Andie chuckled as she filled out her details, then handed the form back and stuffed the brochure into her purse.

After Signora Zitelli had left the table, Valentina laughed. "No wonder she stays in business. She sure knows how to reel in a customer. But you're a professional, and Simonetta's classes really are mostly for tourists. I'm not sure what you're going to get out of it."

"Don't laugh too hard. You'll find out for yourself soon enough." Andie cocked one eyebrow and fixed her with a steady look, a warm glow settling in her chest as Valentina squirmed just a bit and her cheeks flushed for at least the millionth time that afternoon. Hot and bothered was an excellent look on this woman. "I signed you up, too."

"You did not!"

"I most certainly did." Andie squinted at the four wine glasses in front of her, which were now mostly empty except for a few drops at the bottom. She blinked and the image danced before settling into its proper place. "I guess I should've asked first. I'm blaming the wine."

"It's okay. I guess I can go. Simonetta's a sweetheart, and I've always been curious what the *Cucina Mia* classes are like. Why not? It could be fun." Valentina lowered her eyes in that shy way of hers that made Andie's insides tingle. "Time for dessert?"

"Dessert?" Andie groaned, looking from one empty platter to the next. A crumbly bit of bread crust swam in the remnants of foggy green olive oil, fresh from the winery's own grove. A few shavings of pecorino cheese, creamier than anything Andie had ever tasted back home, dotted the table cloth. Other than that, it was all gone, swimming happily in Andie's stomach. "I've already shot my low-carb resolution to hell, so I might as well, but to be honest, I don't think I have the space."

"Maybe just some vinsanto and biscotti?" Valentina suggested. "It's a Tuscan tradition."

"Can we take it home? Or at least have a nap first." Andie yawned involuntarily at the mere mention of sleep, so tempting now that her belly was full and she was drowsy with wine.

"I told you you'd want a nap." Valentina stood and stretched, then took a few steps toward a grouping of cozy-looking chairs near the fire. "What wines do you want to buy for home? Signora Zitelli can start boxing your order."

Andie pondered the empty glasses, trying to recall through the pleasantly fuzzy haze in her brain exactly which wine was which. Giving up, she turned to the signora and shrugged. "I can't decide. How about two of everything?" She reached into her purse, her eyes growing wide as her hand was met with way too much empty space. "My wallet! I think I left it back at the apartment."

"Don't worry about it," Valentina assured her, her eyes closing as she relaxed her head into the overstuffed upholstery of her chair. "Signora Zitelli will put it on the shop's tab and deliver it to town tomorrow. You can settle up then."

"Are you sure?" Andie sat in the opposite chair, but despite its comfort, her body remained tense. She felt stupid for leaving something so important behind. How had she managed it? Then she remembered her restless morning, and seeing Valentina drop the tiny letter by the fountain. She'd retrieved it and tucked it into the wallet for safe keeping, then been in such a rush after oversleeping that she'd forgotten all about it.

The letter. Now that it was on her mind, it was hard to let it go. What had it said? The feminine shade of pink with the little heart had made her think it was a love letter, but if Valentina had a love interest, it was the best-kept secret Andie had ever encountered. After a whole afternoon together and four glasses of wine, Valentina hadn't let on, and there'd been at least a time or two where Andie was certain their flirtation was mutual. Or almost certain, anyway. *God, I sure hope it was.* Her tipsy brain spun like an off-balance top, trying to solve the mystery.

Andie leaned back in her chair with a quiet sigh. Maybe it was just a scrap of trash of no importance. These mental gymnastics she was torturing herself with were stupid. She had work to do, and she'd be going home in three months.

Whether Valentina was as attracted to Andie as Andie was to her, it's not like anything they managed to start could amount to more than a short-term diversion. So why did it even matter?

Because I like her.

It was as simple as that. Did she need any other reason? Because she found her attractive and funny, and she enjoyed her company. Because even if a physical or romantic relationship was completely off the table, Andie would still seek her out for as long as she was in town. And she'd torture herself like this every time unless she knew for sure if Valentina felt the same. But how to find out?

You could try asking her?

Andie wasn't sure if this was her own voice or the wine talking, but rather than dismiss it, she gave it some thought. What could it hurt to be direct? After all, Andie was a famous chef, and made a pretty good living at it, too. She was even decent to look at, though she was willing to admit the flames of hair shooting from her head might be considered an acquired taste. And she could be charming when she put her mind to it.

That was exactly what she planned to do. She'd tell Valentina that, though their time together might be brief, it would be spectacular. She'd tell her that her eyes twinkled like stars in the night sky. She'd be suave. She'd be sophisticated. Assuming Valentina was at least willing to consider the possibility of a romance with a woman, there was no way she could lose! The soothing warmth of the wine that flowed through her veins gave her courage. Andie straightened up and cleared her throat. Valentina stirred in her chair and stretched her legs closer to the fire.

"Valentina, can I ask you something?" After a moment,

she got a low *harrumph* that she took as an affirmative response. Butterflies fluttered in Andie's stomach as every thought exited her brain with a *whoosh*. "It's just, that is, uh, do you like girls?" She gave an involuntary laugh at the end, at least, she was pretty sure the laugh had come from her. It was either her, or someone nearby had done a very convincing impression of an overly hormonal adolescent boy. In the long, deafeningly loud silence that followed, that laugh echoed through her otherwise-empty head on a constant loop.

Oh God, please kill me. Kill me right now, before Valentina recovers enough to speak. Andie wished she could hide beneath her chair until her prayer was granted and she was put out of her misery. She'd pictured it going so much better in her head. Sophisticated! Suave! Damn it, in her imagination, she'd waxed poetic and swept Valentina off her feet. *Do you like girls?* Was that seriously the best she could do?

Valentina opened her mouth and Andie panicked. "You know what, please, *please* let's just forget I said—" But she swallowed the rest of the thought as a hearty snore shook the room. Relief set her whole body shaking. It had been possibly the most embarrassingly awkward attempt at winning over a girl in the history of creation, and yet somehow, she'd been spared having anyone know about it. By some miracle, Valentina was fast asleep and hadn't heard a word.

As Valentina slumbered, Andie reached for her phone, looking for an escape from her lingering chagrin. She pulled up the message Tracy had sent her that morning, to which she had yet to respond. Reading it through once more, the precariousness of her situation set her on edge. Keep her head down, that was Tracy's counsel, but was it really the wisest move? Thousands of miles from her life back home, the sense of powerlessness made her body tremble with anger. It felt as if all the success she'd worked so hard for her whole life was slipping through her fingers like sand, and all because of a spoiled brat who didn't like to lose.

Well, I don't like to lose, either, she reminded herself, jaw clenching. *And I'm not going to start now.* Closing her eyes, she could picture Duncan King's pompous face, and wanted nothing more than to smack the smug grin right off of it. There had to be a way to bring him down, if only she knew where to look. When she opened her eyes, Tracy's message still shone brightly on her screen. Steadying her hands, she composed a reply.

Hi Tracy—

I got your message and have decided to follow your advice by staying put. Shocking, I know. But you need to do something for me. I want to know everything Duncan's up to, everything he says or does, right down to what the bastard has for lunch…

Andie's finger hovered above the miniature keyboard on her screen, wondering what, if anything, she hoped to accomplish. Sure, setting a spy on her adversary gave her a thrill, but what difference could it possibly make?

The screen faded to black. Andie set the phone down and massaged her temples, which throbbed under the latest onslaught of helplessness. If she ended up losing her show because of this mess, what would she do? *Damn Duncan King!* Her foot lashed out, making contact with the side of her purse. *If only it had been Duncan's head!* The small leather bag tumbled over, spilling its contents across the tiled hearth. As she bent to scoop it all back in, the trifold brochure from Cucina Mia caught her eye.

I guess if the celebrity chef thing doesn't pan out, I could always start a cooking school. Andie tried to picture it and couldn't suppress a wry grin. Her, a teacher? No way. She'd left school without graduating and never looked back, and the few experiences she'd had lecturing had been torture. The classroom was no place for her, but the memory of her earlier conversation with Valentina about the fate of some of the cooking schools in the area gave her another idea. Picking up her phone once more, she began to type.

Oh, Tracy, one other favor. There's an old farmhouse near Montamore. It used to be a cooking school that's now closed down. Big commercial kitchen. Can you see if it's still on the market, or any other properties like it? Asking for a friend.

After sending the message, Andie melted back into the cushion of her chair, feeling oddly satisfied for no particular reason. She made a comfortable living, sure, but it's not like she could afford to buy the place for Valentina. Even if she could, it would be one hell of an extravagant gift for a woman she'd just met, and it's not like she was in the market for her own private villa. In all likelihood, the place was long since sold, anyway. Even so, it was worth a few minutes of her time to investigate. Andie's accountant was always telling her to look for ways to diversify her portfolio. Buying property was a pipe dream but helping a company like Cioccolatini di Venere to expand their distribution some other way might be a solid choice if it turned out Valentina was open to the idea of investors.

It was a topic she'd need to bring up at a later date, whether before or after trying to get Valentina to go out with her, she wasn't sure. Both prospects held plenty of challenge, but Andie liked a challenge. As the warmth of the fire seeped into her bones and brought heaviness to her eyelids, one thought gave her hope. No matter how poorly either conversation went, they couldn't possibly go as badly as her performance today.

Valentina let out a muffled snore. Her body was curled into a ball, giving a perfect impression of a plump and happy house cat. With a positively feline stretch, she nestled deeper into the cushion where she slept, and for the second time since they'd met, Andie experienced a pang of jealousy for a piece of upholstery. What she wouldn't give to feel Valentina's body curled against her like that, to run her hands up and down along the length of her back and feel the silkiness of her chestnut hair against her cheek as she whispered softly into her ear. What exactly she would whisper, Andie wasn't certain. She only knew that when the time came, it *would* be suave. It *would* be sophisticated. As she watched Valentina sleep on, gratitude filled her for the reset button she'd been given after her earlier fiasco. She wouldn't let it go to waste.

ELEVEN

"WHAT WERE YOU *THINKING*, CHIARA?" Valentina's voice filled every corner of the empty chocolate shop. She folded her arms and hugged them to her chest as she stared the young girl down. Chiara trembled wildly, but Valentina knew it was only partially from fear. Mostly, it was because she'd walked all the way from the center of the square with her clothes dripping wet from the knees down. Valentina remembered the feeling well. It wouldn't hurt for her daughter to shiver a few minutes more, so she would remember it, too. "How many times have I told you to stay away from that fountain?"

"But, Mama," Chiara argued, "everyone else was doing it!"

"Everyone else?" She cringed at the shrillness of her own voice, but she couldn't help it. Of all the childhood excuses, that one grated on her the most, perhaps because it hit closest to home. From climbing up the fountain in the dead of winter to agreeing to marry a man because all of her friends were engaged, just look where doing what everyone else was doing had gotten her. She took a calming breath and tried to soften her tone. "When you get older, *topolina*, maybe you'll learn that everyone else doing something isn't a good enough reason for you to do it, too."

"But I don't want to be the only one—"

"The *only* one?" Valentina snorted. "*Topolina*, do you know why I call you that? Because you're no bigger than a little mouse, even if you are the tallest of all your friends. The pedestal alone is twice your height, and the stones are slick as ice. You could've cracked your head wide open. I didn't even *think* of trying a stunt like that until I was a good six inches taller than you, and then do you know what happened?"

Chiara's shoulders slumped. "You ended up in the water."

"Yes, I did. Just like you." Valentina shook her head and gave an exasperated sigh. "You know, if we're not careful, our family's going to get a reputation."

Just then, the bells on the front door jingled and Valentina turned to see Andie enter the shop. Her insides dissolved into a swarm of honeybees, inherently dangerous and yet so terribly tickly that it was impossible to maintain her stern facade. She felt her lips twitch upward, and Andie smiled in return, the warm smile that made Valentina's heart pump faster every time she glimpsed it.

But when Andie caught sight of the dripping Chiara, her expression shifted to one of shock. "What happened?"

"Chiara," Valentina fixed her daughter with what she knew was her most scolding look, "maybe you want to explain to our guest what happened?"

"I tried to climb up the fountain," the girl began, looking suitably embarrassed and for once not needing to be prompted to speak in English, "to give a letter to Cupid. And I fell in."

Andie's eyes grew wider as she pointed out the window. "You mean that fountain, out in the square? Isn't that dangerous? It's awfully tall, and the stones look really slick. You could've cracked your head open!"

"You see?" Valentina nodded smugly.

Chiara kept her head bowed, staring studiously at the floor. "I'm sorry, Mama. I didn't mean to fall in."

"Cara mia, it's not the falling-in part that upsets me. You're still a little girl. You're only ten! You have all the time in the world to fall in love. Why worry yourself about it now?"

"You're too old to understand," the little girl muttered, no doubt thinking her mother couldn't hear.

"Upstairs!" Valentina barked, not yet having reached an age where there was anything wrong with her hearing. "Straight to your room. No television and no electronics. If you get bored, you can read a book."

After her daughter had trudged up the stairs, stomping on each one with ridiculous force as she went, Valentina let out a frustrated scream. Andie laughed sympathetically, and Valentina felt her tummy flutter again. "Too old!" Valentina shook her head ruefully. If only she were too old, maybe she wouldn't find her insides tied up in knots every time a certain American came around. What was it about Andie, anyway, that made her feel so dizzy and out of control? "That daughter of mine will be lucky to *make* it to my age with her attitude lately."

"What was that all about?" Andie asked. "What was she doing climbing the fountain?"

"Nothing. A local tradition." Valentina waved dismissively. This wasn't a topic she wanted to discuss, especially with present company.

"What kind of tradition?"

"Oh, you know. The kids bring letters to Cupid. It's silly, really."

"Letters?"

"Yes, why?" Valentina looked at Andie suspiciously, distrusting the slyness that had crept into her expression.

"Well, it's just that I found this." Andie had reached into her wallet and was holding something out for her to see.

Glimpsing the corner of a pale pink envelope, Valentina's chest seized. "What's that?" she squeaked, knowing exactly what it was, and what it said, and wishing she'd never been possessed to write it in the first place.

"Well, that's what I was wondering. It was out by the fountain yesterday morning."

"I wonder who left it there," Valentina mused, doing her best to sound nonchalant.

"You did. I saw it drop out of your pocket."

"What were you doing up at that hour," Valentina asked accusingly, sensing it would be foolish to deny that it had been her.

"I couldn't sleep. When you didn't turn back to get it, I picked it up and put it in my wallet for safekeeping just in case it was important. I meant to give it to you yesterday, only I left my wallet at home."

"Oh, yes, your wine," Valentina said a little too cheerily. "I have it upstairs. Signora Zitelli brought it by this morning. Is that why you dropped by, to settle the bill? There was no hurry, you know." She was just rambling now, looking for an escape from where the conversation would lead.

"Yes. Well that, and to give you back your note, which

you're acting really funny about now." Andie paused as if in thought. "Why *are* you acting so funny? What does it say?"

"What does it say?" There was a hint of anger in her tone as she recalled what the note said. Had Andie figured out what it meant? At the very least, she had to have seen her own name. No wonder she'd asked her what she had when they were resting by the fire. And yes, Valentina had heard every word, and only pretended to be asleep because she was taken off guard and too nervous to answer. Heat filled her cheeks, and she knew she must be glowing red. "Like you don't know!"

Andie frowned, clearly puzzled. "But, I really don't know."

"Please. I can see from here that the flap has been opened." Valentina swiped the note from Andie's hand. "You've read it."

It was Andie's turn to blush. "I might have taken a peek, but I swear I didn't read it!"

"Really."

It must've been obvious from Valentina's expression that she didn't believe her because Andie protested again. "I didn't! It's in Italian!"

This gave Valentina pause, as it was true that she'd written the note in Italian, and she'd seen Andie struggle enough with the language that she believed her when she said she didn't understand a word of it. But she must have seen her name. "You could've translated it."

"I tried! It was too smudged to make out more than a few letters."

"Well, at least you're honest." Her mind flashed back to that moment by the hearth. "But then why did you ask me yesterday if I like girls?"

"Oh no!" Andie groaned, hiding her eyes with her hands. "You heard that? I thought you were asleep. Now you *have* to tell me what that letter says. Trust me, nothing could be more embarrassing than what you witnessed from me yesterday."

"Nope. What it says is between me and Cupid."

Andie blinked slowly, then started to laugh. "So, you write letters to ten-foot tall statues, and I have all the smooth moves of an adolescent boy. Don't we make a fine pair?"

"Yes." Valentina laughed, too. "We're both pathetic."

"You at least have to tell me more about this statue thing."

"Come on." Shaking her head, Valentina took a step toward the door.

"No really. I have to know!"

"So, come on, then." Valentina turned the sign on the front door to closed and took the unusual precaution of locking the door. "Come upstairs and I'll tell you the whole legend. But you're going to have to sacrifice a bottle of wine."

"Sounds like a fair trade," Andie agreed as she followed Valentina up the stairs.

Once in the apartment, Valentina shot a wary glance toward Chiara's bedroom, but the door was shut and she suspected her daughter would have little desire to emerge any time soon. The case of wine that had been delivered in the morning sat on her kitchen counter, and she grabbed a bottle at random and removed the cork, filling two glasses even more generously than Signora Zitelli would have done. She handed one to Andie and led the way back to the living room, carrying her own glass and the rest of the bottle along. She took a seat on one end of the couch and Andie sat on the other end, with the center cushion acting as a safe-zone between them.

"So, Cupid." Valentina took a good, long sip from her glass before she continued. "The village of Montamore was built on the spot where there was once a temple for the goddess Venus."

"The goddess of love?"

Valentina nodded. "Cupid was supposed to be her son, and the statue and fountain in our piazza date back to the days of the temple."

Andie looked shocked. "It's that old?"

"This isn't America. Everything's old," Valentina said. "Including me, if you take my daughter's word for it."

"Kids. What do they know? Although," Andie paused, "I think you should probably give her a break about this and be sure to tell her I convinced you."

"Why's that?"

"I don't think she likes me much, and I'd like to improve her opinion of me."

"If it makes you feel better, I don't think it has anything to do with you. She's been like this ever since Luca moved out."

A look of understanding crossed Andie's face. "Yeah, I've been there. My parents split up, too. But even so, if you could put in a good word for me?"

"I'll see what I can do." Though she laughed it off as a joke, it warmed her to the core to know that Andie cared what her daughter thought. "But anyway, back to Cupid. For as long as anyone remembers, people have been leaving notes on the statue, letters for Cupid asking for his help or advice about love. Maybe that's what they used to do at the temple, too, although no one really knows anymore."

"And people think he answers?"

"Ask anyone in Montamore, and they'll say they *know* he answers. Everyone believes it. It's why the kids are so eager to climb up the fountain with their notes."

"So, you have to get the letter all the way up there? You can't just toss it in the water or something?"

Valentina shrugged. "Oh, who knows. The rules seem to change a little with every generation."

"So, you don't believe it."

Andie had stated it with such conviction that Valentina shifted uncomfortably, not liking what she was about to confess. "Actually, I'm on the fence."

Andie's brow furrowed. "But, with the divorce and all, why would you trust the word of a statue?"

"It's because of that, in part." Valentina crossed her arms in front of herself in an attempt to hold in her embarrassment. "Well, because of how it all came about. See, when I was a little older than Chiara, my friends dared me to ask Cupid to show me a reflection of my true love's face in the water, and I ended up falling in and the whole village knew about it."

"Like mother, like daughter. And did you see someone's face before you fell in?"

"Well, I told everyone I did. They were all so...*expectant*." Valentina shivered, remembering all those eyes on her, waiting. "So, I told them what they wanted to hear. A boy with dark hair and eyes the color of hazelnut cream."

Andie's jaw dropped. "That sounds like Luca!"

"It does, doesn't it?" Valentina's head drooped, ashamed. "But the thing is, I made it all up."

"Because you didn't see anything."

"No," Valentina corrected. "Because of what I saw."

"Be honest." Andie grinned wickedly. "Was it me?"

"No, it wasn't you!" Valentina picked up a pillow from the couch and lobbed it at her, though she was grateful for the levity Andie's comment had brought. "It wasn't anybody, exactly. But it was *something*. It was the start of something that wasn't just a reflection or a trick of the light, and it scared me."

"Well, yeah. That would be terrifying." Andie studied her thoughtfully for a moment, then asked with gentle seriousness, "Who were you hoping it would be? Francesca?"

Valentina's mouth fell open and for a few seconds she was unable to speak. "How…how did you know that?" She reached for her wine glass and took a huge gulp.

"Oh, Val. Falling for your best friend is basically a rite of passage for us."

"Us?"

"Lesbians. Or, bisexuals, in your case?" Andie added quickly. "I mean, given Luca—"

"I don't know." Valentina took another large swallow of wine, finishing off the glass. She set it on the coffee table and watched as Andie filled it close to the top again. "I think you maybe got it right the first time. I always knew marrying Luca was a mistake."

"Then why—"

"Why did I marry him?" Valentina took a sip of wine from the fresh glass, smaller this time, and savored the relaxing warmth of it as it drained down her throat. *Marrying Luca was a mistake, because I'm a lesbian.* There. She'd finally admitted it to herself in the plainest of words, and the world hadn't ended. Despite the gravity of the moment, a weight had been lifted, and she felt like she might float right up to the ceiling. "I think it was because it was what everyone wanted. I'd just finished school and was supposed to be leaving for an internship with a Belgian chocolate maker."

"I didn't know you'd studied in Belgium."

"I didn't. It would've been my first time on my own, and I was so excited. But my father's health took a terrible turn, and I had to stay in Montamore to help with the business. Pretty soon, all my friends were getting married. And, I mean, even you realized immediately that Luca fit my made-up description, and you've only just got here. Can you imagine the pressure I had from everyone in town who'd heard me tell that story, over and over, for years? But it was an awful thing to do."

"Foolish, maybe, but not as bad as you make it sound." Andie inched closer as she spoke, the safe-zone between them reduced by half. "You're hardly the first person in the world to have found themselves in that situation and made the same decision. Minus the magical fountain telling them to, of course."

Valentina paused, considering. Up until that moment, it had truly felt like she was alone. Pondering the possibility that other people had gone through the same struggles and would understand the choices she'd made caused her spirit to rally. "How can you argue with a magical statue, right?"

"Yeah, once you start talking back to statues, you're pretty much a goner. But, what exactly were you trying to ask for in that letter of yours? A new girlfriend?"

"No!" Valentina dissolved into nervous laughter. "No, nothing like that."

"Really?"

"Really. I have enough to do managing a struggling business and a moody preteen. The last thing I need is *romance*." She crinkled her nose as she said the word and Andie laughed.

"Not a fan of romance, I take it?"

When Valentina attempted to shake her head no, she was overtaken by the first signs of dizziness that come from drinking too much red wine in a hurry. Resting her cheek against the back of the couch, she became vaguely aware that somehow the extra cushion between them had all but disappeared. She took a breath that was filled with the clean soapy scent of Andie's shampoo. They were close enough to touch, separated by nothing but a few molecules of air. She was much too close, and much too tipsy, to keep secrets. A nervous sound escaped Valentina, partway between a laugh and a sigh. "Besides, how could I have a new girlfriend if I've never had any old ones?"

Andie processed this revelation for a moment, then tilted her head, resting her cheek against the sofa just as Valentina had done. She looked into Valentina's eyes, and it was like she was looking into her soul. "Are you saying you've *never* had a girlfriend?"

"Never."

"So you've just had sex with women without being in a relationship? There's no shame in that."

"Not...um, no. That's not...no, I haven't actually done that at all."

"So, just making out, huh?"

"Um..."

"Kissed a girl?" Andie's voice cracked.

"No." The word was barely a whisper. At the look of

shock on Andie's face, Valentina curled into a ball, burying her head somewhere between her ribcage and her elbows like a startled hedgehog. She stayed that way until the soothing warmth of a hand on her back coaxed her partially upright.

"It's okay, you know." Andie smiled reassuringly.

"No, it's not," Valentina mumbled into her chest.

"Okay, then. Do you want to?"

"Want to what?" She studied Andie's face warily, unclear as to her intent.

"Kiss a girl. Right now."

Valentina swallowed. "You mean *you*?"

"Sure! I've got a few minutes to spare, and I'd be happy to show you how it's done."

Valentina straightened up in a flash and shot her a scathing look. "Be serious."

"Well, what if I am serious?" She'd expected Andie to laugh or grin, but the woman's face was so hard to read that Valentina couldn't tell if she was teasing her or not. "We're all alone except for Chiara, and with the way you looked when you banished her to her room, I doubt she'll come out any time soon. I have nothing on my calendar…"

Valentina crossed her arms and glared, deciding that it must be a joke. "I wouldn't have told you if I'd known you were going to make fun."

"I'm not making fun," Andie insisted, sincerity filling the spaces between her words. "Well, only a little. I'll admit to being surprised. You've really never experimented a little with your friends, like during a sleepover?"

"Kiss my friends?" Valentina pressed her hands to her cheeks, which had grown warm at the mere suggestion. She drained the last of the second glass of wine, not caring if she'd regret it later. "What kind of sleepovers do you have in America, anyway?"

"The type you should've had, apparently." Andie waggled her eyebrows like a cartoon wolf.

Rolling her eyes, Valentina shifted so that her cheek once again rested against the cool, smooth upholstery of the sofa. She shut her eyes for a moment, as rolling them had made the room start to spin. "Now you *are* making fun, but I guess since I've just admitted I'm a thirty-four-year-old lesbian who's never even kissed a woman, I do have it coming."

"Not at all. Everyone has their own timing, and you really can't control it. Who knows, maybe this is your time to start exploring." Andie had turned, too, so that they were eye to eye once again. She moved her hand, resting it so that it was not quite touching Valentina's knee, but so close that Valentina could feel its presence nonetheless. "I'll just put it out there again, so you know I'm serious. I like you, and I think you might like me, and—"

The intimacy of the pause created a humming that vibrated deep in Valentina's core. Valentina's throat constricted, producing a motion somewhere between a swallow and a gulp. "And?"

"And I know I'm not here for long…"

"No, you're not." The reminder sent a stab of pain through her chest, but Valentina almost welcomed it. She'd needed a jolt of sanity to bring her back to her senses.

"Well, maybe that's not such a bad thing," Andie mused. "After all, you did say you weren't looking for romance."

"True." In the fuzzy haze that was her wine-soaked state of mind, Andie made an oddly compelling argument.

"That's perfect, because I really don't do romance. I'm

terrible at relationships. Which is good, because you might kiss me once and decide to go back to Luca."

"I doubt that." It had been fairly clear she was joking, but just in case there was a smidgen of real concern lurking beneath the jovial tone, Valentina sought to put her at ease. "I really do."

"Yeah, so do I. I'm a fantastic kisser."

Valentina pressed her lips together tightly so as not to reward the woman's ego with the laughter that was trying so desperately to escape her chest. She was less than successful, and the sound emerged as a strangled snort. Valentina writhed with embarrassment, and it was only when she'd grown still again that she realized that her knee now rested fully on top of Andie's open palm. Upon making the discovery, Valentina didn't dare move, or even breathe.

"So, what do you say?" Andie's eyes had grown dark with desire, and she'd gained just enough movement from her trapped fingers to stroke them along Valentina's inner thigh, making all speech impossible. "Why not just keep it casual and have some fun?"

Still unable to answer, or to bear the tortuous temptation of Andie's touch any longer, Valentina crossed her legs, shifting them out of reach of those wandering fingers. "I don't know…"

"People do that here, right, just have fun?"

Valentina's face scrunched with doubt. "In a village where we have a magical statue available as a matchmaker 24/7? There's less casual dating than you might think."

"This little village of yours needs to get with the times!" Andie flashed a cajoling grin. "You can be the trailblazer they're looking for. You've already gone against tradition by ignoring Cupid, and then getting a divorce. You're off to a great start. So why not go all the way and agree to have dinner with me on Saturday?"

"I can't."

Andie buried her face in her palm. "Did I really just list your divorce as a reason to go out with me? I am *so* bad at this."

"We've had a lot of wine," Valentina offered.

"Not a good excuse. Let me try again. Would you be so kind as to have a dinner date with me on Saturday night?"

"No, Andie," Valentina said with a laugh, "that wasn't why I said I couldn't. Saturday night is no good. I'm swamped with work."

Andie gave her a dubious look. "You know, I was just in your shop earlier. I saw that it was empty. You don't need to spare my feelings."

"Not in the shop. In the kitchen," Valentina explained. "We sold most of our stock on Valentine's Day and with Easter coming up, I need to replenish the reserves. Plus, the spring festival is just around the corner. That's pretty much our income for the rest of the year, until Christmas."

"You make it all yourself?" Andie's tone conveyed both interest and surprise.

"Mostly. Except those awful foil Cupids my mother orders for the tourists we don't get."

"Hey, I had a couple of those, and I thought they were great!"

"That's because you've never tasted mine."

"What do you think I've been working so hard on for the past fifteen minutes?" She gave her lips a naughty tongue flick, which sent a spark of electricity directly to the spot between Valentina's legs.

"I meant chocolate, Andie," Valentina scolded, though

chocolate was now the furthest thing from her mind.

"Well, of course you did. So did I. What else would it mean?" Andie batted her lashes. "I'd love to see your technique sometime, and yes, that's actually chocolate I'm talking about this time, I promise."

"Okay, Saturday." Despite her stomach doing a flip-flop, Valentina dropped her voice to a conspiratorial tone. "Not dinner, but Chiara will be with Luca, and my mother and grandmother are going to the movies, so there'll be no one here but me for at least a couple of hours. Why don't you come by then, and I can show you how it's done?"

Andie leaned in as well, so far that her breast brushed against Valentina's forearm, sending shivers down her spine. Her mouth was just beside Valentina's ear, which filled with hot breath as she whispered, "Shouldn't I be the one showing you how it's done?"

"Andie!" The overall effect of her protest was made weaker by the fact that Valentina had wrapped one arm around Andie's shoulder and was clutching her against her chest. "I meant I'd show you how the chocolate was made."

"Sure you did."

Andie's mouth shifted downward, her lips brushing the sensitive spot just behind Valentina's ear. Valentina's breath came in short bursts, her body on fire. Her breasts pressed against Andie's as she simultaneously gasped for air and strained the tendons in her neck to expose every possible surface for Andie's lips to explore. There was no telling how far it might have gone, except that in that instant, the sound of Chiara's bedroom door opening down the hall brought them to their senses and they quickly pulled apart. Andie smirked and Valentina cursed the heat that radiated from her cheeks.

"Saturday, then. I'll come by and you can show me how to *make the chocolate*." Andie drew air quotes as she said the last part and Valentina chucked another pillow at her. "I'll show myself out. Don't forget, go easy on the kid, and give me the credit. See you Saturday."

Valentina put the pillows back on the couch as she waited for her pulse to slow, taking a few deep breaths and smoothing out her clothing before Chiara appeared. It was a false alarm. A moment later she heard the toilet flush and the bedroom door slam shut, but even that was enough to remind her of her daughter's presence, and to put a dampener on her mood.

What am I doing? I have a daughter to think about.

She went to her bedroom window and looked out into the piazza. Andie was halfway across, just passing by the spot where Cupid stood. *Yes, laughing—at me, no doubt.* The last thing she needed was the type of complications that meddling old deity promised to bring, and yet here she'd just done…what exactly? She'd confessed every secret she had in the world, nearly made out on the couch while her daughter was in the very next room, and then invited Andie over at a time when she knew they'd have the place to themselves. She didn't need to question what she'd been thinking. It was obvious. At least, Andie had certainly caught on to her meaning quickly enough.

I should call and cancel. Across the square, Andie disappeared inside her apartment door and Valentina sighed to see her go. She returned to the kitchen and uncorked another bottle from the case of wine that Andie had left behind. She poured it into her glass, watching the blood-red liquid slosh as it neared the top. She drank it down slowly and did not call to cancel.

TWELVE

A RICH COCOA aroma permeated the evening air, so strong that Andie first detected it while still several yards outside the shop. She pushed the door open, oblivious to the "closed" sign that she'd learned to ignore, though even if she hadn't, she would have paid it no heed now. The sweet temptation waiting inside was much too hard to resist. And she was looking forward to some chocolate, too.

Her heart leaped to see Valentina walk through the kitchen door just seconds after her arrival. Valentina was dressed for cooking, in dark blue jeans and a crisp white button-up shirt, the long sleeves rolled up past her elbows. The whole ensemble was mostly covered by a giant white apron, and her hair was tucked under a red-and-white, polka-dot scarf so that just a few dark strands showed. She could've passed for a modern incarnation of Rosie the Riveter, covered with dark streaks of chocolate rather than factory grease.

"You're just in time!" Valentina's welcoming smile lit up the room and raised Andie's internal temperature a degree or two in the process. "I have a new recipe that's almost ready to taste."

"I'll admit, I was still holding out hope that *chocolate making* was a total euphemism." Andie shut the door behind her, and taking her cue from her last visit, turned the lock, just in case. With any luck, the chocolate tasting would be over quickly and they could move on to even more enjoyable activities. By her own admission, Valentina had a lot to learn about the mysteries of Sapphic love, and ever the helpful tutor, Andie had come prepared to start her lessons.

Valentina just laughed. "You won't say that once you try the chocolate."

"It would have to be some pretty amazing chocolate," Andie challenged.

"Oh, it is," Valentina assured her with complete confidence, yet without any hint of boasting. She slipped into the narrow space behind the display case, which was an enormous antique made of carved oak and curved glass that took up most of one wall, and examined the offerings with care, straightening a piece here or there to make them perfect. "What's your favorite type?"

Andie shrugged. "I'm not sure. I mostly had Hershey's growing up."

Valentina let out a horrified squeak. "You're a chef! That can't possibly be your favorite."

"No, I'm a little choosier than that, but only just. I like having dessert, but it isn't my professional specialty," Andie admitted. "To be honest, the most important thing to me when choosing chocolate is finding the type that isn't in individual wrappers. Chocolate is for binge-eating when I'm stressed or nervous, and those wrappers really get in the way."

"I'd pretend to be offended, only I just finished off the last of the Cupids about an hour ago. And you're right, the wrappers were a real nuisance."

Andie looked at the display table where the Cupids had been and discovered that a fresh display of foil-wrapped bunnies had taken their place. "Stressed?"

"Nervous," Valentina confessed. She looked down as she said it, avoiding eye contact, and her cheeks had gone a deep shade of pink. Andie was delightedly certain that it hadn't just been fretting about whether or not the chocolate tasting would meet with her approval that had so rattled Valentina's nerves. Valentina cleared her throat, still looking into the case. "So, what do you want?"

Valentina's lips were rosy with gloss, and they glistened as she spoke in a way that Andie found mesmerizing. She knew the real answer to that question, but Valentina continued to fiddle with the contents of the display case, and was clearly only offering chocolate, at least for the moment.

"You're the expert," Andie said, unable to take her eyes off Valentina's lips long enough to give the chocolates more than the briefest glance. "What do you suggest?" She didn't really care, as long as the choice would hurry things along and get her closer to the real treat of the evening.

Valentina gave the contents of each shelf a long, deliberate appraisal, treating the selection process with the utmost seriousness. "First, you have to decide between dark or milk. I have white, too, but I wouldn't start there."

"So, not your favorite?"

Valentina made a face. "Too sweet!"

"I like sweet! You're sweet," Andie added, seeing no

harm in reminding Valentina what she was really interested in.

"Not *that* sweet." There was a twinkle in her eyes that Andie decided to take as a promise of things to come.

"To be honest, with some of the things I have in mind for later, I'm kind of counting on you not being as sweet as you look."

Valentina choked back a cough. "Nuts?"

"People have said that about me, yes."

Valentina rolled her eyes. "I meant, do you like nuts in your chocolate? Or maybe fruit?"

"Fine. I sense you're really dedicated to ignoring my innuendo right now, so I guess I'll try to pay attention to the chocolate." Andie gave the case a closer inspection, and as she did, her admiration for Valentina grew as she realized the true artistry that had gone into every piece. These were not the standard chocolate-shop morsels of dull, brown chocolate that had been molded into cookie-cutter shapes and filled with the usual choices of caramels and creams. Instead, shelf upon shelf overflowed with confectionery masterpieces.

There were delicate hearts adorned with tiny sugar pearls, pyramids striped with cocoa powder and finely ground nuts, and chocolates the size and shape of robin's eggs that were painted with rose buds. Where before she'd been indifferent, now the indescribable beauty of each option made it impossible to choose. Finally, Andie pointed to a tray of chocolate squares, each as dark as the midnight sky and sprinkled with flakes of gold that appeared like miniature stars atop a bite-sized galaxy. "This one. It reminds me of your eyes."

"Trust me, you have to be careful about chocolate-colored eyes," Valentina said as she placed Andie's selection on top of the case. "They can be more trouble than they're worth, at least in my experience."

"Good thing mine are blue, then. Blue chocolate's hard to come by. But as for a woman with chocolate eyes? I'm willing to take my chances."

Andie plucked the dark square from its fluted paper wrapper, briefly admiring the way the gold flecks sparkled in the light before placing it between her teeth. It was just firm enough to break with a satisfying crack as she bit down, but almost immediately it began to melt against her tongue with a smooth, velvety lusciousness, revealing a thin middle layer of caramel with a saltiness that balanced out the sweetness to perfection. She closed her eyes as it slowly dissolved, the taste filling her mouth and overwhelming her senses. When she opened them again, she found Valentina watching her expectantly. "That was the best chocolate I've ever tasted," she informed her, and it was not an exaggeration.

Valentina beamed with delight. "Just wait. That one was fairly tame. There are much better things to come."

A battle raged as Andie's body fought to see which was more turned on, her stomach by the chocolate, or the rest of her by the unintentional seduction of the chocolate maker's word choice. With the taste of it still fresh on her tongue, the chocolate was winning out. She'd arrived impatient at the thought of sampling anything other than Valentina's kisses, but the sweets had turned out to be just as tempting as their maker. Already her mouth was watering for another bite of chocolate as much as it was for another taste of Valentina's lips, and the unexpected development was really messing with her formerly clear-cut sense of priorities for the evening.

"Here, try this." Valentina wore a mischievous expression as she held out another piece, and it made Andie suspect that the internal dialogue she'd just been having showed plain as day on her face.

"What is it?" she asked, looking at the offering that was nestled in Valentina's palm. It was shaped like a pear, and though she suspected it had been formed from chocolate like all the rest, the outer coating was tinted in such realistic hues that it looked for all the world like an actual piece of fruit. Andie's fingers brushed against Valentina's skin as she retrieved the tiny pear, and her blood pulsed more rapidly through her veins. She turned the pear around in the light, making an effort to examine it closely as it softened in her fingers, hoping to restore herself to some reasonable level of composure before diving in. It wasn't that she was embarrassed that Valentina could no doubt read her lusty thoughts like an open book. It was just that if she didn't pace herself, she'd never last the night.

"See if you can guess what it is," Valentina urged in a voice quiet as a whisper.

Accepting the challenge, Andie lifted the mystery confection to her nose, giving it a sniff like she might a fine wine. "Hints of pear, and maybe some spice?"

"Very good. Now take a bite and see what else."

The outer shell was paper-thin, no thicker than the skin of a real pear. As she bit through it, her taste buds were met with a rush of creamy and richly flavored ganache. "Definitely pear," she paused to swish her tongue around, a smile teasing her lips as the flavors became more distinct, "and is that champagne?"

Valentina nodded encouragingly. "What else?"

Andie shut her eyes, letting her sense of taste take over completely. "Ginger, and…cardamom?"

"Very good! I'm impressed."

Andie opened her eyes and was warmed by Valentina's approving grin. "It tastes like Christmas. I almost said cinnamon or cloves, but I knew those weren't right."

"No, cardamom's a little more unusual," Valentina agreed. "A good winter flavor that's a little harder to guess."

"But, I got it right." Andie captured Valentina's hand in hers, then leaned across the glass case, pulling her closer. Now that her stomach had been placated, she could turn her full attention back where it belonged. "Do I get a prize?"

Valentina pressed her lips together, and there was no doubt she was about to give in, but just as her face started to drift nearer, a shrill buzzer disrupted the silence and ruined the moment. Valentina sighed. "The chocolate's finished heating. Time for the next batch." Though she'd missed out on the kiss for now, Andie found that the excruciating look of disappointment on Valentina's face as she pulled away was a reward in itself.

Andie followed Valentina into the kitchen, which didn't look much like a kitchen at all, or at least not the type to which Andie was accustomed. Instead of a stovetop, there was a huge table with a marble top, beside which stood a line of rectangular boxes made of stainless steel. Each one had a dial on the front, and a light above one of them glowed bright red. It was toward this box that Valentina headed, swiping a long-handled spoon from the table as she lifted the lid.

The buzzer sounded once more, much louder now that they were in the kitchen, and Andie jumped while Valentina remained calm, simply turning the dial on the box. "That little thing is what made all the noise?" Andie asked peering over Valentina's shoulder for a closer look. Its purpose soon became clear as Andie saw that it was filled to the top with melted chocolate, dark and shiny.

"Sorry it's so loud. I'm lucky it works at all, any of it." Valentina swept one hand, the one not holding the spoon, in a gesture around the room. "The shop's been in my family for generations. Everything here is ancient."

"Tradition?" Andie guessed.

"Some of it. I like using the old molds, for instance. They're much more interesting than what you can find now. But the rest of it's just due to cost. I'd love an automatic tempering machine, but it's almost five-thousand euros for the size I'd need. So, for now, I just do it by hand."

"And how do you do that?" Andie asked with interest.

"Oh, you know. The usual way."

Andie frowned, her claim of having virtually no knowledge of dessert-making having been genuine. "And, how exactly is that?"

Valentina gave her a surprised look. "You must have learned the basics when you were in school."

Andie shrugged. "I left high school when I was sixteen, so…"

"No, I mean culinary school." Valentina said with a laugh. "Or college?"

"Never went." When Valentina's surprised expression turned to one of shock, Andie experienced a familiar pang of regret over her lack of formal credentials.

"You've never taken a class?" Far from sounding judgmental, it seemed that Valentina regarded her with a new respect. "You must have studied somewhere. Look how successful you are!"

Andie's regret blossomed into pride. "I started working at a restaurant full-time when I left school, and I've learned everything I know on one job or another."

"That's amazing."

"Not really," Andie demurred, not wanting to let Valentina's praise go too much to her head. "I just learn best by doing."

"I don't, so it's amazing to me."

"Didn't you learn from your mother and grandmother?"

"I guess. But I spent five years at the istituto professionale, as well."

"Oh, great." Andie allowed her shoulders to slump in exaggerated fashion. "I'm over here pretending to be the professional, and you're the one who went to a real school for it." Her jocularity was laced with a dash of insecurity.

"No, it wasn't a proper culinary school. It's just what you might call a high school in English, but one that specialized more in practical skills like culinary arts. It's one of the options we have here in Italian schools. I wouldn't have had the confidence, otherwise, to ever try to run this place on my own."

Andie nodded. "Whereas I jump into everything head first with an abundance of misplaced confidence and worry about learning to swim when I hit the water."

"Like you said, you learn best by doing. In that case," Valentina declared, "I think today you'll learn by helping me!" She handed her a long, flat knife, along with a tool that looked like it was meant for applying plaster to a wall. "Just watch first, then follow along."

Andie clutched one tool in each hand, imitating what Valentina had done, and watched as Valentina wiped the surface of the marble table with a cloth, then lifted the basin out of the warmer and poured about two-thirds of it out onto the cold stone. It spread out fast and thin with the help of Valentina's long knife, soon making a giant chocolate lake which she then gathered up rapidly with the palette knife before repeating the process again. After doing this a few more times, she scooped all the chocolate, thicker now but not yet set, back into the basin and gave the whole mix a vigorous stir.

"Now you try."

The chocolate was poured out again—less this time, or so it appeared to Andie. She was soon grateful for this fact, as she found all too quickly that controlling the viscous liquid took much more skill than Valentina's deft handling of it had made it seem. By the time she had scooped everything back into the container, she was certain the majority of it had ended up in a puddle on the floor or else been splattered down her shirt, but Valentina was nothing but encouraging.

"You're doing well! You really do learn quickly."

"I don't know," Andie said, looking doubtfully at her chocolate-enrobed hands. "I think I've got some way to go. But what does this process do, anyway? It doesn't look much different than when we started."

"It will when it's cooled. Usually when chocolate melts, it sets dull and streaky. This is what makes it shiny and smooth."

"So, you make this yourself? Like, from the cocoa beans?"

"No. We order the blocks of pure chocolate from producers." Valentina set the tempered chocolate back into the warmer and pulled out a large brown square from a box, holding it up for Andie to see. "Fair trade and organic, of course, and the blocks from each country and region have a slightly different flavor, so I can blend them together to produce exactly the taste that I want. So, it's not as much work as you thought."

"Are you kidding? It's impressive as hell. So, what will you do with it now?"

"This batch is simple. It just goes into molds to cool, and that's it. Want to try?"

"Um." Andie held up her chocolatey fingers and grinned. "Maybe I'd better just watch."

"Maybe you'd better wash up. There's a sink over there."

When Andie returned, Valentina filled the molds with lightning speed, a skill acquired from years of practice. When the last one was prepared, Valentina took a stack to the cooling cabinets—a row of what looked like refrigerators, but which Valentina explained were not kept nearly so cold and were used to provide a constant temperature and humidity. When all the molds were stored in one cabinet, Valentina opened another and reached inside.

"And now, there's something else to try," she told Andie as she brought out a single mold and carried it back to the marble table. When Valentina flipped it over and the chocolates came spilling out, Andie's pulse ticked faster at what was revealed.

"They're blue." Andie looked up from the chocolates that were the exact color of her own eyes, and into Valentina's dark brown ones. All the desire that she'd kept on the back burner during their lesson came roaring to a boil.

"Yes, so they are," Valentina replied, and though usually she was prone to look away, this time her gaze remained steady.

"An interesting choice." Andie swallowed roughly at the

last word, her throat impossibly dry. She'd never wanted anyone so badly in her life. She longed to untie the polka-dot scarf and run her fingers through Valentina's hair, to unbutton her plain white shirt and press her lips to the exposed hollow of her throat. Not doing so took every ounce of her will, and yet the more practical part of her sensed that pushing Valentina back onto the marble table and covering every inch of her with kisses might be coming on a little too strong.

"It's a new recipe," Valentina told her, seemingly oblivious to Andie's agony. "The filling's made with an American chili powder, so it's bold. I don't know. Maybe it's a little crazy. But I like it." She touched her tongue to her lips in a way that could only be described as inviting, and it occurred to Andie that she might not be so oblivious after all. She might just be toying with her, like a cat with a mouse. If so, Andie wondered how long it would be before she pounced. She prayed it would be soon.

"Crazy, bold, and American, huh? And this shade of blue." Andie raised an eyebrow. "I wonder where you got the inspiration for these."

"I can't imagine." There was laughter in her eyes, but otherwise Valentina managed to maintain composure. But as Andie plucked a chocolate from the table, her face clouded with doubt. "Wait, I should warn you—"

But the chocolate was inside Andie's mouth, the smooth outer shell had already been cracked before the sudden urgency of Valentina's tone had a chance to register. By the time it did, it was too late. Fire blazed in her mouth, scorching her lips, filling her with a burning that had nothing in common with the pleasurable heat of attraction she'd experienced moments before. The stinging took her breath away. Perspiration broke out on her forehead, and tears seeped from the corners of her eyes, which she'd squeezed tightly shut against the pain.

"—they might be a little too spicy. I wasn't sure how much chili to use. Andie? Are you okay?" Though Andie couldn't see her, she could hear the rising concern in Valentina's tone. "Andie?"

"Water?" It was barely a squeak, but it was all that she could manage. Andie's eyes were still closed, but she could make out rapid footsteps, and the sound of a running tap. At last, a cold glass was pressed into her hands. Once she'd drunk the contents down, she finally dared to open her eyes and take a few ragged breaths. Valentina led her from the center of the room and helped her lean against a countertop for support.

"Andie, I'm so sorry." Valentina's face looked stricken, and there were tears in the corners of her eyes, too. "The first batch didn't have enough chili so I doubled it, only I think I measured wrong, and I was in a rush to get them done before you got here, so I never tasted them. Oh God, what did I do?"

Though still sweating and shaky, the worst had passed, and Andie managed a weak smile. "I'll be fine. It was just unexpected." She placed a hand on Valentina's shoulder, only meaning to offer reassurance. But the next thing she knew, Valentina's arms were around her, clutching her tight. If she'd found the presence of hot chilies in her chocolate surprising, it was nothing compared to the shock she experienced at the touch of Valentina's lips against hers, striking like lightning on a clear blue day.

The kiss was gentle at first, as if Valentina were simply trying to sooth the pain away. As a cure, it was miraculously effective. Andie had assumed she would be the one to make the first move, to coax Valentina back out of the shell she'd retreated into since they'd last been together. Having her expectations flipped upside down was a delightful and dizzying turn of events. Though Andie's lips continued to sting, within seconds she found that she no longer cared. There was nothing that mattered except getting closer to Valentina. She needed to experience more of her. She opened her mouth wider, wanting to shout with joy as she felt the swipe of Valentina's tongue along her lower lip, then the tip of it entering her mouth.

Andie sucked on Valentina's tongue, causing her to gasp and open her own mouth wide. As Andie's tongue entered, Valentina bit down lightly, capturing her between her teeth. Andie stifled a moan, continuing to keep silent only out of fear that Valentina would stop, mistaking it for a cry of pain. The kiss continued unbroken, all memory of the burning chilies gone. There was no place for pain right now, only pleasure.

Wrapping one arm around Valentina's waist, Andie spun her around so that her back was against the countertop. She let the other arm climb upward until her fingers brushed against the silky fabric of Valentina's scarf. With the gentlest of tugs, it slipped from her head, and Andie tossed it aside, returning quickly to bury her fingers in the freed locks. As she delighted in the taste of Valentina's mouth—a taste that was not at all like chocolate and yet somehow just as rich— Andie shifted her hands to the buttons of Valentina's shirt, popping one and then another, and finally a third. It was only then that she allowed their mouths to move apart, her lips traveling along the curve of Valentina's chin, then downward until they were pressed into the hollow of her throat, exactly as she'd pictured. Valentina moaned, her back arching as her bent elbows came to rest on the countertop for support. Andie pushed into her more until finally, after getting her fill of the spot, her mouth traveled lower down her chest.

Two more buttons gave way, and now the formerly crisp shirt lay open and rumpled, exposing a bra of shiny white satin. It was a sensible item, designed to contain and support its generous contents. It could've been the sexiest garment in the world and Andie would've considered it little more than a nuisance standing in the way of what she wanted. Plunging a hand deep into one of the cups, she scooped up the heavy, warm flesh, lifting until the hardened peak inside was freed from its bondage, emerging like a dollop of dark chocolate atop light caramel cream.

Still gripping the soft mound of flesh that surrounded it, Andie pressed her lips to the nipple's rough surface, taking it into her mouth while breathing in the scent of cocoa and sweat that perfumed the cleft between Valentina's breasts. Her free hand moved to the other breast, teasing it with her fingers until she felt its nipple harden and strain against the satin fabric that held it in.

Valentina's chest rose and fell with quick shallow gasps as this time Andie sought to breach the bra's cup from beneath the elastic band. Reaching the other nipple, she gave it a squeeze between the tips of her fingers, while simultaneously sucking and pulling on the one in her mouth. A steady stream of foreign words pierced the air. Unable to understand their precise meaning, Andie vowed then and there to study the Italian language until she knew them all.

Valentina threw her head back and continued speaking

in rapid, demanding Italian as she wrapped a leg around Andie's hip. Kicking off a shoe, she hooked her heel under the waistband of Andie's pants, her woolen sock itchy against the small of Andie's back, not that she minded or really noticed much at all. Lost in sensation, Valentina thrust her pelvis rhythmically, again and again, against Andie's thighs. Dragging one elbow from the countertop, Valentina snaked her arm around Andie's shoulder and then grasped her short hair, using it to pull Andie's head back upward until their mouths could once more reconnect.

It was at this point that Andie remembered the marble table, which had featured so prominently in her earlier fantasy. It was so close, just a few steps away really, but as she shifted her weight to one foot in an attempt to inch closer, she felt Valentina stiffen, her mouth pulling away and her hands pressing firmly against her chest, but not in a way that gave her encouragement.

Valentina shook her head, breathless. "No."

"No?" Andie frowned. Valentina's tone had been unexpectedly stern for a woman who had been devouring her mouth and grinding into her without hesitation just moments before. Perhaps doubt was setting in? "I'm sorry, is this going too fast? We could stop, or—"

Amusement tugged at the corners of Valentina's mouth, softening the seriousness of her expression. "No, *this* is fine. I meant that the table is off limits. It's just not sanitary."

"But how did you know I was going to—"

"Please. It was obvious." By now, Valentina couldn't hold back a chuckle.

Andie frowned suspiciously. "You did say this was your first time, right?"

"With a woman, Andie. I *was* married, remember? I have a daughter. I'm not a complete novice."

"Oh, right. Okay, so maybe we could just try covering it—"

But Valentina had readjusted her bra, pulled the edges of her shirt together and was buttoning the buttons with shaking hands. "Andie, seriously. I didn't even intend for this to go beyond a kiss, but in the event that it did, trust me, this wasn't exactly the location I had in mind. I'm already never going to be able to work in here again without thinking about what we just did. And, oh God, all the things I just said."

"What *did* you just say, exactly?"

"Never you mind. But getting naked on the table is just going too far."

"This table in particular, or tables in general? Because, I have a nice sturdy one back in my apartment that—" At the look on Valentina's face, Andie stopped, settling instead for curling a strand of Valentina's hair around her finger. "We could go upstairs, then, and pick up where we left off?"

Valentina sighed a whimpering sort of a sigh, the type of sigh that did not bode well for Andie's chances of getting the answer she was hoping for. "Mama and Nonna will be home soon. In fact, we're lucky they haven't walked in already."

"You could come to my place. That table idea is completely optional, by the way. There's a nice, big bed, too." Though she suspected the answer would be no, Andie at least had to try.

Valentina shook her head sadly. "Chiara will be home first thing in the morning. I need to be here for her."

A dejected Andie rested her head on Valentina's shoulder. "But, we'll do this again soon, right?" she asked hopefully. She held her breath, uncertain how, having now tasted Valentina's lips, she could go without doing so again.

Valentina was silent, and Andie could tell by the way her chest no longer rose and fell that she was holding her breath, too. Finally, she answered, "Definitely."

"Phew!" Andie let out her breath in a rush. "I was worried for a second that you'd changed your mind about being a lesbian."

"Oh, no. I haven't changed my mind. I just think I'll need more time."

"Time to get used to the idea? Ease into it?"

"No." Valentina flashed a wicked grin. "More time than what we've got right now. I obviously have a lot to learn. It could take all night."

Her unbridled eagerness sent a shot of pure lust through Andie's loins. "On that note, I'd better head home. Only, can I kiss you one more time, to say goodnight?" She stopped breathing once more as Valentina bit her lower lip thoughtfully, before giving a nod.

Valentina leaned closer, stopping inches away and touching her tongue to her lips. "But, just so you know, my lips are starting to tingle. I think you may have gotten some of that chili powder on them."

"I'll be careful," Andie promised, leaning in for one quick kiss before heading for the door. As she crossed the piazza, her heart soared, and her lips were tingling, too, but Andie knew that it had nothing at all to do with the chili powder.

THIRTEEN

THE AROMAS FILLING the downstairs kitchen were not the same on Monday morning as they'd been on Saturday night. Valentina couldn't help but notice the difference as she gazed out the window at nothing in particular. That night, the cocoa smell had been dark and sensual, whereas today it was sweet and light. Mondays and Fridays were the traditional baking days at Cioccolatini di Venere, when they made biscotti, amaretti, and pizelles by the dozens, plus cakes and other treats in every variety. The other days of the week, their selection was more modest, so locals knew that for something special, those were the days to shop.

Valentina and her mother had been working since well before dawn, and almonds, citrus, and anise perfumed the air. There was a hint of vanilla, too, which made Valentina smile as she recalled how Andie had told her she smelled like a sugar cookie. Sweet enough to eat... Closing her eyes, she could almost feel Andie's lips brushing her earlobe, and the soft scrape of her teeth giving the sensitive flesh a gentle nip. And then moving elsewhere, the gentle hesitancy giving way to…

"Valentina, have you finished mixing the batter yet?"

Her mother's voice yanked her back from her reveries, her spine straightening as she instinctively corrected her slumping posture and turned her attention to the wooden spoon clutched in her hand, which had been waiting patiently to be remembered and put to use for a good five minutes. "Just another stroke or two," she lied, plunging it into the thick batter and beginning to stir at a furious pace.

"Where are you this morning, Valentina? You seem distracted."

She sensed her mother's presence behind her even before she felt the weight of a hand on her shoulder. "Just thinking, Mama. Nothing to worry about." She gave her mother's fingers a reassuring squeeze.

"We'll see about that," her mother said, removing her hand. "It wouldn't be the first time that you being in a brooding mood led to something I need to worry about."

"Everything's fine, Mama," Valentina reiterated, but her mother did have a point. The last time Valentina had been so distracted had been during the final months of her marriage to Luca. Her thoughts had been troubled as she searched for a solution to the mess she'd made for herself. She supposed it was fair to say that the end result—having the only divorced woman in Montamore for her daughter—had given her mother plenty of cause for concern. The reason for her current distraction, a distractingly sexy American woman, was as opposite from the previous reason as could be, but she could hardly explain that to her mother without unleashing a fresh batch of trouble, and so she refrained from elaborating. After all, Mama was in a good mood today. Why spoil it?

As her mother pushed a cart loaded with baked goods into the adjoining shop to fill the display case, Valentina set her bowl of batter aside, having completely forgotten what it was she was making, and went back to staring out the window that overlooked the alleyway behind their building. It was bright enough out now to see clearly, a sign that it must be nearing seven o'clock. They'd be open for business soon. She rubbed her temples and tried to clear the fog from her brain. In her current state, she'd be useless for the rest of the day without at least a double shot of espresso. Luckily, she'd had just enough presence of mind to turn on the boiler of the shop's antique espresso maker earlier that morning, meaning that it should be just about ready to go.

As she was turning from the window to pursue her coffee quest in earnest, Andie's face appeared in the window. Valentina jumped, her need for espresso vanishing in a natural surge of adrenaline, then laughed as the woman waved frantically, jumping up and down while sporting a goofy grin. On the other side of the thick glass, Andie bobbed on tiptoe so that most of her head cleared the sill. She was saying something, but Valentina couldn't make it out. Valentina shook her head and cupped a hand to her ear, hoping Andie would understand her pantomime.

She watched with furrowed brow as Andie dropped out of sight momentarily, then reemerged holding up her hand, on which words had been scribbled in ink directly onto the flesh of her palm. *Meet me at my apartment?* the message read. Valentina nodded, mouthing the words five minutes while holding up all the fingers on one hand. Andie touched her forehead in salute and disappeared from view.

"Good morning, Nonna!" Valentina called out in a sing-song voice as she came through the door that led into the shop. No longer possessing the stamina to be of much help on baking days, her grandmother nevertheless was in the habit of waking early to join them as she had always done. She would pull one of the cafe chairs close to the kitchen door to "keep her girls company," though she'd invariably doze off even before the ovens were fully warmed. Valentina's mother usually tiptoed around her to let her sleep but knowing that it annoyed her grandmother to no end when she missed out on anything, Valentina always made a point of greeting her in a loud voice upon walking into the shop so that the old woman could revive herself and then pretend she hadn't been sleeping to begin with.

At the sound of Valentina's greeting, her grandmother woke with a snort that nearly sent her toppling from her chair. "Yes, just resting my eyes, cara. Is it seven o'clock already?"

"Nearly. But something's come up at the Rossini apartment and I need to have a look," Valentina fibbed. "Do you think you can manage without me for a few minutes?"

Usually, Valentina would work in the front with her grandmother for the first few hours on Monday mornings, so that her mother could finish the baking. Technically, it was a one-person job, or it would have been if Nonna weren't so prone to gabbing. In the past few years, the older woman's slowing pace and propensity for gossip had necessitated Valentina stepping in to pick up the slack.

"Of course I can," her grandmother replied with an insulted pout. "I've been taking care of the people of this village since before you were born."

"Of course, Nonna," Valentina agreed diplomatically.

"Have you put the chocolate gateau in the oven?" her mother asked, popping her head up from behind the pastry case.

Chocolate gateau! That's what the batter's for! "Not yet, Mama, but I'll put it in as soon as I return, and fry up the last batch of bomboloni, too. Could you just check to see that Chiara's up and getting ready for school? I'll be back before she has to leave."

"Yes, of course I can, but do hurry," her mother said. "You know how she is on a Monday morning, always dragging her feet. I hope the issue is nothing serious."

"The issue?" Valentina frowned, drawing a blank. "Oh, at the apartment, you mean. No. Just a leaky faucet." Valentina shrugged on a light jacket and unlocked the front door, which for once they'd remembered to bolt. "It won't take but a minute to fix, I'm sure."

"Don't you need some tools?" her grandmother cried out after her, but Valentina was already several steps into the piazza. Since there was no leaky faucet, she saw no need to delay to search for tools. *I'll say I left them there*, she thought, pleased with her growing ability to make up a story on the spot. Considering what she and Andie were likely to be getting up to over the coming weeks, it was a skill worth honing.

Valentina's heart thumped as she crossed the square, but it had little to do with her sprinting pace. *Why does Andie want me to come over?* The note on her palm hadn't exactly delved into specifics. *Does she just want to see me?* Valentina wanted to see her. It was all she'd been able to think about during the blur that was the thirty-six hours since they'd kissed. The desire to see her again had grown to an all-consuming ache. For the first time in years, she'd considered giving in to the urge to touch herself to gain some measure of relief, but she'd found she was unable to go through with it. The stern face of Sister Gloria, who'd taught her catechism class when she was a child, kept popping into her head, immediately killing any desire.

Up until their lips had met, she hadn't been completely convinced she would go through with the kiss. Now that she had, the urge to do it again, to do what they'd done and so much more, was unstoppable. It worried her. Her whole purpose in being with Andie was to satisfy her curiosity, like an inoculation of sorts against the need for any future entanglements. But Andie's touch was like a drug, and she was in danger of becoming hopelessly addicted.

Opening the building's door, she'd half expected to find Andie waiting for her in the first-floor entry, arms flung wide for an embrace, and so it was with considerable confusion that she instead found the small vestibule filled from wall to wall with boxes. Before she had time to make sense of it, Andie's voice rang down in greeting from partway up the stairs.

"Val, would you mind very much grabbing a box and carrying it up?"

She did as she was asked, a warm glow radiating through her chest at the way Andie had called her Val. It was the second time she'd done it. No one had ever called her that. Her grandmother referred to her as cara, meaning dear, and her mother and father had, in typical Italian style, used any number of silly endearments as she was growing up—little one, sparrow, or little potato being some of their favorites— but lopping off the last three syllables of her name was such a charming, American thing to do. She loved it.

They made not one, but three trips hauling boxes up the

stairs. The final one was large and heavy, requiring a team effort to reach the second-floor landing. Valentina didn't mind, as it gave her a chance to look at Andie as they climbed, her walking forward while Andie went backward up the stairs. Neither could spare the breath to speak, but the spark in Andie's eyes told Valentina that the longing she'd endured since Saturday night had not been one-sided.

"What is all this?" Valentina asked when the final box was inside and she'd had a chance to catch her breath. She leaned on her elbows against one side of the box while Andie rested on the opposite end of it.

"Cooking supplies from the network." Andie took a few deep breaths and mopped her brow with her hand, inadvertently smearing ink from her palm across her damp forehead.

Valentina stifled a giggle. "You couldn't just find things here?"

Andie shook her head. "Not this. It's from the sponsors, all the products and appliances I'm contractually obligated to include in my cookbook and feature on air next season."

"They tell you what to use?"

"Oh, yeah. That's how the network makes its money."

"Wow." It had never occurred to Valentina that Andie didn't have final say over how and what she cooked.

"Sorry about having to ask for your help getting all this up here, though." Andie offered a sheepish grin that reduced Valentina's insides to the consistency of molten chocolate. "The courier must've been in a real hurry to get out of here. He'd already unloaded it all before he rang the bell, and by the time I made it down the stairs, I think his truck was halfway to Florence."

"Delivery men can be like that sometimes, but it's okay. I

didn't mind." Valentina bit her lower lip until it stung, acutely aware of the space, not to mention the shipping box, between them. "Is that the only reason you needed me, to help get the boxes up the stairs?"

Andie leaned across the expanse of dull brown cardboard that separated them. "No. Getting you to help was just a bonus. What I needed was this."

Closing the last inches between them, Andie claimed Valentina's lips with her mouth, sending the world around her spinning from the scorching intensity of the kiss. It was better than she'd remembered, better even than the most perfect version that she'd played in her mind during the night as she'd tried to work up the nerve to let her fingers drift between her legs. She let herself fall into the kiss now, deeper and deeper, until her wobbly legs could no longer support her weight. With her body partially draped across the top of the box, she clung to Andie's shoulders for additional support.

"Yeah. I think I needed that, too," was as much as she could manage to say between short gasps of breath when they finally parted.

"We could take this someplace more comfortable," Andie suggested, nibbling at her earlobe in a way that threatened to banish the last shreds of rational thought, while her hands skimmed Valentina's waist, plucking at the edge of her waistband. "Your skin smells like cocoa. How about I strip you naked and see if you taste like it, too?"

Valentina let out a wanton moan, but through the cotton candy haze of her brain, she heard the church bells in the piazza chime and released her grasp on Andie's shoulder. This time the reaction had had nothing to do with bad memories of Sister Gloria, and everything to with the clock striking the half hour.

"I can't," she sighed as she transferred her weight back to her own two feet while straightening the shirt that had, either accidentally or with a little help, ridden most of the way up her torso. "I have to get back to work."

"What did you tell them when you left?"

"That you had a leaky faucet I needed to check. Not that I know all that much about faucets," Valentina said with a chuckle, "but it was the first thing that came to mind. I raced right over, without even frying up the bomboloni."

"You left the shop in the hands of two capable, grown women. Can't they do without you for another half hour? And what on earth is bomboloni?"

Valentina laughed. "It's a doughnut, filled with jelly or sometimes Nutella or Chantilly cream, and rolled in sugar. And yes, my mother and grandmother can manage it without me, but Chiara can't. It's a school day, and if I'm not there to see her out the door, she'll never forgive me."

"I suppose I can't argue with that." The shoulders that had been strong enough to support Valentina's body slumped under the weight of disappointment. "It might be easier to bear if you'd brought over a dozen of those bombo-thingies, though. They sound fantastic."

"Next time." Valentina brushed a finger across Andie's forehead, removing the smudge of ink that had gone as yet unnoticed. "Besides, even if I could stay today, I don't think a few extra minutes would satisfy me."

"Then stay as long as you'd like," Andie suggested, a hopeful twinkle lighting up her blue eyes. "Or, I could take you up on the challenge to see exactly how quickly you could be satisfied. It's not my usual style, but I think you might be surprised. I can be very efficient with the right incentives."

Blushing wildly, Valentina shook her head once more. "I have work to do, and so do you. I mean, look around this place." She gestured to the pile of boxes that littered the floor. "It'll take half the day just to unpack."

"Tonight, then?"

"Family dinner. There's no way I can slip away. And Tuesday and Wednesday I've promised to help Francesca set up the baby's room. Thursday, I have a late meeting with a supplier. This whole week is chaos, and every spare second has to be spent on making chocolate."

"Is it always like this?"

"Easter's only a few weeks away, and the spring festival's right after." Valentina rubbed the back of her neck as tension seeped deep into the muscles. "Our stock is low, and if I don't have at least two new flavors perfected by then, I doubt we'll sell enough to see us through until Christmas. I'd like to be able to see you, but—"

"No, you're right." Andie straightened up, clearly trying to put a brave face on the situation. "Obviously, I have a ton of work to do this week, too. I'm almost two weeks behind schedule, and I have yet to venture into one of the larger towns to find a proper grocery store. That alone could take a full day, especially since that silly micro-car has no trunk and I will have to strap the groceries one item at a time to the roof to get them home."

Valentina snickered at the image that conjured. "Sounds like you'll have your hands full. But on the bright side, those cooking classes are this Saturday, so we'll see each other then. The shop closes early on Saturdays, and I've set aside the whole afternoon just for you."

"And how about the night? Have you set that aside, too?" Andie waggled her eyebrows and Valentina giggled as butterflies tickled her belly.

"We'll see. My mother's taking Chiara to visit some cousins out of town. I just might be able to work something out, assuming Nonna behaves herself."

"From the little I've seen of her, that's a risky assumption. Tell you what, I've got some sleeping pills you can slip her. Kidding," Andie added quickly as Valentina's eyes doubled in size. "Okay, it's settled, then. We just have to make it through the week." Andie sighed heavily, echoing the sentiment of Valentina's heart.

"Not even that long. Just five days." Valentina gave Andie's lips a peck, fighting valiantly against the urge to throw caution to the wind once again.

"I could come by the shop for coffee in the mornings."

"And I wouldn't be able to concentrate the rest of the day for wanting to be with you."

"Well, when you put it that way, I'd better not."

"No, probably not. But I'll see you soon." She turned to go but stopped at the door when Andie called out.

"Hey, Val? What if that faucet starts leaking again. If I give you a call, will you come over to fix it?"

Valentina rolled her eyes. "You can call if you'd like, but I'm afraid the best I can do is walk you through fixing it from across the square."

When she'd made it partway down the stairs, Andie called out again. "Hey, Val? Just so I'm clear, walking me through it was code, right? That *was* phone sex you were suggesting?"

"Andie!" Valentina squealed, her entire body going up in flames as she scurried the rest of the way down to the first floor. Her reaction could mostly be chalked up to embarrassment, but she'd have been lying if she claimed that the proposition didn't hold a spark of appeal, too. In fact, as she made her way back to the shop, she could think of little else. It was shaping up to be the longest five days of her life.

ANDIE WAS STILL CHUCKLING over Valentina's response to her final joke as she searched the kitchen for a knife to crack the seals on the boxes. There was something so satisfying about teasing the buxom Italian woman, who had the capacity to be as feisty and fiery as any of her fellow countrywomen, and yet had trained herself so thoroughly over the years to keep herself in check. It wasn't fair. A woman like Valentina deserved to be herself without apology. Every time she got her reserve to crack, even a little, Andie counted it as a victory. Given a few hours alone in the bedroom on Saturday night, Andie had every intention of breaking her shell wide open so that Valentina would never want to hide inside it again. With any luck, it would be accompanied by Valentina shouting out a long string of very dirty sounding Italian words.

With that happy thought, she began to unpack, and was still at it a few hours later when her phone rang. The number displayed on the caller ID had a New York City area code, but it was unfamiliar to Andie and dampened her mood. Remembering the scandal that had sent her into exile, she answered with a cautious hello.

"Andie Bartlett? This is Jessica Balderelli."

Andie's mouth dropped open as she recognized the caller's voice, the same one that had announced her win and changed her life scarcely a year before. "Jessica? I, uh. I wasn't expecting..."

"No, I'm sure you weren't. After all, no matter what anyone's saying, it's not like you and I have ever really spoken before."

"No, we haven't. What can I do for you, Miss Balderelli?" Andie inquired, remembering her manners.

"You might as well stick with Jessica, all things considered. The fact is, I felt I needed to apologize."

"No, there's no need," Andie hastened to assure her. "This is Duncan King's doing, not yours."

Jessica let out a humorless laugh that indicated she was in agreement. "Well, not apologize, exactly. But it is because of me that you're in a bad position. It's unconscionable that the network is even considering cutting your show."

Andie's blood ran cold, an icy lump settling in her stomach. She'd believed Tracy when she said her show was in the clear, but she saw now that it had been foolishly optimistic of her not to question it. It's not that she thought it was a lie, but as her assistant, Tracy had a vested interest in keeping her calm and focused on her work. On the other hand, if the no-nonsense judge said there was a chance that her career was in danger, Andie would be crazy not to heed the warning. "Please tell me, what do I need to do?"

"Look, nothing's decided, and as repulsive as I find it, I'm urging the network execs to give Duncan what he wants to make this all go away."

"And what is that?"

"He wants what you have. The show, the book deal, the star treatment."

"And the network doesn't need both of us. Which means I'm out."

"Not necessarily. It's just one option of many that they've floated, and I don't think it's ultimately the way they want to go. But this whole thing has shown me a different side of Sizzle and left a bad taste in my mouth. Between you and me, I'm thinking of branching out."

"You mean leaving Sizzle?" Andie burned at the injustice of it. Duncan was the one in the wrong, stirring up trouble with his outrageous lies, and now Jessica, and she, were the ones who would pay for it. "But that isn't fair! You helped build that network!"

"Well, fair or not, it may be for the best. There's a new opportunity that's come up with another network, one where I feel more comfortable with the management style. Let's just say it could turn out to be a real step up, for both of us."

"Both of us?" Andie frowned. "I don't understand."

"It's not a sure thing, but if I get the offer I expect, I'll be in a position to recruit some new talent, and I intend to start with you. I really do believe in your abilities, Andie. That's why I voted for you in the final round. That, and nothing else. And it's why I'm calling now, to give you a chance to prepare."

"And, what exactly," Andie paused to swallow, her throat suddenly dry and scratchy, "am I preparing for?"

"A new show, done your own way, and a book deal, too. We'll have to win over the investors, but after that you'd have complete control and no bowing and scraping to corporate sponsors, or out of touch network executives. No more fear of Duncan or anyone like him. But the only catch is, the concept has to be something really new, a totally fresh approach to a show, which means you can't just do the same routine you've been following up until now. You need to show me more than the Quick and Easy Queen."

"But, at Sizzle, they said that was my brand."

"Well, I'm not suggesting you abandon it completely. You just need to change it up and make it exciting. Give it heart. Sizzle likes to play it safe. Hell, why do you think they're trying to drive people like us out?"

Andie wasn't sure what Jessica meant by people like us. Women? Lesbians? People who didn't play it safe? It didn't matter. She was too flummoxed by the rest of what Jessica had proposed to bother clarifying. "I mean, it sounds like an exciting opportunity, but I'm not sure…"

"No need to answer now. Just tell me you're willing to give it some thought."

Andie squeezed her eyes shut. "Okay, I'll give it some thought."

After the call ended, Andie surveyed the boxes that surrounded her, their disarray reflecting her internal state. She'd thought the hardest task ahead of her was to focus on her work enough to make it through the next five days without seeing Valentina. But a single phone call had shifted her expectations and increased the difficulty of her task exponentially. Her stomach clenched as she realized that her career was in limbo, her entire future at stake, and she was clueless how to proceed.

Andie moved into the living room, leaning against the drapery as she peered out onto the piazza below, past the bubbling fountain in the center, until her eyes came to rest on the intricate lettering of the chocolate shop's sign. In this moment of upheaval, she wanted more than anything to call Valentina immediately. She couldn't remember the last time she'd felt such a connection to someone so quickly. She longed to see her race across the square, and to take comfort in her kisses until she'd sorted out what to do. But she knew it would be a mistake.

Though the rush of emotions she felt each time Valentina was near bore every resemblance to falling in love, the truth was that they'd only just met. Valentina wasn't looking for an emotional commitment, and Andie was just passing through. It was best to keep things light between them. Andie sighed. She was on her own until Saturday, and she'd just have to make it on her own. For the first time since arriving in Montamore, she felt truly alone.

FOURTEEN

"ARE WE CLOSE?" Andie asked, easing her foot off the gas as she swiveled her head to search one side of the tree-lined country lane and then the other.

Close? Valentina swallowed. Very close. A ribbon of heat ran down her left side where Andie's body pressed against hers. She wasn't intentionally trying to be arousing—the rental car's front seat was simply too small for two passengers to sit without touching—and yet every bump or swerve that threw them together threatened to set Valentina off like a spring wound too tight. To be fair, it wasn't just their close proximity in the car that had her this way. It had been everything—every thought, or glimpse, or memory that she'd had, every waking hour, and even in her sleep—ever since the night they'd first kissed.

They had hours to go until they'd be alone, a whole cooking class to get through, and yet, as sweat dampened Valentina's palms, she knew it was becoming increasingly impossible for her to keep herself in check. As if to illustrate the point, Andie flexed her fingers along the steering wheel, innocently adjusting her grip, and Valentina was swamped with longing. A pang of envy shot through her, directed at, of all things, the leather cover on the steering wheel. It was crazy, and yet she truly was jealous of an inanimate object because Andie's hands were on it right now instead of on her.

It had been five days since their brief encounter in Andie's apartment after moving the shipping boxes. She and Andie had both been working round the clock, and between Chiara, and Mama, and *Nonna*, there was always someone around. Privacy in a place like Montamore was hard to come by. When the entire village was on a first-name basis, no matter where you went, there was always someone you knew, and gossip could spread like wildfire. Even so, every minute they spent apart felt like a minute wasted. It was a conundrum, and one that, if not resolved soon, would definitely lead to clouded judgement and risky behavior. And that could get dangerous if her goal was keeping whatever this relationship was that she had with Andie to herself.

The loud clearing of a throat brought her back from the brink of frustration. "Valentina, the turn?"

A bump on the road nudged Valentina's arm deep into Andie's side, the suppleness of her breast so distracting that, had she been the one driving, she would have struggled to keep her focus on the road. As it was, she was having a hard enough time providing directions to the cooking school where they were headed, and she'd lived here her whole life. An unpaved road just ahead offered Valentina a brilliant solution.

"Pull in right here."

Andie turned the wheel just in time, and the little car spun like a carnival ride until it was bouncing and jittering along a dirt path that led straight into a patch of woods. Andie lifted her foot off the gas and their pace slowed to a crawl as the roots and vegetation grew thicker beneath the tires. Andie turned to look at her with a puzzled frown. "Are you sure?"

"Stop here." As the engine cut out, its thrumming was replaced by the sound of Valentina's own racing pulse. The main road was still visible in the mirror, but only just. Anxiously, she bit her lip. They weren't completely hidden, but it would have to do.

"What's wrong Valentina? Are we lost?"

Instead of answering, Valentina turned as much as she could and immediately lunged, clumsy but effective, at Andie's lips, like a bird swooping in on its prey. It was an easy capture, the close confines of the car not allowing much space for escape, though judging by the eagerness with which Andie returned her kisses, escape was the last thing on her mind.

When they finally broke apart, Andie gave a breathy laugh. "That's the second time you've caught me by surprise like that."

Valentina lowered her lids, suddenly sheepish. "I'm sorry."

Andie kissed her again, long and slow this time with all the finesse that their frantic first attempt had lacked. "Don't be sorry. Kissing you is all I've been able to think about."

"Me, too," Valentina confessed. "That's why I had you pull over."

Andie squinted at the road and seemed to notice for the first time that it wasn't really a road at all. "This isn't the way to the cooking school, is it?"

"No, just the first place I saw with some privacy."

"I had no idea how difficult it would be to be alone with you. I wandered by the shop on Thursday. I know I promised I wouldn't but I was hoping to see you for a minute, and both your mother and grandmother were behind the counter. They were just *looking* at me."

Valentina frowned. "You don't think they suspect anything, do you?"

"No, but it freaked me out enough that I turned around and left without waiting for you, although not before buying one of those bombolinos."

"Bomboloni, you mean. Did you enjoy it?"

"My low-carb lifestyle has been ruined since meeting you. I'd be lying if I said that your chocolate-filled doughnut wasn't amazing, but it wasn't as amazing as this." Andie kissed her once more, and Valentina couldn't argue. No doughnut, no matter how good, would ever compare.

"And kissing is completely carb-free, so you can do it as much as you'd like."

"I'll admit, I'd hoped we'd get started on it as soon as I picked you up, but you were so distracted, you hardly said hello."

"My grandmother was watching us leave. The kitchen window that overlooks the alley is a prime location for a busybody."

"We're alone right now." As if suddenly aware of the possibilities, Andie moved to snake her arm around Valentina's shoulder, but drew back as her elbow slammed into the dashboard. "Ow!

Valentina shifted awkwardly to massage Andie's elbow, but with the way she was sandwiched, it was about as close as their contact was likely to get. "If only these seats reclined."

Andie eyed the patch of woods outside. "There's a spot over there that looks comfy, if only I'd tossed a blanket in the back seat. But, alas…"

"No blanket?"

"No back seat." Andie rolled her eyes. "One more reason I hate this car."

"Aw, it's a cute little thing," Valentina offered in the car's defense. "I might buy Chiara one like this when she's old enough."

"Great idea," Andie quipped. "It will all but ensure she graduates high school a virgin."

"Precisely," Valentina agreed with a laugh that turned into a wistful sigh. "Sadly, I think we're out of options, other than waiting for tonight when we get home."

Andie looked out the window again. "You're sure you don't want to give the woods a try?"

"I'm not sure which is worse, the possibility of getting interrupted by a wild boar, or being discovered naked in the woods by the hunting party that's chasing after it."

Andie shuddered. "You make a convincing argument for waiting." She turned the key in the ignition and the car began to make putt-putt noises like a ride at an amusement park. "Just one thing. Do you think the cooking class menu will have a lot of carbs?"

"Andie, this is hardly the time to get back on the diet wagon."

"You misunderstand. If I'm gonna make it all the way until tonight without losing my mind, I'm going to need a distraction, and I've always found stress-eating carbohydrates to be particularly useful in that department."

"We're in Italy. If there's one thing I can predict about

tonight's menu, it's that it will not be low-carb," Valentina assured her.

"Okay," Andie said, starting the car and shifting it into gear, "let the distractions begin."

AS THE CAR bumped along a narrow gravel drive that ended in a clearing overlooking the Montamore valley, Andie spied a sign welcoming them to the Cucina Mia cooking school. The stone farmhouse, nestled in a grove of olive trees that covered the surrounding hills, looked very much like thousands of other such structures that dotted the Tuscan landscape, but bore little resemblance to any school Andie had ever attended. She'd pictured a sterile, clinical setting, a boxy brick structure with stark white rooms and cold, stainless steel appliances. Much to her relief, the kitchen just beyond the main entrance was as warm and inviting as the exterior had been, a discovery that eased her usual schoolroom jitters.

Traditional painted tiles formed a backsplash behind the stove, and every inch of the creamy plaster walls—if not already occupied by wooden shelves that overflowed with spice jars—sported an impressive collection of copper cooking molds with the authentic, dulled patina that comes with age and use. The stove and ovens, which Andie noted with keen interest included a real wood-burning oven, lined one wall, while a generous soapstone sink and countertop ran along the other, the two joining to form an "L."

Three large tables filled the center of the space, two of them draped with brightly printed vinyl cloths, while the third had a bare butcher-block top. Pairs of work stations had been set up at all three tables. Two Japanese women—a mother and daughter, perhaps—occupied the wooden table, while a man and woman who had the lovey-dovey look of a young couple on their honeymoon, were stationed at one of the covered tables. The room was large enough to have accommodated half a dozen more spots, and Andie's heart sank at the reminder of the dwindling number of tourists to this charming region.

Neither set of fellow classmates paid Andie or Valentina any mind beyond a polite nod of the head as they passed. The final table was empty, with two black binders marking their spots. Each was topped with a neatly folded apron, which they promptly donned. Thanks to their detour into the woods, Andie and Valentina appeared to be the last to arrive, and no sooner had they gotten settled than the instructor entered the room.

"Hello, welcome!" Their teacher was a blonde woman at the late end of middle age. She wore a blue print housedress covered by an apron, and had the plump, rounded figure that was the hallmark of a very good cook. It was the same shape that Andie feared she soon would be sporting, now that her carb-lust had been let loose. The woman carried it off regally, but that didn't mean Andie felt any better about the prospect of sharing her fate.

Ignoring Andie for the time being, the instructor headed straight for Valentina and gave her a warm embrace. "Valentina! I haven't seen you in ages. I'm so glad my cousin convinced you to finally try one of my classes. How are your mother and grandmother?"

"Both well, thank you. Simonetta, I'd like you to meet a friend, Andie Bar—"

"Hi! Just call me Andie. Nice to meet you." She thrust

out her hand, purposely interrupting before Valentina could reveal her last name. Though none of the other students had appeared to recognize her, it was possible they'd make the connection to her TV show if they heard the name, and that was the last thing Andie wanted at that moment.

For one thing, she was enjoying the relative anonymity of her stay in Montamore. There'd been an initial buzz surrounding the arrival of a reality TV star, but after the first week of stares and whispers whenever she ventured out, her fellow residents had mostly gotten it out of their system and gone back to their regular lives. Her second, and larger, concern was that being tagged in photos on social media with a beautiful Italian woman by her side was a surefire way to start up the rumor mill back home. She already had a big enough tabloid scandal on her hands without dragging a juicy story of a secret girlfriend into the mix. Fortunately, the instructor simply welcomed her and shook her hand. Whether she knew about Andie's celebrity status or not, she didn't let on either way.

As Simonetta began her introduction to the class, Andie leafed through the binder. She quickly discovered, though, that while the instructions were in English due to the international appeal of the classes, the menu and recipe titles were not. It came as quite a surprise, therefore, when moments later what appeared to Andie's disgusted eyes to be at least a full bushel of tomatoes was plunked into the center of the table. Her face must have betrayed the depth of her dismay because immediately Valentina's eyes grew wide.

"Oh, no, Andie! The first recipe is bruschetta. Do you want to sit this one out?"

Taking in the overflowing abundance of her least favorite food, Andie almost laughed. Though she hadn't brought it up in conversation, this was pretty much par for the course this week. In the five days they'd been apart, nothing had gone according to plan. It had started with the disconcerting call from Jessica, and just gone downhill from there. She'd braved the drive to a neighboring town only to discover the grocery store didn't have half the items on her list. The substitutions she'd chosen had caused her nothing but trouble, and she had yet to have a single recipe turn out well enough to cross it off her list. She was so frustrated with cooking that if it hadn't been for the promise of spending time with Valentina, she would've canceled the class outright. But now that she was here, Andie was determined to turn her luck around.

She shook her head resolutely. "Absolutely not. I'm a professional. Just because I don't care for tomatoes doesn't mean I don't know what to do with them. In fact," she added with mischief in her tone, "I'll race you."

Valentina laughed, but couldn't hide her intrigue. "You mean, a race to see who can chop tomatoes the fastest?"

"Absolutely! I'm a born competitor, didn't you know that? Here we go. Six for you, and six for me." She divided them up between them and had to pause for a recount. Were there really only a dozen? It had looked like a million.

"Whoever finishes first, wins?"

"Well, now." Andie tilted her head, eyes toward the ceiling in her best interpretation of a pensive expression. "Personally, I've always figured as long as you both finish eventually, does it really matter who gets there first?" Andie winked, just to make her meaning clear.

"Andie! I was talking about the tomatoes!" She waved one of the bright red fruits wildly, and Andie snickered as she noted that Valentina's face had turned exactly the same shade as the object in her hand.

"Well, so was I, obviously. I have no idea what you thought I was talking about." Andie did her best to plaster a serious expression over her features as she arranged her tomatoes in a line across the cutting board, and then searched the array of tools on the table. "Now if you could just get your mind out of the gutter long enough to help me find a knife."

"Here." In what Andie could only assume was an attempt at revenge for her earlier sauciness, Valentina sent a curved, metal implement with a wooden knob on each end sliding across the table in lieu of the requested knife. It looked like the type of tool that was sometimes used to cut pizzas back in the States, only smaller. Andie wasn't sure what she was meant to do with it, but she also wasn't entirely convinced the offering was a joke. At moments like these, her lack of formal training necessitated a cautious approach so as not to betray her ignorance, just in case.

Andie picked up the unfamiliar item, turning it slowly in her hand. "So, here we have a…"

"It's a *mezzaluna*." Valentina blinked, everything about her expression signaling that it was no joke.

"Right, that was the word I was trying to recall," Andie bluffed.

"You've never used one before, have you?" Apparently, it had taken her precisely two seconds to see through Andie's ruse.

"Can't say as I've had the pleasure," Andie confessed. "I generally stick with a standard chef's knife. But I'm willing to give it a try. What do you do?"

"You take it like this." Valentina grasped one of the

wooden knobs and, with smooth, practiced motions, reduced one of the tomatoes to a neat pile of slices. "Then you just go like this." Now holding one knob in each hand, she made a series of rapid see-saw motions with the tool, producing a fine dice in the blink of an eye. "See? Easy."

"Yes, you did make it look that way." Andie fumbled with the mezzaluna. After a few false starts, and some giggling on Valentina's part that she was kind enough to muffle with the back of her hand, Andie's cutting board was covered with one of the saddest displays of a pulverized tomato she'd ever laid eyes on. "I think it's safe to say you'll win this contest."

"Don't give up so soon." This time, Valentina slid a five-inch chef's knife in her direction. "You use your preferred method and I'll use mine."

Andie grinned. "Fair enough. Ready?"

Valentina nodded. "Go!"

They tore through the pile of tomatoes, Andie with her knife and Valentina with her mezzaluna, in record time, until the final bits were diced and their tools placed to rest on the table at precisely the same time. Andie frowned. "I'm afraid it's a tie."

"Well, look at that," Valentina mused. "Both finishing at precisely the same time? That's the real holy grail, isn't it, or so I've heard." She looked across the table with what was likely meant to be no more than a teasing glance, but as their eyes locked, the smoldering intensity in their dark chocolate depths ignited a spark of desire so hot that Andie jumped to her feet and began searching for her jacket and keys. "What are you doing?" Valentina demanded, her words reduced to an embarrassed whisper.

"I mean, it's been a good lesson, but I think we should

be heading home, don't you? I have a sudden urge to go to bed."

"You're sleepy?"

"Not in the least."

"Sit down, Andie! We're still on the appetizers." Valentina gave a furtive glance around the kitchen and winced. "Oh, now see what you've done. The teacher's coming over to see what's going on. You're getting us in trouble."

Andie sat back down in a hurry, smoothing her apron and trying to keep her cool as the teacher approached. It was like being back in high school, and if she'd ever wondered what had possessed her to drop out, the pressure in her gut at this moment provided a timely reminder.

"Nicely done, ladies," Simonetta said with a smile. Then somewhat belatedly, Andie remembered that she was an adult who had paid good money for this class, and therefore was in little danger of the teacher calling her mother for flirting with a pretty girl instead of doing her work. "Did you have any questions?"

"Just one," Andie said, acting innocent. "Exactly how many more courses are we making tonight?"

"Six," Simonetta replied.

"Wow. That many." Andie blinked, and once Simonetta had moved on to the next group, she made a show of carefully folding up her jacket, which she'd held clutched in her hand, and setting the keys on top with an exaggerated pat. "There's really no chance of convincing you to duck out early?"

"I'm afraid not." Andie couldn't help but notice that Valentina was sucking in her cheeks to keep her laughter in check. "But we don't want to rush out before we get to dessert."

Andie shot her a dark look. "Getting to dessert was kind of what I had in mind with leaving early."

"Andie, it's barely four o'clock," Valentina pointed out, still smothering a smile. "If we go home now, we'll just have to spend the next three hours watching television with Nonna."

Andie grimaced. "Fine, when you put it that way, I guess we should stay and finish the class. But, I'll tell you right now, Simonetta's menu better deliver a total carb overload. I'm gonna need some professional-grade distraction now."

FIFTEEN

AS THEY MADE their way from the cozy kitchen of Cucina Mia, Valentina paused to look up at the full moon that shone like a bright silver coin in the sky. It was just past eight o'clock, and the grassy parking area outside was empty, the cool night air silent and still. They'd been the last students to arrive, and were now the last to leave, as well. Never having taken a class like this one before, Valentina hadn't been certain what to expect, but the experience of cooking and eating in the company of their fellow classmates had turned out to be a most pleasant one. Even so, after the intense socializing of the past several hours, Valentina found it rejuvenating simply to stand and soak in the peaceful quiet. Rejuvenation, however, quickly transformed to jitters as she recalled the not-quite-spoken but heavily implied promises of what the rest of the night had in store.

Stopping a step ahead of her, Andie reached back, her hand searching for Valentina's in the dark. After a quick glance to reassure herself that they couldn't be seen,

Valentina allowed Andie to take hold, the comforting touch of warm fingers soothing her nerves. It hadn't been a traditional date—the presence of five strangers had seen to that. But even though nothing more intimate than a smile had passed between them for the last several hours, this moment as they walked hand in hand to the car was already one of the most romantic experiences of Valentina's life. She knew nothing of romance, had never expected to experience it. It made her insides quiver in a way that she couldn't interpret. It left her wanting more and wanting to push it all away at the same time, and she wasn't sure how to proceed.

"So, are you glad we stayed for the whole class?" Valentina asked, infusing her tone with all the casual calm that she didn't feel inside as she sought to break the silence.

"You know, I really am. Joep and Famke were a real kick, don't you think?" Andie pronounced the Dutch names with an exaggerated accent that made Valentina giggle. "Can you believe they spoke Italian, Japanese, and English, all fluently?"

"Yes, and every one of them with a much better accent than whatever those names were supposed to be just now," Valentina ribbed. They'd reached the car and Andie let go of her hand so that she could pry the front of the vehicle open before climbing in.

"Sorry, I don't think they teach a lot of Dutch in Brooklyn public schools, not that I stuck around long enough to know for sure." Andie was quick as ever to point out her lack of formal education, and once again Valentina detected the hint of defensiveness that crept into her voice whenever the topic of school was broached. It was clearly a sore subject for Andie, though Valentina wasn't sure why it should be. After working beside her all night, it had been obvious that the woman was extremely accomplished, despite the lack of whatever letters or degrees some people might think a chef should possess. Andie was every bit as good as her formally trained counterparts, better perhaps, because she possessed a natural instinct that many of them did not and soaked up knowledge like a sponge. "Not to mention Kiko and Ayumi!" Andie added, pausing to arch one eyebrow. "There. Did I say their names more to your liking?"

"Yes, much better." Valentina made a scooting motion with her hands to encourage Andie to make a little more room for her. Not that she minded sitting close, but with hips like hers, there were physical limitations to consider. "What about Kiko and Ayumi?"

"Who knew two tiny women from Tokyo would love Italian food so much! I think they ate more than I did."

"I told you," Valentina replied, joining Andie on the seat with a wiggle of her bottom that made Andie suck in her breath in a way that suggested she'd very much enjoyed the experience, "everyone likes Italian food. You're the odd one out."

"Between that first dinner you cooked, and then tonight's meal, I may be willing to revise my opinion about your national cuisine."

"Even tomatoes?" Valentina reached upward and pulled the front of the car shut around them, closing them into their cozy cocoon.

"Perhaps." There being no distance between them in need of closing, Andie simply turned her head slightly to the right and planted a quick kiss on Valentina's waiting lips.

"You read my mind. I've been thinking about doing that all evening."

"Me, too. That, and other things." Andie turned the key and the engine hummed to life, though Valentina could've sworn the sound it made had actually come from her flip-flopping belly at the mere mention of 'other' things.

"Really?" Valentina's laughter came out as a bird-like twitter, and she once more defaulted to teasing to put herself at ease. "You've been so subtle about it, I don't think I noticed."

"Oh, I think you noticed." Andie traced a finger along Valentina's cheek, turning her insides to jelly. "I saw those looks you were giving me when you thought I wasn't watching."

"You mean the ones when I wanted to kill you for getting us in trouble with Simonetta?" Valentina demanded with fake indignation.

"I'll have you know, I was shocked tonight to find out how much of a teacher's pet you are. I've never met a grown woman so worried about getting into trouble in class. But no, those weren't the looks I meant. I was talking about the other looks."

"Oh." Valentina sucked in a breath that whistled through her teeth. "Those looks."

Without a mirror in the kitchen, she hadn't seen the expressions on her face the way Andie had, but it hardly mattered. She knew what she'd been thinking at numerous points throughout the evening, and obviously, so had Andie. Her muscles tensed as it occurred to her that perhaps she should worry that the others had caught on, but then she remembered that their fellow students were tourists. As for Simonetta, the woman had known her forever. If Valentina recalled correctly, she'd even been babysat by her a few times when she was a kid. Like everyone else in Montamore,

Simonetta knew Luca and Chiara. She was as unlikely to guess the real nature of Valentina's interest in Andie as the priest had been when he caught her looking at naked ladies in magazines. If they hadn't caught on by now, maybe they never would. As she became more convinced of this truth, her body relaxed.

As she'd been fretting, Andie's finger had come to rest at the bottom of Valentina's chin. Noticing it now, and emboldened by her newfound feeling of safety, Valentina dipped her head to brush her lips across the warm flesh of Andie's cupped palm.

"Valentina." Andie moved her hand, resting it on the idling car's gear shift. Even in the dim light it was clear that her expression, her whole demeanor, had grown serious. Valentina tensed again. "We've sort of skirted around the subject, and I'm sure it's obvious how I'm hoping the rest of this evening goes, but I need to say this now. There's no pressure. If you'd rather I just drop you off at your door and head home, that's okay. I'd understand."

In the silence that followed, Valentina's heartbeat raced in her ears. It was the point of no return. Her relationship with Andie was destined to be fleeting, but what they might do tonight had the power to change her forever. Was she ready for that? *There's only one way to find out.*

"I appreciate you saying that." Valentina's words were slow and deliberate as she struggled to quiet the snare drum in her chest. "But I had a few thoughts, too, on how the rest of the evening might go."

"Oh?" Though only one syllable, the hope it carried was vast and made Valentina smile.

"Yes. My thought is that when we get back to Montamore, you should park your car in the usual place."

"Ah." The hope dimmed considerably.

"To avoid getting the neighborhood gossips started," Valentina hastily assured her. "Your American paparazzi have nothing on the brigade of Italian grandmothers who keep watch over the streets of Montamore at night. There's no sense in calling their attention to an out-of-place vehicle, trust me. But after that, we'll walk back to my apartment."

Andie swallowed hard. "And then?"

"Well, then I thought you, me, and Nonna could play a few rousing rounds of *Tombola*." Valentina batted her eyelashes with mock-innocence. "Is that not what you had in mind?"

Andie snorted. "I'm not sure what *Tombola* is, but probably not."

"It's a fun game. But, good. It wasn't really what I had in mind, either."

"You still haven't told me what you do have in mind."

"It's…" Valentina's cheeks burned. "Well, you know, my English—"

"Oh, please. In two weeks, you haven't stumbled over a single word. I'm not buying that excuse."

"Fine," Valentina said with a harrumph. "How about this? We can either sit here and keep talking until Simonetta realizes we're still in her driveway and assumes we're having car trouble and comes out and insists we come inside for coffee, at which point we'll probably not make it home until it's much too late to do anything other than go to sleep, or—"

"Or?" It was clear that Andie was making a valiant effort to hold in her laughter.

"Or we can just go back to my place right now and you can find out for yourself what I have in mind."

"Right. Let's go."

With a muted chuckle, Andie shifted the car into gear and they were on their way. It was a short drive, and in no time at all the country lanes gave way to the crowded, narrow streets of the ancient village. They parked behind Andie's building and walked in the direction of the piazza by way of Francesca and Paolo's pizzeria. Out of habit, Valentina peered through the side window into the brightly lit shop, searching out her best friend's face amid the bustling late-night crowd. She'd just caught a glimpse of her and was about to wave when she recalled with a start who her companion was, and instead edged away from the window to walk in the shadows. Of all the people in Montamore who would think nothing of seeing Valentina out for a stroll with the American chef, Francesca was the one person who just might guess the truth.

She felt a twinge of guilt for hiding, but it passed quickly. After all, not having to tell anyone about the relationship was the primary condition of pursuing it. If there'd been any chance that Andie would stick around past the spring, and that one day everyone would have to know about them, well, she wouldn't be doing it at all.

The fountain in the center of the piazza was brightly lit as it usually was at night, the contrast between shadows and light made more pronounced by the exceptional brilliance of the moon. The two women walked side by side, keeping to the darker area at the perimeter of the square, closer to the businesses which, with the exception of the pizzeria, were mostly closed at this late hour. Though Valentina refrained from taking Andie's hand in such a public setting, she remained close enough that she could feel the warmth from her body as they walked. The prospect of being alone with

Andie again, free to touch her as she longed to do, spurred Valentina to quicken her pace, but instead of following, Andie slowed, her attention fixed on a group of young people who'd congregated in the middle of the square, on and near the fountain's lower rim.

"So, is that it?" Andie asked. "Are they doing the ritual, or whatever you want to call it?"

Valentina considered the group for a moment, then shrugged. "Could be."

"I'm still trying to understand how it works. The Cupid statue just sits there, waiting for someone to come along and ask for help with their love life, like they're sending an advice letter to 'Dear Abby' or something?"

"I know it sounds crazy," Valentina sighed. It sounded crazy to her, as well. And yet...

"You believe it." It wasn't really a question, and Valentina shrugged once more, as it was pointless to try to deny that yes, somewhere deep down, she did. "Can I ask you something, then?"

"I suppose so."

"Why invite me back to your place tonight? I mean, not that I'm complaining," Andie hastened to add. "But if there's even a small possibility that you could have divine intervention in finding your soulmate, why settle for anything else? Why not just march on over there and ask?"

"Because, I don't think such a person exists."

"You're sure of that?"

Valentina had rattled off her answer without hesitation, firm in her conviction, but now her eye was drawn to the huge, silvery moon. It looked even more like a coin than before, and seeing it above the fountain, she was reminded of the coin she'd tossed into the water the day of Andie's arrival. Was she really as certain as she claimed? "I'm at peace with being alone," she answered this time, aware that it wasn't quite the same thing. "I have to be realistic. I have a daughter to raise and a business to run, not to mention two aging women who rely on me. It doesn't leave a lot of time for romance."

"And yet, here we are." Andie gave Valentina's shoulder a playful nudge as they started walking again. "Strolling across a piazza on a moonlit night, ready to get up to all sorts of naughty things. I'm afraid, as far as romance goes, this might qualify."

"I suppose it does, but it's not something I can indulge in forever. And, anyway, what about you?" Valentina countered. "You have the same access to that fountain that I do. Aren't you the least bit tempted to write a letter of your own, instead of wasting your energy with me?"

"Well, considering the evening's agenda, I wouldn't call it a waste."

"Fine, not a waste. But you have a life to head back to soon, and unlike me, you'll have plenty of opportunities for finding love in the big city. Don't you have any interest in your destiny?"

Andie looked thoughtfully at the young people, who were laughing boisterously as one after another attempted to scale the slippery stones. "It's only recently that I've been in the position to give any thought to it at all. Before the contest, times were tough. I dated sometimes, even lived with a girlfriend once, although that was way more about paying the rent than finding a soulmate. New York's an expensive town, and unless you're a celebrity, most chefs don't make a lot of money."

"But that's all changed for you," Valentina pointed out. "Maybe now you'd like to know."

A shadow crossed Andie's face, but whether it was just a trick of the light or something else, she wasn't sure. Whatever it was, it disappeared quickly and Andie grinned. "I want to live every moment, and let the future come as a surprise."

"A surprise?" The concept itself came as a surprise to Valentina, and she laughed as she realized how different her perspective must be, growing up in Montamore, compared to the rest of the world. "It never occurred to me that was an option."

They'd reached the door to the chocolate shop. Valentina jiggled the doorknob but found it locked, an indication that her grandmother had headed to bed. She pulled out her key and unlocked it, stepping out of the way to allow Andie to enter first, then shutting it quickly behind her and locking it again. As they approached the stairs, a quick glance at the crack beneath the door to the first-floor apartment that her mother and grandmother shared, revealed no light. Another good sign. "I think we're in the clear. Shall we head up?"

SIXTEEN

VALENTINA CLASPED Andie's hand tightly in her own as they mounted the stairs. Her heart hammered against her ribcage, her breathing coming in short bursts at what awaited them at the top of the stairs. An empty apartment, and the whole night ahead of them. No more excuses, no more restraint. It wouldn't be her first time having sex, but it sure felt like it. Valentina's slick palms slid across the banister, defying her attempts to gain a firm grip. Would she have the courage to see this through?

By the third step, Andie's fingers dug into her hip, seeking a grip of their own. They inched higher, exploring the waistband of her jeans, brushing against the exposed skin along her back. Her stomach muscles clenched, her body trembling under the sudden onslaught of desire like nothing she'd ever experienced. Temporarily unable so much as to lift her foot from one step to another, Valentina paused. Andie caught up in an instant and they stood face-to-face. It was too dark for more than her outline to be visible, but Valentina didn't need to see Andie's expression to feel the desire that radiated from her.

The wall was rough against Valentina's back as Andie's mouth found hers, and the force of the kiss pressed her hard against the plastered surface. For a moment she lost all sense of place, aware only of the heat between their bodies and the relentless torture of Andie's hands trying to gain access beneath the fabric that still covered way too much of her body. Her top bunched and stretched and refused to cooperate. It was only when one of its buttons popped off, plinking as it rolled from step to step all the way down the stairs, that Valentina was reminded that they were only halfway to their destination. There was no longer a question of having courage to go through with this, but of having the presence of mind to make it all the way to the top landing.

Using every bit of willpower to pull away, Valentina made it to her front door. She grasped the doorknob, but it slid out of her damp palm without turning. She growled at the door. "I can't get it to open."

"Use the key."

Valentina dissolved into a giggling fit. Joining her on the landing, Andie regarded her with a furrowed brow. "What's so funny?"

"Use the key!" Valentina snort-cackled. "If you say that in Italian, it means to fuck."

Andie grinned. "Yeah? Okay, say it."

"No!"

"Come on. I want to know how to say it. Weren't you just telling me I should learn a foreign language?"

Valentina shook her head vehemently. "I can't. It's very crude. My mother hates that."

"Your mother isn't here, thank God. And, what, like the word 'fuck' isn't crude? You said that!"

"But that was in English. It doesn't count."

Andie reached for the doorknob, which turned easily in her hand. "Okay, if you really can't bring yourself to say the word, I'll settle for a demonstration."

They made it no more than two steps inside the apartment before the remaining buttons on Valentina's shirt were quickly dispensed of, the garment itself sliding down her arms to land, already forgotten, on the floor. Her bra, which she'd chosen after hours of deliberation, joined the shirt mere seconds later. As Andie cupped one exposed breast in each hand, Valentina ceased to care that the bra's design elements had been overlooked during its unceremonious removal.

"So, what's the word for breast in Italian?" Andie squeezed them gently, brushing her thumbs across Valentina's nipples.

Valentina arched her back as she leaned against the closed front door. "*Il seno,*" she replied, whistling the 's' as she sucked in air through her teeth.

"Il seno," Andie repeated. "You have the most glorious il senos I have ever seen."

Her pronunciation and usage were all wrong, and Valentina giggled despite herself.

"What? Did I not get it right?" A flicker of a frown creased the skin between Andie's eyebrows. Instantly, Valentina regretted her response.

"No," she assured her, placing a hand to either side of Andie's head and gazing into the deep blue pools of her eyes in the dim light. "You're getting everything just right." Valentina stroked Andie's cropped orange locks as she tilted her head down just enough to bury her face deep in the cleft between the two mounds. As Andie peppered kisses along her flesh, the wet heat of her mouth raised goosebumps on Valentina's breasts.

Only when Valentina was thoroughly breathless, chest heaving from the attention she'd shown them, did Andie raise her head from Valentina's bosom. Removing a hand from one breast, Andie slid it down the soft, bare flesh of Valentina's abdomen. Valentina felt a tug as the button of her jeans gave way, then heard the rattling of the metal zipper as it parted. She bit her lip to keep from crying out as Andie's hand brushed along the silky fabric of her underwear.

"And how about here?" Andie asked as her fingers pushed into the molten space between her legs, releasing the faintest scent of musk. "What do you call this?"

Even through the thin layer that separated them, the sudden pressure against Valentina's most sensitive place sent sparks flying. *"Vulva,"* she answered in a strangled hush.

Andie laughed. "Seriously?"

"What?" Valentina strained against Andie's hand, which had gone frustratingly still. Why had she stopped, and why was she laughing? After all, she'd offered the most proper and correct of the many words that had come to mind. "That's what it's called."

"Yeah, that's what it's called in English, too, if you're reading a high school health textbook. And I'm sure that word works just fine if you're at the doctor's office." Andie withdrew her hand from Valentina's jeans. Bringing her fingers to the top of her lip, Andie drew in a deep breath. "I was looking for the word to use when I tell you that I want to breathe you in deep and taste that part of you with my tongue."

Though Valentina opened her mouth to reply, not a single sound escaped. Andie's words had robbed her of the ability to process complete thoughts in any language. But before she could make another attempt, a sound like the death throes of a hibernating bear echoed from somewhere deep in the apartment. Valentina's jaw dropped. Andie's eyes doubled in size and the fingers that had rested so tantalizingly against her lips were now clamped tightly over her mouth in horror.

Eventually, cautiously, Andie loosened her hand enough to speak. "What the hell was that?"

Valentina's face crumpled, and she groaned. "Nonna."

"You *were* joking earlier about her joining us this evening, weren't you?"

"Of *course* I was!"

Andie's voice dropped to a hoarse whisper. "Then why is she here?"

Why, indeed. "It's hard to explain. You'll see." Valentina paused long enough to zip her jeans and shrug on her shirt, buttoning it as she headed down the hall. It was bad enough under the circumstances that her grandmother was in the apartment at all. The last thing she needed was to confront her half-naked.

When they reached the bedroom, moonlight streamed through open curtains. The silhouette of Valentina's slumbering grandmother greeted them from deep within the comfort of a large wing chair. Against her frail chest was the unmistakable outline of binoculars, which upon closer inspection could be seen hanging from a well-worn strap that circled the woman's neck. Valentina made a sound somewhere between a sigh and a groan. "She just can't resist keeping up with everything going on down there."

Andie tiptoed a few more inches into the room. "Are those binoculars?" she whispered.

Valentina nodded. "It's her favorite spot to people watch."

"But, she's in your bedroom!" Andie's words were infused with a level of shock and horror that was wholly appropriate under the circumstances.

"I know." Valentina's shoulders slumped. "I'm so sorry. I really was joking, but clearly she has even less of a sense of boundaries than I thought."

"There's always my place." After a moment, Valentina heard Andie's breath catch. "Wait…is that my apartment over there?" In the block of buildings just beyond the smiling Cupid fountain, many windows were already dark, but in one window on the second floor, a lamp had been left on its dimmest setting, illuminating the interior of an apartment that must have looked especially familiar to its occupant. "And is that my—" Despite the complete darkness of the room one window over, the outline of a headboard could just be made out through the sheers.

"I don't know about you," Valentina whispered with a shudder, "but if we went over there, even for a few hours, I'd never be able to get the image of my grandmother out of my head, sitting here with her binoculars. Watching."

"I may never sleep again," Andie agreed. "I wouldn't be surprised if those things had x-ray vision."

"Oh, God…" Valentina whimpered and Andie wrapped an arm around her. She let her head droop against Andie's chest. "This has really killed the mood, hasn't it?"

"It's okay." Andie lifted Valentina's head gently from her

chest. "But I think for now, it's better if I go. We'll talk tomorrow, though, and figure this out."

She cupped Valentina's face in her hands, her gaze filled with longing and regret. Valentina's body ached deep in her core. She ached in places she hadn't realized existed until they'd been awakened by Andie's touch, and now called out for the release they'd been denied. Chancing no more than the slightest peck of the lips, Andie departed for home. It was a disastrous end to an evening that had started with infinite promise, but as Andie had pointed out, under the circumstances there was nothing more they could do.

Back in her bedroom, Valentina grabbed a blanket from the foot of her bed. She hugged it close to her chest, her arms so empty that it hurt. With tears stinging her eyes, she unfolded the blanket and draped it over her grandmother, tucking it around her as she slept on, oblivious to the pain her antics had caused. Valentina's heart was heavy in her chest, but frustrated as she was, she wouldn't blame Nonna, or even herself.

No, she thought, resting her forehead against the cold window pane and crossing her arms in front of her as she stared down into the piazza. *I know whose fault this really is—stupid Cupid.* His cold stone eyes stared at her as they always did, his face frozen in mirth. "I don't know what you think you're up to now, but this was *not* funny," she muttered. "Not funny at all."

With a primal growl, she dragged a pillow and another blanket from her bed, then headed to the living room to pass the night on the couch. Under the circumstances, she knew she wouldn't get a wink of sleep.

THE TREK across the piazza was the longest, most grueling of Andie's life. Her feet scuffed along the uneven stones, slowing her pace with each step as if the ground were wet cement. The same group of young people from earlier in the evening continued to congregate at the base of Cupid's fountain, their bright and boisterous laughter now at odds with a mood that had darkened considerably in the intervening time since she'd passed them before. By the time she reached home, Andie wondered who had it worse, a condemned prisoner walking to the gallows, or herself, trudging home alone as she'd just been forced to do.

Get a hold of yourself, woman! Andie shook her head at her melodrama. It was one ruined date, not the end of the world. They'd been interrupted at the worst possible moment, it was true, but it wasn't insurmountable. Now, had Valentina's grandmother *not* been sound asleep and actually caught them together, *that* would have been a disaster. This was merely an inconvenience, one that could surely be overcome given that she was still in Montamore for several more weeks.

She snapped on the overhead light as she closed her front door, but it did little to dispel the chill of an empty apartment. Remembering the clear view of the room she'd had from across the way sent a creeping feeling down her spine, and so she shut the bright light off again, leaving only the dim illumination from the lamp that had been left on, then went to draw the heavy drapes closed over the sheers. A sense of claustrophobia overtook her, making her shiver and reminding her that the apartment was still much too cold. She stared blankly at the thermostat on the wall for a minute before turning away and fetching a sweatshirt from her room instead. It wasn't artificial heat that she wanted, but the scalding presence of Valentina's body next to hers, and all the pleasure that it promised.

Or chocolate.

Denied the anticipated night of passion with Valentina, Andie was craving chocolate like a fiend. The lack of a view out the curtained window was a cruel reminder that everything she wanted was just steps away on the far side of the piazza, and yet completely beyond her reach. It may as well have been on the other side of the world. She pressed a hand hard against her stomach, suppressing a pang that was more hollowness than hunger, though it was sometimes difficult for her to tell the difference between the two.

She would kill for chocolate, but she would settle for cake. Or bread. Crackers, even, or maybe some potato chips. Salty or sweet, she didn't much care, to be honest. Andie pulled open the pantry and rummaged through the contents, wondering what health-food-obsessed sadist had stocked her cupboard. It couldn't have been her. There were ingredients galore, but not a snack in sight. What had possessed her to be on her best behavior when she'd gone shopping? Had the possibility of a late night binge truly never crossed her mind? There wasn't a single indulgence that was ready to be consumed, just bags of flour and sugar and nuts. However, she noted with great relief, a large tin of cocoa powder. Now she was getting somewhere.

Brownies? Chocolate cake? There had to be something she could make. She had a few bananas that were turning brown, so maybe she could do something with those. Andie glanced at the clock. It was a little after ten, and the heaviness of her eyelids told her that she should probably give up and head to bed, but the onslaught of thoughts ricocheting in her brain made it a certainty that there was no chance of sleeping tonight. She might not be a pastry chef, but Andie figured if she couldn't whip up something simple and satisfying out of all the things she'd purchased, she hardly deserved to be called a chef at all.

Raiding the contents of the cupboards, Andie spread out the options across the countertop and set to work. Recipes of comfort foods she hadn't allowed herself to make in years came back to her in a flash, and soon she was spooning flour into the measuring cup in her hand, leveling it precisely with the edge of a butter knife to get exactly the right amount. Precision was not one of her natural strengths. When it came to cooking, Andie preferred the mad rush of creativity that came with tossing ingredients into a pan, adding a dash of this or a pinch of that as inspiration struck. Baking was science. Too prescribed, too exacting. But tonight, to her surprise, she found the process calming. Measuring, counting. Even the wavy lines she made as she raked the knife across the flour to ensure she used just the right amount proved as soothing to her nerves as tending a Zen garden might have been.

In her meditative state, her thoughts soon turned to Valentina, but instead of her earlier frustration, she experienced a surprising sense of calm. She wasn't a religious person, but she did believe that all things happen for a reason. Tonight was no exception, and she refused to believe the reason was that it wasn't meant to happen at all. Oh, no. That couldn't be it. The attraction she felt for Valentina was too strong to believe that, plus Valentina had waited so long. *But maybe that's it*, she thought as she stirred the batter for banana muffins, sprinkling in a handful of nuts and watching them swirl around the bowl. Maybe tonight there was something missing, something more that Valentina deserved. Ambience? Romance? Something. Given another chance, Andie knew she could do better. She would do better. Somehow, she could make it perfect.

It was some amount of time later, though with the curtains drawn she had no idea how much, that a knock on the door brought Andie fully back to consciousness. The kitchen counters were piled with baked goods that she could barely remember making. From the looks of it, she hadn't tasted a single bite. The knock sounded again, and Andie brushed her floury hands along her apron and headed to the door.

On the other side of the peephole, Valentina stood waiting, biting her lip. Sweat mixed with flour on Andie's palms, forming a pasty film that was left behind on the knob as she turned it. Valentina flashed a broad smile as soon as their eyes met and leaned in for a quick kiss, but suddenly stopped short and took a deep breath. Her eyes widened, the delicious aroma obviously having had enough time to travel from the kitchen to her nose. "What have you been doing?"

"Baking."

"All night?"

Andie's eyes squinted in thought as she stepped aside to let Valentina enter. "Exactly what time is it?"

"A little after six."

"In the morning?"

Valentina laughed. "Yeah, which you would probably know if it wasn't so dark in here. Why *is* it so dark?"

"You really have to ask?" Andie drew back the drapes, letting in the rays of early morning light. "For as long as I live, I will never be able to get the image of your grandmother and her binoculars out of my head." But Valentina didn't respond, and when she turned around, she saw that it was because the woman was too busy staring at the mountain of baked goods that had been piled on every surface of the kitchen.

"What's all this?" Valentina asked. "Are you thinking of opening a bakery of your own? I'm not sure Montamore's big enough to support two."

Andie's cheeks flushed as she took in exactly how much baking she'd done. "No, I just needed something sweet, and like you said, yours is the only place in town. Under the circumstances, I needed the world's largest distraction."

Valentina winced. "Andie, I'm so sorry about last night."

"It wasn't your fault."

"Maybe not, but still. Our evening was completely ruined" Valentina's plump lower lip stuck out in a pout, but then it transformed into a sly smile and her eyes twinkled. "Nonna's back in her own room now, though, and Mama and Chiara won't be home for a little bit. It's not a lot of time, *but...*" Valentina leaned in closer, and Andie caught a whiff of vanilla scent that she was certain hadn't been there before, and that made her mouth water. "But, maybe we could make up for last night?"

Andie swallowed hard to keep her fluttering insides under control. "You mean, right now?"

"Mm, hm." Valentina looked up at her from beneath lids that were heavy with desire.

Though the temptation was excruciating, she'd had a stroke of brilliance somewhere between frosting a batch of red velvet cupcakes and putting the chocolate chip oatmeal cookies on racks to cool. She'd figured out exactly how to create the perfection that had been lacking before. She smiled hopefully, her night of Zen baking having reminded her that sometimes the best things required precision and planning. "I think what we need is a little patience."

"Patience?" Valentina's brows knitted together in a way that informed Andie that she was less impressed by the suggestion than Andie had hoped she'd be. "Is this your way of saying you're not interested anymore?"

"Not at all! Just hear me out," Andie urged. "I just kept thinking after I got home last night that maybe a few stolen moments isn't good enough. I mean, this is your first time, maybe your only time, so this should be something special. Something you'll always remember." Andie frowned. It had sounded better in her head during her baking fugue. She cleared her throat, determined to see the idea through. "What we need is a weekend getaway."

Valentina's eyes widened. "A weekend? Impossible! There's less than a month until Easter. This is my busiest season."

"Val," Andie tilted her head and gave her a skeptical look. "I think I've gotten to know you well enough by now to know that you have an incredible work ethic. I have no doubt you'll be more than ready for Easter, even if you take a day off."

She sank her teeth into her lip so deeply that Andie feared it would bleed. "But the spring festival is right around the corner, and I'm still behind schedule for that, and Monday is baking day…"

"Baking day?" Andie looked at the countertops overflowing with baked goods and let out a laugh. "I've got you covered!" Valentina let out a nervous chuckle, but didn't look convinced, and so Andie added, "Seriously, Val. Why not use some of this? It's not like I'm planning to eat any of it. I'm not even sure why I made it."

"Well, I..."

"Most everything stays fresh for several days. There's plenty here that you could package up to sell tomorrow, at least to fill in the gaps. If you didn't have to spend all day baking, couldn't you get caught up on the chocolate? Then we could go to Florence next Saturday after the shop closes."

"Florence? I..." The softening of Valentina's resolve was almost visible. "I love Florence."

"So let's start boxing this up so you can fill your shelves."

"Andie, it's a nice gesture and it would give me a head start, but," her shoulders slumped, "I still couldn't get away as soon as this weekend. I have Chiara to think of, remember?"

"How soon, then?"

"Well, let's see." Deep in thought, Valentina's lips twitched into a tentative smile. "The shop closes the Friday before Easter, and doesn't open again until Tuesday. Chiara's with Luca this year, and Mama and Nonna keep talking about wanting to go to Rome. I'm sure I could encourage them to do it. Yes, that could work." Valentina's smile grew wider. "I think I could get away for Easter weekend, assuming I keep to my schedule rigorously."

Easter? Andie was torn between wanting to laugh and cry. Easter weekend was still almost a month away. When she'd said they needed to have a little patience, that wasn't exactly the amount of patience she'd had in mind.

There's still time to say I was joking. The bedroom is only steps away.

But deep down, Andie knew it wouldn't be right. Valentina was the one who had already waited a lifetime to fulfill her desires. Didn't she deserve something more than a fumbling encounter with one eye on the clock? Andie squared her shoulders, accepting the challenge. She had the next few weeks to plan the perfect romantic weekend getaway, and she was determined to make it an experience Valentina would never forget.

SEVENTEEN

"I SEE what you mean about this table." Perching herself on the edge of the rustic farmhouse table, Valentina reclined languidly onto one elbow, twisting her hip until it was displayed in what she hoped was its most appealing angle. Andie's head was down as she pored over her recipe notebook at the kitchen counter, and so Valentina took the opportunity to adjust the neckline of her shirt to affect what she hoped was a casual 'just happened to fall off my shoulder' look. "It has so much potential."

Andie looked up and uttered a choking noise. "Are you trying to kill me? We're only three days in. You can't possibly expect me to last until Easter if you keep that up."

"You're the one who came up with the idea," Valentina reminded her with a giggle. "I'm not the one who insisted on waiting."

"Val, please sit up." Andie's voice had a strangled, pleading quality to it. "And could you start wearing jeans from now on? I can see entirely too much of your legs in that skirt." Andie bent her head lower over her notebook clearly resolute in her determination not to look.

Valentina teased the hem a few inches higher and Andie let out a tortured groan. "Okay, okay." With a sigh, Valentina sat upright and smoothed out her skirt. When Andie whimpered, she crossed her ankles contritely. "I'm sorry."

"No, it isn't that." Andie straightened up and tilted her head from side to side, stretching her neck. "It's these recipes. I don't know what I'm doing wrong, but I can't seem to make them work."

"You're following them exactly?" Realizing what she'd said, Valentina frowned and quickly waved her hands as if to erase the question. "Of course you are. You're a professional. You don't need me to tell you how to do your work."

"Actually, I haven't followed the recipes exactly. That's part of the problem. Some of the ingredients I needed weren't in the stores, so I had to make substitutions, but they're not quite right."

Valentina's face brightened. "I remember in school, we had a lecture on this. There are differences between the food you can get in different countries. Things are processed differently, or there's more fat in the butter in one country than in another, or how big the eggs are. There's a whole section about it in my old class notes. Do you want me to go get them?"

"You kept your old school notebooks?" Andie laughed. "No, of course you did. Why should that surprise me? That seems like exactly the type of thing you would do."

"What's that supposed to mean?" Valentina frowned but Andie responded with a laugh.

"Nothing, except you're a much better student than I ever was."

Despite the reassurance, Valentina continued to pout. "So do you want them, or do you just want to continue teasing me?"

"Can't I do both? You look so cute when you pout. It makes your lips so—"

"Kissable?" Valentina felt a thrill as Andie's cheeks colored. What a rush to know she had the power to throw such a self-possessed woman so instantly off balance.

"Val…"

"Okay, I'll stop." The truth was, Valentina had started to warm up to the idea of their secret weekend getaway, and as much as she enjoyed having a little fun at Andie's expense, she didn't want to ruin things by pushing her too far. "So, did you want the notes?"

Andie nodded gratefully. "Yes, please. I think we could both use the distraction of looking at some nice, dull notes."

Valentina scooted out of the apartment and across the square, slipping through the shop and up the stairs as quickly as she could to avoid the questioning gaze of her mother and grandmother. There were a stack of old binders on a shelf in the kitchen, and unable to remember exactly which one contained the needed information, she grabbed them all and hurried back across to Andie's apartment.

"Here you go." Valentina set the bundle down on Andie's counter with a loud plunk. "It's all in there somewhere."

Andie flipped through the pages of the top book, her nose wrinkling. "They're in Italian."

"Of course they're in Italian, Andie." Valentina rolled her

eyes as she reached for the book. "You're in Italy, remember?"

"As if I could forget," Andie said with a snort.

Valentina regarded her quizzically. "Why are you here, anyway? I mean, not that I'm complaining that you are, but it's obviously not your first choice, and it doesn't make a lot of sense for your bosses to send you here if you can't even get the ingredients you need to do your work."

Andie hesitated for a moment, then sighed. "The truth is, there was sort of a scandal back at the network, and I'm doing my best to ride it out." As she explained the details of Duncan King's allegations regarding her and Jessica Balderelli, Valentina listened with growing agitation.

"That's so awful! And that poor judge, being outed so publicly like that." Her stomach churned just to think of it. If everyone in Montamore found out about her and Andie, Valentina was certain she would drop dead on the spot. "How completely humiliating."

Perhaps sensing the direction her thoughts had taken, Andie cleared her throat. "Maybe you'd better get back to the shop before the matriarchs start to wonder where you've gone."

"I probably should, but before I forget, I did have a legitimate reason for coming over here."

"You mean something other than trying to seduce me away from my work?"

"Seduce you?" Valentina spluttered in mock outrage, then shrugged. "Okay, I guess I was trying to do that, a little bit. But believe it or not, I actually came over here to tell you that those baked goods of yours were a real hit."

Andie beamed. "They were?"

"They were, which had me thinking…"

Andie's smile dimmed slightly as her eyes darted furtively across the piles of recipe notes and ingredients on the counter. "You want me to make more?"

"No, of course not! I know you don't have the time." Valentina bit her lip, afraid what she was about to ask was crossing a line. "It's just that I was wondering if maybe you'd be willing to share a few of the recipes?"

"Is that all?" Andie let out a breath. "Of course!"

Valentina's grinned. "Are you sure? I don't want to steal your recipes."

But Andie waved away her concern. "They're nothing special. In fact, most of them I probably got off of packages when I was a kid."

"Really?" Valentina paused, and idea starting to come together in her head. "You don't suppose I could teach Chiara to make them, do you? I mean, once I get them figured out myself."

"I don't see why not. In fact, why don't I swing by on your next baking day and give you both a quick lesson?"

"Oh, no. I'm sure you're too busy for that."

"Are you kidding? Like I'm not looking for every excuse I can find to spend time with you."

Valentina's stomach fluttered. "Really?"

"Yeah, preferably somewhere brightly lit and with other people around so we don't get too many ideas between now and Florence."

"So I shouldn't mention how easy it would be for us to slip into the supply closet under the stairs back at the shop?" Valentina laughed as Andie groaned.

"You definitely should *not*."

"Okay, I won't mention it." Valentina sucked in her cheeks to stop herself from laughing again. "Friday's our regular baking day, but maybe Saturday would be better, so Chiara can be there too."

Andie nodded. "Saturday it is."

"See you then." Valentina responded with a quick peck on the lips, but didn't allow herself to linger. Despite the brevity of the kiss, her lips tingled for the entire walk home as she counted the minutes until the weekend.

"YOU'RE REALLY sure you don't mind teaching Chiara today?" Valentina wore a tentative expression as she held out the foaming mug of cappuccino.

"No, not at all." Andie's fingertips brushed against Valentina's as she took the mug. She shot a furtive glance to the other side of the counter, where Valentina's grandmother was chatting with one of the regular morning customers. As the old woman was paying them no attention, she allowed her hand to linger against Valentina's a moment longer before pulling away. "I'm just surprised banana nut muffins and brownies were so popular, considering the amazing baked goods you and your mother make."

"I think people liked having something different for a change, and those are so exotic, don't you think?"

"They're American."

"Exactly! And if they're really as easy as you claim, maybe Chiara could learn to make a few of the recipes by herself. It would really take the pressure off me in keeping to my schedule. Speaking of schedules, we'd better head to the kitchen and get ready."

As soon as they'd passed through to the kitchen, out of view of the door, Valentina's hand came to rest on Andie's waist. "Alone, with the whole kitchen to ourselves. What should we do?"

Even that lightest of touches sent shivers through Andie's body, but she threaded her fingers through Valentina's and gently but resolutely moved the hand a safe distance away. "I think we'd better work, or that trip to Florence will be nothing but a daydream."

"Fine." Valentina pouted playfully. "You can watch me make the buttercream chocolates if you'd like, until my sleepyhead daughter makes it downstairs."

Carrying a long pallet filled with white powder, Valentina went to what appeared to be a sink, but which Andie noticed was actually a basin without a faucet. Inside was a fine mesh strainer. Donning gloves, Valentina plunged her hands into the powder and came out with dozens of little lumps, like tiny potatoes, which she gently tossed into the strainer.

"I made these last night," Valentina explained as she dumped the last handfuls in, then gave the strainer a shake. "This is a starch mold to make the creamy centers."

Andie nodded with interest, as fascinated as always with the unfamiliar processes of which Valentina was a master. "I had no idea that's how they're made."

"Well, mostly they're made in factories now, which is different. In fact, we may be one of the last to do it this way. It's a little old-fashioned, but effective. The metal presses that create the molds and the pallets for the starch were some of the shop's original equipment. They're from back in the early nineteen-hundreds, and they'll probably last another hundred years."

"So, how does it work?"

"You just press the metal mold into a pallet of corn starch and it makes rows of indentations in just the right size. Then you pour in the buttercream filling right from the stove and let them cool. Now that this batch had set overnight, all I have to do is brush away the powder with a special, soft brush and then I can cover them in chocolate and sprinkles, and they'll harden right up."

Valentina brought the batch of buttercream centers to a work table, then lifted the lid off a vat of deep, dark chocolate. The luscious smell of cocoa wafted up on a cloud of steam, making Andie's mouth water. Her reaction only intensified when Valentina leaned over to ladle out the melted chocolate into a smaller container, offering up a view of her perfectly rounded bottom that appeared every bit as delicious as a buttercream. Once again, Andie wondered how it was possible to work around so much temptation day in and day out without going mad. Whether Valentina or the candy would do her in first, she wasn't really certain, but if she stuck around long enough, it was a sure bet that one of them would.

"Have you ever done enrobing?" Valentina straightened up and turned to face the work table.

Andie, who was already struggling to pretend that she hadn't been openly ogling Valentina's ass, mistook what had been said and heard it as disrobing instead, which immediately conjured up a mental picture of a very naked Valentina. A strangled cough was all she could manage in reply.

"I'll show you," Valentina said, and only the twinkle in her midnight eyes hinted that she had guessed the nature of Andie's thoughts.

Swirling one gloved hand into the chocolatey pool, she used the other hand to toss herself a rapid succession of buttercream lumps, which she covered and transferred to a drying tray in a single motion that left a perfect swirl on the top in a blink of an eye. It was like magic, right down to the nearly invisible flick of her fingers that deposited the sprinkles on top.

"Huh." Even after a dozen times of watching, Andie still couldn't make out exactly how she was doing it. "It's almost like you've done this before."

"More times than you can count." Valentina wrinkled her nose as she looked at the remaining pile. "And sometimes, it gets tedious. I'm all for the old ways when they're superior, but there are enrobing machines that can do exactly the same thing in a fraction of the time. However..." She shrugged, clearly resigned to the antiquated methods she had at her disposal, but this time Andie was reluctant to let the matter go.

"Is there really no way you could modernize a little, maybe buy a few machines and expand your distribution?"

But Valentina's expression remained doubtful. "We could sure use the money from extra sales. And even putting the financial benefits aside, expanding the business was something my father was working on when he died, so I'd love to do it. I know it would have made him so happy to see that dream come true. But I've never had the head for making deals like he did, and he's been gone so long at this point that I'm sure none of his old leads would be worth anything. It's fairly hopeless. Besides, you need money before you can spend money, and we barely get by right now."

Unwilling to be deterred, Andie's brain continued to spin. "What about e-commerce? That doesn't require anything but an order form on your website and a little bit of time spent figuring out the fulfillment logistics."

"We'd need an actual website first, plus learning what a phrase like fulfillment logistics even *means* could take me years." Despite Valentina's objections, Andie detected interest, but weariness too, as if the thought of doing what needed to be done overwhelmed her. "I don't know. It's not a bad idea. In fact, my father probably would have jumped in headfirst, knowing him. I'm just not sure I'd know where to begin."

Andie brushed her fingers through Valentina's hair, as much to soothe her worry as to smooth the tangles. Valentina leaned her body closer, as if the even the most casual of touches had sparked a magnetic force between them. After a furtive glance around the kitchen, Valentina gave Andie a quick kiss. It was little more than a brush of their lips, yet even that small bit of contact was enough to send Andie's heartbeat skyrocketing.

"Val," she warned, but was incapable of pulling away.

Valentina trailed her index finger along the length of Andie's arm. Her touch, as light as a hummingbird's wing, sent shivers down Andie's spine. She moved closer, touching her hand to Valentina's elbow in a gentle caress, and was rewarded with an arm encircling her waist. But the creaking of the stairs soon broke the intimacy of the moment, and Valentina quickly pulled away, leaving a wreath of fading warmth around Andie's waist where her arm had been. A moment later, Chiara appeared in the doorway.

"*Buon giorno cara.*" Valentina's sing-song greeting was

overly bright as she met Chiara near the door and ruffled the girl's hair, giving her shoulders a loving squeeze, but her efforts elicited little more than a glower in response. "Chiara, Andie's come over to show you how to make those recipes I told you about."

Chiara spoke rapidly in Italian through clenched teeth, and the look on the child's face froze Andie's insides. *How long had she been standing in the doorway before the floorboard had given her presence away?* Andie wondered. *Had she seen them kissing, and if so, was that the source of her anger now?* Andie's stomach churned.

Her diatribe now at an end, Chiara stamped her foot and stormed out of the kitchen, leaving Valentina wide-eyed and trembling. Andie was too stunned to speak. Composing herself as best as she could, Valentina turned to face Andie. "I'm so sorry. There's no excuse for her behavior." It was clear she was still shaken, though she didn't elaborate on the details of what her daughter had said to her.

"It's fine," Andie reassured her, but the wobbliness of her words revealed how much the child's outburst had rattled her.

Valentina shook her head. "It's not fine. I'll have a talk with her later, but I think the lesson may need to wait until another day. If you're still willing, that is."

"Sure. Of course," Andie assured her with much more confidence than she felt. "Do you want me to stay?" She was almost relieved when Valentina declined. She knew nothing about raising kids, so she wasn't certain what comfort or wisdom she'd planned to offer.

A group of young people had gathered outside by the fountain as Andie made her way back home. As their laughter rang out across the piazza, she felt her stomach tighten as if deep down she was afraid they were laughing at her. It was a ridiculous fear, and yet she couldn't shake it. How foolishly optimistic she'd been in her belief that she could win Chiara over before the end of her time in Montamore. It was clear that Valentina's daughter wanted nothing to do with her, and she had no idea what to do about it.

EIGHTEEN

ANDIE PAUSED, her hand resting against the metal strip on the pizzeria's glass door. A calzone was the last thing she needed. Her hand slipped automatically to her hip, but she was surprised when her fingers were not met with the doughy lumps of extra flesh she'd expected. Somehow, despite repeatedly indulging in chocolate, doughnuts, and pizza since the day of her arrival, she'd managed to stay in relatively good shape. Perhaps it was all the walking and cycling she'd been doing. Either that, or Montamore was truly a magical town after all. Buoyed by this thought, she pushed the door open and followed the scent of baking crust until she reached the counter.

"Ah, Andie Bartlett!" Paolo greeted her with a broad smile. "The usual?"

Andie fought back the urge to insist that she had no idea what he was talking about, that she hadn't come into the shop nearly often enough throughout the course of her stay to have established a *usual* order. Instead she nodded silently, then handed over what she already knew was exact change for the order, conceding to herself as she did so that perhaps she'd become a more regular patron than she cared to admit. With nothing else to occupy her time while she waited, she found a seat at a nearby table and buried her face in her phone, trying to look busy.

"Well, hello, Andie!" Andie looked up to see Francesca standing opposite her. The woman rubbed a hand across her round belly. "Do you mind if I sit down for a minute?"

"By all means, please," Andie assured her, pushing the empty chair out from the table with her foot. To Andie's untrained eye it seemed that Francesca might pop at any minute, and she couldn't begin to imagine how uncomfortable it must be simply to exist in that advanced stage of pregnancy.

"Back for another calzone?" Francesca asked it pleasantly enough that Andie only bristled slightly at the word *another*. Was there anyone who hadn't noticed her recent bad habits?

"They're pretty spectacular," she conceded. Her low carb diet was little more than a distant memory.

Francesca beamed. "A five-star review from the famous Andie Bartlett!"

Andie laughed. "Feel free to use it in your marketing material."

"Funny you should say that." Francesca's expression shifted as if she'd just discovered a door that had been left open for her. "As it happens, I'm one of the organizers of the spring festival this year, and there's something I've been hoping to talk with you about."

Andie frowned, not entirely sure where this was going, but nodded for her to continue.

"You see, the festival is one of the biggest days of the year for businesses in Montamore. Some shops bring in half their money for the year in just a day because of all the tourists who come to town." Francesca picked up a brown paper tube of sugar from the table and began to fiddle with it as she spoke, twisting its ends. "But over the last few years, less and less tourists come."

"That sounds like a serious issue."

"It is," Francesca agreed. "I'm sure you've noticed that Montamore isn't a really happening place. We don't have any major industries. Without money coming in from the outside, this town will die."

"Please," Andie said, recalling the chocolate shop's complete lack of online presence, "tell me your festival has a web page, at least."

The look on Francesca's face made it obvious the answer was no. "We have a mailing list, though. And we print up posters and put them in some of the neighboring towns. Which is where I thought you might help."

"You want me to help hang posters?"

Francesca laughed. "No, of course not! I was hoping maybe we could put your name on the list of events. You wouldn't need to have a booth or do any cooking if you didn't want, but perhaps you could sign autographs."

She looked so hopeful that Andie's heart sank as she prepared to let her down gently. "I wish that I could, really I do. But the truth is, me being here is a little bit of a secret."

"Oh." Francesca's shoulders sagged as if someone had just let all the air out of her, and Andie knew she needed to do something.

"That doesn't mean I can't help in some other way. Let me start by making a few calls to some web designers I know, okay?" She'd wanted to do it for Valentina's shop, anyway, and this gave her a great reason to get started. "The least we can do is get a simple page up for the festival. And I may not be able to have a booth, but maybe I know someone who could. Before I came here, I spent a few weeks touring the restaurant scene in Florence. I could reach out to a few of the chefs I met there and see if anyone has any interest in setting up booths at the festival. You never know."

Francesca's demeanor perked up considerably. "That could really help."

"I can't promise anything," Andie cautioned, "but at the very least, they might put up a poster for you, or include the festival in a newsletter."

"Thank you so much, Andie. That would be—" Francesca stopped mid-sentence and let out a rapid stream of Italian, directed squarely at two of her children, who had burst into the pizzeria mid-squabble like a couple of unruly puppies. The children froze instantly, their expressions contrite.

"That's amazing."

Francesca tilted her head in obvious confusion. "What is?"

"The way you got them to listen like that."

"Oh, that." Francesca shrugged. "I've had a lot of practice, is all."

"I don't have a clue when it comes to children." Andie grimaced, thinking back to her most recent encounter with Chiara. She leaned a little closer, inspired by Francesca's cool confidence, to confide. "I'm supposed to help Valentina out by teaching her daughter to do some baking, but so far it's been a disaster."

"Oh, no! What happened?" Andie quickly recounted the details, leaving out her concern that the girl had witnessed her kissing her mom, which was something she was certain Valentina did not want her best friend knowing about. When she'd finished, Francesca nodded. "It's a difficult age."

"So, you think it was just normal for her to get upset and storm out like that?"

"For Chiara? Definitely normal. She has a fiery temper."

"Funny, Valentina seems so even-keeled."

"Well, since it skipped a generation, I think Chiara got a double dose. Plus, Chiara's growing up but Valentina's having a hard time letting go and giving her enough space to spread her wings."

"Surely she's just trying to keep her safe, though," Andie argued, "like the other day when Chiara fell into the fountain."

"Oh, I'm not saying she doesn't still need a lot of watching over, but sometimes Valentina hovers like, how do you Americans say, a helicopter? She thinks she's protecting Chiara, but to a ten-year-old, she just thinks she's being bossy. For someone whose own mother was always on her case and still is, I'm surprised Valentina doesn't recognize when she acts the same way."

Andie nodded slowly while she processed what Francesca had said. "So, how would you approach her? Because I'm supposed to go back over next week and try a baking lesson again, and frankly, I'm a little bit terrified."

"If I were you, I would just start by remembering that she may not be very old, but Chiara's been in the kitchen her entire life, growing up in that shop. She's watched three generations of women bake and make chocolates every day for this town. And cooking, too. Did you know, Valentina's Nonna still makes her own pasta by hand? That little old lady knows how to do things that we can barely imagine. And Chiara's been helping her since she was tall enough to stand on a stool to reach the stovetop."

"Sounds like the kid should be the one teaching me."

"Well, also don't forget that she's ten. She still doesn't know half as much as she thinks she does."

Andie let out a hearty laugh. "Yeah, I may not have kids, but I remember being that age myself."

"Well, then," Francesca said, raising her body from the chair and giving Andie's hand an encouraging pat, "I'm sure you'll get along just fine. I'd better get back to work. You'll let me know if you hear from any of those friends of yours about the festival?"

Andie assured her she would, then collected her calzone from the counter and took the stairs back up to her apartment. She opened her laptop and discovered an email from Tracy in her inbox with English translations of the school notes Valentina had given her. Suddenly recalling Chiara's reticence to speak in English, Andie replied back, attaching the baking recipes with a request to have them translated into Italian. After firing off another round of emails, this time to a web developer friend and the chefs from Florence, Andie clicked the lid of the computer shut and tucked into her calzone. For a newcomer to town, she was sure on the hook for a lot of promises. *Help with websites. Recruiting fresh faces to the festival. Teaching a young girl to make brownies.* Andie chuckled. It was that last task, more than the others, that made her nervous, but thanks to Francesca's advice, she felt more confident that she wouldn't make a complete mess out of it. Hopefully.

ANDIE WATCHED SILENTLY from the doorway as Valentina, unaware of her presence, placed a huge slab of some sort of chewy-looking nougat on the table in front of Chiara and handed her a long, sharp knife. With a guiding hand, Valentina led Chiara through the task of cutting the nougat into bite-sized rectangles. She leaned in close, her hands positioned inches away as Chiara copied the movements. Andie couldn't help but notice how closely she walked the line between helping and hovering, how the closer she got, the more resistance she faced but as she backed away, Chiara's body relaxed and she did as she'd been told. Perhaps Francesca had been right in her assessment of the flaw in Valentina's parenting technique.

From an assortment of tools on the table, Valentina selected one that resembled a thick wire loop on a wooden handle. She placed a rectangle of nougat on the device and lowered it into the bowl, pulling it out quickly and placing it on a parchment covered sheet with a flick of the wrist that produced a perfect specimen fit for the finest chocolate box. Chiara followed suit, producing an almost identical piece. The child had talent in the kitchen. Francesca had been right about that, too.

Even with her back to her, it was obvious that Valentina was about to point out some tiny flaw in her daughter's technique, and so Andie took a step forward to make her presence known. "Nice job," she said, smiling at Chiara, and was rewarded with a smile in return.

"Andie!" Valentina spun around, and the sight of her flushed cheeks and dark shining eyes made Andie wish she could surprise her like that at least twice a day. "How long have you been standing there?"

"Only a minute. I didn't want to interrupt until you were done."

Valentina pointed to another work station where flour, sugar, and other ingredients had been assembled, along with measuring cups and mixing bowls. "I've set everything up according to the recipes you gave me. But I just got a text to say that Paolo had to run an errand and Francie's having trouble with the oven. It's a beast of a thing, and she shouldn't be messing around with it in her condition." Valentina looked toward Chiara, then back to Andie. "Think you can handle things if I run out for a moment?"

"Of course," Andie replied with a confidence that she hoped masked her misgivings. Once Valentina had left, she approached the table where Chiara was either hard at work or studiously ignoring her presence, or perhaps a little of both. "So, what do you want to do?"

"What?" Chiara spun around when she spoke, and it was hard for Andie to tell whether the expression on her face was from being startled or nervousness. Either way, it was a good reminder that the kid was probably every bit as uncomfortable being left alone like this as she was, and it gave Andie an odd sense of comfort and even camaraderie.

"Look, I know your mom wants me to teach you how to bake some of the things I made for your shop a few weeks ago, but can I let you in on a little secret?" When Chiara nodded, Andie continued. "They're pretty basic. I mean, I was making them at your age all by myself, and I didn't know how to do half the stuff you do. My mom didn't even know how to cook."

Chiara's eyes widened. "Not at all?"

"Nope. You know what I heard the other day? I heard that you and your great grandmother make your own pasta from scratch. You want to know what my mom used to make? Spaghetti from a can."

"A can?" In true ten-year-old fashion, Chiara poked her fingers into her mouth, pretending to make herself vomit. Andie couldn't have agreed more.

"Here, I brought these for you." Andie held out the pages she'd printed before coming over, filled with all of the recipes that Tracy'd managed to have translated for her. "I know you can speak English just fine, but I thought you might prefer having them in Italian. Everything's there, brownies, blondies, three types of muffins, and some cookies, too."

Chiara looked down at the tray of nougat in front of her and sighed. "Okay. I guess I have to put this all away."

"Only if you want to," Andie said. She remembered Francesca's advice to trust her gut, and her gut was telling her that forcing Chiara to switch projects midstream would be a bad move. Andie could sympathize. She liked to finish what she started, too, and hated to be bossed around. "We don't have to work on the recipes right now, or at all, if you don't want to. I'm pretty sure you could teach yourself how to make them, whereas I am positive I could never learn how to dip those chocolates like you were doing without someone showing me."

Chiara searched Andie's face, looking puzzled. "You mean, you want *me* to teach *you* how to do it?"

"Sure. Why not?"

With a set of motions so similar to her mother's that Andie thought she would hardly be able to distinguish between the two, Chiara took a rectangle of nougat and dipped it into the chocolate. "See? Like that."

"Slow down there, kid," Andie said with a snort. "I'm old, remember?"

Chiara giggled, then did it once again, but slower and more deliberate.

"Okay," Andie said, after Chiara had produced three more perfect morsels, "I think I'm ready to give it a try." Knowing that she needed to continue to win Chiara's trust, but also determined not to be outdone by a ten-year-old, Andie focused all her energy on replicating the correct motions, eventually producing an adequate finished product. "How's that?"

"Not bad." Chiara grinned slyly. "Not perfect like mine, but not bad."

"Yeah, well, another couple of years, I guess you'll be ready to take over the place."

But Chiara shook her head. "No way. My mother would never trust me on my own."

"I'm sure she will when you're a little older."

"I doubt it." Chiara's mouth had settled into a familiar pout. "She thinks I'm still a baby. You saw how she acted the other day, just because I slipped into the fountain."

"Well…" Andie's stomach tightened, knowing she was on shaky ground. Though Valentina might be overprotective in other areas, Andie felt compelled to side with Valentina on this one. Ten years old was much too young to be looking for love. But she also didn't want to undo whatever rapport she'd managed to build with Chiara that day. "You do have a lot of time ahead of you. Maybe it's better to wait a little while before you start worrying about falling in love."

Chiara scowled at the ground in front of her feet. "That's not why I was up there, you know. It wasn't for me."

"But, then why?"

Chiara sighed heavily, and Andie feared for a moment that she wouldn't answer, but then she looked her in the eyes and spoke. "All the kids, they tease me."

Andie frowned. "Because you don't want to climb up on that silly old fountain?"

Chiara shook her head. "No, not that. It's because my parents are divorced."

"I see." A pain she'd buried long ago resurfaced in Andie's chest. She'd been the only one in her class without a father, and she knew how kids could be. "So you were trying to convince Cupid to get your parents back together?" she asked gently, recalling how often she'd made that wish.

But Chiara shook her head again, more forcefully than before. "I want them to be happy, but I don't think they would be if they were together, no matter what some people say."

Smart kid. "But if not that, what exactly were you trying to ask for? Before you fell in, that is."

Chiara screwed up her face as if trying to decide whether to say anything else. "There's a girl Papa talks to on the computer sometimes. I think he likes her. I thought maybe, if I told Cupid about it, then maybe he would make it so they would fall in love."

"You were asking for your dad?" Andie looked at her incredulously. Of all things, she hadn't expected that. "But you wouldn't have gotten in half the trouble you did if your mom had known that. Why didn't you just tell—oh." Suddenly, Andie understood. "You didn't want your mom to know."

"I was afraid it would make her sad to think about this girl, even though she doesn't want to be married to Papa, you know?"

"Yeah, I know." The girl's earnestness was heartbreaking, with an understanding far beyond her years that Andie couldn't help but be impressed by.

"I didn't mean to leave Mama out, either. I would ask for someone for her, too, only I don't think there are any boys she likes. None of them make her smile the way Papa smiles over the computer girl. Mama's always so sad. I wish I knew why. But you can't tell her I told you about that."

Andie nodded gravely, though of course, she knew the reason why. "I promise not to breathe a word about any of this to your mom. But maybe from now on, you should stay off the fountain, okay?"

Chiara grinned, and her expression was one of pure relief, as if confiding her secret had made everything instantly better. Andie was touched that Chiara had chosen to tell her the truth about the escapade at the fountain, but even so, she envied the simplicity of her youth. The child had no way of knowing that her mother had a secret, too, or how much harder it would be for Valentina to find the same sense of relief that she now enjoyed by telling it.

Andie turned her attention back to the nougat, but Chiara had set down her utensils.

"Andie?" The child's voice was hesitant. "I was wondering. Maybe you could show me how to make those recipes now, after all."

Andie gave a solemn nod. "Of course."

"Mama really liked the ones you called blondies. Should we start with those?"

"You're the boss, kid."

As they got to work, Andie couldn't help wondering whether, if Chiara got the chance to talk to Cupid on her mother's behalf, it might turn out that there was a woman out there somewhere who would bring a permanent smile to Valentina's face. She frowned as something uncomfortably like jealousy stirred within her at the thought. It shouldn't matter, she knew. Whatever resolution there might be to Valentina's situation would come long after Andie was gone. But as she turned back to the table to complete her work, that realization weighed heavily on her heart.

NINETEEN

THE DAY before Easter had brought all of the glories of spring to Florence, with unseasonably warm temperatures that begged for short sleeves and sandals, along with gentle breezes that soothed winter-worn skin. Across the city, every tree had erupted in a profusion of flowers, and along the formal pathways of the Giardino della Gherardesca, in the middle of which their hotel was situated, the petals of a thousand blossoms littered the time-worn paving stones.

Valentina lifted her feet carefully as she walked toward Andie, who waited for her at the bend in the path. Though her shoes were new, they weren't to blame for her unsteadiness, nor was she especially prone to clumsiness, her occasional run-in with slippery Cupid fountains notwithstanding. It wasn't even her close proximity to an attractive woman with whom she would share a bed later that night, though if she thought about that part for very long, it did cause her nerves to rattle like wind chimes in a hurricane. No, the reason was that, after a full day at their hotel's world-class spa, every inch of her body had turned to jelly. Not that she was complaining, but as relaxed as she was, it was a miracle her legs could hold her weight at all.

"Look at you!" Andie whistled softly, setting off a profusion of butterflies in Valentina's stomach. "You look amazing. Now, aren't you glad we couldn't get into our room right away?"

Valentina pursed her lips doubtfully. "I'm not sure if glad is the right word, but I guess there were some benefits."

That had been a twist to the day that Valentina hadn't been expecting. They'd arrived in Florence in the midmorning, heading out from Montamore just as soon as Chiara had left for her father's and her mother and grandmother had caught the train to Rome. She'd had little idea what to expect, as Andie had kept the details of their trip a closely guarded secret, but she'd assumed they'd check in to a reasonably decent hotel somewhere on the outskirts of the city and then, well, then they'd get down to business, so to speak. Their getaway was, after all, just an elaborate excuse to have sex, right? But that hadn't been the plan at all.

First, there was the hotel. From the moment they'd stepped foot on the grounds of one of the top hotels in the heart of the city, Valentina had felt like she'd been transported to another world. The former Renaissance villa was more like a nobleman's palace than a hotel, with frescoes on every surface and statues in every corner. Though she'd visited Florence as a tourist many times before, she'd never experienced anything like this. It was something out of a fairy tale. If she happened to bump into the real-life Cinderella while wandering through the lobby, she doubted she'd be surprised. The only truly shocking thing was finding herself—plain, ordinary Valentina Moretti—in a place like this at all. And yet Andie seemed to take it all in her stride.

Valentina skirted the semicircular, in-ground hot tub where earlier in the day they'd enjoyed a long, leisurely soak. The sun was low in the sky now as sunset approached, and there was just enough of a chill in the air to cause billowing steam to rise from the hot water like magic from a cauldron.

"How did you manage to set all this up again?" she asked.

That had been the next thing that had not gone as she'd expected. They hadn't gone to the room upon arrival. She'd just assumed they would. They'd get the key and drop off the luggage, and one thing or another would happen and they'd soon find themselves stripped naked, fumbling around like two teenagers, with all their best intentions to see the sights of the city forgotten. Instead, she'd discovered that there was a valet to take the bags while they were whisked away to the spa. They'd been there for hours and had yet to step foot in the bedroom at all. Valentina couldn't decide if it was a blessing or torture. She'd been so nervous about finally being alone with Andie that half of her was grateful for the delay, and the other half was growing more terrified by the minute and wished they'd already gotten that aspect of the trip out of the way. At least by now, she'd know what it was all about.

"Like I said before, I had my assistant make a few calls," Andie replied.

I had my assistant make a few calls. Valentina could barely understand the meaning of the words, simple though they were. As if anyone could spend a weekend in a palace, if only their assistant made a few calls. *Well, maybe they can,*

Valentina considered, *if they also happen to be a big-time celebrity*. It was a detail about Andie that she'd almost forgotten, considering what a thoroughly normal life she'd been leading in Montamore. But now that they'd embarked on their long-awaited weekend away, things had certainly changed.

Valentina thought back to the day's activities, which had included massages, and body scrubs, and essential oil treatments. There'd been a facial made with real gold. *Real gold!* Valentina's insides fluttered. *How much does a celebrity chef make, anyway?* It had never occurred to her to wonder about Andie's financial situation, but now that she gave it some thought, she realized she hadn't a clue. Surely she made more money than a chocolate maker, but somewhat less than a movie star—that was about as good a guess as she could manage. However much it was, it couldn't be enough to afford getaways like this, could it? Surely if she had as much money as that, she would have chosen a more interesting location to pass the spring than a tiny apartment overlooking a stupid statue in a place no one had ever heard of.

A twinge of guilt prodded her to consider the possibility that Andie had gone into serious debt for their weekend away, and all because Valentina had been too chicken to risk the off chance of them getting caught by her grandmother in *flagrante delicto*. How selfish she'd been! All Valentina had wanted was to satisfy her curiosity, to find out what it was like to kiss someone she found attractive, to run her hands along a woman's body and be touched the same way in return. They could have done that anywhere. In truth, with the apartment and shop both standing empty the whole weekend, they could've just stayed in Montamore. Valentina's chest tightened as she calculated how much money was being spent on this over-the-top extravagance. She resolved to split the cost of the room, at the very least, but wasn't sure how to bring it up tactfully. "You act like you're used to this type of thing," she commented, hoping to steer the conversation in the right direction to make the offer.

"All part of the job," Andie said with an uncharacteristic humility.

"Andie, we've spent an entire day in a spa where the only other patron was the wife of a Saudi Arabian prince."

"It's just one of the many perks of being a celebrity."

"I had a stylist do my hair tonight, and she even gave me my choice of outfits from the hotel boutique. To keep." Valentina smoothed her palms across the simple black dress she'd chosen, reflecting that even though she really shouldn't accept it, the gift had been a real godsend. Andie's car had been too small to stow two proper suitcases, and they'd had to do some creative packing.

"An excellent choice." Andie grinned. "And here when I told you we wouldn't have to pack much, you thought I was being fresh. The only thing I'm going to enjoy more than watching the way it hugs your hips on the walk to dinner is peeling it off of you when we get back to the room tonight."

"Andie, I'm trying to be serious." Valentina chewed her lower lip, then forced herself to stop, not wanting it to get too puffy for kissing. "I don't want this to sound rude. I mean, I know your show's popular, but…the hotel, and the spa treatments? And I think this is a designer dress."

"I'm sure it is."

"What I'm trying to say is it's too much. You at least have to let me pay for dinner tonight."

"No can do. But would it make you feel better if I told you that most of it was comped?"

"Comped?" Valentina thought it over for a moment, wondering if she really understood the word. "You mean free?"

Andie nodded. "It's how the show-biz industry works. You're right that I'm not a big enough celebrity for this kind of treatment. But the network I work for is owned by a much bigger company that handles some of the top A-list stars. My assistant, Tracy, happens to be friends with a lot of their assistants. Sometimes, they don't mind making a phone call or two on her behalf, and when they do, hotels like this are more than happy to do them a little favor. Upgrading a guest to a suite no one was going to sleep in anyway, or throwing in a spa treatment that costs them pennies to the dollar is a small price to pay if you can get Jennifer Aniston to stay at your hotel the next time she's in town."

"But, the clothes!" Valentina fretted.

"You want to know a secret? The designers give them to the stylists for free."

Valentina's jaw dropped. "Seriously?"

"Especially the young ones who are just getting started. Having a photograph out there of someone famous wearing their designs is marketing that money can't buy."

"What a different world you live in." Valentina shook her head slowly, still struggling to comprehend it all. "Wait, do you actually *know* Jennifer Aniston?"

"No."

"Pity. I like her."

"Should I be jealous?"

"No." If there was one thing Valentina knew for certain,

it was that no other woman could compare to the one she was with tonight. But something else that Andie had said stuck with her, giving her a slight chill. "So, will photographers be trying to take our pictures tonight?" Having their privacy invaded was another thing that Valentina had not been counting on.

"No, of course not," Andie responded quickly, but a shadow darkened her face. They'd been walking the whole time they were talking, and as Andie's head swiveled as if to take in their surroundings, it seemed to dawn on her that they were strolling, arms still snugly looped, along a busy street. She dropped Valentina's arm. "No sense calling attention to ourselves, though."

For someone so used to the public eye, her nervous reaction seemed odd to Valentina, but she decided not to press. Instead, she tried to lighten the mood. "I doubt they'd recognize you, anyway," Valentina assured her with an airy laugh. "Not after the stylist got a hold of you."

Instead of laughing, Andie's brow furrowed. "Do you not like the new look?"

In truth, Valentina loved it. She'd hardly been able to stop staring long enough to focus on walking in a straight line. She'd always found Andie attractive, to be sure, but what the hotel's stylist had pulled off in a few short hours was every bit as amazing as the miracles that Andie's assistant had orchestrated.

Andie wore a midnight-blue pantsuit, in a flowing fabric that was elegantly cut for evening. Her usually crazy locks had been tamed and trimmed, the searing orange tips atop roots of bleached blonde replaced with more natural shades of honey and gold that still managed to glow like a flame, but with a subtlety that was even more striking. The whole style was such a departure from her typical look that Valentina almost couldn't believe she was the same person. Tonight, Andie was a goddess. A dramatic word choice, perhaps, but it was the only one Valentina could think of that truly fit.

"You look amazing," Valentina assured her, keeping the goddess part to herself. After all, just because she'd had a fleeting moment of doubt didn't mean she wasn't still the same Andie Bartlett, a celebrity who was hardly in need of a bigger ego than she already had. "Different, but I like it."

"Good." The last of Andie's worry disappeared, a bright smile replacing her frown. "For where we're headed, even I felt the need to step it up a notch."

"And where is that, exactly?" Despite repeated questions, Valentina had managed to get little more than a hint about their dinner destination, and she was honestly dying to know.

"You'll see," was once more all that Andie would offer.

It didn't take long for them to reach the Ponte Vecchio, the famous bridge that had spanned the Arno river for centuries. From the viewpoint of a pedestrian, the bridge resembled a very narrow street, lined with shops on both sides. There were no restaurants along this stretch, and in fact the bridge had been the exclusive domain of jewelers and goldsmiths for at least four hundred years, so it was with a great deal of puzzlement that Valentina followed Andie as she made a sharp turn from the main thoroughfare when they were only about halfway across, and went instead through a small, unmarked door that led to a staircase on the other side.

"What are we doing here?"

"You'll see." It was a reply that was likely to drive Valentina insane if she heard it one more time.

But once they'd climbed the stairs to the fourth floor, Valentina really did see. Specifically, she saw a secluded terrace, set with a single table for two against a delicate metal railing, beyond which was nothing, save an unobstructed view of the sparkling waters of the Arno below, and a sky that had turned a deep, rosy gold against the rapidly setting sun.

"We're just in time," Andie remarked. She grasped Valentina's hand and gave her a gentle tug toward the table, at which point Valentina realized that she had, in fact, stopped dead in her tracks in utter shock. Whatever surprise she had imagined Andie had in store, this was more.

"This is where we're having dinner? But, how? There aren't even any restaurants here!" Valentina was certain of it, except that everything from the gold-rimmed plates and gleaming glassware to the flickering tea lights and the silver vases overflowing with roses, did strongly suggest otherwise.

"There is, in fact, ever so occasionally, this one table up here that happens to be available." Andie couldn't have looked more pleased with the success of her surprise if she'd tried. "Looks like we're the only ones here, so it must be our lucky night."

"Oh, sure it is. Did your miraculous assistant set this up, too?"

"No, this was all me. It's run from a local restaurant, and the chef is a friend. He came on my show when he was touring New York last year, and he promised if I ever came to Florence, he'd make sure I could have dinner up here. Of course, it was much too cold when I was here several weeks ago, but I figured this time it was worth giving him a call to see if the offer still stood. Usually it would be impossible to book this table for a Saturday night without a year's notice, but technically it doesn't open until next month, so..." Andie ended her thought with a surprisingly modest shrug. "Like I said, it was good luck."

"Andie Bartlett, do you know that you're amazing?" Under the circumstances, Valentina decided there was no harm in giving her ego just a tiny boost.

They'd moved to look over the railing, one on either side of the small table. Taking two glasses of prosecco from the table, Andie held one out to Valentina, who took it and lifted it so that the golden liquid reflected the colors of the setting sun through its tiny bubbles. They clinked the glasses together, offering a simple toast of 'cheers' before drinking. Somehow it didn't feel like enough, and yet what else was there to say? This was only meant to be a casual date. It's not like Valentina had prepared a speech. As she swallowed, the fizzy liquid tickled her throat even as apprehension tickled her nerves.

Whatever it was that she'd pictured when she'd thought about their weekend in Florence—and lying alone in her bed late at night, she'd thought about it a lot—she'd never guessed it would be like this. It's not that she wasn't impressed with the effort Andie had put into creating such an amazing experience for her, because of course she was. It's just that if none of this had happened, that would've been fine, too. More than fine, it would've been exactly what Valentina was expecting. And it was the unexpectedness of her current situation that suddenly had her in a tizzy.

A waiter came to the table, dressed in a formal jacket and tie, and began to explain the evening's menu, but

Valentina only heard half of what he said. Her energy was focused elsewhere, keeping her roiling emotions under control.

What is it about tonight that suddenly has me so confused? Despite their fancy clothes and the private terrace with the sunset view, nothing had changed in their understanding. Valentina was still the divorced mother from a small town unwilling to risk anything more than a brief fling. Andie was the same gregarious and flirty American who had breezed into Montamore a few weeks before, and would breeze back out in another few. So why didn't it feel the same?

Perhaps it was because, for the first time, Valentina had seen a side of Andie she hadn't guessed was there—a soft and sentimental side, a serious side—that was at odds with the public image she projected. What she saw was the type of woman she could possibly fall in love with, if something like that were in the cards for her. Which it was not. And so, perhaps it was regret she was experiencing, for what could never be. But the pounding in her chest didn't feel like regret. It felt like fear. Once, she'd immersed herself so thoroughly in a fantasy that she'd ended up marrying someone she didn't love. How much worse would it be to fall for someone she could never have?

"ARE you going to keep poking at that scallop carpaccio," Andie asked, "or did you plan on eventually trying a bite?"

"Sorry?" Valentina looked directly at Andie, but it was clear from her eyes that she was a million miles away. The waiter had returned with their plates and Valentina had picked up her fork, but though the beautiful arrangement of the appetizer on her plate had been marred by her poking at it with the tines, she'd yet to lift a bite of it to her lips. "Oh. I must have been distracted by the view."

"The view is spectacular, but so is the food. You should give it a try." Andie lifted her own fork to her mouth and her taste buds were rewarded with an exquisite blend of olive oil and citrus that perfectly balanced the sea-brine of the scallops and flooded her senses completely.

Valentina brought the fork to her lips. "Wow."

"See? I told you. But are you sure it was just the view that distracted you? You seem troubled."

"No, not at all."

Andie knew this wasn't true, and it worried her. She'd tried so hard to make this evening, this whole trip, in fact, something special. She'd put every ounce of effort into it for weeks, ever since they'd decided to make the trip. But now, Andie feared that maybe it wasn't good enough. A shot of cold dread hit the pit of her stomach. *Maybe I'm not good enough.* Uncouth, uneducated—how could she ever think she was good enough for Valentina? She put her fork down, waiting for Valentina to deliver the bad news.

"It's just...tonight, it's like a fairy tale."

Relief washed over her in a wave, and Andie rested a hand on hers, catching her deep espresso eyes and holding them steady with her own. "You say that like it's a bad thing."

Valentina pressed her lips together warily, but didn't look away. "I don't believe in fairy tales."

Andie chuckled, shaking her head. "You live within sight of a magical fountain. Your town is home to an honest-to-goodness, wish-granting stone Cupid. That's right up there with a troll under a bridge and fairy godmothers, in my book. How is it even possible to say you don't believe in fairy tales?"

Valentina laughed, too, conceding the point. "Okay, what I meant to say is that fairy tales might be just fine for other people, but I don't believe in them for myself."

"What makes you so different?" Neither of them had broken eye contact, and Andie drank in the sight of her as if she would never get her fill.

"Come on." Valentina squirmed and looked away. "I'm here with you right now, a beautiful *woman*, on a romantic dinner date. Legs shaved, sexy underwear in place…Do you really need to ask?"

"Let's see." The vision that formed in Andie's head made her heart race, and though they had several courses of dinner yet to get through, she could already feel the wetness building between her legs. "Do I really need to ask for more details about the sexy underwear? Yes, I think I do."

Valentina freed her hand from beneath Andie's and gave the top of her companion's wrist a swat. "Not what I was talking about."

"Fine. So you're gay. So what? I am, too." Sensing that the time for joking had passed, Andie allowed her demeanor to become more serious. Her eyes once again fixed on Valentina's, and from the frightened look in their depths, it almost seemed that she was being drawn in against her will. "You think we don't get fairy-tale endings? I just think no one's bothered to write about them, is all."

Valentina swallowed hard, and it was clear how desperately she wanted to believe this. "Maybe that's true. But remember, ever since I was fourteen, I've known that the dreams other people had weren't going to work for me. And the one time I tried to change that by marrying Luca, look what happened."

"Forgive me for being blunt, but you kind of went about it all wrong. For instance, you might have had more luck if you'd started by looking for a wife." Her tone held just enough teasing to keep the observation light and without accusation.

"Well, what's done is done." Valentina sighed. Her unspoken guilt and self-recrimination seemed to swirl around her like a fog.

"But why?" Andie refused to let her give into her own resignation. "You can't give up now! I mean, now that you know what you want…"

"What I want," Valentina interrupted, her tone gentle but firm, "is to raise my daughter and run my shop. That's what matters most. And when you live in a town where everyone knows your business, it's easiest not to be too different if you can help it."

"Well, you've already failed there."

"Yes, I know. I'm the first divorced woman in the history of Montamore. And the first lesbian, too."

That hadn't been what she'd been trying to get at in the least, and Andie cocked one eyebrow at Valentina's ludicrous response. "How old's your town?"

Valentina's brow wrinkled. "I'm not sure. A few thousand years, I think."

"Then I highly doubt you're the first lesbian in Montamore. But none of that is what I meant."

In the candlelight, Valentina's pulse throbbed visibly beneath the thin skin at her throat. "It isn't?"

"No, it isn't." Andie's breath caught in her chest. Could she really not see in herself all the things that Andie could see? "You're an amazingly talented chocolate maker. You're a good mom, and a smart business woman. And sexy. Did I mention sexy? You have no idea what it's been doing to me to sit across from you all night, just watching the flames from the tea lights dance in your eyes."

"I—" Valentina blinked rapidly as tears glistened in her eyes.

Andie took her hand again and gave her fingers a squeeze. "Like it or not, you're already different in so many wonderful ways. It's too late to change that, and you shouldn't even try. There's no reason that someday, you couldn't get exactly what you want, in every part of your life."

A tear slipped down Valentina's cheek. "Sure. Well, the next time a stray lesbian happens to move to Montamore and rescues me from falling into the fountain, I'll keep that in mind." She pressed her lips together and squeezed her lids shut, and Andie knew she was fighting to keep her emotions in check. "Right now, I just want to enjoy this one weekend, and not think about anything else. Is that okay?"

Andie brushed her lips across the silky skin on the top of Valentina's hand, and breathed in the faint scent of the perfumed oils that lingered from the spa. "If that's what you want," Andie assured her, "then that's what you'll get."

Valentina opened her eyes. "Thank you."

"Absolutely." Andie grinned. "Consider me your personal fairy godmother, or your genie in a bottle, or any other magical, wish-granting fairy-tale character of your choosing."

"I see." Valentina shook her head indulgently. "So, can I have as many wishes as I want?"

"Of course!" Andie paused, a deep crease forming in her

brow. The desire to tease was overwhelming. Uncontrollable. She had to give in. "By 'wishes', we are talking about orgasms, right?"

"Andie!" Valentina squealed, an outcome which filled Andie with delight.

"I was just making sure. As long as that's what we're talking about, then yes. Definitely."

Struggling for breath through her laughter, Valentina gave Andie's shin a nudge with her foot beneath the table. "Hush. The waiter's coming."

Andie leaned over the table and whispered, "Not as much as you will be later tonight."

Valentina opened her mouth to reply, but all that came out was a strangled, choking cough. The waiter set down the plates for their next course, a saffron risotto topped with caviar. Valentina, still shaking with laughter as he left, waggled her index finger at Andie's face. "I swear to God, if you do that again, I am going to choke on this exquisite dinner you've arranged and die."

"Okay, I'll be good." Andie passed a hand across her mouth, smoothing away her grin as best as she could. They'd had enough seriousness for one night, and perhaps enough teasing, too. She needed to strive for a middle ground, at least until their dinner was through. "For one thing, chefs really don't like it if their food kills people. Vito would never speak to me again."

"Yes, good reason. I'm glad you have your priorities in place."

Andie snorted but managed to maintain a straight face, more or less. "Well that, and obviously, my plans for when we get back to the room really do require us both to be alive."

"Duly noted." Valentina shot her a saucy look as she scooped up a forkful of risotto, but then Andie could see the uncertainty creeping in, nudging aside her earlier confidence. "So, have you put as much thought into tonight's activities as you did planning the rest of this weekend?"

"Of course." She didn't elaborate, but her eyes traveled down the length of Valentina's neck with such intensity that by the time they reached her breasts, Andie half expected to see scorch marks forming on the dress.

"I see." Valentina took a long sip of her wine. As she returned the glass to the table, Andie could see that her fingers trembled.

TWENTY

THE HOUR HAD GROWN LATE by the time Valentina and Andie made their way back over the bridge and headed in the direction of the hotel. They'd emerged from the rooftop arm in arm, but soon moved to be side by side instead, remaining just shy of touching now that the privacy they'd enjoyed in their secluded hideaway was gone. It didn't matter. They would enjoy being alone again very soon. The very thought of it caused Valentina's palms to perspire. She was almost thankful for the need to keep her distance for just a bit longer, if only for the opportunity to compose herself.

Bright white fireworks flared in the distance as they walked, the starburst patterns reflecting in the dark waters of the Arno, lighting up the river like a million tiny stars. Valentina's first instinct was to suspect that the pyrotechnic display was yet another of the tricks Andie kept pulling out of her sleeve. Even reminding herself that it was a holiday weekend, and that therefore fireworks were to be expected and had nothing to do with them, did little to dispel the overwhelming feeling that Andie had taken this weekend getaway—this whole relationship, in fact—far beyond anything that Valentina had anticipated or prepared herself for.

Relationship. The muscles in her shoulders and neck tensed at the word, and her head got that funny feeling inside it, like she'd stood up too quickly and the room had started to spin. *Or just maybe, is it possible that this is that feeling some people claim you get when you're falling in love?* A lump formed in the pit of her stomach. *What have I gotten myself into?*

A relationship wasn't what they'd agreed on that afternoon in her apartment, not at all. And love? That was *never* what this was supposed to be. In fact, Valentina had been counting on the exact opposite of a relationship. All she'd wanted was a way to satisfy her curiosity when it came to her attraction to women without risking her heart or her reputation in the village, and with absolutely no strings attached. People did things like that all the time, didn't they? Maybe not in Montamore, but in places around the world where people didn't consider a happily ever after ending to be their one and only goal. At least she'd been led to believe this was true. People in movies had flings all the time, so why couldn't *this* have been as simple as *that*?

But as she walked beside Andie now, the air between their bodies crackled with an electricity that arced through her fingertips and traveled up her arms, and she knew she'd made a grave miscalculation. Whatever they had, it bore no resemblance to a casual fling. Had it ever? Perhaps on that morning when she'd stood in front of Cupid's fountain in the darkness, perhaps at that moment it might have been possible for her to regard Andie as nothing more than a convenient means to an end. Or when Andie had first offered to kiss her, sitting beside her on the couch in her apartment. But even that far back, Valentina couldn't swear that it wouldn't already have been too late to escape with her heart completely intact. Who was she kidding? From the very first glimpse of Andie's reflection in the fountain, she'd been a goner.

It didn't really matter. They'd never been left alone long enough to pull off a quick fling anyway. Surrounded by spying family and nosy neighbors, they'd been stymied by the simple mechanics of it. Like it or not, they'd had to wait, and waiting had given them time to grow closer, to become more intimate with one another even as they were denied the chance to be physical. The waiting had proven to be her undoing, of that Valentina was sure. Over the course of weeks, they'd shared meals and gone on adventures. They'd cooked together and laughed together. They'd confided in one another. Weren't those the stepping stones that truly built a relationship, with sex a convenient way to provide reinforcement and fill in the gaps?

At some point, Valentina had started thinking of herself and Andie as not just two people passing by, but as something more. The shift in her perception had been subtle over time, but powerful. They'd become not two 'I's in her mind, but a single 'us'. And so perhaps it was true that there had been a time when she was merely curious what it would be like to be with a woman, any woman. Now that was no longer the case. That wouldn't be enough for her now. It was Andie's hands she wanted on her, the feel of Andie's lips against her skin. Her body pressed against her, and on her. Under her. In her. Andie, and no one else.

Their fingertips brushed as they slipped through the gate

in the garden wall. The contact sent a shockwave through her, a yearning that impacted not just her body, but her heart as well. Caring this much about Andie hadn't been part of her plan, but there was nothing to be done about it. She felt how she felt. Even if she didn't go through with having sex, deep down she knew it wouldn't make a difference. Sex would be a physical expression of a deeper connection that had already been forged between them, but without having sex, the connection would still be there. Somewhere down the road the pain of parting was inevitable. There was nothing that could be done to stop it. She might as well get everything she could out of being together while she had the chance.

Valentina reached out, her fingers curling tightly around Andie's as they walked hand in hand along the path that led to the hotel. There was no one outside, but neither did she care at this point who could see. They were on the hotel grounds now, and it was no one's business but their own. Due to the lateness of the hour, they found only a few people lingering in the bar off the lobby. As they drew near to it, Andie slowed her steps but didn't let go of Valentina's hand.

"Should we stop to get a drink?" Andie asked.

"I—"

As she tried to answer, she found her throat dry and scratchy from disuse, and Valentina realized it was the first time either of them had spoken since they'd left the Ponte Vecchio. "I think we should go straight up to the room." Andie, not needing to be told twice, silently led the way.

The room was as luxurious as any of the best mansions of Europe, its ceiling painted with all the intricacy of a renaissance church, all of its finely carved furnishings brushed with gold. Though she'd never laid eyes on anything half as grand in her life, Valentina barely registered the surroundings except to note the king-size bed that dominated the space. It was topped by a massive canopy of royal blue damask draperies, and piled high with pristine white pillows that, if looked at in just the right way, resembled pale, whispering lips.

Any minute now, she thought she could hear them telling her, *You'll make your way over here, and just think of all the things you might do after that.* Valentina's imagination flooded with a range of possibilities that made the muscles in her belly and thighs clench in sweet anticipation.

"Would you like some wine?" Andie's voice managed to break through her erotic musings just enough to recapture the bulk of her attention. Andie stood with her back to Valentina as she examined a cabinet that had been stocked with drinks.

"No." They'd had plenty of wine already that evening, and plenty of conversation, too. Right now, she was more focused on whatever secrets would be revealed in that massive bed. She inched closer.

"Maybe a few minutes to settle in, relax?" Andie asked, turning around.

"No." Relaxation was not on the agenda for tonight, of that she was certain.

Valentina took a few more steps until she stood in front of Andie, close enough that all she had to do was reach out and they would be in each other's arms. Her muscles hummed, ready to obey her slightest command.

"In that case, do you need—"

"I need for you to stop talking. Now." Valentina reached out and clasped Andie's shoulder, pulling her toward her.

Valentina leaned in, stopping any further conversation with a kiss as rich and luxurious as the room that surrounded them.

When their mouths eventually parted, Andie registered a half-hearted protest. "I told you, I have a whole agenda planned. You're skipping ahead."

Valentina lingered, whispering against Andie's lips. "I know, but if the agenda includes a lengthy chat, maybe we could reschedule it for later?"

"You're sure you don't need more time?" The hunger that burned in Andie's eyes stood in stark contrast to the restraint her question implied.

Valentina drew a breath. "Positive."

Andie touched the tip of her tongue to her lower lip. "Where should we start?"

"I thought you had an agenda all planned out."

"It was more of a rhetorical question," Andie huffed.

Valentina's eyelids fluttered halfway shut. "Start wherever you'd like. You're the expert. I'm here to learn."

Andie's hands were on her in an instant, bunching the silky fabric of Valentina's dress as they sought purchase on the flesh beneath. Her heart raced with the sheer exhilaration of it, but at the unmistakable sound of popping thread, Valentina placed her hand firmly between them and gave Andie a small push.

"Shouldn't you undress me first?" she asked, looking back over her shoulder as she turned around and shifted her hair to expose the zipper.

"I was getting around to it," Andie grumbled, her eyebrows scrunched tightly together.

"Of course," Valentina soothed. "It's just, the stitches were ripping, and it's a designer dress, even if it was free."

Andie unzipped the dress and slid it down Valentina's body with painstaking slowness. Valentina shivered, the goosebumps that covered her skin having nothing to do with being cold. But instead of tossing the dress aside, Andie paused to fold it down the middle, then draped it carefully over a chair. Her grouchy frown had been replaced by a sly half-smile that left little doubt that these delay tactics were payback for Valentina's recent attempt to direct the show.

"Better?" Andie asked when she'd finally finished with the housekeeping. She placed her hands on Valentina's shoulders, slipping a thumb beneath each strap of the bra that Valentina had put so much thought into choosing earlier that day.

"Mm hm." Valentina drew a ragged breath, just managing to squeak out, "Much."

"Good. We wouldn't want anything to happen to your new designer outfit." Andie slid her hands down slowly, following the straps until she reached the cups, then pushed her thumbs as far as they would extend beneath the black lace, gliding them along the plump curves of Valentina's breasts with a sweeping motion that sent teasing promises rippling all the way down to her toes.

Without any hurry, Andie moved her palms along Valentina's sides, tracing her shape until her hands came to rest at the narrowest part of the hourglass. But as she began to ease her fingers beneath the waistband of the black lace underwear, that so perfectly matched the bra, Valentina retained just enough presence of mind to turn the tables again, for fairness' sake.

"Hold on," she said, taking a tiny backward step. "What about your clothes?"

"What about them?" Andie moved to recapture Valentina's waist, but she wriggled free.

"Shouldn't they come off, too? After all," Valentina quipped, "we wouldn't want anything to happen to your new designer outfit."

With a harrumph that walked a fine line between insane frustration and begrudging respect, Andie unceremoniously pulled one arm from its sleeve. Valentina cleared her throat dramatically as Andie let her jacket drop to the floor.

"What is it now? You want me to fold it, too?"

"No. It's just, don't I get to strip it off? You did mine."

"My God, woman. Are you always this bossy in bed?"

"I don't know." Valentina's cheeks grew hot. "This is my first time, remember?"

"You're sure not acting like it is," Andie muttered. But after a moment's pause, she gathered Valentina's hands in hers and lifted them to the buttons of her blouse. "I suppose you're right. Go ahead. It's only fair."

Valentina's fluttering fingers made short work of the row of pearl buttons. She tossed the blouse on top of the jacket, and the pants followed shortly thereafter. There would be no folding. Valentina felt a thrill of excitement to find that Andie had taken similar care in choosing her lingerie, opting for a matching set in muted champagne tones. The sleek lines and simple look complimented the solid strength of Andie's figure so well that Valentina couldn't tear her eyes away, even as she grew desperate to explore what was hidden beneath. Adrenaline made her fingertips ache as she reached out to touch the matte satin fabric.

"Patience." Andie playfully swatted her hand away. "It's not your turn."

Patience was not one of Valentina's strengths. She

watched in agony as Andie grasped the top of the comforter and slowly peeled the covers back to reveal the bed's smooth sheets. Illuminated by the soft light of a single lamp, the surface beckoned with an incandescent glow. Valentina made a swift move toward it, but Andie stopped her, folding her tightly into her arms.

"You're getting ahead of yourself again," Andie pointed out.

"Maybe, but only because you're taking too long."

The sudden release of her bra's band revealed Andie's true purpose, and so she did the same with as much finesse as she could manage in view of it being the first time she'd ever unhooked a bra that wasn't her own. With an expert maneuver, Andie cleared both items of clothing away as if they'd never been there at all.

"Was that fast enough for you?" Andie teased.

"Show-off." She tried not to gasp for breath, but in truth, it had made her head spin.

"You seem winded. Maybe I should slow down again." As they stood undisturbed in their embrace, bare breasts pressed together, the heat between them built to such an intensity that Valentina imagined she would soon melt.

Without letting go, Andie nudged Valentina backward until her thighs made contact with the edge of the bed. One more small push and she dropped, letting go of Andie's body so she could balance herself, palms reaching out behind her as her bottom bounced on the springy mattress. She'd landed with her knees wide enough apart that Andie easily slipped between them. Andie cupped Valentina's chin in her hand and urged it upward until she could see her face.

"Oh, those eyes." Andie's accompanying moan set off a

flood of wetness from deep inside her that Valentina found almost alarming. It had never happened quite like *that* before. "I could get lost in those eyes and never want to leave."

"Andie." Her voice was little more than a trembling whisper. Every muscle shook. Her arms no longer had the strength to hold her up. The terrain was becoming less familiar by the second. Stretching widthwise across the bed, she focused her attention on the canopy high above her head, seeking to steady herself, until the intricate, fanning folds of blue damask became so mesmerizing that she had to close her eyes.

Andie laughed. "No more trying to take control?"

Valentina shook her head, lacking the wherewithal to reply.

Andie's hands brushed her hips, and she felt the tickling of lace against her thighs as the final, inconsequential bit of covering was removed, leaving her completely bare. In fact, she was much more bare than usual, something she recalled the moment Andie's warm breath whooshed across what felt like miles of unnaturally smooth pink skin. Suddenly self-conscious about it, Valentina propped herself up with her elbows. "Is that…okay?"

Andie lifted her head, which had been bent in the process of—well, come to think of it, Valentina wasn't entirely certain what she was in the process of doing, as they'd now reached the point in the evening when her previous experiences diverged wildly from what lay ahead —and looked at her with a hint of confusion. "Is what okay?"

"The woman at the spa mentioned the idea," Valentina squirmed. "I mean, I know Americans can be picky about that sort of thing, and I got started and just sort of ended up taking it all off. Only now, I'm not sure, and—"

"Val."

Valentina swallowed the clump of gibberish that had tangled up with her tongue and waited for Andie to say more. Andie climbed onto the bed and straddled her hips. As she did so, Valentina attempted to sneak a quick peek for the purpose of comparison, but a strip of champagne-colored cloth blocked her view. Andie stretched out on top of her, and her weight came to rest on Valentina's body with the soothing comfort of a heavy blanket.

"I think that everything about you, however you want it to be, is perfect in every way." As Andie pressed her lips to Valentina's neck, the last of the fear and doubt she'd held inside evaporated like drops of dew on a sunny windowpane.

Andie's head shifted lower, her lips caressing their way across Valentina's chest. She squeezed Valentina's breasts closer together and buried her face deep into the valley that formed between them, covering her with kisses. The sudden pinching of both her nipples sent a surge of longing straight to Valentina's core, making her hips buck wildly, completely beyond her control. Clearly taking it as a sign of encouragement, Andie's mouth drifted lower still, but by the time she'd paused to swirl her tongue around the rim of Valentina's navel, anxiousness had reigned in the pleasure.

"Andie?" Valentina reached down and hooked her fingers beneath Andie's arm, giving it a gentle upward tug.

"What, directing again?" Andie left off what she'd been doing and rested her head on Valentina's stomach, her cropped locks shining brilliantly in the lamplight.

"I'm not trying to be bossy, I promise. And I know you

have everything all planned out. It's just…" She searched for the words to make Andie understand. "I miss your weight on top of me."

"Just give it a minute. I'm moving for a reason, you know."

"I know, and I'm sure it'll be worth it, but do you think we could just stay like this for a little longer instead? It felt safe." Valentina held her breath, afraid she'd revealed too much. Their arrangement hadn't changed, so perhaps it would've been better to keep Andie in the dark about what was in her heart. But it was too late now.

"I'll do anything for you," Andie said, and the look in her eyes left no room for Valentina to doubt she spoke the truth. Utterly overwhelmed, there was nothing she could think to say in return, and so Valentina grasped Andie's hand, squeezing it tightly, and raked the fingers of her other hand through the glowing copper locks as Andie's head rested on her belly. They stayed like that for some time and said nothing at all.

Finally, Andie lifted her head and smiled. "I have an idea." Scrambling to her knees, Andie flipped quickly around, taking up a new position so that she was once again stretched out flat along Valentina's torso, her reassuring weight keeping Valentina grounded, but this time her knees were just below Valentina's shoulders, and her head poised strategically lower down. "Now we both get what we need."

Valentina's tummy fluttered in response to the new arrangement. "And what do I do?"

"For the love of God, woman. Nothing." Her tone was more amusement than frustration. "I keep trying to tell you. How do you say it in Italian?"

"How do you say what?" Valentina had lost track of the conversation as Andie's hair tickled her inner thighs.

"Never mind."

Andie's lips traced a meandering line of butterfly kisses along the creamy skin, starting at the knee and flitting back and forth between both legs as she moved further up. Valentina shuddered and moaned as Andie inched closer and closer, until finally, the full heat of Andie's mouth engulfed Valentina's daringly bare flesh. The velvet wetness of her tongue created an intoxicating friction more maddening and glorious than anything Valentina had imagined was possible. Andie's tongue rippled across her folds again and again, pausing every so often for her mouth to suck and her tongue to tease as Valentina's pelvis rose to meet her, demanding more.

Soon, Andie's fingers were there, too, opening her wide, plunging inside her, claiming every part of her there was to claim. In the midst of it, Valentina heard a voice speaking, and even as she became vaguely aware that the voice was her own, she was fairly certain the words were neither English nor Italian. She had no idea what language she was speaking. She had no words to describe the sensations Andie had stoked within her.

What had started as sparks had escalated rapidly, becoming a roaring flame that threatened to consume her completely, and all at once, Valentina was anxious. The way Andie was going, there was no end in sight, and every likelihood she would soon burst apart. They'd be finding tiny pieces of her all over Florence for weeks. She twisted, trying to squirm away, but Andie held her firmly in place.

"Stop that," Andie chided, the brief pause required to

speak giving Valentina a much-needed moment of recovery. "You're almost there."

"I'm probably far enough," Valentina countered. "Don't you think?"

"Don't be ridiculous." Andie picked up where she'd left off, effectively ending the argument.

In search of mooring, Valentina hooked her arms around Andie's legs, grasping them tightly, as if doing so could keep her from being swept away in the tidal wave she suspected was approaching. She pressed her forehead between Andie's thighs. As she breathed in, her nostrils filled with Andie's scent. Desire coursed through her, primal and powerful, drawing her in like the pull of the moon's gravity on the ocean as she buried her face deeper. Reaching her peak, she convulsed with release. Her cry was muffled by a strip of matte champagne satin pressed firmly into her open mouth.

Never in her life had Valentina experienced anything with the same intensity as that moment, and yet even before the shockwaves had subsided, she knew they were far from done. She wanted more. She wanted to give pleasure, and to receive it, until there was nothing left. With her thumb, she moved the fabric of Andie's underwear aside, revealing a forbidden feast she'd denied herself too long. But no longer.

"Val," Andie protested as the tip of her tongue made its first hesitant contact along the crease of her thigh. "It's okay. You can wait."

By way of answering, Valentina gave Andie's underwear a yank, the unintended forcefulness of the action splitting the seam completely. *Wait?* She'd be damned if Andie was going to make her wait a second more. She'd never get what she wanted if she didn't assert herself. After another, much bolder application of her tongue to a spot between Andie's legs that she was fairly certain but not completely positive was what she was aiming for, all protesting ceased. Valentina interpreted Andie's sudden onset of ragged panting as a sign that she'd guessed the correct target, and that Andie was now in full agreement with her timetable.

She didn't really know what she was doing, but it didn't seem to matter. Valentina quickly discovered that the connection she'd felt to Andie from the moment they'd met was as strong or stronger physically as it had been in other ways. Andie gave Valentina free rein of her body to test and explore, leaving her with no doubt when she'd done something particularly well. To her relief, Valentina soon learned that there were no wrong answers after all, but an endless array of possibilities that brought varying degrees of bliss.

Quite some time later, they came to rest with Andie's head propped up by a pillow and Valentina's head on Andie's chest, both exhausted, both facing the right way around beneath the covers. They remained that way silently for half an eternity at least, as Valentina basked in the pleasant warmth that radiated from the smoldering embers that were all that remained of her spent body and mind. She had no idea if she'd ever recover the ability to move or speak again. She didn't think she knew anything anymore.

Earlier that evening, when she'd reminded Andie that this was her first time, she'd mostly been joking. Valentina was no young virgin, after all. She might not have been an expert, either, but she'd thought she'd known enough about sex to know what it was, and what it wasn't. And what she'd been convinced that it wasn't—no matter who you were with, male or female—was the mystical experience that all the songs and poems would have you believe sex to be. She would have sworn that was the case. But now?

She was still the same person she'd been before, and yet utterly different, too. Could the simple act of having sex do that to a person? As she recalled the myriad of ways in which they'd come together, she had the sense that they'd joined more than their bodies, and that a part of their essences had become entwined. Valentina's head began to spin. Was that even possible?

Is that what they mean by making love? She inhaled sharply as the words suggested themselves to her. It was a term that had always made her cringe, and one she'd never understood. But now her head was spinning like it had done earlier in the night, and she was almost certain that love had something to do with it. What else could explain how she felt? Like chocolate after tempering, she imagined that her very molecules had been reshaped through this experience. Where before she'd been dull and lackluster, now she felt shiny and smooth. She wondered, did Andie feel that way, too?

"Is it always like that?" Valentina asked, not sure what she hoped the answer would be.

"Ideally," was Andie's casual reply. Perhaps a little too casual for Valentina's liking, considering how thoroughly her world had been shaken.

"Oh." So, the transformative experience had been one-sided after all. She'd have liked to have thought the evening wasn't entirely routine from Andie's perspective. Was that expecting too much? The beginnings of doubt crept in.

"One thing I know for certain is the answer to my question," Andie said.

"What question?" Valentina prompted, intrigued.

"You are every bit as bossy in the bedroom as I suspected." Andie tousled her hair teasingly.

"I'm not!" Doubt was replaced by indignation, but as Valentina paused to take stock of their evening, she realized Andie was right. "Okay, maybe I was a little more commanding than usual." Valentina's cheeks tingled in the darkness. And it *was* completely dark, the bulb in the lamp by the bedside having at one point met its end as a stray foot sent it crashing to the floor. She hoped it was less expensive than it had looked. A fresh wave of doubt hit as it occurred to her that Andie might not have appreciated the way she'd taken control. "I'm sorry. I'm not sure what came over me."

Andie's laughter resonated in her chest, making Valentina's ear vibrate. "I'm not complaining. It was a little off script, but I think we both got what we wanted."

"So is that it, then, or is there more?" Valentina asked. Andie's laughter had reassured her, and at least some of her confidence was restored. There was still plenty to worry about, for certain, but it could keep until later. Whatever the future might bring, tonight was special, and it was nowhere near done. Valentina rolled onto her side and stretched herself out invitingly, like a lazy cat.

"More?" Andie must have noticed the feline resemblance, too, for she immediately began stroking Valentina's belly.

"Yes, more," she replied, barely managing not to purr. "Or, have I learned it all now?"

"All?" Andie stopped her petting and repositioned herself to look directly at Valentina. She raised an eyebrow. "You mean, have you learned all there is to know about lesbian sex?"

"Yes." Valentina surprised herself by how unembarrassed she was. Usually a question like that would have left her mortified, but not tonight. Tonight, she just wanted to know. She wanted to know everything. "So, have I?"

"In one night?" Andie lifted her index finger and ran it down the bridge of Valentina's nose, stopping when she got to the tip. "Don't get me wrong, we covered a lot, but…"

"So, there's more to learn?" Valentina prompted.

"That's a safe bet, yes." Her voice reflected her mirth.

"Then can you do something for me?"

Andie lifted her finger from Valentina's nose and used it to tuck a stray strand of hair behind Valentina's ear. "I told you, anything."

Valentina snuggled close and whispered in her ear, "Teach me."

TWENTY-ONE

ANDIE STRETCHED her legs out as far as they would reach, the bed's sheets silky yet crisp against her bare skin. *How do hotels manage it?* she wondered as her brain emerged from the blissful fog of sleep. No matter how high a thread count she bought, they were never this luxurious at home. She stretched some more, raking her toes along a surface that was softer still, supple and warm, and delightfully without clothing. *Never mind the sheets. The important question is how did I get lucky enough to manage this?*

Their night together had been everything Andie hoped for, and nothing like she'd expected. In her imagination, Valentina was a shy novice when it came to lovemaking, an inexperienced beginner in need of a good teacher. How wonderfully, spectacularly wrong she'd been. Whatever she'd lacked in finesse, Valentina had more than made up for with the passionate nature she so often tried to hide. She hadn't been hiding it last night. There was nothing Andie wanted more than to spend the rest of the day in bed attempting to recreate the experience as many times as possible, lest she ever be tempted to forget Valentina's true nature in the future.

Valentina shifted as their flesh came in contact, her body perfectly filling any space between them like molten caramel spreading to fill the corners of a pan. Her back pressed against Andie's breasts, whose nipples immediately formed two hard peaks. Her rounded bottom nestled into the hollow made by Andie's pelvis and thighs, as if she'd been created to occupy that space. Electricity hummed. With gentle insistence, Andie maneuvered her knee until her lower leg was sandwiched between Valentina's smooth calves. It was a perfect fit.

Everything about Valentina was a perfect fit, a fact that Andie wasn't sure how to handle. It was something she hadn't been looking for, hadn't expected to find, and her time in Italy was running short. Soon, she'd be back in New York City, while Valentina would remain in Montamore. What sort of a future could there be for them? Deep in the pit of her stomach was a hollowness, a gnawing that she knew even the arrival of the elaborate room service breakfast she'd arranged to be delivered later that morning would do nothing to assuage. But what else was there to do, except seize every minute of the time they had?

Andie cupped her hand around Valentina's shoulder, who made a mewling sound in response but otherwise continued her slumber. Andie's fingers twitched, unable to keep from stroking the velvety skin beneath their tips, she then trailed them toward Valentina's bent elbow, leaving goosebumps along the flesh in her wake. Her fingers rounded the curve and continued down the forearm, until they reached the spot where Valentina's arm disappeared beneath her breasts. Here Andie paused and shifted upward, teasing the soft nub of Valentina's nipple until the skin tightened and puckered in response. Her mouth watered as she recalled the feel of Valentina's nipples against her lips, the taste of them in her mouth. Her palms ached with the memory of the weight of her breasts, and her nose twitched as if once again breathing in the faint smell of lavender oil as she'd buried her face into the valley between them.

Valentina stirred in her arms, rolling with a fluid motion to face her. "Good morning," she murmured, eyes still stubbornly closed against the sunrise that had begun to encroach on the darkness.

Arms and legs encircled Andie, trapping her in a fluffy cloud made of equal parts satisfaction and lust. "Good morning." She dipped her chin to kiss the tip of Valentina's nose.

"What time is it?"

"Why? In a rush to be somewhere?" Andie teased. Before Valentina could reply, a buzzing vibration coming from the direction of the nightstand shattered the tranquility.

"No, but are you?" Valentina cracked open one eye. "I think that's your alarm."

Reluctant to remove herself from Valentina's embrace, Andie flung one arm behind her and rooted around blindly for the phone. She held it to her face and squinted as the bright glare of the screen burned a permanent rectangle onto her retinas. She frowned to see the familiar face of her assistant accompanying an incoming call. "It's my assistant."

"You should answer it."

Andie hesitated a second, then nodded. She swung her legs off the bed, then walked toward the bathroom while

Valentina snuggled deeper into the covers. When she'd closed the bathroom door, she answered. "Tracy?"

"Oh, thank God. You're up."

"Yes, I'm up. Barely." She squinted at the hook on the door where she'd hoped to find a robe, but it was bare. She crossed her arms in front of her, shivering. "Why are you? It must be the middle of the night in New York."

"Just past midnight."

"On Easter weekend." As Andie's head cleared, her confusion grew. "What are you doing in the office?"

"I'm on my cellphone at home."

"Yeah, but on Easter," Andie repeated. "I appreciate your dedication, but this is taking things too far. Go to bed or the bunny can't fill your basket."

"Don't worry, I'm headed that way now, but I had to call as soon as I found out."

"Found out what?"

"Duncan King's been given the ax. I can't believe you pulled it off like that!"

"Me?" Andie's heart raced and the word came out more loudly than she'd intended. She cracked the door open and took a peek, but Valentina continued to snooze. Wanting to watch her sleep, Andie kept the door open but lowered her voice to a whisper. "What did I have to do with it?"

"Remember those documents you sent to be translated? You know, those old notebooks that were in Italian."

"The ones Valentina gave me?"

"Those are the ones! Hey, speaking of Valentina, how did it go last night? Is she there right now?"

"Um, yeah." Andie squirmed, preferring to follow a no-kissing-then-telling policy. "She's here. What exactly is going on?"

"I don't know how you two found them," Tracy's voice nearly sang through the phone, "but when the translator got through, I realized immediately that I'd seen those recipes before."

"Which recipes? I thought I was only sending you some substitution instructions." Andie frowned. What exactly had been in those notes?

"There was an old cookbook, out of print and originally published in Italian."

"What does that have to do with Duncan?" Andie's heart still raced, but she had no idea why. What could any of this have to do with her?

"As part of his settlement with Sizzle, the network had agreed to produce his cookbook. I had the proofs come across my desk a few weeks ago, which is why it triggered my memory. When I compared them side by side, at least a dozen recipes were nearly identical, like way too much to be a coincidence. We had a librarian in the New York Library archives do some more digging, and she was able to find a match to out-of-print, foreign language cookbooks for almost every recipe."

Andie's breath caught in her chest. "Are you saying that he plagiarized his book?"

"That's exactly what I'm saying, lifted from several different and obscure sources, so that I'm sure he never thought he would get caught. But once we were on to him, that was the only excuse the network needed to tear up his contract and send him packing."

As Andie ended the call, her whole body shook, and not just because she'd been chatting on the phone for several minutes while completely naked. Duncan King was finished!

When it came to her career, she couldn't have asked for better news.

Andie steadied her hand enough to place the phone on the nightstand, then crawled back under the covers. Valentina's body heat hit her like a warm breeze on a summer's day and took her breath away. She wanted to wrap herself around her and never let go. The only thing that held her back was knowing that Valentina would find her frozen limbs about as enjoyable as a bucket of ice water. But as if she could read her mind, Valentina rolled toward her, engulfing Andie in a heaven of heat and lavender.

"What was that all about?" Valentina's whisper tickled Andie's shoulder.

"Remember Duncan King?"

"The one who started those rumors about you and the judge?" Valentina's face puckered like she'd sucked on a lemon. "I remember him."

"Well, he's history." Giddiness like champagne bubbles tickled Andie's insides as she shared the news. "Given the ax. All because of you." She clasped Valentina tightly, kissing her on the forehead.

"What did I do?" Valentina asked, snuggling closer into the embrace.

"That old cookbook your teacher copied for you. Tracy had it translated."

"Yeah, it was pretty popular a long time ago."

"Yeah, at least popular enough that the New York Library had a copy in its archives. Turns out, Duncan pulled recipes from that same book, plus a bunch of other out-of-print books, then put them all together and passed it off as his own."

"And they fired him?" Valentina laughed. "Goodness!

Sizzle must be dying to get you back to New York. With him gone, there's no question you're their biggest star."

Andie's spirits deflated like a month-old helium balloon. "I hadn't thought of that."

Valentina scanned her face, her dark eyes filled with tender caring. "What's wrong? Shouldn't you be happy?"

"I am. I just hope they don't need me too soon." Andie forced herself to smile. "I have a lot of work to finish here first, before I'll be ready to go." Work was the farthest thing from her mind. She'd been counting on several more weeks with Valentina, and for the first time in her life, she wasn't willing to compromise for the sake of her career.

"I'm sure work will understand." Valentina's expression faltered, but then she smiled brightly. "This calls for a celebration."

Andie sighed. "Yeah, I guess we'll have to get out of bed and get dressed eventually, anyway."

"Why?" Valentina's brow furrowed. "Putting on clothes would ruin the celebration I had in mind."

As if to demonstrate, Valentina pressed her mouth to Andie's collarbone and began to nibble her way toward her throat. Andie's body responded instantly with an explosion of electric sparks deep inside her groin. She'd just captured Valentina's head, and was weighing whether to encourage her to move up toward her lips or down in the direction of those sparks, when the phone vibrated again.

"Damn." She swiped the phone off the nightstand and once again saw Tracy's photo on the screen as she answered. Prying herself out of bed for a second time was torture, and her tone was sharp as she shuffled toward the bathroom again. "What is it now?"

"I'm so sorry, Andie, but I almost forgot. Jessica

Balderelli wants to meet next week in Rome to talk about your idea for the show."

Andie expelled her breath in a quick puff as she stole a glance into the bedroom, where Valentina was disappearing under the covers with a look of agitation that rivaled her own. At any other time, Andie would have been thrilled to have so many career opportunities to discuss, but right now she had better things to do. "I'd forgotten about that. But how do you know about the show? Jessica's working with a different network to develop it."

"I know. She told me all about it when she offered to bring me on board, which is another reason I'm calling from home. I see how things have been at Sizzle, and if your show's as brilliant as I know it's going to be, then I want in. This would be such a huge step up for me!"

Andie squeezed her eyes shut. She couldn't think about this right now. Besides, she was back in Sizzle's good graces, and so she didn't have to, right? "Tracy, I'm so sorry, I'm afraid I haven't come up with anything. There's no idea to pitch. You'll have to tell her I can't do the meeting."

"Oh."

Even four thousand miles away, Andie could tell that single syllable spelled trouble. "What?"

"It's just, I guess with everything that's been going on, I kind of assumed. All those chefs you've been contacting… and then I wanted to make a good impression on Jessica, and…Andie, I already told her you'd be there."

"Oh." After all Tracy had done for her, Could Andie really bail on the meeting and make her assistant look bad?

"I also sent her the specs on that property. Is that not part of it, either?"

"Part of what?" Andie's head was beginning to spin. "I don't remember any property."

"That old cooking school, the one with the commercial kitchen."

Andie groaned. It was the house Valentina had wanted, the one Andie had daydreamed about giving her, all wrapped up in a bow. But of course, Tracy would have assumed she'd had a practical reason for asking.

"I thought it was related. I'm so sorry, Andie. This was stupid of me. I was trying so hard to prove to Jessica that I could be the miracle worker you always say I am, and I've totally screwed it up."

"It was an honest mistake," Andie assured her. Naturally, her assistant had assumed that she worked for a rational, sane woman, and not one who went around dreaming of buying houses for people she hardly knew. It was a mistake anyone could've made. But as she looked longingly at the lump in the covers under which Valentina's soft, supple body waited for her, she knew that dream would haunt her until her dying day. Even so, she regretted nothing.

"I'll call and cancel for you, first thing tomorrow, and explain to Jessica it was my fault."

"No." In a flash of either supreme brilliance or complete insanity, Andie was struck with a show idea that had the potential to bowl Jessica over, and one that just might solve a whole lot of problems for Andie, too. And as is so often the case with brilliance, one that could also fail spectacularly. "You know what, don't do anything for now. Let me think on it. When did Jessica want to meet?"

"Friday."

Andie's heart sank. "You don't mean this Friday, do you?"

Valentina sat up on the bed and poked her head out from beneath the duvet. "That's the day before the festival, Andie."

Andie nodded. The truth was, she knew all too well when the festival was. She'd spent several hours in the past week alone on the phone with two restaurants in Florence who had agreed to co-sponsor a booth, not to mention all the event details she'd sent to the web designer to design a basic landing page. She hadn't mentioned it to Valentina as she'd wanted it to be a surprise. But the fact that she'd asked for Tracy's help in those matters had led to a misunderstanding that could jeopardize her assistant's prospects for a better job. She had to make it right. "Tracy, how long's the investor meeting?"

"Just a few hours, at most."

"So, I can make it to Rome and back the same day?"

"I don't see why not," Tracy assured her.

"Okay, I'll be there." A mask of disappointment eclipsed Valentina's features as Andie again hung up the phone and returned to bed. "I'll only be gone for the day."

"But it's the day with the most preparation to do, and you said you'd help." Valentina continued to sulk. "Rome's not as close as you think. You might miss the festival completely."

"Val, I know what that festival means to you, okay?" Andie burrowed her hands under the covers and pulled Valentina close, stroking her back until she felt her begin to yield. "I won't miss it."

"Is it that important to your job that you go?"

"It's…" Andie chewed carefully on her words. She didn't want to give too much away until she knew for certain that she could pull this off. There was a lot of work to do before

Friday, and even with Tracy on the job, there were a million ways for it to go wrong. And even if she got her proposal together in time, Jessica could shoot it down. There was no sense getting Valentina's hopes up for nothing. "It's just a meeting, but I do need to go."

Valentina sighed, but nodded. "Okay, as long as you promise not to miss the festival."

"I promise." Andie let her hands drift down Valentina's spine until they rested at the small of her back. She inched them lower still. "Now, what were we doing before we were interrupted? I'm trying to recall."

"Seems like you recall just fine," Valentina quipped, but she made no attempt to wriggle free even as Andie's thumbs traced the crack of her bottom.

The phone rang again.

This time, Andie sat up and snatched the phone without a glance. "Tracy, why aren't you in bed yet?"

"Tracy. Is that her name?" A woman's voice that was definitely not Tracy's filled Andie's ears.

"What?"

"First, for the record, is Tracy the name of the woman you had dinner with in Florence last night?"

An icicle stabbed Andie's gut. "I didn't have—"

"We have pictures, Miss Bartlett."

Springing from the bed, Andie had the presence of mind to snatch one of the complimentary terry cloth robes from the spa that she'd tossed on the floor. Something told her this was not a conversation to have in the nude. She wrapped the robe tightly around herself, as if even now there might be a camera lens trained on her, despite being in a very private second-floor suite.

"Who is this?" Andie hissed when she'd reached the privacy of the bathroom. This time, she shut the door tight.

"This is Gloria Johnson from the *Metro Sun*."

The Metro Sun? Jesus. When it came to journalism, they were about half a step up from the *Star Post*, at best. "What is it you want?"

"An exclusive, Miss Bartlett. Your fans have been looking for you, you know. It's been a real mystery. They would salivate over pictures of you and a mystery woman having a night on the town in Florence. But I'm a serious journalist."

"Sure you are."

"And the *Metro Sun* is a serious newspaper," Gloria continued, ignoring Andie's insult. "Surely you'd much rather I run a real story than some grainy photos of you getting cozy with your new girlfriend. Wouldn't you?"

"Oh, do I get a choice?" Andie pictured Valentina waiting for her on the other side of the bathroom door, so blissfully unaware that all of her secrets were inches away from being spilled. It was the one thing she'd promised, even as she'd worked endlessly to seduce her. Total secrecy. No one would ever need to know. Andie snarled at the phone. If Valentina got caught up in this scandal, she'd never forgive herself.

"That's exactly what I'm trying to offer. A choice. We can run the photos, complete with tabloid-style headline, or you can agree to sit down for a one-on-one, exclusive interview. That way, we keep it classy, and you get to tell your side of things."

"I don't really have a side of things, Gloria."

"Oh, I'm sure that's not true."

Andie cracked the door open. Valentina had risen from the bed and clothed herself in the remaining terry robe and was now lounging near the large window that overlooked the garden. The curtains were tightly drawn, but at any moment she might decide to open them to let in the sunlight. What if Gloria's photographer was waiting outside now?

"When you say keep it classy, does that mean my private life stays out of it?"

"If you mean the woman in the photos, then yes. If you agree to let me send a film crew out to get the interview, she doesn't need to be a part of the story."

Andie's eyes narrowed. "The *Metro Sun*'s a newspaper. What do you need a film crew for?"

"Are you kidding?" Gloria's laugh was high-pitched and unpleasant. "It's the age of the internet. Nobody reads print anymore. Hell, nobody reads. It's all about video streaming. We get paid for advertising, and streaming an exclusive interview with Andie Bartlett about the Duncan King scandal will get clicks. So will the one of the girlfriend. I don't give a shit which one we go with, to be frank. I get paid either way."

With her free hand, Andie balled up the scratchy cloth belt at her waist and gave it a squeeze. *An interview.* What would the network say when they found out. Andie gave a humorless laugh. They would have just two words for her. *You're fired.* She squeezed the fabric tighter, her finger turning as white as the robe. *But if I say no, what will happen to Valentina?* The tips of her fingers grew numb.

"I'll tell you what. Take the rest of the day to think about it. You have my number. If I don't hear from you by five o'clock this evening with a time and location for the interview, I'll assume you'd rather go with the tabloid photos."

With that, the line went quiet. Andie took a deep breath, then slipped her phone in the robe pocket. She paused to check her expression in the mirror, smoothing it until it looked as if nothing were amiss. When she reentered the bedroom, Valentina gave her a brilliant smile. "What was that?"

"Oh, nothing," Andie said. "There's going to be a TV reporter coming to Montamore later this week to do a little interview."

"An interview?" Valentina's smile widened to a grin. "You mean, about the festival? Oh, Andie! I can't believe this. Is this another one of Tracy's miracles? You really weren't joking about her."

"YEAH…SHE'S SOMETHING, RIGHT?" Andie let out a shaky breath. She'd made this mess all on her own, and she could only pray that her trusty assistant would find her a way out of it. Five days to write a proposal for a new show from scratch, and deliver it perfectly to a room filled with stuffy investors, or her career was history. No problem. But what was it that Valentina had just said about the festival?

Airtime for the festival. That wasn't a bad trade. She'd call Gloria and tell her she'd only do the interview if her crew also agreed to film a segment about the festival and she arranged for it to be run on all the local news stations before Saturday. For a spontaneous idea, this one wasn't half bad. Keeping Valentina's face out of tomorrow's tabloids was her main goal, but why not try to give the festival a boost, too?

"A segment on the news could draw in hundreds of tourists. Andie, you're a genius!"

"And there will be a link in the *Metro Sun* to the festival website, for good measure." Andie grinned. Why the hell not, at this point?

But Valentina frowned. "The festival doesn't have a website."

"Actually," Andie's grin turned to a more sheepish smile, "it does. I ran into your friend Francesca the other day, and, well, she mentioned she was one of the organizers, and—"

"Let me guess," Valentina said, her expression knowing, "she roped you into volunteering. I swear, she has no shame." It was clear from the way she said it that Valentina didn't hold this trait against her best friend. "Thank you."

"It was no big deal. I got in touch with a guy, and it took him about fifteen minutes to put something together."

Valentina beamed. "Is there any problem you can't find a solution to?"

"I can think of one." Actually, she could think of several, but only one that Valentina could know about.

"Maybe I can help you solve it. You're amazing, you know that?"

Andie wasn't sure about amazing, but she was resourceful when she wanted to be. Would that be enough to find a solution to the hornet's nest of problems she'd just created for herself and her career? Maybe, maybe not. She could worry about that over the next five days. Right now there was something more pressing, and she definitely needed Valentina's help with the solution.

Andie crossed the room and slipped her arm around Valentina's waist. "I can't stop time. This weekend will be over before we know it, and you already know what it's like trying to get a moment alone back home."

By home, of course she'd meant Montamore, a town where she was no more than a short-term guest. But there was something different about the place from any other place she'd been, something that drew her in and held her. She had a pretty good idea what that something was, and it was standing right in front of her.

Valentina. Montamore. Home. The words filled her with a sense of belonging stronger than she'd ever felt. The sudden pang of impending loss caught her off guard, and she pulled Valentina tightly against her to ward away the emptiness.

"Then we have no time to waste." Valentina leaned fully against her, sighing as Andie slipped her hand between them to untie the belt of her robe. She gave her shoulders a wiggle, letting the robe slip to the floor. She held out her hand and Andie took it, leaving her own robe behind on the floor beside Valentina's as she followed her to the bed.

The feeling of connection flooded Andie as their bodies came together, a million times more powerful than before. Who would have thought that home would turn out not to be a place, but a person. This person. Valentina. But Valentina's home was in Montamore, and so somehow, Andie's needed to be, too. She had one real shot at making that work, but time was running out and there was a good chance she could be left with nothing.

TWENTY-TWO

BALANCED on the edge of a leather chair, on one end of a long boardroom table in Rome, Andie could barely recall the week that had just passed. All she knew was that everything that needed to be done, by some divine miracle, had been done. She had no idea how it had happened, except that she'd been determined that failure on any front was not an option. The details of the booth for the Florentine chefs had been finalized. The interview had been given, complete with plenty of footage of the villagers preparing for the festival. She'd even helped Valentina scrub and polish the woodwork in the shop until she was certain she'd lose the use of her arms for good.

But perhaps most important to her future was that in front of each potential investor who sat with her around the table was a thick folder, its pages filled with a proposal for a show that just might be the solution to all her problems. Jessica Balderelli was seated halfway around the table, leafing through the pages. Beside her to the right sat Tracy, already positioning herself to become Jessica's right-hand woman. Tracy was not reading the proposal. There was no need for her to read it. Once Andie had fleshed out her idea, Tracy had been the one to pull it together into something that resembled a well-thought-out and professional report. If they got the green light, Jessica would be a fool not to hire Tracy on the spot.

Other than those two familiar faces, Andie found herself surrounded by a dozen men in expensive European suits. The network that would be producing the show was mostly women, and yet as these things too often went, the people holding the purse strings were all men. *That's okay*, Andie worked to convince herself. *Men find me plenty charming too, when I try*. All that stood between her and her dreams was convincing them to write her a check for several million dollars. No pressure, right? Andie reached for the pitcher of water on the table, her mouth as dry as cotton.

One of the men, who looked like he probably slept on a mattress made out of stacks of money, flipped the cover of his folder shut and pushed it a few inches away from himself. Andie hadn't been able to tell if he'd read a single word, or if he was content just to thumb through the pages and let the breeze fan his face. Maybe he'd absorbed the information through his pores. "Miss Bartlett, why don't you explain to all of us what makes this proposal unique."

Andie took another sip from her glass, then set it down, hoping the shakiness she felt inside didn't show in her movements. She ran a hand through her hair, then shook out the short locks. It was still the coppery color she'd chosen for Florence and, though it was a more professional look that suited the current audience, she missed the dayglow orange. For some reason, she positively exuded confidence when her head looked like it had just burst into flames. She took a cleansing breath. *No more stalling. You've got this.*

"What makes this show unlike any other is its multi-generational format." The investors nodded, seemingly impressed, and across the table Tracy flashed a quick thumbs-up. *I'm the one who should be doing that to her,* Andie thought. *Multi-generational was her word.* "Most cooking shows have one, and only one, category of cook in mind. The busy mom who needs to make a quick dinner. The aspiring chef who wants to get every detail just right. The kid learning to put together a healthy snack. But that's not how we live, so why keep everyone in separate groups? With my show, families can watch together. They'll watch together, learn together, and cook together. And what they gain from that experience will keep them coming back for more."

There were nods from around the table. Andie held her breath. Were they convinced? When the idea had finally come to her, it had been so brilliant, and yet so simple that she couldn't help feeling she should have seen it all along. How many times had she heard the complaints? The older generation feared their knowledge was being lost. The younger generation felt too harried to prepare meals the way they'd been taught. And the children? More often than not, they were left as Andie had been, to figure it out for themselves. So why not bring everyone together and help them to appreciate the others' perspectives in a fun and entertaining way? It had been right in front of her nose this whole time, but before meeting Valentina and her family, and spending time in Montamore, Andie knew she'd never have seen it.

Finally, the same man who'd spoken before addressed

her again. "So, this will be filmed in the studio in New York?"

Andie's stomach flopped like she was hurtling along the downward slope of a roller coaster. This was the pivotal point of her plan, the thing that her future hinged on, but it appeared that none of the investors had read that far. What if they said no? She opened her mouth, but nothing came out.

Tracy swooped in for the rescue. "If you open to appendix B, gentlemen, you'll see more details of the proposed filming location. I think we can all agree that with a groundbreaking show like this, we need an authentic European setting."

If she didn't think it would shock Tracy and make Valentina angry if she found out, Andie could've kissed her assistant right then and there. The investors, who were all staunchly and unquestionably European, had begun to nod with a certain smugness at the mention of the words "groundbreaking" and "authentic" in connection to their home continent. Tracy had hooked them. Now Andie just needed to reel them in.

"As you can see, we've been able to locate a well-equipped kitchen in a rustic setting that's perfect for our needs." All around the table, photos of Montamore's closed cooking school, with its massive commercial kitchen and abundant country charm, peeked out of the packets.

"And the owner's willing to lease it to us?" the group's spokesman asked.

Andie's muscles tensed. This was it. "Well, that's the best part. There is no owner at the moment. It's owned by the bank and due to come up soon for auction, but we have it on good authority that they'd be willing to take a cash offer at any time."

"You want us to buy it?" The spokesman frowned. "That's highly irregular. What would we do with it after we're done? No show lasts forever, Miss Bartlett."

"Compared to studio costs in New York, buying the building is a bargain. You'd pay the same to own the place as you would to lease something similar for just three seasons. So, my proposal is this..." She glanced at Tracy, who gave her an encouraging nod. This idea, too, had come from her trusty assistant, and Andie was rapidly rethinking the whole kissing thing. *Maybe a quick peck on the cheek?* "If the show goes three seasons or more, you sign the property over to me at the end as part of my compensation. If not, I buy out the difference between the sale price and a standard lease." Either way, in three years' time, Andie would own the old Tuscan farmhouse outright, which meant Valentina's Cioccolatini di Venere was that much closer to finding a new home for expanding their distribution capabilities.

The room was so quiet that Andie swore she could hear the movement of the hands of the clock on the wall. Just as she thought she couldn't take it anymore, the spokesman's voice broke the silence. "We'll look over the details before signing, but if everything is as you described it, I think we have a deal."

Andie's heart was about to burst through her chest. Could this really be happening? Across the table, Jessica and Tracy were beaming. It had to be real.

"Congratulations, Andie," Jessica said, coming around the table to shake her hand as soon as the meeting had adjourned. Tracy followed, giving her a big hug. "This was exactly the type of proposal I was hoping for from you."

"I'll admit, I surprised myself with it."

"It's brilliant. Refreshing and new. And Sizzle would never have taken a chance on it. You know how they like everything to fit neatly into a box over there."

Andie couldn't have agreed more, but the mention of her network employer sent an unexpected shot of nervousness through her. In the unlikely event that she could weather the storm that tonight's televised interview would create, as soon as word got out on this deal, she'd be sunk as far as Sizzle was concerned. "What do you think they'll do when they find out?"

Jessica's expression turned serious. "We've had our lawyers read over your contract to make sure you're not in violation, but we'd be kidding ourselves if we thought they'd take it well."

"They'll cancel your expense account," Tracy added. "Any vendor contracts, sponsorships. The minute I gave my notice the other day, I was completely locked out."

"You've given notice? So, I take it you officially got the job as Jessica's assistant?" Andie asked with a grin.

"Assistant?" Jessica scoffed, patting Tracy on the shoulder. "She's much too valuable to be my assistant. Tracy's my new vice president. This woman's a miracle worker."

Andie laughed as Tracy blushed. "You don't have to tell me. So, your days at the Sizzle Network are done?"

"Completely," Tracy confirmed. "They wouldn't even let me work the standard two weeks, which is why I was able to accompany Jessica to this meeting."

"That was quick. They'll cancel everything, huh?" Andie asked, thinking of her means of transportation back to Montamore. "What about the rental car? How long do you think it will take them to cancel that?"

"Rental?" Tracy's face reflected surprise. "Oh, that's not a rental. Are you kidding? It would have cost more to rent it for this long than it was worth, so I just bought it. Didn't you read the paperwork?"

"It was in Italian. I signed on the line and took the keys. I guess they'll need it back, even so."

"I don't see why. It's in your name, so legally it's yours. The apartment lease, on the other hand…"

Jessica spoke up. "Not to worry. If you end up needing a place to stay, the farmhouse should have more than enough room for you, Andie. Why don't we plan to meet on Monday with the property agents to get things started? Tracy will send you the details."

It was late in the afternoon by the time Andie found herself climbing through the open front of the micro-car. *Her* micro-car. Andie chuckled, feeling a certain pride of ownership as she settled onto the familiar bench seat, which she still thought was ridiculously small, even if it did belong to her now. She started the engine, no longer finding its rattling sounds nearly as disturbing as she once had. Maybe the stupid little thing was growing on her.

She checked the time on her phone, noted the battery was running low, and dreading the possibility of irate messages from Sizzle if word got out faster than expected, she switched it off and placed it in her purse. Only after doing so did it occur to her she should have sent a text to Valentina to let her know she was on her way back, but it was too late now. Besides, at just over two hours, it was a quick trip home.

Home. The word, which had expanded in meaning so much recently, suddenly held yet one more. If all went well, she was on her way to owning a rustic farmhouse of her own. Who would've dreamed? The purchase of the old cooking school would give her permanence in the village, a claim of belonging. Though much of her life was still tied to New York, and likely would remain so, she now had proof that she'd always come back. She knew it would be key to getting what she wanted most, which was not the new contract and show, but Valentina.

She knew Valentina well enough now to realize that tangible proof of her intentions would be vital in convincing her to give a real relationship between them a chance. It wasn't their original agreement, but Andie didn't care. After their weekend in Florence, she had to try. She had to try because she was in love with Valentina, and there was no use denying it. Whatever it might take to win Valentina's heart, she was willing to do it.

Andie started the car and pulled out onto the crowded Roman street. Though she would've preferred to wait for lighter traffic, keeping her promise to Valentina that she would make it back before the festival was more important, and so she gripped the wheel and fought her way out of the city. Only when she'd reached the wide-open space of a back road did she relax, but it turned out to be too soon. Somewhere between Rome and Montamore, on a stretch of deserted highway without a town in sight, what had started as a mere rattle was joined by a whining whistle, and then a series of thuds. With a stutter and a puff of exhaust, the tiny car she'd just been learning to love came to a halt.

Andie was stranded, betrayed by her very own clown car.

VALENTINA CHECKED HER WATCH. It was at least the

hundredth time in the past minute, and her wrist was starting to ache from all the turning. The silence of an empty apartment buzzed in her ears. Chiara was with her father, and her mother and grandmother were downstairs, probably already parked in front of the television. In fact, all around the village at that very moment, the residents of Montamore would be sitting down to turn their sets on, waiting for the news to begin. Tonight was the night that the special report on the spring festival would air, and everyone was eager to see which people were featured and which businesses made the cut. Being featured on TV would be the highlight of at least a decade, if not the entire life, of every person who called the village home. But even though Valentina had been instrumental in bringing it about, she had other things on her mind.

Andie had yet to make it home from Rome.

Valentina paced the floor of her living room. Even with Friday traffic, Andie should've been back over an hour ago. But every time Valentina had attempted to call, which had been almost as frequently as she'd checked her watch for the time, it had gone to voicemail. Valentina checked her phone once more, but there were no messages. There was, however, a new email. One look at the subject line and her heart plummeted to the pit of her stomach. It was an official notice from the Sizzle Network, canceling the lease on Andie's apartment. Effective immediately.

Valentina shivered, though her apartment was warm. Wrapping her arms tightly across her chest, she quickened her pacing back and forth across the floor, wondering what it could mean. Had the network been so eager to get Andie back to New York that they'd ended her sabbatical early? Is that why she hadn't called? Andie had never told her what the meeting was about, but with the firing of Duncan King, they had to be desperate to have Andie back in the spotlight at home. Valentina stopped in her tracks as a terrible possibility presented itself. What if Andie was already on a plane, and had left Italy for good?

She wouldn't do that. She promised she'd be home for the festival. But Valentina's entire body had gone cold. *Home.* This wasn't Andie's home, and though she'd made promises, there were any number of reasons she might have chosen not to keep her word. Andie had made it clear from the start that her career was her life. Her relationships had always taken a backseat to her work, Andie had admitted as much. And what they had together wasn't even that. *What am I to her, really?* And though it hurt like a knife to her chest, Valentina had to face the truth. She was an unimportant woman in an insignificant town in a country Andie barely liked, and that she planned to leave in a handful of weeks, anyway. And wasn't that exactly how Valentina had wanted, even demanded, for it to be? Sure, she may have changed her mind about having a casual fling, but how was Andie supposed to know?

She began her pacing again, but the movement failed to bring her relief, and so finally she stopped and flipped on the television. The segment on the festival had already begun, and it calmed her nerves somewhat to see the familiar sights of her beloved town. She smiled as she saw the pizzeria, then the front of her own shop, followed by a sweeping shot of the central piazza that came to rest on Cupid's fountain. Her smile faded. *Well, I guess they couldn't get away with not showing it, could they,* she reasoned. The reporter was standing so that the waters of the fountain sprayed in a mist behind her. Valentina's chest seized briefly as the camera revealed Andie, standing just beside her. *I guess they couldn't get away with not showing her, either.* Valentina's knees grew wobbly. *She looks so beautiful on TV.* But she was a hundred times more attractive in person, and Valentina prayed that the screen wasn't the only way she'd be seeing her in the future.

Until then, Valentina had paid little attention to what was being said, but suddenly her own face flashed onto the screen, a grainy image of her snuggled against Andie as they'd walked along the Ponte Vecchio the weekend before. They'd only been that way for a second, she was certain. They'd been so careful most of the time. Figuring out how that fleeting moment had been captured took all of her mental energy until Valentina heard the reporter's voice say something that turned her entire body to stone.

"And could love be in the air for famous chef Andie Bartlett and local chocolate maker, Valentina Moretti? We've heard plenty of rumors that the American has found a new girlfriend here in town, but only Cupid knows for sure!"

She'd felt the sensation once before, the endless falling followed by a thousand tiny needles piercing her flesh as the frozen water of Cupid's fountain soaked her to the core. She felt the same way now, though she remained upright, her feet rooted to the floor. Had the reporter just said what she thought she'd said? *Have I just been outed on national television?* Her body quaked from the inside. The phone in her pocket rang, and her mother's stern visage stared her down from the screen.

It then occurred to her that a reporter had just told her *mother* that she was Andie Bartlett's new girlfriend.

She needed to escape. The minute this thought entered her mind, her body unfroze and she raced down the stairs.

Thankfully, the two old ladies who lived on the first floor weren't as spry as they once were and, by the time she heard the squeak of their apartment door, she'd already bolted into the piazza. She thought she heard her grandmother call her name, but she didn't turn. All she wanted was to get away.

But where could she go to get away from this? Her secret had just been announced to the entire village. The entire *country* had just been told that she was in a relationship with Andie Bartlett, with a photograph to prove it. Hell, all of America had probably seen it, too. *Everyone* knew. She could run as far as she liked, but she could no longer outrun the truth.

TWENTY-THREE

THE WORST THING about *sobbing uncontrollably,* Valentina thought as she drew in a spluttering breath, *is how stuffy your nose gets.* Her face was buried in her hands, and her palms were wet with a sticky combination of tears and mucus instead of the usual perspiration. She'd never thought the day would come when she'd miss her sweaty palms, but they were a far better alternative to this.

Valentina's eyes were shut as she sat hunched over on a cold tile floor with her back against the unyielding surface of a closed door. Neither the door nor the floor belonged to her, but in her distress, her memory had gone a little fuzzy as to where she was or why. She just knew that nothing was the way she wanted it to be, and there was no one to make it better.

"Valentina?" It was Francesca's voice she heard as footsteps echoed in the stairwell, but even with her eyes still closed, it took only a second for Valentina to be certain that she was not outside her best friend's door. No, it was definitely Andie's door. She remembered now. Andie, who was not home. Andie, who hadn't kept her promise. Andie, who as of this evening's email apparently didn't even live here anymore. Andie, who was almost certainly not her girlfriend, considering the bleak litany of facts she'd just ticked off in her head, and despite what the entire population of the planet had heard on this evening's news. Andie wasn't her girlfriend, and only now that it was too late did Valentina realize with complete clarity just how much she wished for her to be. A vast chasm echoed inside her with an emptiness that only Andie could fill.

"I don't want to talk about it." Valentina assumed that what 'it' was did not require further elaboration, all things considered.

"You can't just sit in the hallway all night waiting for her."

"Waiting for whom?" Valentina asked, because the first step in convincing herself that she wasn't pining for Andie was convincing someone else. "I'm not waiting for her. I don't want to see her anyway."

"Sure, you don't." Francesca wasn't buying it, nor should she. Valentina's efforts at persuasion had been pathetic. "That's why you're sitting in front of her door at this hour."

Valentina ventured to open her lids enough to peer at her watch through a curtain of tears. It was almost ten. Valentina squeezed her eyes shut as a new deluge of saltwater threatened to overflow. Ten o'clock and she hadn't heard a single word from Andie. The possibility that she was never going to was becoming more real by the minute.

"Isn't it time to go home and go to bed?" Francie's tone was gentle, like one a mother uses when her child's puppy has gone missing, but Valentina bristled nonetheless.

"Nope." Her family was at home, and the prospect of

facing their inquisitive, accusing faces made her want to throw up. "I'm not going home. Not now. Besides, I don't think I can sleep."

"Come on, then. Let's go back to my place. We can talk there."

"But Paolo will be there." No offense to Paolo, but Valentina lacked the capacity for social niceties right now.

"No. He's working late because of the festival. I would be, too, except my head hurts."

"Your feet are swollen, too," Valentina remarked, her vantage point so close to the ground gave her a clear view of her friend's puffy limbs. They had to hurt, standing like that on the hard floor. This fact persuaded her to comply where nothing else would. "Fine. Let's go back to your place, if only so you can prop them up."

They wound their way through corridors and staircases until they reached the part of the building that Francesca's family called home. The children were out, spending the night at their grandparents', leaving the usually chaotic place almost unnaturally quiet. As Francesca sat and propped her feet up on the coffee table, Valentina chose a seat across from her.

"You haven't asked me if it's true," she remarked with a resigned sigh.

"I didn't need to."

"You mean, you knew?"

"Not about Andie, but in general? I've always kind of thought...only then you met Luca, and they say La Fontana di Cupido is never wrong, but..."

Valentina nibbled her bottom lip, debating how to respond, but couldn't see the point in lying anymore.

"Cupid may or may not be wrong. I have no idea. I never saw anything in that stupid fountain."

Francesca looked taken aback. "You mean, you made it up?"

"I shouldn't have, but you all were all so certain of your futures, of who you wanted to be with, and there I was with the whole village looking at me. I couldn't very well tell them the truth." She tensed, waiting for Francesca to press for more and wondering if she would be forced to confess everything to her girlhood crush, but to her surprise, Francesca simply burst out in peals of laughter. Valentina's forehead furrowed. "What's so funny?"

"Oh, Valentina!" Francesca managed to say between gasps of breath. "You thought we had our whole lives figured out back then? Cara, we were fourteen!"

"Yes, but look at you and Paolo," Valentina countered. "You already knew! You gave Cupid your letter, and next thing you know, you and he are on baby number four."

Francesca's laughter subsided and her expression turned thoughtful. "Can I tell you the truth? It wasn't Paolo's name on that letter."

Valentina blinked. "What?"

"You've made your confession, now I have to make mine. The day you fell into the fountain, the boy whose name I'd written on my letter and risked my neck for was none other than Leonardo DiCaprio."

"Leonardo…the actor?"

"That's the one." For a moment, Francesca looked like she might start howling again, but she pressed her lips together and kept her composure. "In my defense, that *Titanic* movie had just been released a few weeks before, and I'd already seen it seven times."

"But," Valentina spluttered, "what about Paolo?"

"I love Paolo, obviously, but what can I say? Those dreamy eyes, and the way Leonardo had that floppy hair." She tried to recreate the look by wiggling her fingers over her forehead. "I couldn't help it. I was obsessed."

Valentina gasped. "I can't believe this. So, did you ever go back to Cupid again after that?"

"Why, to file an amendment?" Francesca chuckled. "No. When Paolo proposed, he said that Cupid had assured him I was the one. I figured that was good enough to straighten it all out. But what about you?"

"What about me?"

"You saw someone that day, in the fountain. I could see the surprise on your face right before you slipped."

"Maybe I was just surprised because I was falling into a fountain in the dead of winter. It's certainly not how I planned to spend my Valentine's Day."

"No," Francesca persisted, "it was before you started to fall. Was it Andie?"

"No," Valentina sighed, "I don't know. There may have been something there, but I was too scared to face it so I looked away."

"You could always go back now and ask."

"Now?" Valentina scoffed. "You mean march out to the center of town right now and climb up a fountain to talk to a statue. It's midnight. What would people think?"

"You're the only divorced woman in the history of Montamore, and they've just heard on the evening news that you're a lesbian, too. I imagine they think you're capable of any sort of crazy thing. But the more important question is, why do you care what they think?"

That really was the question, wasn't it? And the only

answer that came to mind was acceptance. What kind of a reason was that? Yet ever since she was young, she'd wanted to fit in, and had feared what would happen if anyone in her romance-obsessed village had figured out her secret. It was a foolish concern, a child's worry, and here she was a grown woman. If Chiara had made the same argument, she'd have set her straight on the spot.

Chiara. Now that was a worthy concern. Her daughter, and Mama, and Nonna, too. She may not care what the rest of the village thought, but what about them? Could they ever accept the truth they'd just learned?

"Francie, you may not have batted an eye at the news that your best friend's a lesbian, but what about my family? The kids at school will tease Chiara mercilessly if I confirm that it's true."

"Times are changing. You might be surprised."

"Well, what about Mama and Nonna? They're from a different generation. The times don't change so quickly for them."

"All the more reason to get Cupid on your side. They'll accept it, if he says they have to. Everyone will."

For the first time, Valentina considered the possibility that maybe, just maybe, Francie was right. When it came to her family, even if it wasn't easy for them at first, for her sake, they'd eventually come around. But what about everyone else? She doubted it would be as easy as Francie made it sound. But again, she had to ask herself, why did she care if they approved? She'd thought being alone would be the easiest way to get by in this town, but just the thought of Andie never coming back had her in agony. A life without Andie in it wouldn't be easier at all. And it would be emptier than she could bear.

Valentina lifted her chin and looked Francie square in the face. "I don't need Cupid to tell me what I already know. If such a thing exists, then I'm sure Andie Bartlett is the love of my life. I just need to get her back here so I can tell her so."

THERE WAS A SOUND, like the buzzing of a bumble bee, that roused Valentina from the fitful night of sleep she'd passed on Francie's sofa, just as the first rays of morning light were turning the darkness of the apartment's interior to lighter shades of gray. She reached for her phone, which she'd plugged into an outlet nearby, and the symbol that indicated a new text message flashed on the screen. Who would it be at this hour? Her mother? Andie? Hoping for the latter, she pressed her finger to the text icon.

The screen turned brilliant white as the message started to load, but her pupils shrank in a panic and for a heart-stopping moment, she couldn't see what it said. After several rapid blinks, she nearly sang with relief as she finally made out Andie's name, along with a message that read: *So sorry. Car broke down. Be there by noon.* Valentina grinned. Andie hadn't gone back to New York, and so she'd been given a chance, after all, to set everything right. She quickly tried calling, but it went to voicemail as it had before, and so after leaving a quick message to let her know she'd seen the text, a much happier Valentina put the phone away.

With the remnants of sleepiness chased away by excitement, Valentina hopped off the couch. Already, she could hear the sounds of merchants arriving in the piazza. Set up for the festival was well underway, and with the extra publicity, it promised to be a thrilling day. Back at the shop, her mother and grandmother would be heating the ovens for pastries, and probably wondering where she was, among other things. Her stomach clenched at the thought of facing them and whatever questions they had in store, but no amount of dread was sufficient to justify her being late for the baking on festival day. They might forgive her for being a lesbian, but if the shop ran short on *bomboloni*, she might as well plan on finding a new family.

As she crossed the piazza, the familiar rattle of carts was joined by the roar of diesel engines. Valentina could hardly believe her eyes as two trucks, of a size that rarely braved the narrow streets of Montamore, pulled into the square. Each had the name of a different prominent restaurant in Florence emblazoned on its side. They were newcomers to the festival, and though Andie hadn't admitted to it, Valentina was certain she'd been instrumental in getting them there. Between the festival's new website and the addition of two high profile booths, not to mention the added publicity of the news coverage—which, personal ramifications aside, Valentina knew would be beneficial in drawing a crowd—there was a real chance that this would be Montamore's most profitable festival in years. Despite her apprehension over the reception that awaited her at home, she felt her spirits lift.

The door to the shop was unlocked, as always, though the closed sign still hung there. Valentina's mother looked up from behind the chocolate case as she entered. Their eyes met, and Valentina froze. For a moment, it seemed that the world had ground to a halt. Even the sounds of festival preparation in the piazza had faded to nothing more than muffled background noise. Valentina was three years old again, trying to figure out how to convince her mother that the dark brown smears on her face were definitely not the chocolate she'd been told she couldn't have. Slowly, her mother untied the apron she was wearing and lifted it from around her neck, holding it out for Valentina to take.

"Nonna's still asleep. There's baking to do," her mother told her.

And that was it.

Grabbing the apron, Valentina tensed for what was to come, but moments later she scurried into the kitchen as her mother turned her attention back to arranging the truffles in the chocolate case as if she'd never stopped. By the time Valentina reached the sink, her hands trembled. She held them under the warm water, taking deep breaths and watching the soap bubbles circle the drain, until the shaking subsided.

What had just happened?

The look on her mother's face hadn't held a single clue as to her emotional state. Was she angry? Disappointed? Completely unperturbed? It was impossible to say. And why was Nonna still sleeping? Was she distraught from watching the news? Was she ill? Questions whirled around Valentina's brain as fast as the blade on her stand mixer as she prepared batch after batch of batter, but there were no answers to be had. Every time a floorboard creaked, Valentina held her breath, certain it was either her mother or Nonna coming in to have the dreaded talk, and yet as the morning wore on, it never happened. The older women worked in the front of the shop without so much as a word to her, leaving Valentina to stew for hours while she baked.

By ten o'clock, the first round of baked goods was finished and Valentina slipped unnoticed through the crowded shop to check out the festivities in the piazza. She stood in a shadowy spot near the edge of the building, a little removed, so she could watch without being seen. There were people everywhere, more people than she'd ever seen in Montamore before, or at least since she was a child. Every shop was bustling, and crowds had formed up and down the rows of vendors in their brightly colored tents. None of this compared to the fountain, where people young and old covered every surface of the stone basin. While some simply sat to rest, many others were attempting to reach Cupid, or stood waiting with scraps of paper clutched in their hands. At the rate that coins were being tossed in, Montamore would turn a healthy profit from wishes alone.

Valentina's shoulders shook with giddiness, the shadow of her private concerns momentarily brightened by optimism for her town. Even early in the day, it was clear that the success of the festival would far exceed her wildest expectations. She knew it wasn't as simple as a single day having the ability to save Montamore, but for the first time in years she felt hopeful that things might start to turn around. There might be a brighter future for this little village after all, and it was all thanks to Andie.

Valentina checked the time with nervous anticipation. Less than two hours to go until Andie returned. Would she be surprised by the festival's turnout? Proud? *Maybe*, Valentina thought, *but surely not inspired enough to stay.* The joy that had bubbled up so recently inside her subsided, replaced by doubt. She'd made up her mind the night before to tell Andie that she loved her and wanted a future with her, but she still had as little idea now as she had then of what that future could possibly look like. Perhaps she needed to face facts and admit that love wasn't enough. Not even in a town with its very own magical statue of Cupid.

She looked in the direction of her old nemesis. He had nothing to say to her today, being too busy smiling down on the hundreds of people who had flocked to Montamore to show him adulation. But what if she sought his help, as Francie had suggested she should do? Would he have an answer she'd overlooked? She reached into her pocket and touched the cold metal of a coin. Would that be enough to get him to spill his secrets?

As she took a step out of the shadows, she heard a man's voice call to her from the crowd, and turned to see Luca waving her down. Her ex-husband's expression was inscrutable, and instantly the jitters that had plagued her earlier when facing her mother returned. Even if he hadn't watched the news, which was unlikely, there was no way he'd avoided hearing about his ex-wife and her torrid affair with the American celebrity chef. Was it a torrid affair? It didn't matter. It was no doubt what they all assumed, and nothing traveled faster than gossip in a small town. She smiled weakly as she lifted her hand in acknowledgment, then took a step back, seeking the protection of shadows for both their sakes.

"I needed to talk to you," he said, apparently intent on skipping the pleasantries. It was hard to tell if he was angry with her, but if he were, he had every right to be. Valentina had been so concerned with how the village would perceive her after the newscast that she'd never stopped to think how Luca might feel. It was hardly the first time in their relationship that she'd overlooked that detail, and her regret was sincere.

"You saw the news? I'm so sorry, Luca. You shouldn't have found out that way."

His eyebrows shot up. "You mean, you and Andie Bartlett—that's true?"

"It's true enough," she replied, seeing no need to go into the intricacies of whether or not her relationship with Andie had a future. Her eyes widened as another thought occurred to her, and her heart started to beat faster. "Wait. Chiara, was she watching, too?"

"Don't worry. She's just a little girl. She had no idea what they were talking about."

Even with his reassurance, Valentina's head spun with how quickly her personal life had gotten out of her control, but to her surprise, Luca started to chuckle. "Why is this funny?" she snapped.

"It's not." Luca smoothed the smile from his face and his hazelnut eyes grew serious. "It's just there's something I haven't known how to tell you."

"You're not gay, are you?" Valentina had made the joke without thinking, but when he didn't answer for a moment, she froze in complete horror that she'd hit the nail on the head. Then he chuckled again.

"No. But I have been seeing someone, or trying to, anyway. It's a woman I knew a long time ago in school, before I came here. We reconnected online a while ago. The thing is, I've decided to move back near my old home, so we can be closer, and see where it goes."

Valentina's eyes widened. "It's that serious, then?"

He nodded. "There may be some career benefits to the move, too. But I'd be lying if I said it wasn't mostly for her. I've been thinking about it for months, but with the way everyone was always trying to convince us to get back together, I wasn't sure how you'd take it."

"Luca, I think it's wonderful."

"You know I'll still be there for Chiara. Maybe not three times a week, but holidays and summer, and—"

"Of course. You've always been an excellent father." On impulse, Valentina took Luca's hands and pressed them tightly between her own. "I really am happy for you. And I'm sincerely sorry that I wasn't completely honest with you about our chances from the start, or you might have felt free to take this opportunity long ago."

"It's a risk, but I know I'd regret it if I didn't do everything I could to make it work. I'd move to the other side of the world if I had to."

"Luca, did you happen to ask Cupid about it?"

Luca laughed. "No. I've never trusted that statue much, and I think I'd prefer to just see where I can get on my own."

"Smart choice. I'll think you'll do just fine." There was a look in Luca's eyes when he spoke of the woman back home that she'd never seen in all the years they'd been together, and that told her everything she needed to know.

Luca walked away, but Valentina remained where she was, watching the festival. She had her own woman to think about. Luca's words echoed in her head. *I'd move to the other side of the world if I had to.* Did she feel that way, too? If there was no other way to make it work, would she pick up and move to be with Andie? Maybe not year-round, but if Chiara went with Luca in the summer, it was possible, wasn't it, that she could give New York a try? Valentina glanced at the time and drew a shaky breath. Just thirty more minutes until noon, thirty more minutes until she saw Andie again and put everything on the line, and then she might just find out how far she was willing to go.

Keeping to the edges of the festival, she circled the piazza slowly until she reached the far side, determined to wait by Andie's door for her return. It wasn't technically Andie's apartment anymore, but as the property manager, it was up to her discretion how the property was used, and they would need a quiet place to talk. But as she reached for the door to the foyer, she heard Paolo call out.

"Valentina! There you are. Thank God." His voice sounded strangled, and when she spun to face him, Paolo's face was ashen.

"Paolo, what is it?"

"It's Francie. Her head aches so bad she feels sick, and her legs are swollen to the point she can barely stand. I can't leave the pizzeria unstaffed in the middle of the festival, but when I called for an ambulance they said they couldn't get through the streets with all the extra traffic. But she needs to get to a doctor."

"I'll take her." Valentina's hands were already digging through her pocket for her keys. Andie might be the love of her life, it was true, but if she were, then she would understand. If Francie and her baby were in danger, everything else, even Valentina's future, would have to wait.

TWENTY-FOUR

THE STREETS of Montamore were packed with festival goers as Andie slowly rolled into town. The first glimpse of its impossibly narrow streets filled her with sweet relief. Though her time in Rome had been a success, the trip home had been a disaster. Despite the assurances of a very nice mechanic she'd managed to track down just after sunrise in a tiny town a few miles from where she'd broken down, she'd been convinced that every rattle or ping spelled the end of her car for good. She'd held her breath most of the drive back. But now, as she pulled into the last spot available on a stretch of road for residents only, she allowed herself to relax. She'd made it, and in just a few more minutes she'd have the joy of witnessing Valentina's reaction as she shared her big news.

As she elbowed her way through the central piazza, the best comparison that came to mind was Times Square on a holiday weekend. Andie glowed with pride. Though she'd been unable to catch the segment on the news, it must have been a success. Now that she no longer had cause to be terrified for the future of her career, Andie couldn't help but think that the interview was the best thing that could've happened. Granted, she'd avoided all communication from the outside world by keeping her phone off since Rome, save for the brief text she'd sent to Valentina when her battery had recharged. By now, there was no doubt that her old network knew about the interview, and possibly her new contract, too. She preferred to deal with those consequences after she'd had a little more time.

Reaching La Fontana di Cupido, Andie stared in amazement. There were people everywhere, leaving letters and tossing coins into the basin's water, which was turning a little murky from all the paper. Across the way, long lines snaked out from the booths belonging to the two restaurants she'd personally persuaded to attend. She lifted one hand to indulge in a triumphant wave, but the chefs were too busy with festivalgoers to notice her. In fact, all around her, people were too busy to give her a second glance, despite her celebrity status. Frankly, Andie was relieved. It would make it easier to find Valentina, and she was the only person Andie really cared about right now.

She surveyed the piazza and weighed her options. After a night spent sleeping on the side of a country road with her knees bent at ninety-degree angles and her feet hanging out the car window, a hot shower in her apartment would be nice. But the chocolate shop was in the opposite direction, and that was where Valentina would be. A shower could wait.

She stepped into the shop, blinking as her eyes adjusted to the dim interior. Like outside, the shop was packed. While her mother and grandmother worked behind the counters, Valentina was nowhere to be seen. As Andie pondered the possibility of sending her a text, or more specifically debating whether to risk an onslaught of angry messages from Sizzle by turning her phone on again to do so, another group entered and the bells on the door jingled. Valentina's mother looked over at the sound, and as their eyes locked, a chill ran down Andie's spine. Celeste's expression was as cold as an Arctic wind. She had no idea what she'd done to offend the woman, but she had no desire to find out and quickly exited the shop. But that wasn't far enough.

"Miss Bartlett." It was Celeste.

Andie froze in place. She'd only made it a few steps, but somehow Valentina's mother had caught up with her in record time. There was an open hostility that seemed to ooze from her, a personality trait that Andie had never seen in the woman before. Sure, Celeste could be a little difficult and disapproving, but this was something else, and it made Andie nervous.

"Hi, Celeste. I was just trying to find Valentina."

Celeste's expression changed when Andie said Valentina's name. There was something almost wild about it, and for reasons she wasn't sure of, Andie got the impression of a mother bear protecting her cubs. "Oh? To turn in your key, I assume?"

Andie frowned. "Excuse me?"

"Your key." Celeste blinked, then sniffed. "I get copied in on the emails regarding the property management accounts. I see you've ended your lease, and so I assumed you'd come by to drop off the key."

"I...oh." *Perhaps*, Andie thought, *I should have read my messages after all*. "The lease was canceled, you say?"

"Heading back to New York, are you? I hope you enjoyed

your visit." It was clear from the way she said it that she hoped no such thing, and Andie still couldn't figure out why. Was she upset about the rental? But the property wasn't even hers.

"I guess I'll need to pack," Andie said, feeling dazed. She'd anticipated several ways this day might go, but the current scenario hadn't been among them.

"The instructions say your company will send a service by to collect all of the equipment next week."

"Yes, well, my clothing, though." She wasn't about to leave it behind just because Celeste suddenly looked intimidating, and although she now understood where Valentina had come by her commanding bedroom presence, the current circumstances weren't nearly as much fun as when Valentina did it.

Celeste gave a curt nod. "Bring the key back as soon as you're done. Just drop it in the planter. No need to come inside." With that, she turned and went back into the shop, and Andie could've sworn the temperature on the street went up by ten degrees, at least.

What on earth had gotten into her? Andie wondered. *And where is Valentina?* Her head was spinning as she tried to find a path through the crowds back to her apartment, but she hadn't gone more than a few feet when she saw Chiara coming toward her. Andie was relieved to see that, unlike Celeste, the girl appeared to be welcoming, if a little out of sorts.

"Hi, Andie." Chiara's eyes darted one direction and then another before settling onto Andie's face, earnest and wide. "Can I ask you a question?"

"Sure." Unaccountably, Andie's stomach tied itself into a

knot. What could a kid have to ask her that had her looking so nervous?

"Is it true what they're saying?"

"Oh," Andie nodded solemnly, beginning to understand. "You've heard about the apartment. Yes, it's true, but I won't be going far, at least not yet. You still have to show me how to make that homemade pasta your Nonna taught you to make." *In fact, that would make an excellent episode for the new show...*

"No, that's not it. I meant what they are saying about you and my mama."

"What *who* is saying?" Andie's stomach flipped once more. "Wait, *what* are they saying?"

"They said my mama was your girlfriend. It was on the news."

Andie's chest tightened, and little black dots floated at the edge of her vision. All of a sudden, Celeste's odd behavior made perfect sense. Andie swallowed hard and tried not to give in to the panic that was rapidly rising within her. "Well, what did your mama say about that?"

Chiara shrugged. "I don't know. I was with my papa."

"I see." *Stay calm. Maybe there's been a mistake. There's no way Valentina was outed by the evening news.* "Well, what did your papa say?"

"Nothing." Chiara rolled her eyes. "He thinks I'm too much of a baby to understand."

"But you do?" Andie proceeded with utmost caution. "You do understand?"

"That girls can like girls and boys can like boys?" Chiara shot her a scornful look. "Of course. That's how it is now, you know?"

"Oh, that's how it is now?" Despite the fact that every

single nerve ending was now alight with dread at the prospect of facing Valentina, Andie had to stifle a laugh. She'd just been schooled in Homosexuality 101, by an eye-rolling tween. "Well, that's a very good thing to know. Thank you. But Chiara, what exactly did they say on the news, if you don't mind telling me?"

Chiara tilted her head, considering. "They said that my mama might be your new girlfriend, and they showed a picture of the two of you walking together."

"A picture?" Andie groaned. *Of course, the pictures from the Metro Sun.* She should never have trusted that damn reporter to keep the story under wraps.

"Yeah, you were sort of hugging, I guess? And Mama looked really happy. And then they said that only Cupid knew for sure." Chiara's expression grew thoughtful. "Hey, Andie? I know I told you I wouldn't try it again, but do you want me to go talk to him about this?"

"Talk to whom?"

"Cupid. Remember how I told you about Papa and that woman on the computer?"

"Umm…I guess so?" *Is she going somewhere with this, or am I having an aneurysm?*

"Well, it worked! He's even planning to move to be with her."

"That's nice, but what does this have to do with me and your mom?"

"See, that day I didn't know what to write about her. But now that I do, I could go try again. There are lots of people around the fountain, so I'm sure I wouldn't fall in."

"You would do that?"

Chiara nodded. "I want Mama to be happy. When she's with you, she is."

Andie's heart turned instantly to the consistency of a gooey caramel. What a kid. "You know what? Maybe you'd better not. I know you'd be careful, but if someone had to fish you out of that fountain again, your mother would never forgive me."

"That's probably true."

"Maybe you could just point me in the direction of your mom, though? Because I think we need to talk."

"I can't. She's not here."

"Not here?" Andie tried to blink but her lids had frozen in place. "Where is she?"

Chiara's brow wrinkled. "The hospital. Aunt Francie's sick."

This news was the final straw. Andie's body began to tremble. Was the entire world suddenly stacked against them? Despite Andie's best efforts, Valentina's secret had been revealed in the most public way possible. She had to be furious! Andie would willingly turn her life on its head three times over for Valentina if it would fix the mess she'd made. But it wouldn't. And at that moment she was in need of a shower, and had clothes to pack, and she didn't even have a place to stay, at least not until after the meeting with the property manager on Monday. Andie's breaths came short and shallow, and her stomach felt queasy. She needed to get away, but first there was one thing she needed to do even more.

She grabbed a piece of paper from her bag and scribbled down the address of the cooking school property, then folded it and handed it to Chiara.

Chiara took the paper and smiled. "You want me to bring him a letter after all?"

"No. It's for your mom. Tell her Monday, that's where I'll be. Can you do that?"

"Monday," Chiara repeated back. "I'll tell her."

It was very little under the circumstances, but it was all that Andie could think of to do. Valentina would be in no shape to talk with her best friend in the hospital, and even were that not the case, she'd probably be too angry to answer her phone. Face-to-face was her only hope.

Andie watched as Chiara headed toward the shop, and could've sworn she saw Celeste scowling at her through the glass. She did her best to shake off the sudden chill that image brought to her spine as she made her way to clear out her belongings from the apartment that was no longer hers. She had little doubt that if she wasn't gone by sundown, Celeste would be happy to gather a posse of grannies to ride her out of town.

Monday. It couldn't come soon enough.

VALENTINA DROVE the last mile along Montamore's curving main road with one eye closed. She was just awake enough to know that she couldn't close them both at the same time, but so exhausted that keeping them both open was simply not an option. It was late. The sun was long since down, and the festival ended, though as she pulled into the central piazza, the extra-bright glow of lights from the windows all around it was startling. It took a moment for her sleepy brain to realize that it was a result of all the occupied apartments, usually dark, but tonight filled with guests who'd booked a room for the night. Montamore looked alive again.

Valentina, on the other hand, felt like death warmed over. The trip to the hospital had come at the worst possible time. Not that there ever was a great time for hospitals, but when Andie had been expected to arrive at any moment, the last thing Valentina had wanted was to be heading away from the village. And it wasn't Francie's fault, but by the time they'd arrived, it had become increasingly clear that it was a false alarm. The doctors had mostly confirmed their suspicions, but not until after several hours of waiting.

The funny thing was, at any other point in her life, Valentina knew her attention would've been focused a hundred percent on her best friend. But as she'd sat there, shifting uncomfortably in a plastic waiting-room chair, all she could think of was Andie. Andie, arriving in Montamore and finding her gone. Andie, with no place to live. She'd tried calling, of course, until that terrible nurse had come by and told her she couldn't use the phone. Hospital policy, she'd said. Well, the woman had smelled like stale cigarettes and exhibited all the warmth of Attila the Hun. If the hospital wanted to start banning things, it seems like either of those would've been a good place to start.

Valentina could feel her blood pressure increasing. She was getting worked up over it again, but she was too tired for that tonight. She trudged the last few steps to the shop, sighing with relief as she spied its dark interior. Her family was in bed. It would take every last bit of her energy to make herself climb the stairs without first having to embark on a lengthy explanation of the last two decades of her life. It was a conversation they needed to have, but one she'd much rather do face-to-face in the morning.

The knob twisted easily in her hand. Of course. The town might be filled to the brim with people from out of town, but it would never occur to Mama or Nonna to treat them like strangers. Valentina sighed. They were so open and accepting when it came to the tourists, but she feared she wouldn't be treated the same way. Not now that they knew about her and Andie. She could never fully please her mother on the best of days. What a disappointment it must have been to her to confirm that she would never have the perfect daughter she'd always wanted. All the scolding, all the disapproval, and what had she gotten for her troubles? The village's first divorced lesbian. Then again, her mother had always been keenly sensitive to her faults, so maybe she wasn't so surprised. At least Nonna might not mind too much. Now that the festival was behind them, tongues would be wagging about her all over Montamore for sure, and Nonna would be right in the middle of it. Gossip central. It was the old woman's idea of heaven.

Inside the shop, she rested against the door, leaning back until she heard the latch click. She wanted to stay in that spot forever, to close her eyes and never move. Instead, she reached across her body with one arm to turn the lock, not feeling quite as inclined to trust the entire world as the rest of her family was. Her eyelids fluttered, dangerously close to shutting completely. Then a light snapped on, and she jumped several inches into the air as adrenaline coursed through her.

"You're home." It was her mother who spoke, her face still carved of stone. Nonna sat beside her, looking almost as displeased. Apparently, the conversation she'd thought could be put off until morning was going to happen, right here and now.

"I'm sorry. I was at—" Her brain stopped, the word eluding her. Shakily, Valentina sank onto a cafe chair. The energy it had taken to send her flying into the air had been the last of her reserves.

"The hospital," Nonna supplied. "We know. Paolo told us, and we sent Chiara over to help with the little ones. How's Francie?"

"Better. Dehydrated, mostly. They're keeping her overnight for observation just in case, but the doctors were pretty much agreed that it seems to have been a false alarm."

Her mother nodded. "Good."

And like that morning, that was all. As her mother turned and took a step toward her apartment without another word, Valentina couldn't stand the silent treatment another second.

"Mama, stop." Exhausted or not, this had to end tonight. "Nonna, you stay, too. We need to talk about this."

"This?" her mother sniffed. "I'm not sure I know what you mean."

"Seriously? Please."

"Oh, you mean finding out from the news that my daughter has a famous American girlfriend, and didn't bother telling us?"

"We were the last to know," Nonna pouted. "The very last."

"Wait." Valentina blinked and her tired eyes produced three copies of each of the women. She blinked again and the scene in front of her returned to the correct head count. "Nonna, is that the only reason you're upset, because someone else got the scoop on some juicy gossip?"

"I'm the one people come to when they want to know things, piccolina," Nonna said. "I've *never* been the last to know something before."

"Oh my God, that's what all this silent treatment is about?" Valentina shook her head as a memory surfaced of the time when her mother and grandmother had both given her father the silent treatment for a full week because of something or other that he'd done. *I can't believe this,* she thought. *They're not even focused on me at all. They've got their damn feelings hurt!*

"Can you imagine how humiliating that was for her?" her mother asked.

"And what about me?" Valentina spluttered, indignation giving her a second wind. "It's not like I was thrilled to have my sexual orientation announced on the evening news for all the world to hear. Try *that* for humiliation."

"Well, now," Nonna shrugged, "it's not like it was that big a secret, right?"

Valentina's mouth fell slack as she stared at her grandmother, trying to make sense of her. Perhaps it was the exhaustion to blame, but she could've sworn the woman had just claimed that her attraction to women wasn't a secret. "Of course it was a secret, Nonna."

"Hmm. Not a very good one," Nonna countered.

"I never told a soul!"

"Maybe not," Nonna said, "but we have eyes, you know."

"True," her mother added, because apparently this conversation hadn't already killed Valentina enough. "Of course, to be fair, when she married Luca, the rumors did die down for a bit, Mama."

"You have a point." The old woman's eyes grew misty with remembrance. "Oh, what a surprise it was when that boy showed up in town. Up until then, most people figured that story about the boy with the hazelnut cream eyes was made up."

"Such a strange color for eyes," Valentina's mother added.

"But, it was made up." By now, Valentina's head was held in the open palm of the arm she'd rested on the wrought iron cafe table for support. "The whole thing."

Both her mother and grandmother went completely silent, looking stunned. "But then why did you marry him?" her grandmother finally asked.

"Because everyone wanted me to. You two most of all!"

"Because we thought he was the one Cupid had chosen for you," said her mother.

"As I recall, I didn't like him all that much," Nonna chimed in, "but who was I to argue?"

Valentina lifted her head from her hand and straightened her back. "Are you telling me that if I had come in here twenty years ago and announced that I'd seen a girl in that fountain, everyone would have been just fine with it?"

Her mother blinked. "Of course."

"It sure would've made the boys on the village bocce team happy." Nonna chuckled. "They had quite a wager going that you'd say exactly that."

A queasy sensation settled into Valentina's stomach as she took this in. "You're telling me that the day I fell into the fountain, the village bocce team were placing bets on whether or not I was a lesbian?"

"Well, I mean…" Nonna paused and pursed her lips. "Yes, I guess they did."

"How many people in town were betting against it?" Valentina grimaced. "Never mind, I don't want to know. Was there anyone who didn't have an opinion on the topic?"

"Montamore's a small town, cara," her mother reminded her. "We all have opinions on everything and everyone."

Valentina shut her eyes. "All these years, no one ever said a word."

"Of course not," her grandmother said. "They all thought Cupid had spoken."

"I hate that fucking statue," Valentina muttered under her breath.

"Valentina!" her mother scolded. "Language."

"Oh, *that's* still a rule? Good to know." Valentina's eyelids popped open. "After all of this, it's almost a relief to know that my language still upsets you."

"You know how I feel about profanity."

"I don't think I know how you feel about anything," Valentina countered. "All I know is that you've always wanted me to be perfect, and I always fall short."

Her mother sighed. "Cara mia, all of those expectations, you put on yourself."

Valentina blinked back tears. "You're trying to say you've never been disapproving of me?"

"Disapproving?" If her mother wasn't genuinely surprised by the accusation, her face did an excellent job of pretending to be. "I've been strict, I do know that. Maybe too much so. Your father spoiled you so much when you were little, and you needed a little discipline to balance it out. I guess it became a habit even once you were grown. But I've never disapproved."

Valentina sniffed as a single hot tear escaped and rolled down her cheek. "I thought you did. I thought everyone would disapprove, if they knew who I really was. I never thought anyone would understand if I told them how I felt."

"Oh, cara mia," Nonna said. "How could you think that?

Valentina sniffed again and wiped her face with her hands. "Isn't that what it's like everywhere? It's what they say on TV."

"You watch too much TV," her mother interjected.

"But you're not judgmental, or anything," Valentina shot back.

"Valentina." Nonna's voice brimmed with all the warmth and kindness her mother's sometimes lacked. "Montamore's not a typical place. This village was built on a temple dedicated to the Goddess of Love, you know. People here could never hold the narrow ideas about love that they do in other places. She'd never allow it."

"I always thought that was a made-up story. I never believed any of it. I'm not sure I do now." Valentina's insides trembled at her confession. *Is it worth the risk to believe?*

"Well, you may not, but we do." Her mother smiled an uncharacteristically sweet smile than made her look as young and beautiful as Valentina remembered she used to be. "So tell us, twenty years ago, was it a girl's face in the fountain?"

"Was it the American's face?" Nonna prompted. "Was it Andie Bartlett?"

"Oh, dear. I hadn't thought of that." Her mother suddenly looked troubled. "Perhaps I shouldn't have been so quick to send her packing."

Valentina gasped. "What?"

"Well, I kind of thought she was an opportunist," her mother said, growing defensive. "I thought she was just trying to get her picture all over the news and then up and leaving you behind to deal with the consequences."

"Mama!"

"I'd just seen the email about the lease, and right after

that came the segment on the news. What was I supposed to think? It's not like you told me any different, young lady," her mother scolded. Valentina hated to admit it, but she had a point. "So when I saw her come into town earlier today, I demanded the key back, immediately. I may have been a little harsh. But I was just trying to protect my own, and don't tell me you wouldn't do the same for Chiara."

Horrified, Valentina turned her head to look out the window and across the square. "You mean, Andie's not asleep in that apartment right now? Where did she go?"

Her mother stayed silent. Nonna chewed on her lower lip.

"Mama where did she go?" Valentina demanded, more forcefully than before.

"Does it matter?" her mother sniffed. She was back to her old self once more.

"Yes, it matters!" Valentina's body flushed with heat and her vision narrowed. "Of course it matters. I'm in love with her. I've been as afraid to tell her as I was to tell you, so it's no wonder she was going to leave, but I have to find her and tell her, before it's too late." She reached the end of her diatribe and gasped for breath.

"You're certain?" Her mother was impossibly calm. "You're positive you love her?"

"Yes!" Valentina answered in between heavy breaths. "Yes. It might be the only thing I've known for certain in my life. Do I need to march out to that fucking statue—and yes, I said it again and I really don't care—and settle this once and for all?"

Her mother's lips had become thin lines as soon as she used *that* word. "That won't be necessary. Here." She held out her hand, and there was a slip of paper there. "I should give you this."

"What is it? A letter for Cupid?" Valentina quipped. "I was joking about that."

Her mother didn't crack a smile. "No. It's an address. I don't know where she is now, but I know that's where she'll be on Monday. She gave it to Chiara this afternoon to give to you."

Valentina watched her mother warily, unsure whether to trust her. "And then you took it and held onto it."

"Just until I knew. I always regretted I didn't question you more about Luca when I had a chance."

"Well, now you know." Valentina's shoulders slumped, her fading anger leaving her even more exhausted than before.

"Now I do. And so now I'm giving it to you to decide for yourself what to do."

Valentina mustered the last of her strength and stood, then forced her legs to drag her to the stairs. "What I'm going to do is go to bed, and given the way I feel right now, I just may sleep through Sunday completely. And on Monday, I'm going to find her and I'm going to do whatever it takes to keep her in my life forever. So what if I'm the first lesbian in Montamore, right? If what you say is true, they'll get used to it."

"Why on earth," her grandmother called out when Valentina was halfway up the stairs, "do you think you're the first lesbian in Montamore?"

Valentina paused and turned. "I don't know. I guess I just assumed. I'm the first divorced person."

"Well, yes," Nonna said. "But that's different. There have been plenty of lesbians over the years."

"Oh," her mother said, turning to talk to Nonna, "do you recall all the gossip about Sister Gloria, back in the day?"

Valentina choked. "Sister Gloria, from catechism? But she was a nun!" *A mean nun, who made me afraid to even touch myself, for years!* And because the woman had done such a thorough job of it, Valentina said that last part silently in her head.

"My goodness," Nonna said to Valentina's mother. "We really did shelter her, didn't we?"

"Well, she was always such a sensitive child. Look how worked up she gets." They both seemed to have forgotten that she was still within earshot, and no longer fourteen years old.

"Okay," Valentina called out as loudly as she could, "I'm going to bed now. Right after I scrub my brain with bleach. Please don't do any more gossiping until I close the door. Good night."

When she reached the inside of her apartment, Valentina shut the door and stared at the slip of paper, which had been clutched tightly in her hand. The address looked familiar, though she couldn't quite place it. Wherever it was, Andie would be there on Monday and wanted to see her. They needed to talk. All of Valentina's secrets were out in the open now, if they'd ever been secrets at all, of which she was no longer so sure. If she could be as honest with Andie and tell her how she felt, what would happen?

I'll find out Monday.

TWENTY-FIVE

VALENTINA CHECKED THE ADDRESS, then checked it again before pulling her car onto a long, gravel driveway. The directions to the place had brought her to a farmhouse in the countryside, so very much like every other farmhouse in the countryside that it felt vaguely familiar to her, even though Valentina was certain she'd never been there before. Grass and weeds grew high around the property, and it seemed likely it had stood unoccupied for some time. There were no signs to announce where she was, not so much as a house number, so Valentina had to trust that her GPS had sent her to the right place. The location seemed to match, and yet why Andie had wanted her to come here was a mystery.

When she'd ventured out of the house Sunday afternoon and into a sun-drenched piazza filled with villagers who suddenly all knew the most intimate details of her personal life, Valentina had assumed that would be the most frightening experience of her life. She'd been wrong. The scariest moment was now, hearing the crunch of pebbles beneath her feet as she got out of the car, not knowing what was ahead. It wasn't just the purpose of the day's excursion that was unknown to her. It was her entire future.

She could've called Andie on Sunday, and really she should have, but she hadn't been sure which was worse, the prospect of the call going to voicemail again, or having Andie answer only to tell her that Monday would be their final goodbye. She didn't think she was strong enough to handle either, and so she'd sat with the phone in her hand and never dialed. As she scanned the farmhouse for signs that Andie was there, unease coiled in her belly. The note hadn't specified a time, so Valentina had opted for early. Maybe Andie hadn't arrived yet, or because of their lack of communication, she simply didn't know if Valentina was going to be there. Maybe she wasn't coming at all.

But after a few minutes of picking her way gingerly around the front of the property, the terrain being too uneven and overgrown to allow for pacing, the sound of a car coming up the drive reached Valentina's ears, and the sight she saw when she turned made her heart sing. The world's tiniest car was bopping along the gravel, looking so cheerful it almost made her laugh as its bright aqua paint glistened in the morning sun. She'd never loved a car so much, although maybe it wasn't so much the car as its driver. Valentina walked briskly to meet her, but as Andie got out, the gloomy expression on her face stopped Valentina in her tracks. She wanted to rush to her but was afraid of being pushed away.

"Andie," she said, her throat so tight she could barely force the words out, "you're here."

Andie squeezed her eyes shut, pain etched on her face. "Oh, Val. I'm so sorry."

"Why?" Her stomach dropped. *Here comes the bad news.*

"You were outed on the evening news."

"Is that all?" Her shoulders shook as a titter of nervous laughter escaped. If that was it, maybe she'd been too quick to give up hope.

"Is that all? That was your worst nightmare! It's like what happened to Jessica Balderelli, but even worse. Keeping our relationship secret was the one thing you asked of me, and I let you down."

Andie's lip began to quiver, and it was clear she was on the verge of crying. Valentina couldn't bear it. She closed the distance between them and crushed Andie to her chest. "No. No, you didn't."

Andie clung to her, and Valentina could feel her struggling to maintain control. "But everyone knows."

"It's okay." Valentina ran her fingers through Andie's hair. She noted how the familiar orange shone at the tips and wondered if Andie had kept herself occupied the day before by giving the color a touch up. It seemed like something she might do. She pressed her lips to the top of Andie's head. "In fact, it's kind of a funny story. It turns out the entire village has known for years. They'd been making bets about when I would come out."

"And you're okay with that?" Andie's doubt was evident.

"With them making bets? I mean, it might have been nice if someone had told *me*, but if you mean am I okay with things in general, I'm a lot more okay with it than I ever thought I would be."

"And your family?" Andie relaxed her grip on Valentina's body enough to look her in the eyes. "Are you saying they're okay with it, too?"

"My family is full of surprises." Valentina wiped a stray

tear from Andie's cheek and smiled. "I guess it's not the disaster I thought it would be. In fact, you shouldn't be apologizing. I should be thanking you. Not carrying around that secret is a huge weight off my shoulders."

Andie's own shoulders relaxed, as if she'd started to accept that Valentina spoke the truth, but some caution remained. "Even so, I'm really sorry about how it happened. I *knew* they had the picture, but—"

Valentina frowned. "How did you know they had the picture?"

"I—"

She wasn't angry, but she had to know. "Come on, Andie. There's no point in making up a story, trust me. You might as well just spill it."

"Fine. Remember last weekend at the hotel, when I first told you about the interview? You thought it was Tracy who had set it up, but the truth was, a reporter from the *Metro Sun* tracked us down in Florence. She told me they had a compromising photo, and she'd run it if I didn't do an exclusive interview for them. I wasn't sure what to do, but when you assumed the crew was coming to feature the festival, I figured I'd just go with it."

"But Andie, if your network didn't set up that interview…" The truth hit her, and her pulse ticked faster as she realized what it meant. "You were fired. That's why they canceled the rest of the lease, isn't it? It was right before the interview aired. They must have found out. I can't believe it. Your job's the most important thing in your life, and you lost it because of me. This is all my fault!"

It was Andie's turn to reassure. "It's not your fault. I would've been quitting anyway. Really, I should be thanking you."

Valentina shot her a doubtful look. "Come on, we're being honest about everything from now on, remember?"

"That's the absolute truth. Look, I asked you to come here because it's easier to explain if you can see it in person. But while we're being completely honest, I would've given up the job if I'd had to, even if I had nothing else."

"You don't mean that." But the truth sparkled in Andie's eyes, and Valentina had to believe.

They'd drifted apart as they'd talked, but now Andie wrapped her arms around Valentina and pulled her close again. "I do. Look, I know this isn't what we agreed on, or what you wanted, but the truth is, I think I've fallen in—"

Several staccato blasts from a horn stopped her words, and they both jumped.

"What was that?"

"Shit. What timing. The realtors are here." Andie's regret was evident. "I have to go meet with them about the paperwork."

Valentina swallowed her frustration and offered a weak smile "It's okay. Go."

"As soon as I'm done…"

"Oh, yeah. You'd better believe we'll be getting back to this later." Valentina was counting the minutes until she heard for sure how Andie's sentence would end.

A dark car pulled into the driveway, its generous size eclipsing Andie's diminutive ride. The doors opened and a well-dressed man and woman got out of the front, accompanied by a woman in a no-nonsense pantsuit who had been sitting in the back. This woman smiled and Andie lifted a hand in greeting, then motioned her over.

"Val, this is Tracy."

"*The* Tracy?" Valentina shook the woman's hand warmly. "I've heard so much..."

"Me, too." Tracy laughed as Andie gave her a warning look. "Discreetly, of course."

"Oh, of course," Valentina responded, joining in Tracy's laughter.

"Andie," Tracy nodded toward the man and woman, who were waiting by the car, "they're ready whenever you are. Jessica will be by later, but you can get started on your portion."

Andie turned to Valentina. "I have to take care of this, but maybe Tracy will show you around until I get back." With that, Andie followed the man and woman through the gate and disappeared deeper into the farmhouse.

"Shall we?" Tracy took a step toward the gate. "I'm sure you're curious to see everything."

"Oh, very." Valentina was indeed curious. She had no idea why the property itself was important, or what Andie's meeting was about. She aimed to figure it out without making her complete ignorance obvious. "So, you're Andie's assistant?"

"Not any more. I'm the new vice president at Lezione di Cucina Enterprises."

Valentina nodded at the business name. "Lezione di Cucina. Very straightforward. That's just Italian for cooking lessons, you know." Valentina squinted at the farmhouse, which was easier to see from the opposite side of the gate, and a memory surfaced. "There used to be a cooking school around here that had that same name."

Tracy gave her an inquiring look. "Has Andie not explained?"

"Explained what?"

"You haven't been inside yet, have you?"

Valentina shook her head. "No, should I?"

"Oh, you'll want to see it." Tracy opened a heavy wooden door and motioned her through. "Come on!"

Once they'd stepped inside, Valentina stopped in her tracks to take in the massive industrial kitchen, its sturdy and well-aged countertops providing a pleasing contrast to its gleaming modern appliances. She'd seen it before, but only in photographs. "Oh my God, now I know where I am."

"Our company doesn't just use the same name as the old school," Tracy explained. "This is the same place. And pretty soon, it will be the set for a brand-new cooking show that's going to take the whole world by storm. Guaranteed."

As Tracy went into more details about the show's concept, a mixture of pride and excitement blossomed in Valentina's chest. "Finally," she said when Tracy had finished speaking, "she'll be doing a show that truly makes use of her talent. Andie really is brilliant."

Tracy nodded in agreement, then added, "You're the one who inspired it, you know."

"Me?" Valentina's eyes widened. "No, that's not likely."

"It is. She never would have had the idea if it hadn't been for coming here and meeting you."

They'd toured the kitchen as they talked, and now stood by a doorway on the other side of the room. Tracy swung the door open and inclined her head toward the room on the other side. "Oh, this is the best part."

"Better than this?" Valentina looked back around at what she could only describe as her fantasy kitchen. "I don't see how." She followed Tracy through the doorway and as she saw what awaited, she blinked slowly, confused. "It's just an empty room."

But Tracy shook her head. "It's more than that. It's exactly the size of space needed to hold all of the equipment to expand your chocolate shop to double the capacity, at least. I know because Andie insisted I confirm it before anything went into the proposal."

All the times they'd discussed expanding Cioccolatini di Venere, Valentina had assumed it was nothing more than a daydream, but Andie had taken her seriously. All around her was the proof, and as she took in the space with this new vision in mind, she could see that it was perfect. With a space like this and use of the kitchen in the other room when filming wasn't taking place, her business could expand significantly without losing the personal attention and local qualities that Valentina valued most. Her heart leapt to realize how completely Andie had understood her vision, and knew there was no one else with whom she could have made her dreams a reality.

Valentina swallowed the lump in her throat. "I don't even know what to say. How lucky for me that the show required a setting like this."

A conspiratorial expression crossed Tracy's face. "I probably shouldn't mention it, but this show could easily have been filmed in New York. The studio there was perfectly well-equipped. Andie wouldn't hear of it though. It had to be Italy, she said."

"Had to be Italy?" Valentina laughed. "When she got here, she didn't even like Italy."

"I guess she found a reason to change her mind," Tracy said, and left it at that.

Valentina thought back to the day she'd first seen Andie's face in the water. How much things had changed, for both of them, since then. Andie had been counting the days until she could go back to New York. Valentina had been positive she would spend her life alone. And now? She knew how her own feelings had changed. And if she'd guessed correctly, then Andie had been about to say that she loved her, right before they'd been interrupted.

That was what she was going to say, wasn't it? It had to be. Without talking to Andie about it, she couldn't be certain exactly how she saw their futures unfolding, but Valentina was certain that when it came to their relationship being a quick fling, both of them had most definitely had a change of mind, and heart.

Tracy pulled out her phone, looking at the screen. "Jessica will arrive soon. I need to go see how Andie and the realtors are getting along. It shouldn't be much longer." She placed a guiding hand on Valentina's shoulder and ushered her to a door that led outside. "There's a courtyard right through there. The garden's a little overgrown, but I know I saw a bench. Would you like to wait out there until Andie's done?"

The garden was a tangle of weeds and vines, but Valentina could just make out where planting beds had once been. The stone walkways were sound, and with a little work, it could quickly be restored to make a top-quality kitchen garden. Valentina picked her way carefully through the mess of growth until she reached a stone bench in the middle. Its surface had been baked to a pleasant warmth in the sun that soothed her to soak in as she sat. She breathed in deep and could detect some rosemary that was hidden somewhere nearby, and which perfumed the air with a tangy scent. Maybe basil, too. It felt right, being on that bench in that garden at that moment, as if her whole life she'd been waiting to sit there.

Her eyes were shut, lost in thought under the intense light of the spring sun, when she heard a creaking sound, like a door on rusty hinges. She looked back from where she'd entered the garden and frowned. The door was closed. The creaking sounded again, and this time she seemed to detect that it was coming from a different direction, off to one side. She turned on the bench, and froze.

There was an alcove, nearly hidden by the vines that had grown up around it, and inside the alcove was a door. It was a wooden door, heavily carved and rustic in style, exactly the type of thing that belonged on an old Tuscan farmhouse. She'd seen it once before.

The hinges creaked again, but she could barely hear the sound over the pounding pulse in her ears as the door, freed from the rust at last, began to swing toward her. In the bright sunlight, the very edge of a head began to appear from behind, short locks glowing orange like a flame.

Tears welled in Valentina's eyes but she wouldn't blink, couldn't look away. Not like before. She knew who was behind the door, and was ready to embrace her and everything the future promised, and never let go.

That stupid Cupid, she thought as she rose from the bench. *He knew it all along.*

EPILOGUE

IT WAS a brilliant spring day in Florence as Andie and Valentina paused halfway across the Ponte Vecchio bridge and slipped through the doorway that led to a set of steep stairs. It was their first time back in the city since the weekend break they'd taken the year before. In fact, much of the time seemed to have passed in a blur.

Production had started on Andie's show the preceding May, and premiered in September to international acclaim, and Andie had spent most of the winter months testing recipes for her latest cookbook. With hard work and Valentina's constant help, not to mention that of Nonna and Celeste and Chiara, her career was stronger than she'd ever imagined. There were days when Andie could hardly believe it was real.

Meanwhile, with the help of some startup capital from investors that Tracy had found, Valentina had transformed the empty room at the farmhouse into a state-of-the-art facility that had allowed her to double production without sacrificing quality. With the new e-commerce-enabled website that Andie's designer had created for it, Cioccolatini di Venere's products had started to reach boutique shops across Europe and beyond. Andie had provided the resources, but Valentina had brought the talent, and Andie couldn't have been prouder.

Andie reached back as she mounted the first step, and the butterflies fluttered in her belly as they always did as Valentina took her hand. As they climbed the stairs to the rooftop, bells rang out from churches across the city. It was Easter. They wouldn't have time to eat up here on this visit. After experiencing her first authentic Tuscan Christmas, which involved cooking for the entire month of December, Andie had insisted on a meal out this holiday, and the restaurant at their favorite hotel was the perfect solution.

Valentina's family was waiting for them back at the hotel, along with Andie's mother, who'd made the trip from Miami for the first time. Having all of the women from both of their families together let loose on Florence without them, was just a tiny bit terrifying. But neither of them could imagine a trip to Florence without at least glimpsing the Arno from their special spot, and so Andie had arranged to stop by for just a minute or two. And, aside from staring at the sparkly water, there was something else Andie needed to do.

"Listen, I've been practicing my Italian," Andie said, once they'd watched the water flow past silently for what seemed an appropriate amount of time. "Mi piace vedere i tette di Firenze."

"Tetti," Valentina corrected, between peals of laughter that Andie might have found annoying if Valentina's laugh wasn't so enticing. "Tetti. It means rooftops."

Andie frowned. "Yeah, I know. Wait, what did I say?"

"You said that you enjoy looking at all the tits in Florence."

Andie's cheeks tingled. "That's definitely not what I meant to say."

Valentina raised an eyebrow. "I should hope not, or we'll need to have a talk."

"No need to talk. I don't enjoy looking at anyone else's tits but yours. I promise." She took a long and admiring glance at the aforementioned area, just to prove she was telling the truth.

"Andie!" Valentina's face had gone scarlet, just as Andie was hoping it might.

"Okay, here, let me try another phrase."

Valentina grimaced. "I'm not sure how much more of your Italian I can take."

"No, this one's pretty good." Andie closed her eyes, hoping to get it right after weeks of practice. "Sei il tesoro più prezioso che ho trovato…" She paused to remember the rest and Valentina, clearly thinking she was done, rewarded her with a peck on the cheek.

"Mm, very poetic. You're my precious treasure, too. Come on, though, it's about time to head back. We don't want to be late for lunch."

"Wait. I wasn't quite done." Andie's insides were starting to quiver as she took a breath and started again, slipping one hand into her pocket just to make certain the small box she'd placed in it earlier was still there. "Sei il tesoro più prezioso che ho trovato e che vorrei custodire per sempre."

Andie pulled the box from her pocket and felt it start to slip. Her heart thudded in her throat as she tightened her grip. How many times had she teased Valentina for her slick palms, yet here she was about to send a ring worth several thousand dollars splashing into the swiftly flowing Arno. She knew she should be on one knee. She'd planned to be, but she was too shaky to try. She didn't trust herself even to open the burgundy leather box. Instead, she simply held it out to Valentina, who looked somewhat stunned.

"That was supposed to be 'You are the most precious treasure I have found and one I would like to cherish forever,'" Andie added after an eternity in which Valentina still had not spoken. *Please tell me I didn't say something obscene*, Andie prayed. *Val still hasn't blinked. Is that good or bad?* "Did I get it right?"

"I…well," Valentina finally stammered, "I think so. But if you mean by it what I think you mean, you could have made it easier and just said *sposarmi*. I would have gotten the gist."

"I know. There *are* easier ways to say marry me, but you were worth the extra effort. Besides, I love Italian."

"Since when do you love Italian?" Valentina scoffed.

"Since I fell in love with the most beautiful woman in Italy." Andie felt warm and tingly as she watched Valentina melt into a puddle at her feet. "You never answered the question."

This time Valentina blinked slowly, at least three times, before speaking. Andie was happy to see that her blinking skills were returning. "Which question?"

"Will you marry me?" This time, Andie managed to pop the box open, sending sparkles of rainbows across them both as the light reflected off the diamond inside.

Valentina grinned. "Ti amo e voglio passare il resto della mia vita con te."

Andie's head spun from the speed at which the words rolled off Valentina's tongue. She'd been hoping for a simple *sì*, but if Valentina had said that part, it had been well hidden. "Could you say that one more time?"

"Let me see if I can translate it for you." Valentina wrapped her fingers around the hand that held the box, trapping it safely between the two of them. The other hand she placed in Andie's hair, which had grown out just a bit more than usual but was a truly impressive shade of orange for the occasion. She pulled her closer until their lips met, and the kiss they shared left Andie with no doubt that Valentina had just said she loved her and wanted to spend the rest of her life with her.

A MESSAGE FROM MIRANDA

Dear Reader,

There's something magical about Tuscany, and so when I decided to set the third book in the *Americans Abroad* series there, I knew it needed to have just a little touch of magic. And a lot of food. And wine. And most of all, I knew that if I was going to call it *Letters to Cupid*, it needed to be brimming with romance. I hope it didn't disappoint.

Getting this book from first draft to publication was a monumental task, and life threw in several bumps in the road, as it tends to do. I especially need to thank Claire Jarrett for her superb help with story development, and Holly Schneider for her wonderful dedication in editing, especially on a tight schedule.

Best Wishes,
Miranda

Printed in Great Britain
by Amazon